Attaché

Extraordinaire

Attaché Extraordinaire

by

John M. Danielski

www.penmorepress.com

Attaché Extraordinaire John M. Danielski
Copyright © 2022 John M. Danielski

ISBN: 978-1-957851-07-5. (EBOOK)
ISBN: 978-1-957851-08-2 (Paperback)

BISAC Subject Headings:
    FIC014000FICTION / Historical
    FIC032000FICTION / War & Military

Editor: Chris Wozney

Please send all correspondence to:

Penmore Press LLC
920 N Javelina Pl
Tucson AZ 85748

Dedication:

to Carolyn Leavenworth Meyers,
a great lady who passed far too soon.

Special thanks

to James S. Danielski
for his creative consultations.

Prologue
10th November, 1814
Packet ship Speedwell, 15 miles Northwest of Rotterdam.

Enduring an electrical storm at sea is a fearful ordeal, since water, lightning, and human skin sometimes combine in a lethal affinity. Fear becomes terror if you add ear-splitting thunder, bone-chilling cold, and a pitch-black night. A howling North Sea gale slammed mountainous waves against the little *Speedwell.* Vaporous coronas of violet light enveloped her mastheads and spar tips, the ionized air of St. Elmo's Fire giving her the ghostly appearance of the legendary Flying Dutchman. On *Speedwell's* forecastle, steel sparked as two swords clashed against each other.

Thomas Pennywhistle's cutlass blocked his opponent's lunge, but the rolling foredeck shoved him toward his foe's saber. He reared back, executed a fast half-turn to the right, and slashed sideways with his blade. He should have connected with the man's neck, but the ship's down-roll jerked his adversary just out of range.

A stab of lightning revealed Pennywhistle canted at a 45-degree angle relative to the slippery deck. A burst of frigid sea spray caused him to lose his footing. He rolled hard to the left and corkscrewed to his feet. His enemy had also fallen, but righted himself faster. He charged, bellowing curses, slicing rapidly from side to side.

Pennywhistle dodged at the last second and chopped downward as the man blew past. His cutlass ripped a deep

Attaché Extraordinaire

trench in the man's left calf. He screamed and toppled onto the oak planking, brushing against Pennywhistle as he fell. Pennywhistle reflexively touched his coat pocket, pressing against a tiny book that had the power to alter the future of Europe.

The driving rain, just short of sleet, suddenly ceased, but the wind increased sharply. Four lightning lances ripped the cloud-darkened sky, accompanied by deafening booms of thunder. One bolt connected with the main topgallant mast, setting its tip afire. The enormous heat swiftly conducted that fire down the full length of the mast and below decks to the places where it was stepped. A small chunk of flaming wood landed on Pennywhistle's boot.

He kicked the brand away, but it distracted his attention and he failed to hear swift footsteps behind him. Fortunately, he was not alone, and his wife missed nothing. The rain made it impossible for her to rely on her weapon of choice, so Sammie Jo pressed her American backwoods skills into service and hurled a tomahawk. The wind caused the blade to miss, but its blunt end struck the second assailant's left temple. His raised saber dropped from his hand as he sagged to the deck. She dashed to Pennywhistle's side just as his cutlass skewered his first foe, piercing his heart.

Another bolt illuminated the apprehension on his face as he shot a glance toward the starboard bow and then at the helmsman, spinning the wheel helplessly and swearing loudly. "The ship is going to broach!" he shouted to his wife. The shrieking winds made normal tones impossible.

"Broach? That don't sound good!" his wife yelled back in alarm.

"The ship can't keep her bow into the wind and is sliding sideways. The wheel is useless. These two must have cut the rudder cables. It's just a matter of time before a big wave hits and we capsize."

"But they would have been signing their own death warrants! Why would they do such a thing?"

Lightning crashed into the deck just behind them, causing both to recoil.

"My opponent may be holding their family hostage. And if the storm had not struck, they probably planned to escape, using one of the ship's boats. Who puts that kind of fear into men?" He shook his head in disgust.

A raptor's cry pierced the air. He swiveled his head and saw what represented a contingency plan. A peregrine falcon of bluish grey perched on the starboard gunwale. The large size indicated this was a female falcon. She cocked her black head to the left as if awaiting instructions. Pennywhistle glanced down at the corpses and noted that one wore a falconer's glove. The bird had a small circular container strapped to her back: the pocket-sized codebook his assailants sought would fit inside it. He had never heard of falcons being used as messengers, but from what Ghillie Gunn had taught him as a boy, there was no reason they could not be. They had to be very close to shore since the falcon could only have been launched after the rain had ceased. Peregrines could reach speeds of over 200 miles per hour in a dive and her handler ashore would have had the book in much less time than it took two men to row ashore. Peregrines were reckoned earl's possessions in classical hawking, and he wondered if the puppeteer of the dead men held the Continental equivalent of that rank: graf or count.

The bird shrieked and took flight as a heavy belaying pin glanced off her claws. Pennywhistle turned and found that his wife had thrown the pin. He raised his eyebrows at her.

Attaché Extraordinaire

"A falcon like that poses danger to Plymouth," she said, in answer to his unvoiced question. "A predator will kill a parrot just as well as a grouse."

The wind increased in force yet again and blew flaming shards onto the fore and mizzen masts. "We've got about ten minutes before *Speedwell* becomes a fire ship. There is no way to lower a boat in this weather. We'll have to jump for it. Thank God, we are strong swimmers. Sadly, few if any of the sailors are. They will probably break into the spirit locker and use stupefaction to block terror. "

A reeling sailor who staggered past them brandishing a large jug confirmed his hunch. A second joined him. Suddenly both froze as if immobilized by a block of ice then keeled over, stone dead.

"My God, these two assassins poisoned the rum supply!"

"What poison would kill so quickly?"

"Oil extracted from the liver of a pufferfish. Its odorless, tasteless, and paralyzes the body within a minute of ingestion."

A presentiment of danger caused him to look up. He grabbed his wife and shoved her sideways. A falling spar hit the deck where they had been standing then bounced up and over the side. "Jesus, that was close!" exclaimed his wife.

Pennywhistle flashed a wry smile. "Not sure if Jesus had anything to do with it, but we have our ticket out of here!"

She shot him a puzzled look.

"That spar is a life raft. It's only half a mile to the Dutch Coast and dawn is not far off."

"First we have to save Plymouth!"

"It will be cutting things close!"

They made a mad dash to their cabin, or rather a series of dashes, since they could run only when the deck was level.

They dodged reeling sailors and the corpses of those who had already succumbed to the poison. When they reached their cabin, Sammie Jo freed Plymouth from his cage. The blue and green parrot immediately took up his accustomed post on her right shoulder.

Pennywhistle donned a flapped tweed cap, stout greatcoat, Inverness scarf, and thick leather gloves. He took the target of the attack, a pocket size book, and inserted it into a waterproof pouch, which he then placed in a buttoned coat pocket. He handed Sammie Jo a spare pair of gloves and socks, as well as his heaviest hooded boat cloak, a close-fitting garment which protected her from head to ankle.

The pair picked up a large chest by its wooden handles and hustled it onto the quarterdeck: it represented an innovation Pennywhistle had devised after having spent years at sea and witnessing more than a few shipwrecks. It was purpose built, containing clothes, blankets, weapons, tinned food, and a purse of gold coins. It was airtight with a combination lock and featured a thick layer of Portuguese cork, ensuring that it would float. It was painted a garish orange, a color in the worst of taste, yet highly visible and hence most likely to be spotted by potential rescuers.

They heaved the chest overboard in the direction of the detached spar. Sammie Jo whispered some words to Plymouth, an exceptionally intelligent animal, and he bobbed his head in understanding. He unfurled his wings and headed for shore.

A huge wave smashed into the *Speedwell,* nearly knocking them off their feet. Pennywhistle grabbed her hand. "The next big one will finish the ship. It's now or never. The cold water will trigger a gasp reflex, so just before we jump take a deep breath and hold it for as long as you can."

Attaché Extraordinaire

"Got it."

They braced themselves against the port gunwale. He guessed the water temperature was in the low forties on the Fahrenheit scale, so hypothermia posed a real danger. They had an hour at best before they lost so much heat that they would be unable to move their limbs. Though their woolen clothing would weigh them down, wool still retained heat well, even when wet.

Another bolt of lightning slashed across the sky. "There it is! And not twenty yards away." Pennywhistle eagerly pointed to the bobbing spar.

He squeezed her hand hard. "Jump!!"

They hit the sea with their hands joined. The cold administered a cruel shock as the roaring waves sucked them under. The roiling waters rolled them over and over but could not break their grip. Disorienting vertigo and stunning cold assaulted them, Neptune's power was terrifying, but they drew emotional strength from their locked hands, because it symbolized their joined hearts. Just when their lungs seemed about to burst, a rogue current spat them to the surface.

They sucked in lungfuls of air. Another wave shoved them sideways and up. The spar flowed toward them, a firm, straight beam borne diagonal to the waves, and they grabbed on with all their might.

"Not a moment too soon," wheezed Pennywhistle. He canted his head to the left, directing his wife's attention. Their eyes widened at the sight of *Speedwell,* lying on its side. The stricken ship turned upside down when a mountainous wave smashed into it.

"Start kicking, keep it steady, but not too vigorous. We must conserve our strength." Pennywhistle hollered. "The waters here shoal rapidly. We may be able to walk the final hundred yards or so."

Their kicks moved the spar slowly. The rising tide made the current a friend. The wind was also blowing toward the shore. The sky lightened, changing from charcoal to pewter. The wind howled less loudly, and the fury of the waves diminished.

Pennywhistle's teeth chattered and he shivered, but when he spied a large dorsal fin twenty yards to port, a jolt of primal fear triggered a burst of heat, arresting the reaction to the cold. He eyed its movement, assessing it as its owner was assessing him. That owner was nine feet long and appeared to be a mackerel shark. They usually fed on the fish after which they had been named, but they had been known to attack humans. His left leg had taken a small sword cut, and sharks could scent blood from miles away.

The shark began to circle.

His wife spotted the fin and her face lit with shock. "Shit!"

A strange noise caused him to turn his head away from the shark. It was the chittering of a pod of dolphins. They had an odd affinity for mankind, and he had heard of them protecting shipwrecked sailors and even carrying them to shore.

The circling fin stopped abruptly then shifted sideways. Three bottle nose dolphins had butted it hard. The dolphins continued butting until the fin tore off in the opposite direction.

Two exceptionally large dolphins pulled alongside the spar. They began bobbing up and down energetically, making sounds that Pennywhistle took to be a form of greeting. Dolphins were among the smartest of beasts: an Edinburgh scholar had written a paper claiming they had developed an actual language. They gradually edged closer, and Pennywhistle realized he was being offered a lift.

"Grab on," he yelled to his wife. She looked startled but trusted his wisdom.

Each locked their hands round the dorsal fin of the closest mammal. The dolphins seemed untroubled by the added weight and moved swiftly through the water. They understood their passengers need for air and so ran very near the surface. To his surprise, Pennywhistle found himself enjoying his aquatic cab ride.

When they were two hundred yards from shore, the dolphins made noises and waggled their dorsal fins. Pennywhistle found his boots could touch bottom in the troughs of the waves. They were close enough. He released his grip and slogged forward. Sammie Jo followed his lead. The dolphins chittered goodbye then sped back out to sea.

The top of a pale sun had pierced the horizon. It promised little warmth but seemed to be chasing the gale away, since the wind had dropped, and the cloud cover had turned spotty.

"We d-didn't even have to t-t-tip the cabby," his wife jested through blue lips and shuddering teeth.

There was a flurry of blue and green wings as Sammie Jo felt a pressure on her right shoulder. Plymouth had returned.

"Ahoy mate!" He chirped.

She stroked his head lovingly, and then continued trudging toward shore against the resistance of the surging water. Each footstep seemed an exercise in mountain climbing.

"The chest! The chest!" exclaimed Pennywhistle. "There it is!" He pointed to the bobbing container not more than 200 yards away.

John Danielski

It took ten minutes to reach the chest and twenty to reach shore. By the time their leaden feet touched the sandy beach, both were shivering hard. Pennywhistle summoned his last reserve of energy and dragged the chest onto the beach. With numb, aching fingers, he opened it and extracted two heavy Hudson's Bay blankets. He spread one out and laid the other next to it, unfurled.

He and Sammie Jo peeled off their wet clothing as fast as near exhaustion would permit and donned the dry attire from the chest. He beckoned her to lie next to him on the blanket. When she had done so, she summoned Plymouth to join them. Pennywhistle drew the other blanket over them, forming a tight seal. "We need to warm ourselves for a bit."

He pulled her close and held her tight, a gesture of love as well as survival. They said nothing for the next hour, but as the minutes passed, color returned to their faces. The numbness in their fingers and toes changed to pins and needles and then normal feeling. "I am going to get some food from the chest," he whispered. His wife nodded in understanding.

He returned with two large bars of pemmican, a mixture of tallow, dried meat, and berries, an invention of American Indians that Sammie Jo had brought to his attention. Pemmican could be eaten raw and was a rich source of energy. He had also plucked up a box full of hard candy, two small bottles of ginger beer, what Sammie Jo called root beer, and a handful of cashews for the bird.

The pair ate silently for the next quarter hour; the humble meal seeming a royal banquet. By its end, they were halfway back to feeling civilized. Plymouth daintily consumed the cashews and fluffed his feathers to dry them. "Want bath," he remarked.

Attaché Extraordinaire

Pennywhistle felt sufficiently recharged to gather up some driftwood and beach grass. Using a flint and striker, he started a small campfire. It generated scant heat, but it did much for their morale.

"How is your back?" asked a concerned Sammie Jo. "Your wound must hurt powerful bad. You were lucky you did not pop any stitches."

He forced a smile into his voice. 'Nothing I cannot manage. Much preferable to death."

"Where do you figure we are?"

"According to what the navigator told me, two hours ago we were seventeen miles from Rotterdam. I should say we are currently about fifteen miles from it, overland." He looked off into the distance, spotted a large church spire, and nodded. "I believe that is the Oude Kerk Scheveningen in The Hague. We should be able to hire some horses directly."

"But it looks a couple of miles away," sighed his wife. "Not sure if I am up for a walk just yet."

"No matter, we can rest here a couple of hours. I am so relieved that I sent Margaret on ahead with the rest of the caravan. Her ship will have missed the storm; the rest of our valuables and equipment should still be intact."

"Only seven hundred more miles to go," His wife wearily observed. "Just a hop, skip, and a giant leap of faith."

"The Congress of Vienna won't be ending anytime soon. Unfortunately, the man who tried to kill us has similar staying power."

"You're sure he resides in Vienna?"

"Positive. He is one of four chief aides to Czar Alexander, but I do not know which one."

"You're certain that he will come at us again?"

John Danielski

"I would love to tell you that the rest of our journey will be safe and uneventful but... he'll be back."

Chapter 1

*30 November, 1814. The Province of Neiderosterreich,
Hapsburg Empire.*

Ta ta ta ta da! Trrrup! Trrrup!

The shrill, staccato blasts of an English fox horn resounded off the canyon walls with the urgency of a fire bell in the night. Late afternoon clouds scudding across the cold, muddy sky acted as an aural roof, turning the canyon into a massive echo chamber. The rising wind circulated the sound that Thomas Pennywhistle did not wish to hear.

He jerked back on the reins and his mount reared briefly; his alarm mirroring his master's. Pennywhistle was not a skilled rider, but his thoroughbred was superbly intuitive, anticipating his actions and adapting to his imperfect seat. He gave the reins a quick pull and applied his spurs. Spartan spun 180 degrees and galloped toward the source of the sound.

Though Johnny's fox call had sounded a tally ho, today Pennywhistle was the fox, not the hound. Johnny's azure eyes widened with alarm as he pointed in the direction of the warning signs that Pennywhistle had made him memorize. The hounds today would be men on horseback who sought a very particular trophy far more valuable than a fox tail.

"Well done, Johnny!"

Johnny saluted his acknowledgment and his stripling frame stiffened with pride as his eyes brightened with confidence. An orphan who had once stolen Pennywhistle's purse, his mark had instead become his patron.

Johnny perched atop an ornate blue and gold carriage bearing the arms of the Countess Leith, part of a caravan that included a family, retainers and friends, a newspaper correspondent, three manservants, two ladies' maids, thirteen horses, and a Polish Wolfhound named Bounce. Two large baggage wagons followed the carriage.

Officially, Thomas Pennywhistle, Major, Royal Marines, and Knight of the Most Honorable Order of the Bath, was being seconded to The Congress of Vienna as His Britannic Majesty's Naval Attaché.

The Congress was an unprecedented pan-European gathering designed to sort out the legacy of The Napoleonic Wars and likely redraw the map of Europe. He owed his appointment and knighthood more to celebrity than service; having brought the dispatches to Whitehall announcing the seizure of Washington by General Ross and Admiral Cockburn. The nation was starved for a victory in a stupid little war, and newspapers had designated him as the public face of a New World achievement. That tabloid triumph had brought him to the attention of the Prince Regent.

His formal accreditation would facilitate covert missions well outside the bounds of diplomacy. He had been secretly tasked by the Prince Regent to use any means necessary to recover the Clarke Letters. He would also be stationed to serve justice to the individual who had stolen them, the same man who had murdered his brother and dispatched the horsemen he currently faced. He had yet to decide if that justice would be administered by a gavel or a gun.

Attaché Extraordinaire

Now, as he urged Spartan to yet greater speed, his heart quavered when he thought of his two great loves in the convoy: his wife and the unborn child she nourished in her womb. He felt sure it would be a son, though a daughter would delight him nearly as much. Either way, he would not be the last of an ancient line.

As he drew even with the rear of the caravan, Pennywhistle's gaze discerned a dark block of movement at what he estimated was slightly over a mile. The wintry air shimmered in rhythm with the steaming breaths of large animals, likely horses in close formation. By the volume of vapor, at least fifty were approaching. The heavy basalt stones of the old Roman Road transmitted loudly the measured, military *clop clopping* of many hooves. The sound reverberated menacingly off the canyon walls and mimicked the beat of some Domesday clock counting down his fate. He was facing half a troop of cavalry, or at least men who had been trained as mounted troopers.

God's Blood! Thought Pennywhistle. *I expected a few men, but nowhere near this number. Surprising that my opponent waited to spring his trap until we were so close to our destination; on the other hand, this defile is an excellent place for an ambush. If they have friends coming from the east, they can box us in and finish us at their leisure. They likely know the local terrain from a reconnoiter; they may have a lookout signaling them even now.* He unshipped his Ramsden spyglass from its saddle holster and extended it to its full 32-inch length. The piece improved his vision by a factor of 25.

He slowed his mount to a walk and swept the Ramsden over the canyon top in search of a sentinel. He noted a stray beam of sunlight bouncing off a signaling mirror. He then panned the glass more deliberately over the approaching horsemen to confirm his estimate of their numbers. He swiveled in his saddle and pointed his glass in the opposite direction: no movement. He only had to worry about attack from astern, at least for now.

He halted Spartan on a small knoll twenty yards to the caravan's rear and plucked a map from the circular red leather case in his left saddlebag. He unfurled it and carefully traced the contours of the present road with his index finger. They were familiar; each night he studied the details of alternate routes, in the event his preferred mode of transport should fail. It was wise to plan for the eventuality that would "never happen", so that if it did you would be prepared. While Pennywhistle considered Bonaparte a mischief maker of Olympian proportions, he had learned a valuable lesson from him: the Corsican's mastery of maps had transformed an upstart into an Emperor. Pennywhistle's own maps were based on the most recent topographical surveys.

His present position lay astride a spur of the *Via Militaris Styria,* laid down two thousand years ago by the Romans. He was a hundred miles southwest of the Legionnaire's camp that eventually became the great city of Vienna and three miles north of the mining center of Leoben, where a youthful Bonaparte had compelled the Austrians to sign a humiliating peace treaty. It was a road he had never expected to traverse, because he had planned on making most of his Viennese journey by water.

After the shipwreck, he had reunited with his caravan and hired barges to carry it up the Rhine. Riverine passage was ten times faster than land travel, thirty times as cheap, and offered greater safety and creature comforts.

They had left the Rhine at the former city-state of Reichenau. A bumpy, exhausting land journey of 100 miles

Attaché Extraordinaire

had taken them to the head of navigation on the Danube at Ulm. But they had been forced to depart from the Danube at Amstetten, due to unseasonably early ice and to adopt a more southerly, circuitous land route due to equally early snow. Despite the uncooperative weather, they had made good time. He thought they had been circumspect, yet clearly, their progress had been followed and anticipated.

The imposing canyon walls were not continuous. Ahead, the Roman Road passed through a narrow fissure, while the smaller track bisecting the road's north/south axis burrowed through an opening barely wide enough for two carts. The approach to that track skirted an alpine lake a quarter mile wide. Currently, the water was coated with a layer of ice that was probably much thinned by the recent thaw.

He furled the map, and then panned his glass carefully over the interlopers as they rounded a curve. Their advance was steady, deliberate, and designed to conserve the energy of their mounts. A casual observer would take them for an assemblage of sportsmen. They wore cloaks the color of terra cotta tiles in twilight, and trousers that of sea mist at dawn, subdued hues found in no current military wardrobe. Marble gray hats with wide brims and bell crowns, and black Marlborough riding boots also proclaimed civilian status. Hunter saddles and gentlemen's tack were meant to complete the illusion. Yet, the lack of variety in the horsemen's attire functioned almost as a uniform and suggested a military mentality.

And closer inspection revealed other items which belied their imposture. The small, sleek horses were of a similar height and weight and possessed the same chestnut-colored coat—what you would expect of horses belonging to a particular cavalry troop. The dueling scars on several riders' weathered faces, their exceptionally erect postures and heavily muscled physiques, and the set of their teeth reminded him of alert beasts that were products of a single litter.

He suspected these were hussars, light cavalry troopers in mufti. Hussars were daring young men as famous for their horsemanship and swift swords as for their willingness to converse with their fists and wager on anything that moved. An informal test for an officer candidate was to give him three horses, three bottles of champagne, and three harlots, order him to ride 20 miles, bullseye three targets, and return within 36 hours. As fighters, hussars were fearless; as scouts, relentless. These men had found what their master had sent them to find, and their purpose was straightforward. Pennywhistle's own purposes were anything but straightforward and his choices in the days ahead would come in shades of shifting grey.

The real leader of the horseman, he was sure, did not ride with them. The riders were puppets, and their string puller resided in a Viennese Palace. Pennywhistle swore softly in frustration. His shadowy opponent had nearly succeeded in killing him on four occasions. The deep sword slash on his back was a souvenir of one. He frowned as his doctor's ignored verdict came back to him. *You need two months more bedrest before that cut will fully heal.*

He searched his opponents' saddles with his glass, checking for weaponry. The various components were concealed in what was designed to look like an expensive gentleman's ice fishing kit—an exotic new sport enjoyed by the Hapsburg emperor himself. Their scabbards were designed to resemble holders of ice augers, but the stirrup hilts of their swords protruded. They looked to be the Blucher version of the British Pattern '96 Light Dragoon Sabre, a single blow from which sufficed to amputate a man's arm. Alongside each hip was an additional holder; he could make out the butts of what he guessed were Prussian imitations of the French Pattern 1777 cavalry musketoon. In addition, each rider carried two pistols, whose holsters were designed to resemble fish pouches. If the pistols were copies of French Year XIII cavalry pistols, they fired the same .65 ball as the musketoons.

But though the collective power of the opposition was formidable, it shared one defining characteristic: all of it was medium or close-range stuff. The horsemen fielded a total of one hundred thirty shots before the first re load. His own caravan had far fewer guns; however, their weapons outranged their opponents by a considerable distance. And there was one other factor that might provide him an advantage. Given the recent outbreak of international peace, there was a fair chance that, though these young men had been trained for combat, they had never experienced it.

His enemy would be counting on force and numbers to defeat men. Pennywhistle's perspective was based on literal horse sense. You did not have to beat a mounted trooper, you just had to beat his horse. Frighten a horse and he would balk. Terrify him and he might stampede in the opposite direction, taking an unwilling rider with him. Unhorse his master and allow the beast to gallop away, and you faced only a foot slogger. Unseasoned horses reacted badly to loud, frightening stimuli outside the parameters of their training.

Well-trained and experienced cavalry mounts were rare in 1814. Bonaparte's invasion of Russia had killed more than 200,000 warhorses, and the German Campaigns of 1813 had taken a heavy toll of Prussian, Russian, and Austrian mounts. The Belgians pulling his wagons were veterans of the Peninsula, famous for their large size and calm nature under fire. The seasoned County Kildare hunters in his entourage found gunfire no more frightening than the clanging of a familiar town hall clock.

If his opponents were Prussian hirelings, as their movements led him to believe, they would follow a well-rehearsed pattern straight out of von Scharnhorst's manual. They would close the distance at a steadily increasing pace to make sure their horses did not arrive blown. They currently moved at the trot, 8 mph. At 400 yards they would switch to the canter, 12 mph; at 200 yards they would transition to the gallop, 25 mph. The final 50 yards would be at the charge, 30 mph. Prussians were disciplined and skilled and they followed orders, but predictability could become a liability in combat.

He inserted the fingers of his left hand into a pocket of his slate grey watch coat, rubbing them slowly over a slim book which never left his person during the day and resided under his pillow at night. *The Little Code Breaker and Pocket Cryptographer* was the real objective of the approaching horsemen, for it was the key to deciphering scandal-laden letters, which could be used to blackmail or disgrace the British Monarchy. His hidden antagonist knew the power of the letters he had obtained, but not the full contents, for the most damaging portions had been encrypted. The cache of letters was like a malevolent genie that could only be released by the decryption tables of Pennywhistle's hundred-page volume.

Pennywhistle's heart performed a steeplechase as sweat beads tickled his hairline. The pupils of his eyes dilated, occluding the emerald green of the irises. His angular, Plantagenet face reddened as his capillaries widened to accommodate the blood necessary for combat. His fair, Celtic complexion soon assumed a copper color, not unlike that of the native inhabitants of America. A lance of naked fear jabbed his brain, but he was thankful for it and welcomed it as a friend, transmuting its power to paralyze into a heightened perceptivity and intuition.

His breath quickened; a jolt of electricity ripped through his veins. The ancient song of battle coaled his primal furnace as its hot melodies rang deep in his bones, seducing his senses into an extraordinary sensitivity. Yet Pennywhistle was sick of fighting; he longed for a lasting peace as only a veteran can. Penniless widows, starving orphans, and crippled soldiers pleading for stray coins were the real legacies of war. A dozen years of hard service on three continents had left Pennywhistle with a cold contempt for poets who wrote of the glory of war.

He again surveyed the approaching horsemen. Their slowly gathering pace furnished him with the best ally of all: time. He felt it stretch as if it were cosmic taffy that transformed the lifespan of a moth into that of Methuselah. The ticking of his Blancpain in his pocket sounded preternaturally loud. He resisted the impulse to pull it forth and note the time. His quickening mind schooled his eyes to break the movements of his opponents into discrete actions that could be swiftly analyzed.

A large grey stallion galloped up and stopped next to Spartan. His rider, the Earl of Grosvenor, wore the face of a phlegmatic man reluctantly speaking words of alarm. "We may have a problem."

Pennywhistle nodded vigorously.

"No, not those horsemen, Mother Nature. I have ridden this route several times and I do not like what I am seeing." He pointed to the cliffs above. "Take a look with your glass."

Pennywhistle panned his glass over the snowy foothills of the Alps.

"What do you see?"

"Lots of snow, ice, and rock."

"I see a cocked pistol with a hair trigger; an avalanche waiting to happen."

"Good Lord!" exclaimed Pennywhistle as he lowered his glass. "You may be right. But one threat at a time. Nature's wrath is only a possibility. I shall trouble you for more information once we are on the far side of peril."

"Tom!" His wife's voice caused him look away from the threatening cliffs. She had jumped from her carriage and sprinted to his side.

"Fu—uh...uh... uh... tarnation! You said there would be more trouble and I'll be God... gol durned if you ain't right. Reckon we ought to thin the herd a bit."

She was learning to mimic the manners of an English lady, but her life as a huntress always lurked below the surface—a muscled, hour-glass figure of Junoesque proportions. Her penchant for expletives occasionally resulted in a blue stream that would startle a sailor, but she was working hard to limit them to only one or two outbursts per day.

She shielded her cornflower-blue eyes with her palm, surveying the approaching troop with the remarkable eyesight that had made her the victor in every Maryland turkey shoot she had entered. "I told Dale and Gabriel to ready the *amusette* and they are attending to it. I think I got time for a fair number of shots before anything too bad happens." She trawled up a predatory smile that came nowhere near her eyes.

Pennywhistle favored her with a brisk "thumbs up". Rather than being a Roman signal to spare an opponent, it was a sign that a gladiator should raise his sword and finish his enemy. Even as he did so, the former sergeant-major Andrew Dale and freedman Gabriel Prosser wheeled the *amusette* alongside Sammie Jo.

Attaché Extraordinaire

The ironically named *amusette* was a combination super rifle and light artillery piece. What had started life as a fortress rampart gun had been modified for mobility, with a dovetail foresight and windage adjustable rear sight. Its seven-foot barrel perched atop a smaller version of the two wheeled "grasshopper" carriage that had proven popular in the American War of Independence. Stocked in black walnut with a cheek piece and concave brass butt plate, it weighed two hundred ninety pounds. Its smoothbore predecessor had fired a 110 caliber round, good to 1200 yards; the rifled version's range was considerably greater. Anyone hit by such a round did not so much die as disintegrate.

Sammie Jo's innovation was mating a spyglass to the weapon. She had hired the lens-maker, Thomas Earnshaw, to ensure that the glass was properly calibrated to function in conjunction with the existing sights. The result exponentially increased the effectiveness of an already deadly weapon.

"Now, boys" she said, "use them handspikes careful like, to jockey Last Call into position." Dale, Gabriel, and Pennywhistle looked at her in puzzlement. She returned their gazes with the weary expression of a mother explaining the obvious to slow children. "Every good weapon needs a name. You wouldn't launch a warship, lessen someone had already christened it. I figured this one needed a name that said its verdict was final."

Pennywhistle nodded in agreement and realized he should not have been surprised; after all, her long rifle bore the appellation The Widowmaker. As she directed Dale and Gabriel maneuvering the piece, he thought back to his original discussions with her. She had discovered the *amusette* in a storage shed on the rolling field behind his godmother's townhouse, and had examined it as enthusiastically as a child happening upon a sled on a snowy hill. She brought the matter to his bedside during his month-long recovery from an assassination attempt. Her enthusiasm for what she imagined it could do was infectious, yet she seemed surprised when he had simply said, "go ahead and see what you can make of it. I shall see to it that anything you need is forthcoming."

"That was as easy as taking as taking firewood from a forest!" she'd replied.

"Why the puzzlement?"

"It's just that most gents don't put no stock in a new-fangled notion if it come from a maid's mind. They think a woman's head is like a cloud: pretty but empty. The men I grew up with would have told me to go to hell or had a long guffaw at a dame offering an opinion on a shootin' iron."

"The short-sightedness of conventional men is my gain," he had replied. "I rely upon intelligence and cleverness, far more than faith, to deliver me from evil. It is only logical that since my own wife possesses both in abundance, I should allow her to follow those talents down whatever road they will lead."

Marry her and marry chaos. Only discord can come from such an unnatural match of breeding and estate. Her world and yours are night and day and no one can live in twilight. The warnings of Pennywhistle's gentlemen friends had been well-intended and heart-felt, but his pairing with Sammie Jo was a match of kindred spirits willing to look at life through an unconventional lens. The times were rapidly changing as an agricultural England was being replaced by an industrial one: nearly as many people resided in cities as lived in the countryside. This new England needed people willing to give audience to novel ideas and fresh perspectives.

Attaché Extraordinaire

Sammie Jo lent her own shoulder to the handspikes; not to add strength but exactitude. When the *amusette* was finally in the right spot, she rose to her full height and rubbed her hands together in gleeful anticipation of its use.

"So, Hawkeye, what is its range? I have a general idea, but I am sure you can give me a more exact one."

Sammie Jo's lovely features turned as hard as a marble Minerva, yet they were infused with a leonine energy found in no statue. It was the energy of defense, a cause that the Roman Goddess championed. Her voice changed from silk to leather as she reverted to her native Southern drawl.

"I can hit a man at 1,600 yards," she said confidently, "but that don't matter right now, because those cavalry fellows ain't more than 400 yards away."

The hussars spurred their horses to the canter.

"Amazing!" He knew her estimate was based not on bravado but testing.

She had explained to him a month ago, "I must have fired two hundred rounds while you were abed recoverin', Tom. I listened when you said that practice makes perfect, and that excellence is a habit, not an act. I know that weapon as well as a Ma knows her child."

"Thanks, boys," said Sammie Jo to Dale and Gabriel. "Now why don't you get the sabots and utensils so we can get this show on the road." Each sabot was an oval sack of flannel that contained powder, wad, and ball. Dale laid out six and an equal number of priming quills for the pan. Gabriel spread out a rammer, wormer, and swab as well as a bucket of water. He placed wooden chocks a few inches behind the wheels to limit recoil.

"I do believe my predilection for the scientific method has rubbed off on you, my dear," remarked Pennywhistle with satisfaction. "Your testing was impressively systema..."

"Uh... yes, sure, uh... right,' she mumbled in response. So great was her concentration that he might as well have been a thousand miles away. "Hitting that gent leading the pack will be like taking candy from a baby." Her accompanying smile was full of knives and needles.

She placed her hands firmly on her wide hips and nodded in satisfaction. "You boys load her up while I adjust the sights."

Gabriel and Dale acknowledged with informal salutes. Dale passed the first sabot to Gabriel who inserted it carefully into the breech. It was a tight fit, allowing for almost no windage. Greater windage would have eased loading but increased the leak of gases, reducing the range and hitting power of the round.

Dale performed the ramming ritual with a smooth, easy grace rather than the ham-fisted motions of the average British soldier.

Sammie Jo ran a wire pick through the touch hole to make sure the vent was completely clear. She then inserted the contents of a priming quill into the pan—30 grains of superfine double strength powder that would give the fastest ignition. She made sure to leave a tiny opening in the powder trail between the last grain and the touchhole to facilitate ignition. Satisfied she was ready to do damage, she walked round to the breech of the piece, flexing her knees slightly as she put her eye to the lens of the glass. It was five feet off the ground while she was just half an inch under six feet.

She slowly rotated the eye piece clockwise with her left hand as she quietly hummed "Yankee Doodle." Its rhythm steadied her nerves and paced her actions, just as a drumbeat did for a marching soldier, but the tune also had a personal meaning. A doodle was a silly fellow and many Britons condescendingly thought of Americans thusly. She often hummed it under her breath when she had outsmarted a Regency buck who thought her beauty meant she need not be taken seriously. She reduced her motions to tiny tweaks and until the face of a cantering hussar came into focus. The range had dropped to 325 yards: still too far for any of the enemy weapons to be of use.

His features looked boyish and homespun, though a scar on his right cheek suggested his face belied his real nature. His expression was carefree and confident, as if he had just proposed marriage successfully. He looked like a subaltern who would be popular with his troopers; one whose death would be quickly noticed. He was probably a martial sprig of an aristocratic family since hussars were considered an elite body. Rules for ordinary folk did not apply to such men.

She loathed the type, although she knew her backwoods prejudices were showing. Her husband had once told her that General La Salle, one of Napoleon's most famous hussar officers, had remarked, "If you are doing your job right, you should never live past thirty." The lad in her sights would never even reach the quarter century mark.

She draped a padded roll of cloth over her right shoulder; its interior contained two inches of Portuguese cork. The recoil of the piece exceeded even that of a Nock volley gun—a weapon that had fallen into disuse because it had a nasty habit of dislocating shoulders. So, she seated the rifle butt hard against the pad and then made one final adjustment on the lens. She breathed deeply four times—an abbreviated version of the meditation ritual her husband had taught her. It ramped down her predatory excitement, then remolded those powerful energies into a concentration that blanked out all distractions and focused every facet of her consciousness on the face of the hussar officer.

Rather than experiencing pity or pathos, she felt the throbbing pulse of the hunt: an ancient blood rhythm that relegated compassion to a dark and silenced place. While the head of her target would never be mounted as a trophy on a physical wall, it would repose on one that existed in her mind. His resolve to take part in this assassination attempt, to play the predator, had turned him into prey. She gently put her finger on the trigger and then took a breath and held it. At the bottom of a slow exhale, she applied pressure.

"*Crack!*" The loud report sounded like Zeus bellowing a demand for obedience. The *amusette* kicked like a rhino, but she had anticipated the reaction and her grip remained firm. The smoke cleared a few seconds later. "Yes!" She clapped her hands together in satisfaction as she regarded her handiwork.

The round blasted the youthful hussar from his seat. He flew high in the air, or at least his torso did. The lower part of his body slumped from the saddle and slithered down his mount's side to plop hard on the basalt stones.

At first his fellow troopers did not understand. They saw a distant puff of smoke and heard the report of a rifle, but it did not really register. They were supposed to be the ones springing the ambush. One minute there was a trooper and his horse; the next an empty saddle and a confused mount. The advance ground to a spontaneous halt.

"Look! My God! My God! What hit him?" shouted one shocked NCO as he pointed to the remains. The wreck of a body left but one conclusion: they were under attack by people who were supposed to be unarmed. Their civilian targets were actually displaying hussar spirit.

Joshua von Halle pulled his horse alongside the stunned sergeant. "Compose yourself, Weber. You must be an example to your men." His voice came out as a cross between a hiss and a bark. Von Halle was the troop's senior member at age thirty, as well as its commander. His pinched, narrow face suggested an eager ferret and his storm-grey eyes flashed like lightning as he realized his quarry meant to put up a fight.

"Yes, Herr Rittmeister, of course, of course," said the sergeant abjectly, like a child being reminded that he was expected to care for his puppy. "I will do my duty!" Prussian discipline steadied his voice and carriage.

Von Halle diverted his horse and rode around the remains of the trooper, assessing the cause of his demise. He spoke crisply to Mueller, his manservant; a trusted confidant of advanced years, who had also served his father. "Looks like grapeshot severed the body, but those people cannot possibly possess artillery." He scratched his temples in bafflement.

A careful man would have taken cover, and then sent two scouts forward to discover the lay of the land. But he was a hussar and their reputation was based on impetuosity and attack, not defense. Fortune favored the bold! In von Halle's experience, gained at the Battle of Leipzig, there was no problem that could not be solved by a fast charge administered with ferocity and skill. His men lacked his seasoning, but he had spent hundreds of hours drilling them hard and had made real soldiers of people who had been gawking farm boys a year before.

The range was too great for their guns to be effective, so von Halle decided on cold steel. He spoke *sotto voce* to Trumpeter Braun next to him. Braun blew the appropriate commands. Forty-eight troopers and two subalterns formed themselves into four neat lines that filled the road. The lines were separated from each other by a horse's width, and the boots of the troopers in each line were so closely aligned that they almost touched. The hussars placed their hands on the hilts of their sabers but did not draw them. There was no point in fatiguing the wrist before calling it decisively into action.

Gabriel and Dale had reloaded. Satisfied that she had gotten the attention of the men by killing an officer, it was time to disrupt the unit's communications. She focused her sights on Trumpeter Braun's mount, held her breath, and gently squeezed the *amusette's* trigger.

Braun's horse disintegrated into misshapen clump of flesh, mane, and hooves. Its rider shot through the air as the trumpet flew from his lips. His head impacted on a roadside boulder, turning his face into strawberry-colored mush. Since the command to advance had not been blown, the lines remained stationary. The horses began neighing in agitation and only reluctantly obeyed the frantic jerking of their reins by their white-faced riders, who were equally bewildered.

"Well done, Sammie Jo!" said Pennywhistle, observing the damage through his Ramsden. "Might I suggest..."

"Already there, Sugar Plum," said Sammie Jo, her eyes never leaving her scope's lens. "Time to take out the commander and then the remaining subaltern. Officers always have the best mounts, the ones with fire and spirit. I just have to spot those two. Horses run in packs and will follow the leader, just like privates follow generals." She stepped back and motioned for Gabriel to adjust the handspikes to swivel the piece as she pressed her eye to the lens. "I just found the subaltern, so he goes first."

Dale and Gabriel reloaded the *amusette.*

Attaché Extraordinaire

Sammie Jo fired, and the head of a tall subaltern's mount exploded. The impact threw the rangy man five feet, and he landed in a patch of moss and lichens. He slowly sat up with the surprised expression of a man who finds himself naked at a fancy-dress ball. His men stared at him with equal puzzlement. Their horses whinnied and neighed loudly in terror. The subaltern retched, put his hand to his head, and passed out.

A short, wiry horseman on a massive black mount cantered up to Pennywhistle's side: Lord Steven Thynne of the 1st Lifeguards, who had saved Pennywhistle's life in Spain. He rode with such grace that he seemed almost a centaur. "I think I see what you have in mind, my dear fellow. "Mind if I make a contribution to the amusement?"

"Be my guest," said Pennywhistle.

Thynne withdrew a Baker Rifle from a saddle holster. The weapon's best range was 200 yards, but it was lethal at greater ranges if the pop-up rear sight was adjusted by an expert marksman. Thynne calculated the distance to a particularly balky horse at 300 yards, brought his piece to the point, and fired.

The shot hit the horse in the right fetlock. The stallion reared and whinnied loudly in pain, tossing its rider. It then raced off as fast as its three working legs could carry it. Two horses next to it also reared in panic, though their riders managed to retain their seats.

The two baggage wagons pulled up behind Pennywhistle and Thynne. Johnny had taken the reins of the first wagon; Dale and Gabriel crouching along its sides with their Baker rifles primed and ready. Sammie Jo knew they were just itching to get in the fight and had said she could reload the *amusette* from here on. Andrew Junior, Dale's son, captained the second wagon. Grimsby, Lady Leith's peg-legged butler and a retired Royal Marine sergeant, sat next to him on the buckboard, also carrying a Baker. Emboldened by Thynne's success, the three Bakers barked almost in unison and three more horses plunged to the ground.

Though some commanders felt that the distasteful business of actual killing should be left to the "Other Ranks", while a leader concentrated on issuing directions, it was a philosophy that Pennywhistle did not share. He owed his friends his active participation in the defense of the caravan. He raised his Ferguson Rifle and fired, bringing down yet another horse and rider.

Sammie Jo massaged the trigger and a crack like Cerberus barking thundered off the canyon walls, shaking bits of snow off the cliffs above. The head of von Halle's horse sagged, and the dying body dropped in response to gravity. Von Halle pitched hard onto the road; bounced slightly, then unfurled to his full length. He staggered to his feet but bobbed and weaved like a man who had had one too many schnapps. The horses around him reared in fear and confusion and were on the edge of becoming unmanageable. The grand charge that he had planned would never happen.

Von Halle clapped his head twice to chase away the dizziness that threatened to envelop him. *What the hell was happening?* His superbly trained troops seemed to have devolved into a mindless rabble. He began shouting commands but his words came out oddly slurred. He swore savagely. This could not be happening. To his chagrin, he saw two of his newest troopers gallop away; he could not be sure if the riders or horses were in control. He drew his saber and shouted, "Stand fast! Remember your duty! Remember the Fatherland! Remember..." His last words never cleared his throat because his head exploded.

Attaché Extraordinaire

Von Halle's death extinguished the last semblance of order within the troop. They reversed course with the speed of a spinning top and sped back whence they came, as if they were being pursued by the Furies. Panic was not just an idea but a disease that burned away countless hours of training in an instant. It affected horse's primal instincts even more than those of men.

Sammie Jo stepped back from the *amusette* as Johnny brought her horse forward. She leapt into the saddle and immediately extracted the *Widowmaker* from its holster. She gently applied the spurs to her horse and moved alongside Pennywhistle.

She leveled the *Widowmaker* and aligned the sights on the head of the slowest member of the fleeing herd; wanting to add some extra encouragement to the equine survival instinct. She squeezed the trigger gently: the horse stumbled, fell, and rolled heavily, crushing his rider beneath. The other horses galloped even faster.

Lady Leith's elegant carriage pulled up just astern of the two wagons. Dale's wife of less than a month, Deborah, occupied the coachman's seat.

A fourth rider joined the mounted trio, eliciting shock from all three.

"Margaret, we are perfectly capable of handling this. You should stay safe in the carriage," said Pennywhistle with deep concern.

"My lady," said Thynne in a soft voice that was courtliness personified, "your rank and age make it clear that you must stay out of harm's way."

"Hell's bells!" said Sammie Jo indignantly. "Don't you two dare pull that frail old woman stuff. I seen Margaret shoot and she's damn good. If she wants to take a crack at them folk hell bent on killing her, give her the chance!"

"Thank you, Sammie Jo," responded the Countess Leith with a mixture of hauteur and amusement. The spry septuagenarian, who possessed one of Scotland's most distinguished pedigrees, was Pennywhistle's godmother. "I remind you, Tom, that I paid for a large part of this expedition and as chief financial officer, I claim the right to participate in its defense," she said, with the gravity of an archbishop pointing out the truth of transubstantiation.

"Very well, Margaret," said Pennywhistle. "Your point is well taken, so do your worst."

She pulled a Collumbell Rifle from her saddle, raised it to the point and then lowered it slowly with a sad face. "Ahhhh! Blast! I waited too long. The range is too great for this piece."

The Earl guided his horse close to Lady Leith's and the two exchanged subtle looks that hinted at an incipient romance. "I want those working for the killer of my son wiped off the face of the earth," he said, "but we need to be gone from this place as soon as possible. I have been monitoring the snow cover on the heights and it has shifted. I fear the gunfire has had a deleterious effect." He pointed to the overhanging cliffs.

The Earl was a stately looking man who had fought alongside Pennywhistle's father in the American War of Independence. He had shared his humiliation at Cornwallis's surrender at Yorktown and had entrusted his beloved son to Thomas's elder brother, Peter, as aide de camp. That son had shared Peter's fate.

Pennywhistle was humbled by the way his friends had pitched in during his hour of need. The Earl was right. It was unwise to stay where they were.

Chapter 2

"Tell me what you know about avalanches," said Pennywhistle in the manner of a student seeking counsel from a professor.

"I will speak from experience, for I have survived two in my time." The Earl's voice was urgent, yet measured. "One further down this very road, and one in the Canadian Laurentians. The first I managed to outrun on a fast horse, but I was buried by the farthest edge of the second. Fortunately, the grave was shallow and I had a friend to dig me out. Being buried alive is something one never forgets; it is a lesson in the puniness of man. Afterwards, I made a study of avalanches."

Grosvenor's voice became yet more serious. "The warning signs are all in front of us. See! The snow rests precariously in tear-shaped clumps. Such a shape could give way at any moment. Then the angle to the road approximates forty degrees, so the snow will move fast and far. And there have been fluctuations in weather the past few days."

"Are you referring to the recent thaws?"

"Yes, thaws and strong winds are destabilizing."

"And right now the wind appears to be rising," observed Pennywhistle with alarm. He removed his black top hat and let the wind rustle his sandy red hair, wishing it would cool his fevered brain.

John Danielski

"Just so," responded the Earl as he unfurled his pocket telescope and surveyed the ominous, snowy outcrops. "The masses of snow that have accumulated are enough to crush men and horses to death when the laws of gravity, acceleration, and momentum act upon them. To make our situation worse, the snow will not be slowed by the trees. Spruce and fir trees make effective barriers because they have lower branches, but most of the trees here are lodgepole pines, and they will do little to absorb the onslaught of an avalanche.

"Could a loud noise fire this metaphorical pistol?"

"With avalanches, one never knows. Noise is less important than concussive pressure."

"Could the intrusion of a random animal unbalance things? Such as a deer, a lynx... or us?"

"It could be something as small as a rabbit. Our caravan could certainly be a trigger. Those retreating hussars and the gunfire may have already loosened the precarious stasis."

"Hmm," responded Pennywhistle. He could still not shake the sensation that he might just have won an opening skirmish, not the battle itself. He so devoutly wished the end of fighting that he wondered if he was thinking clearly.

Between France's Declaration of War against Austria on April 20, 1792, and Napoleon's abdication on April 6, 1814, Europe had known only 441 days of peace. Though centered in Europe, the conflagration had encompassed the globe, with battles being fought as far away as the Rio de la Plata and Nagasaki. France's desire to spread Robespierre's call for *liberté, égalité, fraternité,* added to the Corsican's quest for *la gloire,* had cost Continental nations more than five million dead and two million wounded, 3.6% of a total population of 190 million. The wars had rendered untold numbers homeless and had spread disease and famines, while embargoes had ruined whole industries. Like camp followers, revolutionary ideals had accompanied French armies, challenging traditional notions about the rights of men, nations, and religion.

Pennywhistle prided himself on anticipating the attack he had just repulsed, then wondered if that pride was intellectual arrogance in disguise. He had no shortage of mental hubris and wondered if it had made him as predictable to his opponent as the hussars had been predictable to him. That possibility unsettled him, and it also cautioned him to husband his resources. A memory of Marengo sprang to mind: a battle on the verge of being lost by Bonaparte, won when Desaix's fresh division arrived at the last instant to rout the worn-out Austrians.

A few drops of rain alighted on his collar, indicating that the temperature was rising. "We have but an hour of daylight and should seek shelter as swiftly as possible."

"You're sure, Tom?" Sammie Jo's predatory eyes glowed, hungry for action. "Them hussars might decide to turn around and come after us again, all quiet like, under cover of darkness. That's what I'd do. It might be good to put more of the scare into them. I'm up for a little hard riding and fast shooting, and I don't think I'd lack for good company." She nodded at Thynne, Earl Grosvenor, and Lady Leith.

"I appreciate your zeal, Hawkeye, but I think this unpredictable weather makes a pursuit unwise. The road could ice up again after nightfall."

Thynne nodded in agreement, but his expression darkened. "But that's not all, is it, Tom? The tone of your voice tells me there is something else worrying you."

Pennywhistle sighed in frustration. "I have always thought a leader should keep his doubts to himself; however, this is not a military organization but a band of volunteers who have put their hearts and souls into following my quest. You are putting your lives at hazard when you could have lounged safe and comfortable back in London." He squared his shoulders, and his voice became that of a doctor delivering a terminal diagnosis. "Very well then. My opponent may have a second stroke planned. We need to keep a tight order and be on guard against surprises."

Lady Leith spoke with puzzlement. "I agree with you about the weather, Tom, but shouldn't that also cause a second attack to be stood down?"

"While a second attack in peculiar weather seems illogical, surprise in war conveys a huge tactical advantage. A man is never so vulnerable as when he lowers his guard after having beaten a threat. My adversary is an extremist. Such a man is undeterred by nature. Instead, he is possessed of such hubris that he believes even elemental forces can be bent to his will. He will have sought out minions who act with audacity rather than circumspection."

Sammie Jo spoke brusquely. "Whoever is after you, Tom, he must want that codebook mighty bad. He seems crazy to get it."

"I think his motives are not entirely rational, Sammie Jo. There is something very personal about his struggle with me that has nothing to do with crowns, causes, or cabals."

"But Tom, don't that give you an advantage?" wondered Sammie Jo. "You have told me that letting hot blood and quirky obsessions affect thinking through a problem is like punching holes in the hull of a boat just before you hoist the sail."

"Quite right, my dear. I am painfully aware of my own flaws and limitations, but fanatics are often blind to theirs.

Attaché Extraordinaire

They are consumed by self-righteousness, possessed by a sense of superiority so profound that they will brook no arguments with their judgments. And since no one man can be perfect in all his judgements and plans, he invariably comes to grief, usually through one of the Seven Deadly Sins."

Thynne, who had been surveying the horizon to the southeast with his glass, snapped it shut and spoke with an undercurrent of alarm that contrasted with his normally nonchalant tones. "My dear chap, I do believe you are right about a second threat. There is a disturbance above the tree line that looks like snow, stirred by the passage of many men."

Pennywhistle whipped out his glass and panned it over the woods astern of the alpine lake. Thynne was not wrong.

Thynne speculated, "Perhaps it is a work gang of miners using their shovels as snowplows. The mines in this area bring in revenue to the Hapsburgs, and the miners probably have the additional duty of keeping the roads clear in bad weather."

The Spiegel Mine, the largest iron mine in the Empire, lay only two miles away. Three roads branched out from it, and the one through the forest ahead connected it with the old Roman Road to Vienna. Since the Emperor Francis had stripped the Empire of regular troops to fight Bonaparte, the mine would likely be guarded by the Austrian equivalent of British fencibles, men with thin military training who might never have fired their weapons with live rounds. Mining was hard on the lungs, so they might not have much endurance. Pennywhistle suspected that several chests of rubles sent to the town mayor and mine manager had provided his opponent with a ready-to-hand second thrust. As often happened, it would be a rich man's war and a poor man's fight. Just like the hussars, they could be explained away as civilians, out on a task other than assassination.

John Danielski

The noise of tramping feet could now be heard. Pennywhistle wondered how many men they were facing. If only there was a way to get a God's eye view! He had done some hot air ballooning in America, but though his caravan was well equipped, it did not include such an exotic item. Yet perhaps there was another method. A warm breeze had sprung up that reminded him of the quirky Bora in the Adriatic. The clouds were dissipating, and the temperature was rising. Though the aid he had in mind hailed from the tropics, a flight could perhaps be managed.

"Sammie Jo, would you please fetch Plymouth from the carriage? And bring your sewing basket as well."

"What do you need him for... oh!" Her eyes sparkled with understanding.

She trotted back to Lady Leith's carriage, dismounted, and opened the door. Once inside, she removed Plymouth from a cage sheathed in a heavy blanket. While the cover kept him warm, it also obscured his view of the outside world. He was a social animal, brimming with curiosity, and limited vision had made him cranky. She stroked him gently with love and reassurance. He fluffed his feathers and trilled back at her. She guessed that after his imprisonment he was eager for adventure.

Plymouth was a foot-and-a-half long Grand Cayman Parrot who had adopted the couple. He had shown up with a singed wing and Sammie Jo had nursed him back to health. He regarded Sammie Jo and Pennywhistle as members of his flock. He needed a lot of attention but rewarded it with unstinting loyalty. Sammie Jo doted on him, and he had become her constant companion. Under her tutelage, he had learned new tricks. Regency society ladies delighted in his antics, for he was much more entertaining than the usual gentlewoman's lapdog, which generally greeted people with yaps and snaps.

Though at first Pennywhistle had treated him as an amusing novelty, he'd become fascinated by the animal and had begun to study him with the scientific curiosity of a zoologist. As the bird came to trust them more and more, he'd gradually displayed unexpected capabilities. He was not simply an avian entertainer equipped with a remarkable ability to mimic human, animal, and street sounds, but a creature blessed with real cognitive gifts. He obeyed fifty commands and had a vocabulary of over 1000 words. He greeted people by name. He understood what he said and could respond to questions of a basic nature. He was able to fashion simple tools. Furthermore, and not unlike humans, he thrived on touch and praise. Most significantly and relevant to their present need, he grasped the concept of numbers and even the idea of zero.

Though his eyes lacked the sharpness of a raptor's, Plymouth's vision exceeded a man's, with a wider perception of colors and a 300-degree field of vision. He had a small blind spot at the back of his skull, but he bobbed his head constantly to compensate. He could not give Pennywhistle the exact numbers of the approaching men but could furnish a rough estimate.

Sammie Jo returned with Plymouth on her shoulder. He ruffled his wings and swiveled his head several times to assess his surroundings. "Better! Better," he cackled. The temperature now was far more congenial to his kind than when he had entered his cage that morning.

Sammie Jo made a hand motion to Plymouth, who immediately flew to Pennywhistle's shoulder. "Ahoy, Captain!"

Pennywhistle responded by gently stroking the crest of Plymouth's head and then doing the same to the tuft of feathers around his neck. The bird nuzzled his hand and gave several quick chitters that were the equivalent of a cat's purring.

"Good day to you, my friend. I need your help."

"Aye, aye, Captain!"

He formed the fingers of his right hand into a V: a signal that a command was about to be given. The bird's eyes snapped to attention.

"Bad men. Bad men. Bad men." Pennywhistle made a grotesque face and jabbed his finger toward the forest three times. The bird not only understood words, but gestures and emotions as well.

"Awk, awk, awk! Bad men! No good! No good!"

Pennywhistle decided on a variation of a test he had employed repeatedly to assess the bird's understanding of numbers. He had made the test seem a game, and Plymouth loved games. Taking the sewing basket from Sammie Jo, he quickly scissored off strips of green, yellow, and red thread. He tied each color into a bundle: green was thinnest, yellow next in size, and red the thickest. The first represented a platoon, the second a company, and the third a battalion. Plymouth watched with absorbed interest, as he liked colorful things.

Pennywhistle held the bundles close to Plymouth. "Bad men, bad men. How many? How many?" He pointed to each bundle three times.

"How many? How many?" Plymouth did a creditable imitation of the urgency in Pennywhistle's voice.

Pennywhistle waved his arms upward several times, the signal he wanted the bird to fly. "Find, find, find!"

Attaché Extraordinaire

The bird bobbed his head. "Aye, aye, Captain." He unfurled his wings to their full three-foot span, fluffed his feathers briefly, and departed with a *whoosh*.

Thynne gaped in astonishment. "An avian scout? Can he be relied upon?"

"Damned right he can, Steven," said Sammie Jo with asperity. "He sees better than people do. He once spotted a lost pearl earring and brought it back to me in his beak. Tom here trained him to use bundles of thread to provide a count of men. Plymouth is a member of the family and senses when we are in danger."

Pennywhistle began to worry when Plymouth did not return after five minutes. Then he realized the bird was probably enjoying his liberation from the cage and playing this particular game to the hilt.

Vroof! There was a sound like a ship's bilge being flushed and he felt a smart pressure on his right shoulder. Plymouth emitted a series of short trills as if to say, "*Did you really doubt me?*"

"Well done, mate!" said Pennywhistle in glad relief. He stroked Plymouth's head and neck, then handed him a cashew from his pocket as reward.

"Thank'ee kindly, Captain." The bird seized and nibbled the treat.

Pennywhistle again held up the bundles. Plymouth flapped his wings and put his right foot on the yellow bundle. "Awk, awk, yellow! Yellow!" The enemy had a company; roughly sixty men. He briefly considered the option of retreating to safety, but if they spent the night in Leoben, news of the presence of a foreigner and his entourage would spread like wildfire. "Never leave a castle in your rear," de Saxe had warned. Therefore, he would engage them now, on his own terms.

The sound of shuffling, stamping feet increased in volume.

Petting Plymouth calmed him as well as the bird. A sudden inspiration crystalized into a plan. Nature could be his ally. The frozen lakes at the Battle of Austerlitz flashed through his mind: a headlong retreat of Russian troops onto their surfaces had shattered the ice and sent hundreds of Czar Alexander's men to a watery grave.

Once the course of the forest road exited the trees, the path traversed a broad plain that skirted the alpine lake. After three quarters of a mile, it joined the Roman Road. The trick was to persuade his opponents not to use the road but instead choose the fastest route between two points, a straight line over the frozen lake—a lake whose ice may have been substantially weakened by the three-day thaw.

Four inches of ice was generally reckoned necessary to support the weight of a man, and a group of men burdened by equipment would need even thicker ice to cross safely. But to plan he had to be sure, and that required someone to vet the ice personally, someone who did not weigh much. Johnny! He could not weigh more than eighty pounds.

He waved urgently at Johnny. The boy had been watching him; he jumped down and raced forward as intently as a diving eagle spotting a leaping salmon. Before Pennywhistle got a word out, Johnny demanded, "How can I help?"

"I warn you, what I am about to ask will be dangerous. If you decline, I would unders—"

"Dangerous!" exclaimed Johnny with a combination of excitement and glee. "Then I am your man!"

"Capital!" replied Pennywhistle. He pointed to the lake. "I need to know the thickness of the ice on yonder lake. I want you to fire a pistol into it and then measure the depth of the ice through the opening. I don't have a ruler handy so a pen will have to do." Pennywhistle produced a quill from his watch coat. "The plume is twelve inches. Make note of how much of the plume covers the thickness of the ice."

"I can do that!"

"I appreciate your eagerness, but the ice may not support your weight and I have no wish to send you to the bottom of the lake. Before you commit to walking on it, put your foot on the edge of the ice and push hard. If it seems firm, advance out, taking only short steps. If at any point you feel the ice weakening, retreat as fast as you can, because you will have obviated the need for a gun and quill. Once you have an answer, get back here as fast as you can. Time is of the essence." He reached into his coat and handed Johnny a small pistol. "Be careful! Tread lightly!" He feared the boy's eagerness might cause him to take foolish risks.

"Don't you worry none," said Johnny, and dashed off.

Sammie Jo trotted over. "I assume that Johnny's errand has something to do with what Plymouth spotted?"

"Indeed. We are about to be set upon by sixty men and I need to know how thick that ice is before they debouch from the forest."

Sammie Jo swiveled in her saddle to observe Johnny's progress. "He is walking that ice like a duck with a load of buckshot up his butt."

"Good. He is distributing his weight. The fact that the ice bears his weight has already answered part of my question."

The report of a pistol cracked the wintry air.

"What is he doing?"

"I don't have an augur, so I had him use a pistol. I need to know the thickness of the ice."

"Are you trying to see if the ice can handle our horses?"

"No, Hawkeye, I merely need to know if it will bear the weight of a man."

"I thought maybe you were a-fixin' to stage a cavalry charge."

"I considered it, but given the weather, I want them to bring the fight to us."

"Ain't that giving up that offensive you are so keen on?"

"Tactically, yes; strategically, no. Wellington in the Peninsula often took up a defensive position that dared his opponents to attack, when he knew the ground and they did not. You recall, I have always stressed the importance of a thorough reconnoiter before engaging?"

"Information is the key to victory, and a proper scout is the first step in securing that information," Sammie Jo intoned in a creditable imitation of Pennywhistle's voice.

Pennywhistle smiled. "I do ripple on about battle maxims rather a lot, don't I?"

Sammie Jo grinned back. "You love to lecture like a rooster loves to announce dawn, but I confess, you have taught me a heap o' stuff. And I ain't never seen your mind nor instincts play you false when it comes to battle."

"Thank you, Hawkeye! If our opponents do not conduct a proper reconnaissance, it will be because they are eager to get the job done as soon as possible, in order to return to the comforts of warmth, hearth, wine, and wives."

Sammie Jo's expression turned sly. "Give them a little homicidal philanthropy?"

"God's blood, you have been reading Gibbon!"

"He is your favorite author, so I thought we should get acquainted."

Attaché Extraordinaire

A blur in blue raced up to Pennywhistle's horse then halted as abruptly as an iron filing caught by a magnet. Johnny breathlessly burst out, "Ice is four and a half inches!"

Pennywhistle scratched his temple and then looked at the sky as if the heavens might supply some inspiration. "If they test the ice and proceed cautiously, they will either make it across or realize it is too dangerous and turn back to take the safer, longer route, where they will have the advantage of cover and numbers," he explained to his wife. "We need to goad those men to charge over the ice, where our few rifles will have the advantage of range, and our bullets can weaken the ice beneath them. Alpine lakes are cold and deep, and even men who can swim will be hampered by weight of their clothing and equipment, and by hypothermia."

He sighed and rubbed his chin philosophically. "I wonder if it might be possible to spare those men. The ice is borderline, perhaps vulnerable to bullets alone. Perhaps we can stop the militia's journey early enough that they can wade to shore and retreat to those homes and hearth fires, abandoning the pursuit."

Sammie Jo's expression turned hard. "Perhaps? Perhaps? What kind of talk is that? You said it's all about weight, and mercy can't trump the laws of physics. We got to be sure they don't come after us, and the only way to do that is to wipe them out, every last God-da... er... cursed soul! Men who would kill passing strangers because someone paid them means every last one of them varmints is lower than a snake's belly in a wagon rut. You never believed in the "I was just following orders" defense for murder, and now ain't the time to start. We stop them right here, right now!"

Pennywhistle blanched at Sammie Jo's words, but then his eyebrows arched in understanding. "Truly, there is no creature so fierce as a mother protecting her child in her womb! You are right; the quality of mercy would be strained in this situation. Let's get everyone back toward the intersection of the cart track with the Roman Road. That looks to be the highest ground and will give us a clear field of fire."

Chapter 3

The caravan moved to the modest hillock. Gabriel uncoupled the horses, and he, Dale, and the manservants pushed the two large baggage wagons together to form a barricade. Lady Leith's carriage was positioned five yards to the rear. The riders dismounted. Their thoroughbreds and the Belgians were turned over to the servants and Dale's son, who would act as horse holders.

Gabriel, Dale, Grimsby and Thynne lay on top of the baggage in the first wagon, using its side as an extended rifle stand. Sammie Jo, Lady Leith, and the Earl took up similar positions on the second wagon. Pennywhistle stood alongside, observing the enemy through his Ramsden.

"Sure you don't want to use the *amusette?*" inquired Sammie Jo.

"I'm still concerned about a possible avalanche. Besides, multiple rounds of small fire will break up a larger region of ice. The weight of our opponents will do the rest."

Pennywhistle surveyed the column as it emerged from the woods, 300 yards away. There was a lot of pushing and stumbling, and the marching men resembled elephants in cement boots. The men were dressed in heavy, dun-colored moleskin trousers, jackets of muddy blue, and wide-brimmed circular hats of hard black leather. Muskets and cartridge boxes that looked to have been new when Marlborough marched to the Danube were slung over their shoulders, and all carried shovels in their gloved hands. They were all short of stature, and coal dust was imbedded in the creases of their faces, marking them as men who spent a lot of time underground.

A bugle blew, and the column responded slowly; cold, numb-fingered men shuffled to a halt. A man who was slightly taller than the rest waved a sword and shouted a command. Two men, however, seemed to be arguing violently, and one of them shoved the other. The column evaporated as the men formed themselves into a circle to watch the fight. Pennywhistle had no idea why the men were fighting, but the prospect of death in battle often caused smoldering resentments to burst into flame.

"Stay away from my wife," yelled one combatant. "Not going to let you shoot me in the back so you can have her!" He threw a punch to emphasize his point.

"Who'd want that pox-ridden hag!" shouted his opponent as he blocked and responded with a left jab.

The two exchanged blows with increasing fury.

Each combatant had his supporters, and men erupted in cheers or boos, depending on the progress of their brawler. The taller of the two finally landed a solid left hook to the chin that staggered his opponent. The man stumbled backwards and then dropped to the ground. Half of the crowd burst into cheers. The same officer, who had earlier waved his sword, stepped forward and waved it again, this time not as a weapon of war but as a sheep herder would use a staff. He formed them into a long line on the plain in front of the lake. They gradually straightened their line into something that looked reasonably military.

Attaché Extraordinaire

Pennywhistle watched, pleased by the disruption. He wanted these men excited: prisoners of roiled emotions demanding an outlet, angry men itching to teach someone, anyone, a lesson. The actors were in place for the parts he had assigned them in the drama about to unfold. Bonaparte himself had been the grandest of actors and had captivated millions by treating the continent of Europe as his stage. This was a much smaller stage, but no less deadly.

Pennywhistle unfurled his Ramsden. He slowly surveyed the expressions on the men's faces and then smiled wryly. They reminded him of country horses at a race awaiting a starting gun. The officer who would be their collective metaphorical jockey did not look like he would have much control.

"I just wish I had a way to prod them a bit," Pennywhistle muttered.

Johnny, who had been hovering by his side, overheard. "I have an idea!" He raced off towards the ice.

"No, wait!" shouted Pennywhistle. He started after the boy, but Sammie Jo grabbed his arm.

"Let him go. The ice can hold his weight, but it might not take yours. You couldn't catch him anyway."

"Blast it all!" Pennywhistle cried out in self-reproach. "The young can be such fools! I should have gone myself—"

"No!" exclaimed Sammie Jo, with the passion of a Spanish Inquisitor confronting an atheist. "You are in command and need to act a ship's captain, not go haring off like a midshipman! You always told me that for a commander to be effective, he must be willing to hazard the lives of those he loves best. In a war young men die, and even the most conscientious officer has no power to alter that outcome.

Remember that powder monkey that was cut in two at Trafalgar?"

"William Borders."

"How old was he?"

"Seven."

"Compared to him, Johnny is an oldster."

"I take your point, but I do not have to like it."

"If you liked it, you would not be the man I fell in love with."

He followed Johnny's progress through his Ramsden. To his surprise, Johnny had stopped by the second baggage wagon and acquired a companion: the Earl's dog, a Polish Wolfhound named Bounce. It was a friendly beast rather than an aggressive one, well suited to his chief function of delivering the *London Times* to the Earl's bed rather than hunting. At the lake's edge, under the cover of a spreading bush, Johnny proffered something that Bounce took in his mouth. Through the spyglass, Pennywhistle could make out that it was a loosely rolled up newspaper. Next, Johnny unpocketed a grenade, cut a length of fuse that Pennywhistle's practiced eye estimated had a two-minute burn time, and wedged it into the small aperture atop the projectile. All of this he shoved inside the roll of the newspaper, tied off the end with a bit of string from his other pocket, and lit the exposed fuse. He whispered something in the dog's ear, then gave him a quick slap on the rump. Bounce took off at a lope for the enemy line.

My God, thought Pennywhistle. *He remembered the story I told him about Americans using mine dogs to blow up British ammunition wagons in their War of Independence.*

The dog came to a halt in front of a puzzled sergeant who was of roughly the same build as the Earl. The dog opened his mouth and dropped the newspaper at the man's foot. He then reversed course and lumbered back toward Johnny.

The confused sergeant heard a hissing noise as he bent down to pick up the paper. The grenade detonated in his hand, blowing it off as well as blinding him and removing most of his nose. It happened so fast he did not have time to cry out before he hit the ground.

Once his comrades had recovered their wits, they shouted in angry surprise. They looked to their officer with the bloodlust of revenge in their eyes.

The officer responded by barking out the commands to fix bayonets and advance. He then placed his hat upon the tip of his sword and waved it in the air. The men surged forward.

Pennywhistle moved briskly among his people. "We have their attention. Now we need them to ignore the cracking of the ice. Start shouting insults! As loudly you can. I want the denizens of both Heaven and Hell to feel deafened by your cries."

Everyone responded with alacrity, glad to dispel tension in a way that contributed to their safety. Sammie Jo let off a panoply of her favorite expletives. After months of trying to corral them, it delighted her to let them run wild. Lady Leith's shouts were not profane but featured some very pithy insults. Dale's and Grimsby's contributions in a lower register featured colorful Service curses. Thynne's insults reflected his genteel upbringing. It was like a man wanting to say, "Move your arse, now!" but having it come out, "Hasten forward quickly, there."

But it was Johnny who angered their pursuers the most. He pulled his trousers down and made a farting gesture in the direction of their pursuers—a traditional Saxon expression of contempt.

Pennywhistle stifled a snort of laughter, then frowned. He wondered why the officer in command had not yet ordered his men to fire. Looking through his glass, he saw that their cartridge box flaps were loose; their cartridges might have absorbed enough moisture to render their contents inert. The bayonet charge might be sheerest necessity, yet terrible folly against an enemy who demonstrably had firepower, even if their numbers were small.

His musings were interrupted by Johnny shaking his arm. "Did I do it right? Did I? Did I?"

"You showed real initiative. That is the stuff of which Great Captains are made. Now get back to the wagons, pick up a rifle, and show me that what my wife has taught you has taken effect."

"Ha! I aim to please!" Johnny exclaimed just before he took off.

Pennywhistle shouldered his Ferguson and waited; would the ice hold or would it give way under the stamp and slide of over 100 boots? If it held, this would come down to a handful of rifles against all those rapidly approaching bayonets in the hands of exceedingly angry men. Shots were going off now from the wagons, but only the rifles had the range. Out on the ice, one man fell and another staggered, but pressed on.

As if in response to his question, beneath the covering sound of firing guns, he heard a noise like an ogre cracking his knuckles.

Two more men cried out and fell to rifle bullets. Several of their companions cursed and loaded their guns to return fire. Clearly, not all of their powder had taken on dampness. The officer in charge berated them. He, at least, knew enough to calculate effective ranges.

The ogre cracked his knuckles more loudly.

Attaché Extraordinaire

The enemy advance quickened as they apprehended the danger, but they were past the point of return. They were committed, because Pennywhistle's position was closer than their starting point.

The ogre's knuckles cracked sharply again, but the ice still held.

"Fire all together!" Pennywhistle shouted, and pulled the trigger of his Ferguson.

The rifles discharged with a deafening sound. The shooters all aimed low, allowing for the rise of bullets. The screams, shouts, and groans that followed told him most of the rounds had struck. A dull chorus of *thud-thud-thud* followed as bodies collapsed onto the ice. The impacts increased the ominous sounds of frozen fissures widening.

He heard his friends reloading. *Three volleys*, he had told them. The first to immobilize, the second to disorganize, the third to sink.

"Fire!" yelled Pennywhistle.

Their rifles and his blasted out a second time. More screams and thuds followed as bodies fell. The shouts of the hapless officer were devoid of authority. Terrified voices answered in panic, not obedience.

The humanist in Pennywhistle felt pity. He shivered as a spear of recrimination pierced his equanimity. Four months ago, an encounter with The Grim Reaper had transported him briefly to a realm of love and peace, a place furnishing infinite possibilities for gentle and improving instincts. At some level, what they were doing felt wrong.

Crack Crack Crack. This time the noise from the lake sounded like lightning bolts a cricket pitch away. The fissures were visible now.

Pennywhistle purposely directed the third volley, not at the men, but at a point twenty yards to their left. It was the metaphorical straw that broke the camel's back. There was a crack like a chorus of thunderclaps as the ice gave way entirely. Since the sun was three quarters of the way down, all Pennywhistle could see was a silhouette of shapes that disappeared. Shouts and screams choked off abruptly as the chill of the water constricted lungs.

As he was sinking, the brawl's winner's last thoughts were of his wife. He wondered if she had been unfaithful. The brawl's loser thought, *she wasn't worth it.*

The militia commander wished he had left his wife a will.

The sound of splashing assaulted Pennywhistle's ears. It swelled to an awful crescendo, then gradually faded away like the final *pianissmo* notes of a Satanic symphony. The absence of sound emphasized the absence of life, the silence of the grave completely unlike the soundless calm of nature in repose. The lack of noise felt as eerie as it was oppressive. Pennywhistle sucked in a long breath of air to calm himself. The cold chilled his bones.

Pennywhistle felt relieved yet sad. The threat was gone, but the miners had been collateral casualties. Professional soldiers accepted death as a concomitant of their occupation and understood its awful randomness. Militia were intended for the defense of home and family, and these men had probably been roped into a madman's machinations. He wondered if they had even had a chance to spend any of the pittance they had been paid. Probably not; the coins had likely only added to the weight that dragged them to their deaths.

How could his nemesis have arranged two ambushes to arrive at nearly the same moment? Pennywhistle's appointment to the Congress was public knowledge and the progress of his caravan was conspicuous, but to coordinate two thrusts from opposite directions was a difficult thing, even when performed under the direct supervision of the planner. Yet his real opponent was nowhere close. He scratched his head in thought and his expression darkened. He hated the conclusion that he reached because it suggested he had made a bad mistake. He'd thought he had spotted a sentinel, but even that man must have been given advance information to position himself where he did. His opponent's information was too detailed and exact to have come from the outside. No, there was a traitor in his caravan.

Pennywhistle trusted his friends implicitly. Logic and loyalty argued against their betraying him. But since arriving on the Continent, he had added two servants to the caravan, replacements for two retired Royal Marines who had been rendered *hors d'combat*. Both newcomers were Dutch and had come with good recommendations. Both had performed well, and he had felt he had made a good bargain. And yet, if someone were engaged in clandestine skullduggery, he would not want to call attention to himself by performing his duties badly. Rather the opposite, to earn the trust and confidence of the man that he was betraying.

Sammie Jo shook his arm hard, and he blinked. "Sorry, Sugar Plum! I could see you were lost in thought, and we ain't out of this yet." Her voice rippled with alarm and she pointed in the direction of the hill where the narrow cart track descended to meet the Roman Road. "Why don't you use your glass and take a closer look?"

He unshipped his Ramsden. He panned it over the heights, then sucked in his breath in horror and began counting. He slammed the glass shut in exasperation. Horsemen were coming down the hill, single file. They were probably the other half of the troop that he had defeated earlier.

"God's death, Sammie Jo, these people will just not quit! That maniacal devil has mounted a triple threat!'

"Ain't that damn near impossible to pull off?" said Sammie Jo with surprise. "You've told me that the more complicated the plan, the more likely it will go wrong."

"Very true! I think each link here was intended as a separate effort, a series of redundancies operating on the theory that if one failed another would succeed. Much like Russian nesting dolls; the one on the outside is a precursor to those that lie within. The man in Vienna is not only persistent, but thorough to a remarkable degree."

He stopped talking abruptly, for he had had a Eureka moment and descended into the deep silence of profound concentration. Watching him at such moments always amazed Sammie Jo and frightened her just a little. Her man contained hidden depths beyond her power to imagine. It was like viewing a silent mental steam engine in action: the pistons of thought producing the energy of creativity. When he spoke again a minute later, she recognized that the confidence in his voice meant a full-blown plan was ready.

"Our present situation is a not a bad one. The track leading to our position is narrow, while we have the use of the little improvements that I had built into Lady Leith's carriage."

He gave her a quick summary of his strategy and she nodded thoughtfully.

"That's a whale of a plan, Tom."

"Right now, we need to deal with the immediate threat." He began to stride towards the carriage, then stopped abruptly and smacked his forehead at having missed the forest for the trees.

"Something else, Tom?'

"Your observation about my opponent's hubris. I think I may be guilty of exactly that and it has caused me to miss something that is literally striking me in the face." He brushed away falling snow from his eyebrows. "All of the movements and commotion cannot have improved Nature's temperament. The approaching men and their horses may act as lit matches in a powder magazine." He pointed to the snow-capped peaks in the near distance.

Sammie Jo's jaw dropped. "Snow 'til the cows come home! You think that—"She jerked her head in the direction of the shattered ice over the lake. "—we might have sent a bee up Nature's bottom?"

Pennywhistle nodded.

Sammie Jo clenched her fists in frustration. "But Nature can't tell good men from bad. Whatever she does to them, she does to us."

"True enough; however, we are forearmed with knowledge. We need to relocate our people a good five hundred yards to the rear for a clear field of fire. Nature could act anytime in those minutes, and we will need to move at the first sign of trouble."

"I thought avalanches don't give no warning," remarked Sammie Jo.

The Earl had trotted over in time to hear Sammie Jo's concern. "A common misconception, but there will be warning signs. First splinters in the snow appear, like cracks in a pane of glass. The ground vibrates as the stronger layer of snow displaces the weaker. From that point, you have about a minute until the main collapse. A damned difficult thing to outrun, and the width and depth of the resulting snow field are impossible to guess."

Sammie Jo pulled a face. "I feel like a fly with Mother Nature holding a fly swatter."

"We are always supplicants before Nature," agreed Pennywhistle, "but though she is unpredictable, once she commits to a particular action, she acts according to the laws of physics." He unshipped his spyglass and panned it to the east. "I see a rock outcrop not far distant which might serve as an effective shelter against the snow blast. You and I will man the carriage and Johnny will be the rear lookout. You handle the horses and guide our progress while I attend to the 'other things.'

"Those 'other things' you added to the carriage, do you really think they will work?"

"Caltrops worked well for the armies of Louis XIV, and Frederick the Great employed them on occasion. As for the others, they are... well... experiments. I cannot honestly say that they will work. However, I consulted with Sir Humphrey Davy, and he said their theoretical basis is sound. If a man who is considered the father of modern British chemistry tells you something will work, I think you may set aside most of your fears. The only problem he foresaw is mixing the chemicals too far in advance of their use. My arrangement solves that problem."

Sammie Jo responded dubiously, "Well, if I got to go, I can't think of no better way than riding side-by-side with the man I love."

"No!" exclaimed Pennywhistle, "Our task it to make sure that we live! Think of our son!"

"Or our daughter."

"Equally excellent!" His demeanor transitioned to deep anger. "I am utterly damned if some Russian hirelings will deny me a chance to see my child grow to adulthood. Fuck that bastard in Vienna!"

Sammie Jo gasped. Her husband never swore and had worked hard to correct her penchant for doing so.

"I cannot believe I just said that." Pennywhistle's voice rippled with chagrin.

Sammie Jo smiled. "It's good to step down from The Cross every so often."

"Let's get moving," said Pennywhistle decisively, "and hope we live to continue this discussion."

"Amen to that! I will get the carriage lamps lit," said Sammie Jo. "Hell, I will add a couple of torches, too! No sense in being subtle."

Pennywhistle and Sammie Jo set off in opposite directions. While their movements were swift, they were also disciplined and directed. The trust and love both had engendered meant their commands were obeyed without question or hesitation.

Gabriel was a genius with horses, and despite the cold and falling dark, soon had them hitched to the wagons and carriage. His many years supervising stables came in handy because the carriage had to be backed into the narrow cart track, since there was no room to do a turn around. The result was a very tight fit, with the large wheels of carriage nearly scraping the needles of the tall pines corseting the road.

Thynne and Dale positioned the baggage wagons a thousand yards in front of the tree line, turning them sideways to be used both as a lures and barricades. Lady Leith's carriage took up a position in front. The shooters loaded their weapons and took up their positions atop the baggage.

Pennywhistle noted that the advancing column was perhaps four hundred yards distant. He wondered if they could perceive the outlines of his caravan. No matter, when he ignited the carriage lamps, their lights would be noticed.

Johnny held a lamp close to Pennywhistle as he mixed two separate assortments of chemicals that he hoped would work the magic of deliverance. It should have been a painstaking process, but the constraints of time caused him to work with a haste that he found unsettling. When the task was done, he poured the results into two canvas bladders suspended beneath the cab of the carriage. The first bladder took the majority of Chemical Assortment A. The second took the remainder of Assortment A, but had a separate compartment for the contents of Assortment B, to prevent their intermix until the time was right. He attached narrow ropes to three release latches and then crawled under the carriage to bring their ends to the buckboard at the front of the cab.

Nature continued unpredictability, this time redirecting acoustics. The stygian silence of the forest departed, and sounds became amplified. He heard hoof beats on crunchy snow distinctly, now much closer than when he had first spotted the horseman. Time to get moving!

He rocketed onto the buckboard and plopped down next to Sammie Jo.

"Is that a comet just landed, or only my husband?"

"Grace is rarely a function of haste. Time to shed some light on the situation!" He signaled to Johnny, on the roof directly astern, and the boy lit the two large carriage lamps at the back of the cab. Sammie Jo did the same for the two at the front, then ignited two three-foot torches soaked in pitch. She handed them to Johnny, who waved them about.

"Very good, Johnny. I want them to be the fiery equivalent of the signal flags the Navy uses."

Attaché Extraordinaire

Pennywhistle unshipped his glass to make a final survey. The enemy cavalry was now less than three hundred yards away. The column was moving faster; they had seen the lamps and torches. He directed his glass toward the lofty peaks but saw no movement. His upcoming actions would be like extending a dance invitation to the Devil and expecting him to match your step, marking him as either lucky or a fool. The minutes ahead would decide, though he might not be alive to observe the outcome.

He swung his hand-held lamp side-to-side twice; a signal to commence firing after thirty seconds. While they were technically laying down a suppressing fire, they probably would not hit anything. They did not have to; this was about the sound of bullets, not their impact. The noise would serve as a lure to the cavalry and, more dangerously, a nudge to Nature.

"Let's go," he said with quiet resolve. "A slow trot, if you please, Hawkeye."

Sammie Jo flicked the reins, and the four horses began to move.

The crack of rifles erupted, and Pennywhistle felt the heavy air displaced by zipping missiles. Through his Ramsden, he saw several branches snipped from pines.

The carriage moved forward while Johnny's motions with the torches sent the lights gyrating. He was enjoying baiting cavalry even more than he had the infantry.

The cavalry closed the distance to two hundred yards. They could have moved faster, but it was possible that the man in charge apprehended some danger from the snowy cliffs above. So far, Nature remained a sleeping giant.

A volley burst out from the wagons, and he saw one rider fall.

"Be prepared to apply that whip fast and hard at a moment's notice," he said to Sammie Jo. "Once that snow starts to move, it will gain momentum fast."

"I got that. We ain't dealing with something that has any brakes."

The advancing cavalry closed to one hundred yards distance. Another volley blasted out and another man went down.

Nature continued coy, so it was time to deploy his infernal devices.

He flicked the lever that released the chemicals in the second bladder, causing them to mix. The result was a vile-smelling, inky smoke. He pressed another lever that dropped a flap on the bladder, liberating a rapidly swelling cloud that blotted out their view of the narrow road astern. The cloud drifted toward the cavalry column.

The hoof beats slowed, though they did not stop. The sounds of violent coughing were followed by prolonged retching.

He squeezed a third lever that unlatched the first bladder. This released a slick, composed mostly of picula; his old professor had renamed it petroleum, after the Latin *petra*, meaning rock. It trailed behind the carriage.

Screams and thrashing followed, some human and some equine. He heard assorted curses, as masters struggled to right their mounts. His friends acknowledged the noise by discharging another volley. Judging from the human cries, some rounds connected.

The hoof beats resumed. He reached for the fourth lever, which released the box of caltrops on the rear luggage board. Caltrops were large crows-feet of sharp iron spikes; weighted to always land with the points up. It was a cruel weapon, and extremely effective in a narrow corridor. He had never bonded with horses, but regretted he would cause them lingering pain rather than a mercifully quick death.

The caltrops trailed out, followed by equine neighs and screams. The hoof beats stopped completely.

He waved his hand lantern three times in a prearranged signal to Gabriel, who got the Belgians ready. Pennywhistle surveyed the outcrop that he had noted earlier. It was thirty feet high and was wide enough to divert a wave of snow. It would make a safe bivouac for the night.

A deep rumble shook the ground.

"Is that what I think it is?" croaked an alarmed Sammie Jo.

"Yes! Now it's a race. Make for that outcrop."

A loud ripping sound assaulted his ears as the snow fractured into giant slabs; their jagged edges would act as Nature's guillotines. Each was ninety feet long, three feet deep, and had the consistency of marble. The noise changed to a low *whooshing* as the slabs began to move, the sound *molto fortissimo*.

In the first two seconds, the white tsunami surged to ten miles per hour; by twelve seconds, it had reached its terminal velocity of eighty miles an hour. At that speed, the noise changed to a deep base, a *whumpf whumpf, whumpf* that made it sound as if every elephant on the planet had declared war against man.

Rampaging Nature generated an instinctive terror that made Gothic novels exercises in mannered civility. Sammie Jo shivered but kept cracking the whip, pushing the horses to within an inch of their collective lives.

Thynne's horse, Mandrake, was the fastest of the lot and he reached the outcrop's opening ahead of the rest. He turned Mandrake and waved violently. "C'mon, C'mon!" he shouted at the top of his lungs, but his cries were drowned by the snow's *whumpf, whumpf, whumpfing.* Desperate to find a more effective signal, Thynne unshipped a torch from his saddle and lit it, holding it high, once the flames flared up.

The snowy wall made Gabriel, who was not a small man, feel diminutive and insubstantial. His felt his chest convulse and shudder, erratic and painful, trying to match the booming of the avalanche.

Pennywhistle experienced a flashback to a hurricane off Antigua. Hurricanes generated a similar primal terror, but an avalanche compressed days of fear into seconds. An avalanche could kill you by blunt force trauma or suffocation, either burying one alive or filling your lungs with so many airborne particles that you ceased to breathe.

The *whumpf whumpf, whumpf* felt like a giant vice applied to everyone's temples. Whole stands of trees vanished with a crackling noise. The sound changed as the torrent absorbed obstacles: forest, boulders, and miscellaneous animals. The aural war between treble and bass resulted in an unholy sound that oppressed ear drums, compressed the brain, and made nerve endings shriek for mercy.

Two of the enemy horsemen were the first to fall to the snowy holocaust. One man had dismounted his disabled horse when the snow slammed into him. To his horror, an ice mask formed over his face, making breathing impossible. A companion was struck by five boulders: one decapitated him while the rest acted as a giant meat grinder.

Sammie Jo concentrated on Thynne's torch and willed the horses to move faster. The carriage's front wheels hit a rock and bounced hard. Sammie Jo barely kept her seat; Johnny lost his and tumbled into what shortly would become a snowy abyss. Behind, Deborah swerved her wagon to avoid the rock—

and Johnny. Ahead of them, Grosvenor and Lady Leith gained the entrance.

Thynne saw Johnny fall. He applied spurs to Mandrake and the pair became a blur of speed.

Johnny crashed to the ground and rolled several times. Barely conscious, he looked up and saw a giant black horse and a man leaning far over in the saddle, his scissored legs acting as anchors. With a grip like a steel vice, Thynne's hand grabbed Johnny's collar and yanked him up and onto the saddle. Fluidly, he resumed his normal posture and spun Mandrake toward the outcrop. Mandrake sensed the urgency and demonstrated why he had cost a king's ransom.

Gabriel felt his heartbeat steady and sucked in a deep breath that nearly froze his lungs. He believed in a gentle approach to horsemanship, but now he thought the Good Lord would forgive him if he applied a whip to the horses for the next few seconds. To reassure himself, he hummed the go-to-meeting hymn, "Michael Row the Boat Ashore".

The juggernaut of snow plowed to within twenty yards of the rear-most wagon helmed by Gabriel. The cloud given off by the snow wall made the ambient air so heavy that it was difficult to breathe. The air was heavy, not just with snow and ice, but pebbles, dirt, branches, and bits of turf. The smell was a mixture of mud and tree scents, pine being the strongest.

Pennywhistle felt a nasty taste in his mouth as some of the grit collided with his tongue.

Sammie Jo thought the horses were about to collapse because they had even more trouble breathing than people, but with one final burst of speed, they rounded the outcrop into sanctuary. The wagons followed as the advance tendrils of the avalanche nipped at their wheels.

Once inside the outcrop, everyone wanted to breathe a collective sigh of relief, but the snow-choked atmosphere oppressed their lungs, covering everyone with a mix of ice crystals, pebbles, and mud. The thick, white wall blanked out all vision. But the shuddering roar gradually diminished as the snow blew past, lessening with distance and as trees absorbed more and more of the force.

Pennywhistle, Sammie Jo, and the rest alighted and surveyed the devastation wrought by the avalanche. Sammie Jo spoke for all of them. "It don't do to fool with Mother Nature."

"Sleigh rides are one thing, but that slay ride I could have done without," mused Thynne. He patted Mandrake's head. "I owe my life to you, and not for the first time." Mandrake gave a snuffle of acknowledgement.

"M-mine too," stuttered Johnny between shivers. "I will never look at a snow-covered mountain the same way again."

"But at least we know there won't be no more threats against us," said Sammie Jo.

"Until we get to Vienna," Pennywhistle corrected her. "After that, my opponent may try again, although he will have to be more subtle."

"How are we going to get there, Tom?" inquired Sammie Jo. "The road ahead is sealed shut."

"We will find a way. A detour will add a few days to our journey, but it can't be helped."

Gabriel detached himself from the rest to do some exploring. He returned thirty minutes later, with welcome news. "Sir Thomas, there be a cave round the curve over yonder that might be a good place to bed down for the night. It's a cheese cave the size of a barn. Must be hundreds of round cheeses on them cave shelves.

Attaché Extraordinaire

"Ennstaller Steirerkas," offered Pennywhistle.

Gabriel looked at him in puzzlement.

"The kind of cheese most likely in the cave. This region is famous for it. Good reconnoitering, Gabriel. A cheese cave may not be what I had in mind for accommodations, but it's far better than shivering in the wagons all night.

"At least we have plenty of food, thanks to those picnic hampers you laid at Reichenau," said Sammie Jo.

"At this point, the company is more important than the food, Hawkeye." Pennywhistle faced his companions. "It is said that a man's life can be defined by the quality of his friends. I am fortunate to have you as mine. I sincerely apologize for almost getting you killed."

Lady Leith protested tartly that he had, in fact, saved their lives because of his quick thinking.

Over the next hour, he and his friends created a creditable bivouac that was almost comfortable. Johnny could not stop shaking from the adrenaline residue. Lady Leith pulled him tight and whispered soothing words as she stroked his hair, lavishing on him the affection that she would have given the child that she never had. Johnny calmed and stretched out. She fed him a few bites of a baguette and he slipped into the deepest of sleeps.

Dale was the least demonstrative of men, but he could not restrain himself from giving repeated hugs to his wife and son. They returned his embraces.

The Earl thought of his own lost child. Rather than surrender to tears, he took out his violin, handling it tenderly, tuned it, and began playing the third *Sei Solo a violino* of Bach, one of his son's favorite airs.

Gabriel had never encountered Bach, but liked what he heard. He joined in with his trumpet, providing a counterpoint that incorporated contrasting rhythms. The unusual mixture generated an unusual but pleasant sound.

A how-do-you-do with death burned off a huge amount of energy and acted as a powerful stimulant to the taste buds. The adults were glad to partake of the humble meal of raisins, baguettes, tinned pork, and lots of cheese. Sealing meat in a container was a recent French innovation. An Englishman had improved the method by substituting cans for bottles, although the English referred to such things as "embalmed meat." Two bottles of Riesling provided a refreshing accompaniment.

After a leisurely dinner, Pennywhistle took out several maps, and then he and Gabriel set out on an extended reconnoiter. They returned with a confirmation of Pennywhistle's hunch: the large outcrop had a rear exit unaffected by the avalanche. Even better, they had discovered a small cow-path that had not been obliterated by the passage of the avalanche; though barely navigable, it would eventually lead to a thoroughfare that would link up to the main highway to Vienna.

Pennywhistle announced their findings to his relieved friends, who had feared they had become snowbound. Then they all turned in for the night.

"How bad is the pain, Tom?" said a concerned Sammie Jo as her husband grimaced.

"It's been better."

"Do you want some of my medication? Or maybe the emergency stuff?"

"No, we need to conserve your medication, as we are almost out." That medication was made from Maryland willows and contained salicylic acid; an effective pain killer favored by the Piscataway Indians. "As for the laudanum, I will stick to our bargain that it should only be used for the most excruciating pain, since it is addictive and clouds the mind. I have no wish to succumb to the Soldier's Disease."

He held Sammie Jo close in their makeshift bed and stroked her hair until she drifted off to sleep. He lay awake, thinking about the odd turn of events that had brought her into his life. His brief encounter with "The Other Side" had taught him that many events were not random, but part of a larger plan that interacted with his free will. He would have died today, along with Sammie Jo, but for the rocky outcrop. Its presence was providential, not a mere coincidence.

He laid his head next to Sammie Jo and willed sleep to bring relief to his weary bones, but it would not come. He finally gave up on Morpheus, dressed, and went out for a long walk in the cold night air. He needed to exorcise the demon determined to deny him rest. If his suspicions were correct, there was a traitor sleeping in their midst. He did not want to believe his judgment had been so mistaken, but a spy was the only explanation that answered for the day's events.

It had to be one of the two Dutchmen. The first had replaced a Royal Marine private who had been killed by a runaway hay wagon. The second had replaced a corporal of long service who had been found dead in his bed one morning. Pennywhistle had attributed the private's death to a freak accident and the corporal's to the ravages of age. Though the deaths had occurred within a day of each other, it had never crossed his mind that one or both might not have been accidental. He had been so focused on threats from the outside that he had never considered one from within. The way the innkeeper had been able to proffer replacements so quickly suddenly seemed highly suspicious.

Chapter 4

"I despise failure, *Herr Major*." said Klaus von Steinwehr in a voice as sharp and menacing as spears tipped with curare. He leaned back in his leather chair with the confidence of a superior predator and glared at the man standing on the other side of his desk.

"Men who fail me suffer unpleasant fates, von Gilsa. You have betrayed my faith five times. You have squandered my money, my resources, and my reputation." His iceberg blue eyes became scalpels, slicing fissures of threat into the imagination of the now terrified von Gilsa. "You left England as a fugitive because of a very public scandal created by your blundering. The British tabloids got hold of it and began asking questions, whose answers might eventually lead back to me, or worse, to my prince. I warned you to use discretion and subtlety, because your target had the ear of the Prince Regent. You, however, were about as *subtle* as a chimpanzee wielding a meat cleaver. A clumsy, ineffectual chimpanzee. You were supposed to dispose of Pennywhistle and deliver a certain object to me. Instead, Pennywhistle arrived in Vienna along with his entourage yesterday, with the object of my attention still in his possession. You neglected to inform me, and the only reason I know is because I heard it mentioned that he is to present his credentials formally to Lord Castlereagh this evening. My sources tell me that he has taken up temporary

Attaché Extraordinaire

residence at the British Embassy. Since the embassy is cramped, it is possible he will seek more permanent accommodations, and those outings may give you a chance to get at him, to finish your job and redeem yourself." He stabbed a finger to emphasize his anger. "*I* have been doing *your* job, von Gilsa!"

Von Gilsa's eyes darted about and his face turned the sickly grey of fear mixed with despair. A tendon in his neck started twitching. He considered himself a man of iron, but he faced one of steel. "I am truly sorry, *Herr Kolonel*. Mistakes can be corrected, and I pledge on my sacred honor to do all in my power to—"

"Stop!" thundered von Steinwehr. "I care nothing for your pretensions of honor, your hollow promises, and your pretended determination. I have heard them all before. This city is filled with experienced soldiers that I could have chosen. The only reason we are having this conversation is my wife's intervention on your behalf. If that codebook is not in my hands very, very soon, I may be forced..." He paused ominously."...to reevaluate my position. Do I make myself clear, von Gilsa?"

Von Gilsa's cower deepened and he shivered slightly, "*Ja wohl, mein Kolonel.* I will put things right."

Von Steinwehr sighed with the irritation of a professor explaining Spinoza to a child. He pointed to a small fishbowl which contained an Amazonian Candiru: a fish that fed on blood. "A gift from a well-wisher, meant to amuse me during long hours of paperwork. This is a curiously aggressive creature, but I grow weary of its simplicity." He rose from his desk and plucked the fish from the bowl. "I have a better use for it."

John Danielski

He walked a few feet to a tall wooden stand, on which perched a hooded Peregrine falcon. "Magnificent animal, isn't she? Medusa is a Valkenswaard: the most savage, the most dangerous variant of the Peregrines. She is the outcome of many generations of cross breeding by Dutch falconers, the best in Europe." He put the fish under her beak, letting her scent it. She seized and devoured it. He stroked her head lovingly. "There, there, my pretty! I promise you a better evening meal, a runty puppy."

He returned to his chair and steepled his hands. "That bird is of much more use to me than you are. I trust that you do not want me to see you as a human version of the fish. In any case, I have wasted enough time on you, von Gilsa. I have a meeting with the Czar in two hours for which I should have been preparing. I shall expect a written report of your progress in two days. Now, get out of my sight!"

Von Gilsa snapped a salute and a quick, "*Ja wohl, mein Kolonel,*" He did a quick about turn then scuttled from the room like a roach evading a broom.

Von Steinwehr rifled through the mass of official documents plaguing his desk, his high forehead creased by vexation. Disgusted and impatient, he swept them onto the floor. He already had more than enough information at his fingertips to handle the Czar.

Klaus von Steinwehr was a man with a mission, an all-consuming one that had come to define him. He was a 39-year-old colonel of Rhenish heritage in the Russian Service. He had once been Graf von Steinwehr, the Landgrave of Reichenau and desperately wanted to be so again. Reichenau had been a small country, ruled by his family since the Middle Ages. It contained valuable real estate because it fronted on the Rhine. His patrimony had been stolen from him by Napoleon after Prussia's fall in 1806, and incorporated into the Confederation of the Rhine, part of Napoleon's efforts to reduce 300 German statelets, duchies, principalities, and free cities to 39 much larger and more efficient entities. But that efficiency had cost hundreds of families their hereditary holdings.

The Congress was redrawing the map of Europe, and he wanted the new cartography to include Reichenau. The man he served, Czar Alexander, was a key power broker who could make that happen, but Alexander faced opposition from the French, British, and Austrians who feared granting Russia a large role in central Europe.

Klaus von Steinwehr had enjoyed a distinguished career as a soldier before joining Alexander, fighting under various flags, but always devoted to opposing the Corsican who was the cause of his present discomfiture. He had gotten close to Alexander because of his moral adaptability and skill with what the Russians called "wet work": strong-arming, disappearances, assassinations. The Russian Court was a hotbed of cabals and conspiracies, and Alexander had needed a man who could make problems disappear without even a whisper that the Imperial Family might be involved.

Von Steinwehr considered himself a man of honor, attempting to model himself after the legendary Siegfried. He found parts of his job distasteful and possessed sufficient introspection to fear the man he was becoming. Yet, even paladins had to adapt to the demands of harsh necessity, and he considered the present state of affairs a temporary one. Once his great task was accomplished, he would return to the ideals of his instructors at Heidelberg: ruling his returned kingdom with an equal measure of sagacity and firmness. He might even become a modern Frederick the Great—an enlightened ruler who had been a writer of poetry, a friend to Voltaire, and one of military history's Great Captains.

Although he presently served the Czar, he neither liked nor respected Alexander. The Czar was intelligent, but logic was not his forte. He often ignored considerations of state in pursuit of his next bedmate. Von Steinwehr had never seen a man so relentlessly driven by the brain between his legs. On the rare occasions when he was thinking of matters of state, Alexander wanted leverage against the British, who seemed to be leading the charge against Russian ambitions. Any man who gave him that leverage would be well rewarded, even to the extent of reconstituting a vanished state. Von Steinwehr had offered leverage in the form of letters that compromised the British monarchy, and the lascivious Alexander would derive pleasure as well as power from using the contents to blackmail members of the British government. The threat of publicizing their embarrassing contents could be used to compel Lord Castlereagh to soften his oppositions and see things the Czar's way. If Castlereagh came round to a new perspective, the other powers, who respected Castlereagh's intelligence and honor, would follow his lead.

Trouble was, von Steinwehr had so far only been able to deliver on half his promise. He had shown Alexander the letters and whetted his appetite, but the real meat could not be revealed because the most salacious parts had been carefully encrypted. He had committed numerous murders to obtain the letters, but they were mostly useless without one slim volume which held the key to unlocking the encryption. The man who held that volume knew exactly what he possessed and had shown himself unwilling to give it up without a fight. That man was Thomas Pennywhistle.

Von Steinwehr had researched his opponent with the thoroughness of a seasoned campaigner, and his conclusions

Attaché Extraordinaire

had been validated by Pennywhistle's conduct. The man was resourceful and relentless in achieving his objectives, taking hit after hit but always moving forward like a scarlet juggernaut. While von Steinwehr would have preferred a target lacking courage and sense, he afforded Pennywhistle a measure of grudging respect. He was a worthy and interesting opponent. Those did not come along often.

Von Gilsa had failed because, like Napoleon's Murat, he had more dash than brains. Von Steinwehr had tried to furnish him with detailed plans but had come to understand that the man could only execute the simplest of directives. Ordinarily Von Gilsa would not have left his office alive, but he was his wife's cousin and her childhood friend, and she regarded him with uncharacteristic affection.

His wife, Ingrid, stabilized and energized him, an equal partner in his plans. She absolutely believed that the ends justified the means and that a great end justified extreme means. She urged him to bear in mind the legacy he would leave his children.

His three daughters, an infant, a six-year-old, and a ten-year-old, were the joys of his life. Playing with them, he could forget the brutality of the real world and enter one where fairies ruled, unicorns roamed, and licorice and lollipops were the foods of the day. Whatever was happening at the Congress, he religiously allotted an hour each evening to be with his family and connect with what really mattered in life. The innocence and depth of his daughters' imaginations reminded him that there was indeed hope for the world. He trusted that he could bring some of those qualities to his time as the future ruler of Reichenau.

Reluctantly, he pushed aside his reveries and picked up one of the papers he had tossed on the floor. It detailed the agendas of the nine committees that conducted much of the real work of the Congress. He skimmed the topics, passing over the ones concerning Switzerland, Germany, and diplomatic protocols, until his eyes fixed upon a topic that caused him to jerk upright: "International Rivers." That was of great concern to him. He guessed the British would be pushing for unfettered navigation on the rivers of Europe, consistent with their advocacy of free trade on the high seas. The elimination of trade barriers would mean the elimination of tolls—and Reichenau survived on tolls. That could not be permitted to happen! He would push Alexander to appoint him to that committee, and he would do so today. It would not be difficult; that committee's work lacked glamour.

Von Steinwehr's eyes narrowed, and the fingers of his left hand slowly clenched as a realization struck. Pennywhistle was the British Naval Attaché; riverine matters would fall within his purview; he would almost certainly be assigned to the committee. It would be interesting to converse with his opponent to get a better idea of his vulnerabilities. He, Von Steinwehr, would have the advantage, since Pennywhistle had no idea who was directing the attempts on his life. Yes! This promised to be a memorable meeting.

Chapter 5

"I apologize for sending an underling to accept your credentials, but the Czar was being importunate, and I simply could not get away when you arrived. Your report is extraordinary! Extraordinary, Sir Thomas," remarked Lord Castlereagh with an excitement that was at odds with what Pennywhistle guessed was a reserved, almost shy nature.

Pennywhistle had never met Castlereagh before, but made it a practice to diligently research those under whom he would serve. He was curious to see how his conception of the man corresponded to the actual individual.

The British Foreign Secretary, Robert Stewart, Viscount Castlereagh, bore the title of Minister Plenipotentiary at the Congress. Plenipotentiary derived from the Latin words *plen* meaning full, and *potens* meaning powerful, and it referred to a diplomat invested with the complete power of independent action on behalf of his country. The term had been employed informally since the mid-18th century, but the Congress was the first gathering to formalize its use.

Castlereagh was the same age as Bonaparte and Wellington. He had blonde hair and a long, angular face, boyishly handsome in a way that made him look twenty years younger than his actual age. His usual expression was neutral and detached; one could not be sure if it came from aristocratic reserve or the academic contemplation of the Cambridge don he had almost become. That he smiled little and habitually dressed in sober black surprised no one. Demeanor and dress combined to make him hard to read, a useful diplomatic advantage.

Yet, like the Congress itself, he was not exactly what he seemed. He had a combative side that was fueled by a fierce sense of honor. Upon discovering that George Canning had intrigued against him when both were ministers in Spencer Percival's Cabinet, he'd challenged Canning to a duel. Dueling was common enough, though illegal, but unheard of between the King's Ministers. When the first shots had missed, Castlereagh had demanded a second round. This time, he'd hit Canning in the thigh.

Pennywhistle understood the concern for honor but regarded duels as harmful to the body politic. He had fought one long ago and it had thrown his life into chaos. He'd learnt his lesson and never fought another.

Castlereagh had also paid a price for exacting vengeance in so direct a manner: three years of political exile. During the time of his eclipse, however, Castlereagh formed a network of powerful supporters. Elected to a safe seat in Parliament in 1812, he quickly gained the position of Speaker of the House of Commons, his Irish peerage having only ceremonial, not legal, force in England. He then replaced Richard Wellesley, the Duke of Wellington's brother, as Foreign Secretary. As such, he had worked indefatigably to bring down Bonaparte. He had used his personal experience building political networks to construct international diplomatic ones. Under Castlereagh, Britain had become both the banker and arsenal of Europe. This Congress gave him a chance to bring years of effort to a conclusion.

Attaché Extraordinaire

"You are lucky to be alive, Sir Thomas. That you were able to compile such a lucid *precis* of such distressing events tells me that what I have heard about you is well-founded." The admiration in his voice transitioned to the tones of a monkish scholar speaking with priestly kindness. "I am heartily sorry for setting in motion the chain of events that got your brother killed. I had no idea a packet of letters sent by the Bourbon king as a gesture of amity would be intercepted by a murderous interloper. I met your brother Peter but three times, yet the sterling impression I formed of his character was borne out by his admirable record of clandestine service. It is a pity that his deeds and accomplishments must forever remain hidden."

Pennywhistle's green eyes inventoried Castlereagh's grey ones. They were thoughtful, yet radiated a restless energy, the eyes of a humble man, nonetheless determined to leave his mark upon history.

"I sometimes feel that I was given the knighthood my brother earned," responded Pennywhistle mournfully. "He was so good at his job that he fooled me as thoroughly as he fooled everyone else—nearly everyone else. I underestimated him."

The tall case clock in the book-lined, oak-paneled study struck five. It was one of 22 official rooms that constituted the business end of an embassy housed in the Palais Starhemberg on the Minoreitenplatz. It was cramped but convenient, within easy walking distance of both the Hofburg Palace and The Austrian Chancellor's residence at the Ballhaus—so named because it had once housed a tennis court. The French Representative's residence at the Kaunitz Palace and the Czar's residence at the Amelienberg were close by, as well.

John Danielski

"The sun is over the yardarm, Sir Thomas. Would you care for a whiskey? I have Glen Livet, Glen Garriott, and Glenturret, as well as Jameson's and Bushmills."

"What would you recommend?" Pennywhistle seldom drank spirits, yet whiskey was a ceremonial beverage often used to commemorate a special occasion.

"As an Irishman, I prefer Bushmills."

"Then Bushmills it is." Pennywhistle recalled Castlereagh had played a key role in Britain's union with Ireland in 1801.

"Neat, or with tonic water?"

"Neat. It is cruelty personified to adulterate a superb elixir."

"A man of refined discernment!"

He arose from a heavily gilded rococo desk and walked over to a Sheraton sideboard containing Waterford decanters. He opened one and poured two glasses. He skirted the desk and offered one to Pennywhistle.

"Forgive my manners, Sir Thomas, please sit down. This is an embassy, not the Admiralty." Pennywhistle had been standing as a show of deference.

"Thank you, milord." Pennywhistle smiled briefly, accepted the glass, and then folded himself into a red leather wingback chair of seemingly unending depth. He swirled the glass under his nose a few times, and his nostrils flared in pleasure, inhaling the fragrance as appreciatively as a woman would a vial of Parisian perfume. The aroma's promise silenced the pain whispering at the edge of his consciousness.

After Castlereagh had done the same, Pennywhistle raised his glass. "To the King!"

"The King! Long may he reign!" responded Castlereagh.

Pennywhistle sighed inwardly; George III was barking mad. The Prince Regent was the real power.

Attaché Extraordinaire

Both took slow sips over the next few minutes, saying nothing. Civilized gentlemen understood that a good talk should come after the first swallows, not before.

Castlereagh broke the silence. "I have no great fund of small talk, so let us attend to business directly."

Like many intellectuals, Castlereagh had a reputation for speaking chiefly of ideas, while average men talked of experiences. Lady Leith had informed Pennywhistle that Castlereagh was a solitary man whose chief confidant was his vivacious wife, Emily. She was one of the four female arbiters of "The Season" at Almanack's back in London.

"We have diplomats at the Congress from 216 states, principalities, free cities, and princely houses as well as a papal ambassador and legions of disguised observers from places as far away as Iran and Aden. There is a Jewish delegation representing several German cities, a group dedicated to stopping piracy on the high seas, and even a group committed to stopping the intellectual piracy of books and music. Yet the term 'Congress' is something of a misnomer, Sir Thomas, since it has never met in a formal, plenary session. The Congress is really series of individual negotiations. Though I sometimes speak with my opposite numbers at The Hofburg Palace, the chief principals and their aides generally transact business in social settings: balls, soirees, fetes, festivals, frolics, and all manner of parties great and small."

A frown flickered across Pennywhistle's face at the thought of diplomats at frolics. He wondered what insights they gained after slamming into furniture and each other while under the influence of nitrous oxide. Sir Joseph Priestly probably never imagined his discovery would be treated as laughing gas, though it was no laughing matter if crucial decisions were reached while under its power.

"The Congress is a peculiar mixture of courtesy and rudeness, as well as reserve and recklessness. Frivolous wit competes with blunt words, just as court intrigues compete with *affaires de coeur*." He sighed in distaste. "Some residences have become little better than aristocratic brothels. Business is also done at the symphony, at the opera, at Marie Antoinette style picnics in the Vienna Woods, at dinners formal and intimate and even during sleigh rides and boar hunting.

Salons are particularly useful for covert diplomacy. The one hosted by the Princess Bagration is sometimes referred to as 'Russia's more important embassy.' It is bad luck indeed to attend one and not end up meeting a king, a prince, or a field marshal. My wife hosts one, Tuesday nights." His voice took on a note of pride. "Hers feature supper, violin and guitar music, and dancing, in addition to spirited discourse. They are so well attended that it is impossible to gain entrance after ten pm."

"Are you saying that in Vienna, pleasure is business?"

"Roughly speaking, yes, and the reverse is true as well."

Pennywhistle's eyebrows drew down in puzzlement at the contradiction. "Business is pleasure?"

Castlereagh nodded. "The ancient Prince de Ligne put it well. 'The Congress does not go forward, it dances.' The frivolity that attracts all the attention obscures the serious purpose that lies at the heart of this gathering. I see Britain's task not as collecting trophies but as restoring Europe to peaceful habits. Our host, the Emperor Francis, houses the greatest assembly of royalty in history at the Hofburg Palace. Though he has one foot in bankruptcy and one on a bar of soap, he has formed a special committee to devise and execute elaborate outings based on the whims of the delegates and

Attaché Extraordinaire

their entourages. Those entourages are very extensive and have increased the city's population from 250,000 to 350,000. It is not just diplomats you see, but those who support their extravagant modes of living: tailors, couturiers, hair stylists, cobblers, jewelers, florists, carriage makers and scores of other occupations." His voice rippled with contempt: an abstemious man forced to deal with voluptuaries. "It distresses me to say the Congress has attracted thousands of ladies of easy virtue as well as hordes of displaced aristocrats, adventurers, soldiers-of-fortune, and every type of criminal under the sun. Legions of confidence men and schemers as well as an epidemic of pickpockets plague the Congress. Guard your purse carefully."

Pennywhistle tilted his head in acknowledgement.

"I should also add The Emperor Francis has an extensive network of informers at those social events who report to the very capable chief of the Ministry of Police and Censorship, Baron Franz von Hager. Von Hager has placed innumerable spies among the servants that staff the residences of foreign dignitaries. Coachmen, for example, have been instructed to befriend those they transport and report their conversations. Humble footmen, unnoticed by most at formal dinners, have big ears. Ladies gossip freely as parlor maids go about their business.

Our delegation is the only one that has not been penetrated by von Hager. I have rejected the lower-level personnel sent over by the Austrians and personally hired every doorkeeper, chambermaid, and kitchen helper."

"That must have taken a great deal of time to interview them all."

"It did, Sir Thomas. Ever since I arrived in the city, sleep has become a precious commodity, because I get so little of it. I also insist on a careful accounting of all documents. I require that all important ones be signed for when they change hands and those no longer relevant be destroyed. The Austrians regularly intercept, read, and reseal diplomatic mail so we have our own set of couriers. I would ask you to take special care about what you say and to whom you say it."

"My policy is to be courteous to all but intimate with few and let those few be well-tried before giving them my friendship. My lord, could you tell me something about your opposite numbers?"

"I will give you blunt assessments of each, Sir Thomas, since you are a man of discretion. I would add that the endless rounds of parties confer one priceless advantage; repeatedly seeing your opponents at uninhibited play gives you great insight in how to handle them at the negotiating table."

A loud crash in the street below interrupted Castlereagh's talk, and a look of distress descended on his face. Pennywhistle recognized the noise as that of two carriages crashing violently into each other. Vienna's streets were crowded with them, and they were often driven with more speed than circumspection.

Castlereagh put down his drink, rose from his chair, and walked to the French doors overlooking the Minoreitenplatz. He opened them and looked down.

Curious, Pennywhistle rose as well, and took up a position behind Castlereagh.

Two men were arguing violently in front of the wreck of a gentleman's phaeton and the Viennese equivalent of a hansom cab. One was clearly a gentleman, dressed in extravagant attire that featured large yellow boots. The other was a cabbie, dressed plainly. A woman stood to the side of the gentleman, looking deeply upset. Though her attire was expensive, it was not that of a lady but a courtesan.

Attaché Extraordinaire

"You damn fool. I could have been killed. You drive like a blind man. You should be locked up." The gentleman's voice was English and far from sober. His expression was that of a man eager to kick someone in the teeth.

"It is you who are the idiot," hissed the cabbie. "You should be banned from ever driving again. I tried to get out of the way, but you were going far too fast." The voice was probably Austrian since the man's heavily accented words were barely recognizable as English. He was livid and completely sober.

"I will see that your license is revoked, you Austrian dimwit. I am a British Ambassador. And it is who I shall make sure you never drive again. You will also pay for the damage to my phaeton."

"Over my dead body, you English *dummkopf*," said the Austrian. "Go back to your stupid little island and take your whore with you. Your kind is not welcome here! He grabbed a driver's whip with his left hand. "The only payment you will get from me will come from this whip."

"I don't need a weapon, you coward. We can settle this thing with fists. I'd enjoy teaching an upstart like you a lesson."

Traffic around the scene had stopped and many had stepped down from their vehicles, eager to watch a fight.

Castlereagh's face blanched and Pennywhistle looked puzzled.

"He is my brother," said Castlereagh with quiet distress. He sighed in exasperation. "You must excuse me, Sir Thomas. I must retrieve my sibling before this gets out of hand. Something similar happened two weeks ago and a repeat could cause the embassy embarrassment. Please, sit down and finish your drink. I will return as soon as possible."

Castlereagh did not quite run but exited the study with an unusual haste. Pennywhistle recalled that his brother Charles had a reputation as a problem maker. "Gallant, dashing, and thoroughly mad," was how one wag had put it. Though he had fought bravely in Spain, Wellington had called him "a brainless fool." From what Pennywhistle was seeing just now, he was the antithesis of a good diplomat. He undoubtedly owed his present appointment as ambassador to the Austrian Court purely to nepotism.

Pennywhistle continued to watch Charles demonstrate the correctness of Wellington's estimate of him. The Austrian cracked the whip, but Charles ducked and landed a solid blow to the chin that sent the Austrian reeling backwards. Charles charged ahead but the Austrian recovered enough to dodge and avoid a flying tackle.

A small crowd chanted derisively, "Lord Pumpernickel! Lord Pumpernickel!" Pennywhistle gathered it was the local nickname for the Englishman, possibly derived from his outlandish yellow boots.

The Austrian aimed a left hook at the Englishman, which missed. Charles dove at him and both went down in a heap, rolling over and over as the growing crowd hooted at the spectacle.

At that moment, Lord Castlereagh and two assistants arrived. The two assistants quickly separated the two combatants. Castlereagh handed a purse to one of the assistants, then placed a few coins in the woman's hand and spoke a few quiet words to her. She nodded and scuttled away.

He then took his brother forcefully by the arm and frog marched him from the scene. "Damned blackguard deserved what he got, Robert. You should have let me finish the job," Charles grumbled drunkenly. "Bloody beggar insulted England's honor!"

Pennywhistle could not hear Castlereagh's response, but from the lines of tension in his face, he gathered it was on the order of "shut up and keep moving."

The assistant spoke some soothing words to the cabbie and passed him the purse of coins. The cabbie's glower changed to a surprised smile as he held aloft a gold coin after examining the contents of the purse. The crowd seemed pleased that English gold had been used to fix the problem and slowly dispersed.

Pennywhistle shut the French doors, resumed his seat, and took a long, slow sip of his whiskey. The incident made him realize just how heavy a burden Castlereagh bore, not only having to manage affairs of state but keeping a wayward brother from becoming an international embarrassment.

When Castlereagh returned, he looked flustered and embarrassed. "Very sorry about the interruption, Sir Thomas. I thank you for your indulgence. I put Charles to work stamping passports. That is something he is good at." Castlereagh resumed his seat and took up his glass. "Now, where were we?

"You were about to give me assessments of your opposite numbers. I gather this is an assemblage of men with large egos who sniff offense with every tainted breeze."

"Your instincts are sound, Sir Thomas." Castlereagh sighed and for an instant, his neutral mask dropped, revealing a truer face—that of an idealist pained at having to compromise because of the double-dealing that he confronted daily. "While the able Count Nesselrode is Russia's official plenipotentiary, Czar Alexander frequently takes control of issues that interest him. Though it is a breach of protocol for a monarch to speak directly to the chief representative of another country, Alexander has no hesitation about approaching me when he feels the need. He thinks himself smarter than Bonaparte, which he most certainly is not. He is unpredictable and contradictory, with a theoretical love for man but a personal contempt for men. His Swiss tutor has trained him in the Enlightenment ideals of Rousseau, yet he will, with no warning, often revert to the posture of a Romanov autocrat. A shameless, unabashed rake, he sees every woman as fair game and marriage poses no barrier to his advances. I talk louder to him than others, since he has a bad hearing loss in his left ear. I hunted with him once and found him a poor shot; his vanity refuses to allow him to wear spectacles. And he is nothing if not vain."

Pennywhistle's eyebrows signaled understanding.

"My relations with him have been chilly, though I have detected a recent thaw. He made the unilateral decision to exile the Corsican to Elba, where he could retain his title as Emperor. He is now the ruler of a pocket principality with 12,000 inhabitants. A stupid move in my estimation. My colleague Metternich, who was appalled at the Czar's decision, believes that Bonaparte will reappear on the European stage within a year. He is a contagion and should be quarantined. I would have sent him to St. Helena; a volcanic rock 2800 miles from South America and 1200 from Africa."

"I agree, my lord. I believe Bonaparte once said, 'I never see a throne without being tempted to sit upon it.' To believe such a man will change his stripes and become pacific is as ridiculous as believing a prowling tomcat will revert to being a playful kitten."

A hint of a smile played at the corners of Castlereagh's mouth. "Yes! Bonaparte has something of a feline character.

Attaché Extraordinaire

Unlike dogs, restless cats cannot be commanded to sit." He took a slow sip of his whiskey. "Prince Karl von Hardenberg of Prussia is intelligent, pragmatic, and more aggressive in military matters than the vacillating sovereign he represents."

Pennywhistle scratched his temples absentmindedly as he realized that he had much to learn.

"Prince Klemens von Metternich of Austria avoids skirmishes and plays the long game, a marathon man rather than a sprinter. He is handsome, witty, brilliant, and vain. Like me, he plays the cello for relaxation, often participating in a string quartet with the Emperor Francis, who is an excellent violinist. Though reactionary in that he wants most of the changes caused by the late wars erased, I agree with him about the need to maintain equilibrium in Europe. He, like Alexander, is a ladies' man. As Austrian ambassador to France, he once had an affair with Bonaparte's sister Caroline, giving new meaning to the term "foreign relations." Unlike the Czar, who has no children, he dotes on his son and daughter, though his relationship with their mother is unhappy.

He is currently enjoying the affections of the Duchess Sagan. Alexander is trying to poach her from him, despite his heated dalliances with the Princess Bagration. Curiously, The Princess lives across the courtyard from the Duchess at the Palm Palace and was once in love with Metternich. The clash of hearts and vanities has created an intense dislike between the two that extends to matters of state.

"Lust and love influencing the lives of millions," remarked Pennywhistle as his lips pursed in disapproval.

Castlereagh inclined his head in agreement. "Lastly," he sighed in exasperation, "there is Talleyrand. He is cursed with a club foot, but there is no greater master of the diplomatic pirouette. He is unique, having served the Bourbons,

Bonaparte, and now the returned Bourbons. A thoroughgoing aristocrat that *La Revolution* could not kill, he started his career as a bishop; a strange occupation for a man who believes nothing of Catholic dogma. Bonaparte finally dismissed him because of his constant intriguing, but he got his revenge in 1814, becoming the key French figure in The Emperor's ouster. He is wily, unprincipled, and devious. He is also the most skilled adversary whom I have ever encountered. One of his mistresses described his unique appeal, 'how can you not love a man with so many vices?'

Talleyrand's hostess is his niece by marriage, the 21-year-old Dorothée Talleyrand-Perigord. She is beautiful, intelligent, and uses her considerable charm to keep dinner parties witty, warm, and worldly. Curiously, she is the sister of the Duchess Sagan.

Talleyrand has the best trained and educated staff in the city and his cooks are kitchen magicians. They have created brand new dishes such as *Bombe a la Metternich, Clam Marintez Torte, and Nesselrode Pudding*. The last was too sweet for my palate; A pineapple size dessert of chestnuts, currants, raisins, soaked in Maraschino and covered in whipped cream. The lavish dinners in the city are dangerous if you value your waistline. Talleyrand's dinners are considered events not to be missed and he once remarked, 'I need more saucepans not secretaries.'"

"I gather gluttony is just one of many vices that flourish here."

"Everything at the Congress is on a grand scale, including vice. Yet the complicated interplay sometimes results in the right things being accomplished for the wrong reasons. Not exactly what Locke and Montesquieu had in mind for good governance, is it?" He gave a wan, ironic smile.

Attaché Extraordinaire

"The historian Herodotus comes to mind. Some consider him the father of history, while others consider him the father of lies. The truth lies somewhere in the middle."

"Exactly! Talleyrand is a habitual high stakes gambler and dresses as if the French Revolution never happened—silk breeches, diamond buckled shoes, and long coats of purple, scarlet, and apple green velvet. His attire is always made from the costliest materials, I assure you. He profits from the diplomatic endeavors in which he has been involved. It is said that $5 million of the $15 million that President Jefferson paid for the Louisiana territory found its way into his pocket. When Bonaparte abdicated, Talleyrand filled the void and became, in effect, the French government. He alone has made France a major player at this conference when all the other powers sought to exclude her."

Castlereagh's saturnine eyes assumed a sparkle. "There is a wry bit of doggerel making the rounds which sums up what happens when you have so many sovereigns in such a small space. Would you care to hear it?"

"Very much so, my lord."

"'The Czar of Russia, he makes love for everyone. The King of Prussia, he thinks for everyone. The King of Denmark, he speaks for everyone. The King of Bavaria, he drinks for everyone. The King of Wurttemberg, he eats for everyone. The Emperor of Austria, he pays for everyone.'"

Pennywhistle's mouth crinkled in wry amusement; jests often contained truth. "I have a general acquaintance with the issues under discussion here, my lord, but could you favor me with some specifics about your policies?"

"Of course, Sir Thomas." Castlereagh steepled his hands as if bringing competing thoughts together. "The balance of power is my guiding principle and I see Britain as its bedrock:

Britain should intervene on behalf of an imperiled weaker power to balance things out and prevent a war. I want to maintain equilibrium in Europe to ensure we have no further wars like the ones just concluded. I desire a mechanism of alliances that will prevent any significant power from dominating the Continent as France did under Bonaparte and will forestall any revolutions that might give rise to a future Napoleon. I could accept a France reduced to her natural frontiers: the Channel, the Rhine, the Alps, and the Pyrenees, if she is ringed with buffer states not affiliated with any Great Power."

"A *cordon sanitaire;* most sensible," replied Pennywhistle.

"I have tried hard to keep maritime matters under our tight control," Castlereagh continued. "Since The Royal Navy owns the seas, I have so far been successful. As naval attaché, your primary official task will be to do everything to further that policy. We have returned most of the colonies captured in the late wars but have retained the ones necessary for our security, The Cape, Mauritius, and Ceylon being keys to the safe passage to India. Keeping shipping lanes clear of danger is not only good military policy but a furtherance to free trade. Malta presents problems. It is the linchpin for our dominance of the Mediterranean, but the Czar objects to our possession. Your help in smoothing out that spot of trouble will be appreciated."

"Free seas and free trade are like two lenses in one pair of spectacles; both needed to give the proper view."

The door to the study opened slowly and Charles Stewart walked halfway through the doorway with an unsteady gait. "Sorry to interrupt Robert,' slurred Charles, "but I have batch of notes from creditors and was wondering..."

Attaché Extraordinaire

"Yes, yes, yes," said Castlereagh impatiently. "I will provide you with whatever funds you need. Now please, shut the door and go sleep it off."

"Thank you, Robert. I do not know what I would do without you." Charles about faced uncertainly and slowly closed the door.

"Family can be taxing sometimes, can't they," said Pennywhistle in sympathy.

"You have no idea, Sir Thomas,' replied Castlereagh as his eyebrows arched in exasperation. "At least as a diplomat you can choose your allies. Let us return to business. You also are involved in a much thornier issue: stopping the slave trade." A deep frown transformed his countenance into that of a world-weary old man. "The work of that committee is heart-wrenching, and the debates acrimonious. Because of our navy, we alone have the capacity to end that foul practice. France and Spain have every interest in seeing it continue because of their overseas colonies. The Sugar Lobby is immensely influential in those countries, and the industry relies upon the labour of forced servitude. That supply must constantly be replenished, because...." He looked distressed.

"The climate is death for those who perform hard manual labor," Pennywhistle filled in.

Castlereagh inclined his head in quiet acknowledgement. "While the *business* of capturing slaves for the express purpose of selling them has been going on for thousands of years, every tenet of religion and philosophy decries the foul practice, and men of conscience must strive to put an end to it once and for all. Though I am no follower of Mr. Wilberforce, I believe slavery degrades anyone involved in it."

"As do I, my lord. My batman was freed in the Chesapeake and fought bravely in a war that..." His lips wrinkled in disgust. "...should be swiftly concluded. He continues in my paid service by choice, since he has sufficient funds to live an independent life."

"I concur about the American War, said Castlereagh quietly. "Its end would strengthen my bargaining position by immediately freeing up at least a million pounds. The original *casus belli* is now moot. I have instructed our negotiators in Ghent to drop any *uti posseditis* demands for the retention of occupied American territory. Britain thrives on commerce; the Americans were once numbered among our key trading partners, and I should like to see them become so again."

"I agree, my lord. I seek a peaceful world where my military services will be unnecessary. Since I will soon be a father," he flashed a quick smile, "I have thought much about what I would wish for my heir. I would agree with President Adams that 'I study the arts of war so that my children may study the arts of peace, their children mathematics, philosophy, and agriculture, and my great-grandchildren the joys of music, poetry, and sculpture.'"

"Congratulations!" Castlereagh smiled the sad, envious smile of the childless. He raised his glass in a salute, which Pennywhistle returned; each took a quick sip as a toast. "No one has ever stated my ultimate aims any better. Most of the general ideas agreed upon by our various governments here represented have their details hammered out in committees. There are nine, each varying in prestige and composition. Each one is configured to address a particular issue.

There is a meeting of the International River Committee the day after tomorrow and I want you there. I am sorry to say that it will mean spending most of the evening reading background material. Just as we want free navigation on the high seas, we favor it on Europe's waterways. Before the late wars, there were no fewer than thirty-eight toll stations on the

Attaché Extraordinaire

Rhine between Basel and Rotterdam, administered by nineteen different authorities. Because of them, a cargo of salt that cost four hundred thalers in Basel cost seven hundred thalers by the time it reached Rotterdam. A customs dispute between the Duke of Nassau and the Landgrave of Reichenau once brought all traffic on the river to a standstill for two months. Tolls are relics of the past and we want none on the many new canals now being built. Since we are a manufacturing nation, it is in our interest to make sure commerce is unhindered by trade barriers."

"I shall begin my reading, directly after we conclude here."

Castlereagh resumed. "I have been informed that you have a good memory, so I think that would make you a candidate for the Committee on Statistics. That committee wields far more power than the bland title indicates." He paused briefly and cleared his throat, the action of an inherently modest man about to speak of himself. "I am in a unique position. Unlike the other powers, Britain has no territorial ambitions on the Continent. Since my opposite numbers do have, that puts me in the position of a plain dealing gentleman who can serve as an impartial arbiter of their disputes. I am the sheepdog that prevents the members of this conference from scattering, and from territorial fighting. Britain's banking system provided a large share of the finances for their six coalitions against Napoleon. My colleagues know we would not be having this Conference, save for British gold."

"As I understand matters, my lord," interjected Pennywhistle, "you do not want a reconstituted Polish Kingdom under Alexander's influence and you do not want Saxony reduced to a shell. You wish the return of Hanover to George III and for most of the German consolidations made by

Bonaparte to remain, in some form. You desire France to have the borders of 1789, not 1792."

"Correct, Sir Thomas. Along with the French and Austrians, my chief fear is Russian influence in central Europe. Prussia has fallen under Russia's influence, which is worrisome. Prussia wants Saxony's lands added to her own and Russia is willing to back her in that cause. Prussia is yet not the equal of Britain, France, Russia, or Austria, but wants to become so. Possession of Saxony would boost Prussia's population to ten million and increase her land by a sixth. Saxony is a point of contention because of geography. If you drew a north-south line from Copenhagen to Rome and an east-west one from Warsaw to Paris, Saxony would be at its center.

With Saxony gone, Prussia would border Austria, and that is something Metternich most definitely does not want. If France got the borders of 1792, she would retain part of the Low Countries, which I desire reconstituted as the Kingdom of the Netherlands. The Low Countries must never again be under French control. There is also a possibility that, in return for Prussian support on the Polish question, Alexander would continue to back Prussia's further expansion. That would be a grave threat to European equilibrium. I have tried to avoid offending Prussia. If she could be detached from her affinity with Alexander, she could serve as a useful buffer against his ambitions in central Europe."

Pennywhistle massaged his temples slowly, as if assisting his brain to digest a great amount of potentially explosive information. "These are complex matters, requiring wisdom to resolve," he said thoughtfully. "De Ligne's observation about the Congress dancing is a point well taken, as the players here are in a swirl of changing partners. That such business is transacted at balls seems strangely fitting."

Attaché Extraordinaire

"I just hope I have wisdom in sufficient supply for the challenges ahead." Castlereagh clinched his fingers together, wrinkled his nose, and sighed in frustration. "And now we must discuss your unofficial duties. I wish I could grant you *carte blanche,* but I cannot. A scandal would not only weaken my position, but it could also drive this fragile coalition over the edge. I ask you to tread carefully because your diplomatic immunity will protect you only so far and will not excuse violence."

His scholarly eyes turned fiery as his voice became low and conspiratorial. "And I would presume a good bit of violence will be necessary to get them back. I will do my best to cover for you, but if things turn out badly, I will have to issue a blanket disavowal. I might say it was a temporary insanity, a good soldier driven mad by terrible memories. It would mean the ruination of your career and reputation, but it would save you from the gallows."

His voice softened. "I regret the position in which this job has placed you. It is unfair to a man who has brought so much honor to his country."

"I accepted this position with my eyes fully open, my lord. I harbor no illusions. I must be as much Machiavelli as D'Artagnan." He neglected to add that he had accepted for reasons having more to do with family than country. He wanted justice. Or was it vengeance? In his heart of hearts, he was not sure.

"I should like to continue this discussion, Sir Thomas, but the chiming of the clock warns me that I must prepare for another evening of... dancing. My wife loves dancing. Besides, several aides of the Prussian King, with whom I must speak, will be attending this ball. I will have the background papers delivered to your quarters. I trust you find your accommodations adequate?"

"I do, but Lady Leith does not like to share a palace, so she and my wife will be seeking a different residence."

"I must warn you that real estate is scarce and expensive."

"That will not prove a problem, my lord." He smiled. "By the way, I love dancing. A true gift of the gods."

Castlereagh snorted a quick laugh. "I wish you could go in my place." He rose, as did Pennywhistle. "May Dame Fortune smile upon you, Sir Thomas." He shook his guest's hand firmly, and then was gone.

Pennywhistle was left alone with unpleasant thoughts. He only had one lead to recovering the letters, and it was a thin one. One of the two Dutchmen was a mole, to use the term Sir Francis Bacon had coined, and that mole could be followed back to his master. Once Pennywhistle knew the name of his adversary, he could shift from defense to offense. But was the mole van Meegeran or van der Horst? He could detect no flaws in either man's character or behavior. As he slowly finished his whiskey, he pondered how he could get each man to reveal his true intentions. He would not get much sleep tonight.

Chapter 6

Sammie Jo awoke at dawn, feeling refreshed. She slipped quietly from beneath the covers, not wishing to disturb her husband, who was fast asleep. He had spent most of the night reading a ream of papers with his characteristic diligence. He would probably still have been at his desk, scribbling copious notes, but for her taking charge. At 3 am, she had silently shucked her night dress, stealthily approached his desk from behind, and begun massaging his shoulders. She'd felt him relax as her strong fingers chased away incipient tightness in the strong, well-defined muscles of his neck and shoulders, but he'd continued compiling notes.

So, she'd begun raining kisses on the nape of his neck until he put the pen down. She'd then walked in front of his chair and let the firelight outline her womanly curves. She knew her power, and her husband had reacted strongly. The problem with an intellect like her husband's was that it possessed a bulldog's tenacity. It had its own agenda that sometimes made its owner oblivious to his physical needs for rest, meals, and other things. It was her job to oppose that intellect on occasion, to make sure it was not just his mind that was sated.

She'd taken him by the hand and led him to bed, her love and desire swathing him more warmly than any blanket. Their coupling had been slow and languorous. When the moment of release came, simultaneous for both, he sighed quietly, smiled, and sank his head deep into the pillow. He'd slowly drifted off into sleep, and she had joined him soon after.

She dressed herself in a simple, puffed sleeve, high collared dress of a buff color; she had yet to find a replacement lady's maid. The previous one had left, with her blessing, to marry a tailor, a good and worthy man. She knew the transformative power of love and welcomed any opportunity to further its domain.

She also knew Lady Leith was looking forward to joining her in a day that would be devoted to finding new quarters. And her husband had given her another task, one which she found distinctly odd. He did not say why he wanted it done, but she trusted that he had thought the matter through.

Her knock on Lady Leith's door was answered by the woman herself rather than her maid. She was dressed in a frock that was a twin to Sammie Jo's, save that it was rendered in slate grey. But there was a significant difference in their apparel: Sammie Jo's earlobes were bare; Lady Leith's earrings each sparkled with a diamond that would have been impressive in a necklace. Her clothing might be subdued but her earrings sent a message that she was not to be regarded as insignificant.

The smell of fresh, strong coffee tickled Sammie Jo's nose. Like her husband, she considered tea an insipid beverage fit only for geriatrics.

"I guessed you would not be sleeping in when a day of house-hunting, or palace hunting, awaits," said a chipper and cheerful Lady Leith. "Come in and join me on the settee. I have already sent my chief footman to procure the earliest harvest of today's pastries, and I anticipate his return shortly. This city is famous for its arabesques of cakes, chocolates, and creams, and I thought a sampling of them would be a fine way to start the day."

"You're right, Margaret. I love the smell of fresh pastries in the morning, and as my husband's favorite author said, "When in Rome do as the Romans do.""

The two proceeded to a study furnished in Empire fashion — ironic in that it had been popularized by the Empress Josephine, the first wife of Britain's most implacable foe. The walls featured blue silk upholstery with white and gold fringes, four porphyry tables topped with Sèvres vases in green and gold, and eight silver filigreed chairs inspired by those of ancient Rome. Two crystal chandeliers hung from a ceiling painted with cherubim and seraphim. Though intended for repose and reflection, the room was better suited to being a miniature reception hall.

Sammie Jo and Lady Leith took seats on the red velvet settee, which Sammie Jo found uncomfortable. "This room is intimidating, Margaret. All those angels above make me feel like they are eves-dropping in preparation for Judgment Day."

A maid appeared with a silver coffee samovar on a wheeled tray. The slight woman smiled cheerfully and placed the samovar on a small ebony table in front of the settee. She turned the spigot and filled two blue Sèvres porcelain cups. She handed one to Lady Leith and one to Sammie Jo.

"Thank you, Maggie; that will be all."

"Very good, milady." The maid did a quick curtsey and departed.

Sammie Jo had noticed all of Lady Leith's servants were as cheerful as the maid. She treated them as people, not objects, and encouraged a degree of familiarity unusual in British households. A woman who had once slapped the Prince

Regent was not the kind to worry about what conventional people thought.

Sammie Jo took a long, slow sip and smiled. "That's what I call a tornado in a cup! Most English coffee tastes like brown gargle."

Lady Leith laughed. "I know Tom's preferences from long acquaintance and have taken the trouble to acquire a detailed knowledge of London's vendors to find Brazilian coffee."

Just as Lady Leith finished an invigorating pull on her cup, she heard a knock on the study door. She guessed who it was and what he brought. "Come in Carlton!"

Carlton the footman came through the door, wearing a grin of triumph and bearing a large circular tray laden with a bewitching variety of pastries. Sammie Jo's nostrils flared as her eyes widened in wonder. The tray held the stuff of culinary dreams.

Carlton set the tray down next to the samovar. He waited a few seconds before speaking, wanting his mistress's eyes to take in the magnitude of his achievement.

"I consulted with the embassy's pastry chef and visited the three bakeries that came most highly recommended. I had the Earl's batman accompany me, since he understands German. I asked for two specimens of the three most popular pastries at each bakery. One each for you and Lady Pennywhistle." He pointed to individual pastries. "We have apple strudel, cherry strudel, and peach strudel. We have *Mozart tortes Thermidor, punshkrapfen*—that's punch cake to you and me, milady,—and *Kardinalschitte* with crème..."

"Stop!" said Lady Leith in pleasant protest. "I appreciate the tutorial, but this is an occasion where tongues should taste, not speak. Let us solve the delightful mysteries of flavor at our leisure. I commend your efforts, Carlton. There will be a bonus added to your monthly pay."

"You are most gracious, my lady." He extracted a formidable collection of forks, knives, and serviettes from a wicker basket which dangled from his arm. He placed them on the table. "You may need these for some of the pastries. I should be happy to serve."

"We will manage fine on our own, Carlton. For now, you are dismissed."

"Very good, my lady." Carlton bowed and exited.

"I think I have gained twenty pounds just looking at this array," exclaimed Sammie Jo in delight. "I do not know where to begin."

"Then allow me to make a recommendation: the *Kardinalschitte*. I shall try the *Mozart torte*." Lady Leith took a knife and cut a slice of cake that was three layers of soft meringue and genoise sponge cradled in thick layers of rich cream. The meringue was flavored alternately with vanilla, chocolate, and strawberries. She placed the slice on a plate and handed it to Sammie Jo.

Sammie Jo sank a fork into it, but before it touched her lips, she savored the aroma. "If it tastes half as good as it smells, then the archangels have set up a secret bakery on earth!" She took her first bite, and what came out were noises that seemed more appropriate to the bedroom. "*Oooh! Oooh! Ohhh.*" She took another bite. "*Ahhh, Ahhh Ahhh.*" Her eyes glowed with bliss. "I feel like a cat in a fish market!" Completely ignoring her companion, she pitched into the remainder of the slice with the vigor of a miner who had just struck a vein of gold. The plate was soon empty. She took a long pull of coffee and sighed in contentment.

Suddenly, she flushed red. She had completely forgotten her recently acquired manners. "I can't believe I just did that, Margaret. Lordy! I pitched into it like a moth in a mitten!"

Lady Leith laughed merrily. "Don't worry, my dear. Viennese pastries have a reputation for inducing a delightful form of madness. I too succumbed, when I first encountered a strudel. Your reaction is perfectly natural. This city is as much about food as it is music." Lady Leith took a small bite of her torte. "Even more delights lie ahead. "Taste this torte and tell me what you think."

Sammie Jo accepted the torte, and this time took a bite that she hoped was ladylike. Her eyes blinked in amazement as she slowly savored a concoction of chocolate, marzipan, pistachio, and Viennese nougat, which had the consistency of French truffles. "I do not see how it's possible, but this is even better than the *Kard... Kard... Kardinalwhatever*. Makes me want to eat the whole tray; waistlines be damned."

Lady Leith refilled Sammie Jo's coffee cup and then did the same with her own. "What we can do, Sammie Jo, is take a bite or two of each. That way we get the taste and will not have to commission a whole new wardrobe."

"That's a right fine idea, Margaret."

The next hour passed quickly, fueled by cream, cake, and coffee. Lady Leith showed Sammie Jo a plan of the city and described in detail what a residence should have. "I spoke with Lady Castlereagh yesterday; she has had the Second Secretary contact a realtor. I received word that the realtor had been in a carriage accident and his wife will stand in for him. She will meet us at the first appointment. I told Gabriel to have the carriage ready by ten, which allows us plenty of time to reach our first appointment at 11."

Attaché Extraordinaire

Sammie Jo put aside her plate. "That is fine, but I got some other errands to perform. We need to visit a few theatres."

"Theatres? Why? We will have plenty of balls to attend that will provide their own theatrics. The first is tomorrow night."

"It's not about entertainment but business of a kind. Tom wants me to find an actor; one who resembles him in build, gait, and face. *Doppelganger* was the term he used. I gather that means his twin. "

"Do you mean," said Lady Leith in puzzlement, "we are to hold auditions?"

"In a manner of speaking. He said he wants an actor so much like him that he could fool me at a distance. Presumably, his godmother as well. I know it all sounds peculiar, but Tom is up to something, and I am pretty sure it is aimed at the man behind the attacks."

"Any idea what that something is?"

"I can hazard a guess. He knows he will be followed and is looking to use a decoy to send his minder off in the wrong direction. He said his opponent specializes in misdirection; Tom wants to use that against him by visiting a variety of odd locations, making his opponent look for a pattern in actions that really make about as much sense as a bird hit in the head with buckshot flying in crazy circles."

"So, in a way you are auditioning a second husband?"

"Yes, I suppose so, but this one don't have to speak."

"A silent man," said Margaret archly, "would be a miracle!"

"It would be indeed!" laughed Sammie Jo. "Can you imagine the Congress if all of the delegates were quiet men?"

There was a discreet rapping at the door. Lady Leith looked at the case clock and knew Grimsby was serving notice that the carriage was ready. Time to furl tongues and concentrate on finding a place to stay, where they would not be underfoot of the embassy's overworked staff-of fourteen.

Chapter 7

"A wife should be to her husband as the first mate is to a ship's captain" Ingrid von Steinwehr observed. "She must calm him when he is troubled, embolden him when he is uncertain, and above all, inspire him to follow his dreams.

"You do all that and much more," replied Klaus, favoring her with one of his rare smiles.

Ingrid stood only five feet four, but she was strongly built. She had auburn hair, piercing blue eyes, and a judgmental face that matched her iron character. Stopping just short of pretty, she nonetheless had a striking countenance. Her voice was a contradiction of her nature; it was soft and soothing.

"That assistance can come in many forms, Klaus. I realize that you dislike the balls we have had to attend and prefer business be conducted along traditional avenues. I, however, enjoy them, not just for the dancing but for the opportunity to socialize with the wives of other diplomats. There is much useful information to be gleaned from the ladies at such events, since they do not bridle their tongues, and their husbands often let slip secrets of state after their bedroom appetites are sated."

"The front door may be bolted but the rear one is left unlatched?"

"Exactly! I have taken the trouble to get to know Emily, the Viscountess Castlereagh. Well, perhaps 'get to know' is too strong a phrase." Her eyebrows arched in exasperation. "Her conversation is a torrent of trivial information. It is just a matter of listening and agreeing with her sentiments at the right moment. She mentioned the arrival of the new naval attaché and his wife. She seemed impressed by the man but said she had not yet met the woman. She let slip that they were seeking more spacious quarters. I asked if she had a particular realtor in mind. I said that you and I were also seeking new accommodations. She replied she did not, but said the embassy's Second Secretary would handle it; when she had a name, she would pass it on to me."

"Very clever, Ingrid," replied Klaus with amused satisfaction.

"The name of that realtor is Karl Stottler. I made some inquiries and found out he had a checkered past, and a wife who is known to assist him. It occurred to me that he might be amenable to an alternate course of action if a small sufficiency of cash came his way."

"I think I see where this is going, Ingrid. It is a bold strategy to impersonate his wife. Do you think you could be convincing as a realtor?"

"Mostly it is a matter of knowing what a woman looks for in a residence and pointing out how the one that you are showing fits those specifications. I spent yesterday afternoon with Stottler and his wife. They will be taking an extended holiday. I hope you will forgive me for draining our petty cash fund."

"I feel certain the money was well spent."

"He was very forthcoming about what a realtor does and gave me a tour of the three properties he intends to show to the Pennywhistles. He also pointed out their chief selling points. Last night, I wrote down most of what he said and memorized it. I think I can generate a very convincing line of patter." She crossed her arms and bobbed her head in satisfaction at her cleverness.

"How do you know you will be dealing with Lady Pennywhistle and not her husband?"

"It is because I know you. You are always busy, needing a twenty-five hour day to complete your agenda. Her husband will likely be even busier. He is a new man in an important position and will have a lot of catching up to do. Finding a house and making it a home is woman's work and he will delegate that task to his wife, both from necessity and inclination. You once told me that the French tried to stir up trouble in Ireland because it is the backdoor to England. A wife is also the backdoor to her husband. I know exactly who she is, while she will have no idea of who I am, probably thinking me just a friendly woman who wants to make a stranger feel welcomed and comfortable. I can find out all manner of information simply by asking seemingly innocent questions."

"I, of course, would funnel questions to you."

"Exactly. There will probably be several meetings with her before she decides on a residence. That would give me plenty of opportunity to pump her for information. I have heard she is American and naïve, likely vulnerable to European sophistication."

"You certainly have plenty of that, Ingrid. You make Lady Macbeth seem an amateur."

"What a wonderful thing to say, Klaus! When I am done, we will know the exact location of your opponent's lair as well as its vulnerabilities. All three of the residences I will be showing contain safes. I have the combinations."

"Very good, Ingrid! If the book is not on his person, or at the embassy, it will surely be in his safe. The last thing he will expect will be for an outsider to have the combination."

"That book is the key to our future, Klaus. I am determined that you shall have it. Considering what transpired last week, I think an old aphorism applies. "If you want something done right do it yourself."

"Your opponent might still live after this is done. Does that bother you, Klaus?"

"No, Ingrid. The recovery of Reichenau is all that matters. I have been so focused on killing him that I have made things personal. That has skewed my logic, fueled my mania, and caused me to act unwisely. So long as he does not know who I am, I pose no threat. He cannot come after a shadow. If he loses the book, his reputation will suffer. From what I know of English gentlemen, if his honor is smashed, he will resign as quickly and quietly as possible and return to England. It is also possible that if he loses the book, he will be sufficiently embarrassed not to reveal the truth to anyone. He may even take the gentleman's option of a snifter of brandy, a locked study, and a loaded pistol."

"And now husband, I must prepare for the meeting. I went to a second-hand store yesterday and purchased a drab grey frock appropriate to the wife of a realtor of the middling orders. Its dull fabric and unflattering drape will be depressing to wear but should be a convincing disguise."

"It is a great pity you must conceal your beauty. And yet your real beauty is not that of your skin but that of your mind. I am indeed a lucky man!"

Attaché Extraordinaire

"Before I depart, how fare your discussions with Alexander?"

Klaus frowned and rubbed his hands together vigorously, as if trying to remove an unpleasant substance. "As well as can be expected. One minute he is agreeable to my ideas and the next he vacillates. He wants respect, yet he also wants to be loved. He wants to be seen as a conquering hero, yet also as the rescuer of Europe and the Savior of the Russian people. He seeks to mix pragmatism with romantic impulses, which is like putting stew on top of a cake. In my quest to understand the English mind, which Alexander publicly disdains but secretly admires, I have been reading Byron's *Childe Harold*. Alexander is as much a wandering outlaw of his impulses as is Byron's peculiar protagonist. The difference is that one is only concerned with mad personal adventures while the other is deciding the fate of a Continent."

"Do you think the codebook represents a tipping point for the Czar?"

"I do. He knows that Castlereagh is personally immune to blackmail but understands he will alter his positions if the British monarchy is placed in jeopardy. I have whetted the Czar's appetite with the plain text part of the Clarke Letters. He has viewed the first acts of a play and is a Hotspur to see its denouement."

"He would be a bad man to disappoint," observed Ingrid.

"I must play a double game, Ingrid. I must convince Alexander that Reichenau can provide him a Russian base on the Rhine whilst telling everyone else that it will be independent and neutral."

Ingrid's face paled, "But Alexander is your patron. You know how he deals with disloyalty. You have often been the agent tasked to punish that disloyalty, and the blood spilled has given you nightmares."

"I would need some influential new friends. But if there is anything that I have learned from this conference, it is that nations have no permanent allies, just permanent interests. Today's enemy may be tomorrow's friend. A man like Castlereagh could be very useful."

"Pennywhistle's employer? That is bizarre."

"Perhaps, but the British are great pragmatists."

Von Steinwehr paused, drew in a deep breath, as his scarred face turned as hard as his voice. "You knew what we were getting into when we started this game, Ingrid. You and I both wanted a home, but one that should be worthy of the ruler of a country. God designed me to rule, not work as a martial hireling of lesser men. Our children deserve a long, happy life of high station and great comfort, consonant with their birthright. You always beat me at chess, Ingrid, but my game is not one where assets have fixed values. Bluff, bluster, and guile determine their worth."

"Calm down, Klaus. I hear the voice of mania." His malady followed a lunar cycle and Ingrid considered it the behavioral equivalent of the four seasons. In the first phase, he was calm, brilliant, and rational. In the second, he turned ridiculously optimistic; speaking rapidly, sleeping little, and hatching schemes that were both outlandish and alluring. In the third, he slept much and became so melancholy that he could barely leave his residence. In the fourth, he became world weary and reflective; appalled at the awful things that men did to each other.

Klaus blinked, as if someone had thrown ice water in his face. "My God, you are right. I do not think my reasoning is flawed, but I need to relax. The usual method would work just fine. When did you say you had to leave?

Ingrid kissed him passionately; their bond of flesh was as strong as that of mind. She drew back and regarded him with a mixture of lust and amusement. "Immediately."

He pulled her tight and kissed her even more passionately. "Almost immediately."

Chapter 8

Pennywhistle awoke refreshed but disappointed that Sammie Jo was no longer beside him. He found a short note from her on the table next to the bed. Her penmanship was beautiful and even more impressive on the embassy stationary. His own was functional at best; a left hander, his horrified mother had beaten him into writing "with the proper hand." She had been a fanatic, just like the opponent who had tried to kill him on the Vienna Road. Yet the monomania of fanatics often created strange blind spots. She had remonstrated loudly about handwriting but had said nothing about the use of the "sinister hand" when used for painting, and so Pennywhistle had become a capable artist.

The note was also a model of his bride's breezy terseness:

Gone house hunting. Should be back early this evening. Borrowed Gabriel, so you are on your own today. Hugs and kisses.

SJ

He was independent by nature, so the lack of a gentleman's gentleman to dress him posed no problem. He selected a charcoal-hued tailcoat of the finest broadcloth, high collared and double-breasted with silver buttons. He donned a white

Attaché Extraordinaire

shirt of Indian cotton, a raven-colored silk stock, and an iron-grey waistcoat above anchor-grey breeches that buttoned two inches below the knee, white silk stockings, and black shoes with silver buckles. He would have preferred the more modern ankle-length pantaloons, which fitted tightly, or trousers which fitted more loosely, but they were considered too informal for important venues; the Duke of Wellington had once been denied entrance to an exclusive club because he was clad in trousers. He departed his quarters and headed to his office, looking forward to his 11 o clock appointment.

His back pain was almost non-existent, thanks to his wife.

The night before, he had recognized the name of a friend on the embassy roster: a man he had not seen in nine years and with whom he had sadly lost track. He had served as Luke Higgins's mentor and guardian angel on board *Bellerophon* at Trafalgar. He had thought Higgins might make a career of the military and was surprised to find him serving as a diplomat. But that might well be Miss Lydia's doing. Though he had never learned if Higgins had married his sweetheart, he had the impression that proving himself once in battle was more than enough for her. It gave him plenty of heroic cachet that would be useful in a civilian career, where she could have him home each night. Being "a Trafalgar man" opened a lot of doors and being able to say, "I fought with Nelson" impressed men who did not do so easily. Becoming Third Secretary of a major embassy at twenty-five was a major achievement.

Higgins might provide the answer to one of his problems.

Paperwork was the curse of diplomats; several piles marred his desk. He sat down and began sorting through the batch that had just arrived. His quick reads were interrupted a minute later when the case clock struck eleven. Immediately after the final chime, there was a discreet rapping on the study's doors.

"Enter."

The doors opened slowly and in walked a man with his hand extended and a broad smile on his face. Pennywhistle blinked in surprise. It was Higgins, all right, but the boyish officer had been replaced by a grown man. The bright red hair and freckles still reminded him of a leprechaun, but his face had filled out and he was now, probably, five nine, a gain of five inches from his height at Trafalgar. He had been-razor thin before, but now his chest seemed broader and his shoulders wider.

"So wonderful to see you, Sir Thomas. I was delighted to read of your knighthood and overjoyed to find you were assigned here." His expression darkened. "Terrible thing, that attack on you in London. Did they ever catch the culprit?"

Pennywhistle shook his hand joyfully. "No. Please Luke, let us dispense with formality. We are both diplomats, not soldiers, so make it Tom."

"Tom, it is then," said Higgins uncertainly. He had never addressed Pennywhistle as anything other than Mr. Pennywhistle on *Bellerophon*.

"Now please take a seat and make yourself comfortable. I would love to reminisce with you and hear of your progress, but I called you here on a delicate matter of business. I have left instructions that we should not be disturbed, though what I have to say will not take long."

Pennywhistle locked the doors and then proceeded to the sideboard, where he poured two glasses of freshly squeezed orange juice. It was a luxury that he knew his guest would appreciate, since it was impossible to obtain at sea. He handed one to Higgins and then sat down, reminding himself to brief

Higgins, not lecture him. He took a short pull on his juice then got straight to the point. "I was supposed to be the Assistant Naval Attaché, but just before leaving London I received word he had passed and that I was now to fill the chief position. "

Higgins made a face. "I never liked the man. He was a terrible snob and always referred to me as "that jumped up bog-trotter." He took a long sip of his juice as if to banish his memory of the man.

Pennywhistle concealed his surprise. The Higgins he remembered was the least judgmental of men. "I intend to fulfill my official duties, but I have been given a special task that takes priority over them. I have been granted special permission by Lord Castlereagh to tell you that my unofficial mission involves the recovery of some letters that could be very damaging to the House of Hanover, as well as the reputations of some very prominent men."

"A grave matter indeed."

"I need your help. I require you to follow a man who may be the contact for the fellow who nearly caused my death on the road to Vienna."

Higgins reared back. "I had not heard that you were attacked on the way here. That is monstrous! Monstrous!"

Pennywhistle sighed in response. "I do seem a magnet for mayhem. I think the people behind the Vienna Road attack are the same ones who attacked me in London. I believe this servant will lead me to his immediate master and that master will lead me to the ultimate overlord, the possessor of those letters. I would do it myself, but since this man was hired by me, it might clue him in that he was being followed if I were spotted. I know you have never done any clandestine work, but you were always a quick study on *Bellerophon*, and I trust that has not changed. "

"The cloak-and-dagger stuff sounds deuced exciting. "

"I will give you a quick course in surveillance before you start. "

"This is all very mysterious." Higgins rubbed his hands in glee. "Most intriguing!"

"Don't get carried away. This is a dangerous endeavor. The man behind the attacks on me is ruthless. He will stamp you out like a bug if he thinks you are an impediment to his plans."

"My life has been quiet of late, Tom. I love being married to Lydia, but our household is ordered and sedate. A job that brings some adventure and contributes to the safety of the realm is most welcome. And now, I have some information for you." He pursed his lips and knitted his eyebrows in distaste. "Another of our shipmates is in the city. One that I was initially displeased to have reappear. However, he has proven a handy source of information on the behind-the-scenes machinations of the Congress. He plays cards with many of the key aides of monarchs and ambassadors and has amassed a small fortune from his nightly encounters."

Pennywhistle scowled. "Wilson?" Peter Wilson had been a fellow Marine officer on *Bellerophon*. He was a coward whom Pennywhistle had considered killing outright at the height of the battle. He was also a genius with cards.

"Wilson. I cannot tell you that he has turned over a new leaf or reformed his character in the slightest. I only heard of his presence from the Second Secretary, who had been thoroughly fleeced during an evening of cards. I initially met with him out of sheer curiosity. It's funny; he is still a blackguard, but I sense a certain guilt about his conduct during the battle. While he is not the picture of a patriot, he has on occasion passed on gossip that Castlereagh has found useful. It may be his odd way of seeking absolution."

Attaché Extraordinaire

"I would not want to depend on that rotter for anything. Still," he sighed. "I should not look a gift horse in the mouth. The Congress is about compromise, so I suppose some personal ones will be necessary from time to time."

Higgins changed the subject, wanting to lighten his friend's mood. "I see a wedding ring on your finger. I should love to hear about the woman who snagged a marriage-phobic man."

"I should be equally curious to find out how Miss Lydia became your wife."

"Since the official business is done, perhaps the embassy can spare us both for an hour," said Higgins cheerfully. "Are you hungry? I know a pastry shop a block away that has the best strudel in the city. Several varieties of excellent coffee too. I recall that you have a connoisseur's tongue for that beverage, just as you have a disdain for tea. What did you call it, "an old woman's drink?"

Pennywhistle chuckled. "I do have a caustic tongue sometimes. "I could use a pleasant diversion." With that, Pennywhistle finished his juice, as did Higgins, a moment later.

As they were exiting the study, Higgins remarked, "do you ever get the idea that Wilson and myself showing up in your life is not just coincidence?"

"Definitely! I think powers far greater than you or I have arranged things. It remains to be seen why."

Chapter 9

It was only two hours until midnight and Castlereagh was tired. He had had a long and exhausting day speaking with various representatives of the German Confederation on the Saxon Question. The vast majority wanted the continued existence of Saxony because they feared the developing hegemony of Prussia. They understood that the King of Saxony might suffer a reduction in his domain because of his support for Bonaparte, but they wanted to limit the territory he would cede to Prussia. two fifths of the land and 900,000 people were figures they could live with, though they were not at all happy about the prospect. King Frederick Augustus was a stubborn but principled man, and far better liked than either Frederick William III of Prussia or the man many saw as leading him around the nose, Czar Alexander. The Saxon Army, while small, was loyal, well trained, and experienced; not a force to be dismissed lightly.

Castlereagh had saved the worst appointment for last. He entered the ornate Baroque music room in the Hofburg Palace, accompanied only by an aide who would serve as an interpreter. He hoped Alexander had brought one, too, though he often insisted on speaking directly in English. Alexander spoke passable French, as did Castlereagh, but the Czar liked to show off his command of a language that he spoke with more confidence than skill. Precision of language was important in diplomacy, since treaties often turned on the exact meaning of a particular word or concept. Alexander had trouble with idioms, resulting in malapropisms such as "niche in time saves nine," or "bird in the hand is worth two in the boot."

A glaring anomaly in the pacific atmosphere was the presence of Alexander's massive bodyguard, Boris, hovering in the background like a storm cloud at a picnic. His right hand casually squeezed a billiard ball that seemed seconds away from turning to powder. Castlereagh wondered if he practiced on animals. Boris served to remind him that cruelty and blunt force underlay Russian power, despite Alexander's belief that he was a champion of Enlightenment.

The Czar rose from the long table and advanced to shake Castlereagh's hand. He was just under six feet tall, with a striking face and red hair. He had a receding hairline that he took pains to conceal with an artful comb over and a figure that, though once reckoned manly, had developed an incipient paunch, thanks to the abundance of good food in Vienna. To Castlereagh's relief, he had brought a translator, who remained seated. Castlereagh realized he was being granted a considerable privilege, since the Czar was coming to him. Normally, one had to stand before the Czar; permission to sit in the presence of His Imperial Majesty was allowed only by special dispensation. He knew Alexander found his customary reserve annoying but understood that the Russian also respected his tactful honesty, intellect, and—something rare in St. Petersburg—his incorruptibility.

"Your Imperial Majesty, it is an honor to see you again," Castlereagh said joylessly, as he shook Alexander's hand firmly.

"My Lord Castlereagh. I have decided to dispense with a secretary today, since I prefer our talk to remain unrecorded. I thought it would allow more frank discussion and facilitate the development of compromise. I wish to make the Continent a place where all can call their homelands 'home sweat home."

Castlereagh groaned inwardly. The interpreter was just window-dressing. "A fine sentiment, Your Imperial Majesty, and I am agreeable to keeping our little chat beyond the reach of historians."

Both took seats on opposite sides of the heavily gilded porphyry table. There was a brief awkward silence.

"Your Imperial Majesty, allow me to begin with a discussion of the Saxon question. I have been consulting with members of the German Confederation and they find your suggestion of the dissolution of Saxony to be extreme. I would add, however, that they are open to compromise and would not oppose a reduction. The size of that reduction would be a subject for negotiation." There was a long, disquieting pause as Castlereagh's words hung in the air, as if instruments of Damocles.

When the Czar spoke, his expression was thoughtful. "I think Frederick Augustus needs chastisement of the severest sort for his support of Bonaparte. An example should be made of him so that Germans will think long and hard about lending support to any future usurpers. We all wish to ensure that Bonaparte was a once-in-a-millennium phenomenon. I am a reasonable man and would consider lessening the punishment of Frederick Augustus, in return for the German Confederation looking favorably upon the reconstitution of an independent Poland. Under my protection, of course."

"An independent Poland would find favor with me," replied Castlereagh. "It is a question of just how independent it would actually be. As with so many things, that could be negotiated. If you would soften your position a bit on other matters, I think we could work something out. We both want the same thing, after all: A Continent free of war and turmoil, where trade and commerce flourish and amity among nations is the order of the day."

The Czar smiled. "That is all I have ever wanted. A Continent at peace, with lasting alliances in place to ensure it stays that way. All working together under the blessed banner of Christianity."

Castlereagh maintained a neutral expression but blanched inwardly. The Czar's messianic complex was as vexing as it was dangerous. It fueled his impulsiveness, often making him think that a random thought was an inspiration from On High. Castlereagh was not sure how to respond, so he simply said "indeed", a word favored by the British when one sought to acknowledge a statement rather than taking any position on its validity.

"Before we continue to more weighty concerns, my lord, there is a minor matter I should like to discuss. It concerns a small state erased by Napoleon. One that I would be gratified to see restored. Its name if Reichenau. I am sure you will have heard of it but have probably not given it over much thought."

Castlereagh narrowly prevented himself from blinking in surprise. What was the Czar up to? What benefit would he gain from reconstituting an unimportant state that was a medieval relic? He recalled that the rulers of Reichenau had been robber barons who had obstructed free trade on the Rhine; charging the sort of tolls that he wished to erase. He seemed to remember the last ruler of that tiny state had been oppressive and out of touch with its people. Castlereagh was a supporter of self-determination, in so far as it was consonant with the balance of power. Still, the entire Congress was about *quid pro quo,* and Reichenau could be a bargaining chip.

"I confess I am surprised at your endorsement, Your Imperial Majesty. I would have to study the matter before adopting any official position."

"Of course, my lord, like me, you are not a man given to impulsive actions." The Czar failed to see the irony in his words. "I respect your erudition and feel certain that upon reflection, you will see the merits of my position."

"Tell me, Your Imperial Majesty, if Reichenau returned, could it be under a new ruler, perhaps chosen by the people themselves, from a list of acceptable candidates supplied by us?"

"I regret to say, no. I would insist on the Landgrave who was ousted by Bonaparte. I believe Metternich would want that too, since he dislikes illegitimate newcomers and favors old bloodlines."

"That could complicate matters." Castlereagh allowed the hint of a frown to play on the corners of his mouth. "A new ruler and the abolition of tolls might have to be a precondition for negotiation."

The Czar knew von Steinwehr would never stand for such conditions but did not want to start a fight too soon. "I too would have to study the matter before taking a position. You mention a *quid pro quo.* I am happy to say I may soon come into possession of some information which will be of interest to your Prince Regent. I cannot tell you more until I understand the exact nature of this information. When I do, I will communicate with you at the earliest possible moment." He smiled pleasantly.

The smile alarmed Castlereagh. It was not a friendly one, but one that said, 'I know something you don't know, and that something is very bad.' Castlereagh wondered what he was talking about. The Czar would never give up a key piece of information out of generosity. He suddenly saw Pennywhistle's face in his mind's eye and made a connection with the Czar's words. Was the Czar about to acquire the Clarke Letters and use them for blackmail? It certainly tracked with the way business was done at the Court in St. Petersburg. He calmed himself with the knowledge that the most damning information was under the lock of encryption, at least for now. He would speak with Pennywhistle tomorrow morning and ask him to redouble his efforts. Now he needed to change the subject, to give himself time to think.

"Returning to the Saxon question, I wonder if a resolution might be made easier if you and I dined with Frederick Augustus; something quiet and informal. Not a state dinner, merely a pleasant talk over good food. I know you and he have not spoken personally, and I find misunderstandings are more easily straightened out if the principals can meet each other as persons, not sovereigns."

"I would be agreeable if you would serve as the intermediary. The one thing I share with Frederick William is a respect for you."

"I thank you for that, Your Imperial Majesty. I shall arrange that dinner in the next few days."

"I have been thinking of Malta of late," observed the Czar, "And I think the resolution of that question could be part of a greater agreement that could include both Reichenau and Saxony."

Castlereagh kept his face neutral but groaned inwardly. He decided the best course was just to let the Czar talk until the impulse was exorcised from his system. He knew he was in for several hours of blather, but it could not be helped.

"I am not sure how such disparate issues could be linked, but I welcome your thoughts. I am sure they will be unique, creative, and offer me perspectives that I had not considered before."

Alexander beamed, since he fancied himself an intellectual and relished the approval of a man who was the genuine article. "I think it is time to send for some champagne. I know it is premature to celebrate, but I believe we are on the cusp of some very important, very good decisions."

Alexander barked instructions at the translator, who departed to inform the servants on the other side of the door that the Great Men needed refreshments.

The servants had anticipated the request and had numerous bottles of champagne chilling. Less than two minutes later, a tall servant wheeled in a cart with a large bucket of ice that contained three bottles of champagne and two large glasses. Next to the bucket was a sizeable plate of crackers, caviar, and small wooden spoons.

"Will there be anything else, Your Imperial Majesty?'

"No, that will be all."

"My Lord Castlereagh, have you ever tasted caviar?"

"No, I have not, Your Imperial Majesty." All Castlereagh knew about the black muck on the plate was that it was a form of fish eggs.

"Then you are in for a heavenly delight. Your culinary education is not complete unless you have tasted caviar." The Czar grinned like a child wanting an adult to appreciate his favorite kind of candy. He laughed and popped the cork of a champagne bottle, poured two glasses, then spooned caviar onto two large crackers. He walked round and handed a glass and a cracker to Castlereagh.

Attaché Extraordinaire

Castlereagh realized it was a remarkable moment: the Czar of Russia acting as a servant! He was seeing something of the real man beneath the ruler's exterior. Despite his pretensions, he was something of a lost child. Considering that his father had been mad, his mother distant, and he had grown up in a court where intrigue and assassination were always in the background, that characterization was as apt as it was useful to know.

Castlereagh managed a wan smile. Hard negotiation lay ahead, but part of that was simply wearing your opponent down. He dreaded the champagne and would have preferred a large pot of coffee. He needed a clear head for what was to follow, but there was no way he could get out of drinking with the Czar. The Russian capacity for absorbing huge amounts of alcohol was legendary, and the Czar was no exception. Castlereagh was an abstemious man who disliked intoxication. He would just have to pace himself carefully and take tiny sips while the Czar took gulps.

He reminded himself that the Czar needed British trade far more than the British needed Russian products. When the Czar had closed his ports to the British, the hemp, iron, and wood trades had nearly collapsed, bankrupting more than a few magnates upon whose support Alexander depended. Magnates of that sort had been behind the assassination of his father, and the Czar was wary of provoking them.

Castlereagh noticed that the Czar was staring at him expectantly, so he took a quick sip of champagne and a large bite of the cracker. The first was good, the second anything but. He nonetheless forced a smile and gave the response Alexander wanted. "Delicious! What a remarkable combination!"

"I knew you would appreciate the taste. Caviar is a magical substance that bewitches all who partake of it." Satisfied that he had introduced a philistine to civilization, he returned to his chair. He took a relaxed pull of champagne and began speaking in magisterial tones. "My father had a deep spiritual connection with the Knights of Malta. Not only was he the patron of the order, but numerous of their members hailed from Russia. I would not relinquish such a connection lightly, but would be willing to do so in return for a favor. Your Commodore Hoste captured Ragusa in the late war. That city-state likely means little to you, but Metternich would be very glad to have it back and might support the restoration of Reichenau if I could make that happen. The Austrians are now the most influential power in Italy and the Adriatic, and it would make good geographic sense to add it to their domains. In return, Metternich might come round to your position on the slave trade."

A hulking man in a colonel's uniform entered the room, strode forward briskly, gave Alexander a document, and departed. Castlereagh caught a glimpse of a remarkably ugly face that might have been borrowed from a gargoyle on St. Stephen's Cathedral. Castlereagh took another sip of the champagne. It was going to be a long evening of maintaining a polite facade, followed by a long, sleepless night filled with despair, indigestion, and self-doubt. Thank God for his wife Emily, who would listen patiently and reassure him that he was doing the right thing.

Chapter 10

Sammie Jo hated the condescension of the English, but she disliked the smarminess of the European variant even more. Their snobbery made her feel as lost as last year's Easter egg.

Upon her arrival in England, she had been viewed as an exotic barbarian, a beautiful rustic with strange ways and an unusual way of pronouncing words, which had more in common with the English of Shakespeare than that of Regency England. English women were supposed to be sugar and spice, while she was more like whiskey and ice.

She might be just a country girl at heart, but she read people well. Instruction in the arts of manners by Lady Leith had sharpened those instincts and enabled her to navigate the social season. The superficial polish she had acquired, along with her beauty and willingness to speak forthrightly, had won her the respect of men who liked strong women and the admiration of women who wished to be something more than mannered milksops. Her outbursts of profanity shocked people, but these had become less frequent and less protracted. Right now, she wanted to curse a blue streak.

This was the third residence that Frau Ingrid Stottler had shown them, and her condescension had deepened with each tour. The residences all possessed legions of turrets, towers, and domes that put Sammie Jo in mind of the Arabian Nights and castles that might have belonged to Cinderella's prince. They were grand in design and epic in scale. Two had been designated palaces by great families who had once enjoyed Hapsburg favor. Vienna was a city of palaces, containing over four hundred.

The potential domiciles all contained elaborate silver and gold filigree work and spectacular floors and ceilings. Intricate chandeliers, and marble pilasters. Imposing Palladian windows were additional hallmarks of their interiors. The walls featured gigantic tapestries replete with mythical beasts and ancient gods, as well as portraits of expensively dressed people, long dead. The fireplaces were so large that you could pitch bell tents in them. All had water closets and pumps with gold spigots connected to hidden wells.

The housing shortage in Vienna had driven rents sky high. The three residences Sammie Jo had viewed were only available because their former tenants could no longer afford the rent. All of the palaces had been built over a period of years, in sprawling blocks that each represented a slightly different architectural style. The one Stottler was currently showing them was the earliest wing of the Auersperg Palace. The current representatives of that family lived in the wing across the courtyard.

Soap was in as short supply as housing. Wags said it was because the Congress had a lot of dirty laundry.

Sammie Jo sensed that Frau Stottler, her realtor, viewed her as an American adventuress of no breeding and fewer morals, an opportunist who had snagged a title through luck and the liberal employment of her beauty and backwoods wiles.

Warning bells clanged in Sammie Jo's head; something was off about the woman. She smiled and laughed too much.

Attaché Extraordinaire

But her smiles were those of Dismal Swamp gators and her laughter sounded more like the titters of a scavenging fox. She sensed that true joyous, gurgling laughter was as much a stranger to this woman as a vagrant was to a throne room. She was like a catbird faking the call of an oriole to steal a nest and appeared a changeling, a hard woman compelled to impersonate a soft one in a profession where easy charm was of great moment and strength of character a liability.

Sammie Jo sensed a fundamental toughness as formidable as her own. The German's superficially deferential speech and poised handling of a formidable aristocrat like Lady Leith suggested that toughness was allied to cleverness. Sammie Jo pegged her as a predator, but she guessed Frau Stottler thought she was dealing with a silly goose.

Playing the role of the untutored rustic came in handy when dealing with Europeans flaunting their superiority; her husband had been right about the usefulness of being underestimated. Frau Stottler had missed her intelligence entirely, so she would give the woman what she expected, a scattering of folksy Americanisms that would mark her as gullible.

"Aw shucks, I can't decide among all these superfine choices." The words meandered from her tongue like a parade of turtles with their back legs tied. "It's like asking me to be the judge of the prize pig at the county fair. Or making me decide if I like catfish better than crawdads."

Stottler smiled in delight.

Lady Leith watched with great interest. She recognized two females contending for dominance. One had sophistication and experience, the other instinct and cleverness.

"I should be gratified to assist you in any way I can," said Stottler unctuously, "though it would be helpful if I could understand a little more about your tastes and expectations, so I could better match you to a residence."

A smile warbled Sammie Jo's mouth as her mind raced. Was Stottler an information broker, selling to the great and mighty? Being a realtor would give her a detailed knowledge of the floor plans of houses, useful for a burglar seeking classified documents or briefing papers that had carelessly been left lying about.

Sammie Jo played a hunch. "One thing my husband told me to ask about is safes. He sometimes handles secret information that needs a secure hiding place. The house with the stoutest safe would be the one I would probably choose."

It only lasted for a split second, but Sammie Jo caught the 'I have you now' expression on Stottler's face. "You are in luck, Lady Pennywhistle. The residence we are in has a safe that was installed two years ago that features the most up-to-date security refinements. I could show it to you directly, if you like."

"That would be mighty fine, Frau Stottler, and would really dill my pickle. Bless your pea-pickin heart. Important stuff without a safe is like a one-legged cat in a sandbox!"

Lady Leith gave Sammie Jo, a quick, disapproving glance, indicating she was moving into definite "ham" territory with her "li'l ole country gal" act.

Sammie Jo took the hint and resolved to tone down the cornpone canting.

The safe was well-nigh impenetrable unless someone detonated a bomb nearby. Its hiding place in an elaborate armoire was an ingenious additional protection. Frau Stottler opened it without a second's hesitation. The usual realtor would have used a written combination. Something was most definitely going on.

Attaché Extraordinaire

"We'll take it," exclaimed Sammie Jo with an impulsivity that caused Lady Leith to regard her with a stunned surprise.

Sammie Jo shot her a quick glance that said, *I know what I am doing.*

Frau Stottler beamed. "And for how long will you wish to lease it?"

"Three months ought to do it. My husband said he expects the Congress will be wrapped up in that time. We would like an option to extend, if it runs longer."

"I can provide that. Do you wish to know the rent?"

"I ain't worried about that." She glanced at Lady Leith who nodded in acknowledgement that cost would not be an obstacle.

"Now, when can I sign the lease? I would like to move in the day after tomorrow."

"It is on the bureau in the study. If you will follow me, we can take care of the matter straightaway. "

Sammie Jo signed the lease and after a celebratory glass of champagne with Stottler and Lady Leith, the realtor departed promising to return the following day with a list of reputable movers.

She had offered help in hiring additional servants, since the residence would require a considerable number. The word spy could easily be substituted for servant and some of them on the staff would provide intimate surveillance.

"What the blazes was that all about Sammie Jo? I thought you'd at least want to talk the matter over with me."

"It was not the house that sold me, it was the way the realtor showed off the safe. That is, if she even is a realtor or her name is Frau Stottler."

Lady Leith gave a start. "You think she is an imposter?"

John Danielski

Sammie Jo spoke with assurance. "You're darn tootin'! I think she's lying like a no-legged dog. She sucked up information like a twister gobbling houses. Why was she standing in for her husband anyway? We are valuable clients with big purses. Even if a realtor was at death's door, he'd want our business. And if he had to send his wife in his place, wouldn't she act like she was trying to charm the dew off a honeysuckle, not snooty? The Second Secretary made the appointment and directed us here. He never gave us a physical description of Herr Stottler. He certainly never told us if he had a wife."

"All true." Lady Leith regarded Sammy Jo with deep satisfaction. Here was another person who could ferret out falsehood and see through disguises, very much like her godson.

"I think she is part of something, Margaret. I think the real Stottler... well, I am betting he ain't even in the city. I think this woman is planning to rob us, not of gold and jewels, but the codebook. Hell!" Sammie Jo exclaimed as if a chandelier had just lit in her head. "That means she works for the fella that tried to kill Tom and me! That's why I made such an issue of the safe. She took the bait faster than a monkey cracks a coconut."

"That is very bad."

Sammie Jo smiled sardonically. "It ain't bad at all. Something I have not told you. Tom wants to use a decoy codebook to fool his opponent. I think we have just given him an excellent idea of where it will be kept, and his accomplice conveniently has the combination. I think Tom will be pleased that I have just defined the battlefield."

Lady Leith cupped her hands on her cheeks. "Stars and Garters! I know who Stottler is!"

Attaché Extraordinaire

"Who?" asked Sammie Jo eagerly.

"She is not just the accomplice of the man who tried to kill you two; she is his wife. The one person a ruthless man could trust completely would be his wife."

"Do you think today was a reconnoiter? A chance to find out what I was like and what to expect?"

"Very possible, Sammie Jo. She was sizing you up. I think, however, she came away with exactly the wrong impression, seeing you as a simpleton."

"Tom says deception is a powerful weapon in war."

"We should have Frau Stottler followed when she leaves tomorrow,' said Lady Leith. "My lady's maid is smart and observant. She also knows a good bit of German."

"We might finally be able to put a name to the man who has been after Tom. Once we have a name, he can settle an old account."

"We are become spies and scouts!"

"What do you say we celebrate our new-found secret identities with some coffee and strudel?"

"An excellent plan. Espionage makes me hungry."

Higgins was right. The coffee at Zindel's Pastry Nook was delicious; strong Brazlian—Pennywhistle's favorite. He had never had much of a sweet tooth, but the cherry strudel was a delight. So much so, that he ordered another when he had his coffee cup refilled. The first cup had disappeared quickly as he explained to Higgins the basics of surveillance: maintain a discreet distance, use the shelter of crowds, shift position frequently, change sides of the street regularly, check store front reflections, both for your mark's image and your own, to make sure that you are not being followed. Common sense really, and Higgins had a lot of that.

"This shop's location is convenient, Luke. It is on the route Van Meegeran should take." Pennywhistle extracted his pocket watch and checked the time." I expect he will pass our location in the next five minutes. His destination is the Fugelsang Harness Shop opposite the Amelienburg Palace. That palace is a 16th century wing of the Hofburg, where Czar Alexander and the Russians are housed. I told him that it catered to the elite carriage trade and that a yoke from it would be an appropriate replacement for the one on Lady Leith's coach, which was damaged in the Vienna Road attack. Assigning him this task will give him the impression that I repose trust in him, rather than suspecting him of being an information conduit. I believe the man behind the attack on the Vienna Road is one of the Czar's four top military aides. I wish to see if the Dutchman meets a contact or enters the palace. He would have no earthly reason to do so unless he is exactly what I believe him to be, a man planted in my entourage to replace an old Marine. I believe poison caused his death. One of this Dutchman's friends probably placed it in his food."

"Poisoning?" exclaimed Higgins in shock. "You are dealing with some very dark fellows, Tom."

"Indeed. My opponent is ruthless and relentless. Our contest will not end in a draw but in the death of one of us. "

The large bay window fronting on the Singerstrasse proved its worth. "Wait! That's him, Luke." Pennywhistle pointed at a short, swarthy man with a distinctive bow-legged stride. He was dressed in the dun-colored attire of a working man instead of the Leith livery. He wore a flat brown cloth cap with a short bill that was common in the city. "Your target. Sorry to make you dine and dash, but the game is afoot."

Attaché Extraordinaire

Higgins took a good, long look at the slowly walking man and fixed his image in his brain. "I will report back to you in a few hours. I will take particular care to furnish you with an exact description of any persons with whom he may speak."

"Good luck!"

Higgins departed and the slow-motion chase began. The city itself was small, shaped like a snail's shell, and radiated outward from the Ringstrasse, which followed the pattern of its medieval walls. Much of it had been rebuilt in the seventeenth and eighteenth centuries in the Baroque fashion, giving it an air of prosperous beauty and grace. It was the greenest city in Europe, with plenty of parks and wooded areas that were carefully maintained. Beethoven stated frequently that many of his musical inspirations came from long walks in the Vienna Woods.

The Dutchman had no idea he was being followed. His movements were steady and anything but furtive; no quick glances over the shoulder, backtracking, or walking in circles to detect pursuit. Higgins was quiet and careful, but as the minutes passed, he felt confident enough to move closer to his quarry. His grey cloak attracted no attention, just a diplomat going about his business in a city overflowing with them. There was no reason that sort of gentleman would be following a working man.

Van Megeeran entered the palace gardens forty minutes after Higgins had begun his surveillance. In summer, the gardens were vast acres of green and a rainbow of floral colors. The rigors of autumn had muted those tones and mantled the foliage with a light coating of snow. The late afternoon sun lent unexpected warmth and caused the melting snow to sparkle like sugar crystals on top of strudels.

John Danielski

Opened to the public in 1779, The Amelienburg Gardens were a mixture of the French and English fashions. The first featured flowers, shrubs, and trees laid out in an orderly, symmetrical pattern. They highlighted the structure of the palace they fronted: plants near the main building were pruned low and taller plants farther away were edged with paths and cascading fountains. The second was far less geometric and much more natural, reflecting the Romantic Movement, designed to showcase the raw beauty of nature rather than the mathematical management of Enlightenment planners. The result was a harmonious blend whose happy result stood in contrast to a Congress where Enlightenment logic sometimes butted heads with Romantic emotions.

The gardens were popular for strolling and there were plenty of people enjoying them when Higgins entered. It was a good place for a rendezvous: public, yet replete with places for a stealthy conversation. A clandestine rendezvous could be explained as a chance meeting. And yet, Vienna had plenty of other parks closer to the British Embassy. Van Meegeran struck Higgins as a blunt instrument, not a connoisseur of gardens.

Higgins stationed himself behind a large fountain featuring nymph astride a pair of dolphins. He had a clear view of the Dutchman, but the reverse was not true as the statuary provided an effective shield. The Dutchman loitered near a statue of Diana, clearly awaiting a visitor. The visitor appeared a minute later. He was tall and spare with a face that was distinctive, because it resembled the Prince Regent, or at least a Prince Regent, before the ravages of age and dissolution had exacted their tolls. His attire was that of a gentleman. Higgins could not hear a word of the short conversation, but he saw Van Meegeran pass a small valise to the stranger. The stranger handed the Dutchman a purse, presumably containing payment for his efforts.

Van Meegeran nodded acknowledgment and then began walking toward the park's exit.

The Dutchman was no longer important. Higgins followed the stranger closely, stopping from time to time to shelter behind trees and statues. He guessed where the man was going, and his guess was a good one. He entered the palace through a subsidiary entrance rather than the main one. The guards took no notice; he was obviously well known to them.

Higgins put the events together. Pennywhistle was right. The Dutchman was a mole and reporting to a man who was a diplomat of at least middle rank, probably working for Alexander. He speculated about the contents of the valise, but then decided it was pointless. Pennywhistle would tell him what he needed to know in due time.

The Dutchman's mind was occupied with no speculation whatsoever. He reminded himself to purchase a yoke, glad that it had furnished him an excuse to leave the embassy. He was a man of simple tastes and flexible morals. He had been well paid to poison the man whom he had replaced, and his employer was satisfied with his efforts so far. At least, the man who was his contact. That man was obviously the agent of someone with considerably more power. The permutations of the Congress interested him not at all, because he was about opportunity not politics. The Congress furnished plenty and he was already thinking ahead to the next job. He saw a bright future filled with plenty of wine and women, though he was not much given to song. He had come to the city as a runaway apprentice and felt he had done well for himself.

But he missed something that a wiser man would have noticed. His employers were ruthless, and it never occurred to him that one more murder would bother them not at all. His employers had even made it clear that they disliked loose ends and warned him that severe chastisement would follow, if he left any. He never thought he might be one of them.

An anonymous looking man followed the Dutchman. He was what the Russians called a cleaner, a man who dealt with low level toxins that could still cause problems. The man ahead was spillage, but he had brought the right detergent. He would leave no stain.

Chapter 11

Pennywhistle was pleased with Higgins's report. When Higgins had mentioned the face of the Dutchman's contact, Pennywhistle knew exactly who he was. He had met the man at a ball held after his investiture as a Knight of the Bath. He had heard the hardness in his voice that mirrored the darkness in his eyes. His name was Rittmeister Anton von Gilsa, a Prussian hussar in the Russian service, operating out of their London embassy. In an encounter that lasted only a fraction of a minute, each had concluded that the other was a man you underestimated at your peril. Yet von Gilsa was still an underling who executed the schemes of someone else, someone also in the service of the Czar.

He decided to speak to Van Meegeran and see if he could surreptitiously wheedle additional information out of him. But two hours had passed since his talk with Higgins and the Dutchman had not returned: his groomsmen still lacked a new yoke. It was odd; the Dutchman was a dedicated and speedy Calvinist, not a man given to dilly-dallying in the performance of his duties. Had he spotted his tail, panicked, and flown the coop? No, he was sure Higgins had been discreet and remained undetected.

He wondered if von Gilsa had any bad habits that rendered him susceptible to blackmail. He struck Pennywhistle as tight-lipped and dedicated but even hussars could be persuaded to talk if their touchy sense of honor might be exposed to public ridicule and official censure. He hated using such low tools for leverage, but it was far better than violence; his opponent certainly would not hesitate to do the same to him if he could.

He needed new information from an old acquaintance. Enemy might have been a better choice of words, but he no longer gave much thought to Peter Wilson's cowardice at Trafalgar. While he possessed intelligence, guile, and cleverness in abundance, asking Wilson to be brave was like asking a horse to speak French. Pennywhistle was not a believer in superstition, but Wilson's miraculous survival of Trafalgar almost made him believe in gambler's luck.

Wilson was a creature whom gentlemen did not like to admit existed: a professional gambler. Games of cards were the province of gentry and lords. Even monarchs participated on occasion. The hubris of such men would not permit them to admit that they could be bubbled out of cash by a man who played cards with a cold calculation that employed mathematics, a superb memory for the cards in each rubber, and an unerring ability to read their behavioral tells. To Wilson, his opponents were insects under a microscope of his own devising.

Gambling was a cancer, not just in Regency England, but throughout the whole of Europe. Intemperate men sometimes blew through whole fortunes in a single evening. He was trusting his intuition that von Gilsa was a gambler. It would be in line with the reckless behavior associated with hussars. Von Gilsa was likely a mid-level Junker aristocrat. If he played cards, he could be found at *Les Ambassadeurs,* a fancy club that attracted some of the biggest names at the Congress. Knowing Wilson's ability to ferret out big money, he would probably have made it his Viennese Headquarters. If any man could give him information about the foibles and sins of the men playing there, it was Wilson.

He decided to walk to the club, desiring a better understanding of the sights and sounds of the city. While Sammie Jo had warned against strenuous exercise, a pleasant stroll was good for his mental well-being. It had been risky to walk the streets after dark until two months ago. A mad killer had been stalking the city and murdering people with a ritualistic viciousness that seemed lifted from the mythical *Neocronomicon*; a satanic book written in blood with pages crafted of human skin. The murders had stopped as abruptly as they had begun, leaving the authorities with no clue as to their author or his motives.

He saw a pattern that the local gendarmes had missed, but he was there to help England, not to solve crimes. The murdered men had all been affiliated with the Congress. They were the kind of men who operated behind the scenes, faceless but powerful minions that people were starting to call bureaucrats; after the desks on which they scribbled their thoughts. They possessed the expert, specialized knowledge that The Great Ones needed to reconfigure the map of Europe. Their loss meant a want of information, and information was the lifeblood of the Congress. The murdered men had all been pro-French and no friends of the Czar.

The murders had riveted the attention of the city, though the reasons varied by class and station. The humanity of the lower orders was repelled by the horror of the crimes, yet the danger also brought excitement into weary lives of unending toil. That the victims had all been their betters, the sort of people who oppressed their daily existence, generated a certain sneaking satisfaction, like seeing the town bully beaten up. His depredations had been theatre performed at irregular intervals by a monstrous main character who seemed even more frightening, because only a few had ever glimpsed his face. Imaginations played ghastly tricks and their impressions were far worse than anything received through the eyes.

To the participants of the Congress, the abominable murder of members of their own shook their faith in their protected status. They thought it quite possible the murders were carried out by a deranged anarchist, an outsider dedicated to blowing up the societal order and perhaps even ending the dominance Christianity held over Europe. The murders carried the scent of revolution and reinforced the inherent conservatism of the Congress.

Dale's new wife, Deborah, had run a successful, if radical, newspaper in London that had been recently transplanted to Kent. With Lady Leith's help, she had persuaded several papers to let her act as their Viennese correspondent. She had been speaking with the editor of Vienna's largest newspaper about the matter, since he had followed the killings closely and London readers loved the outré and outrageous. He was curious what she had discovered.

As he walked along the riverbank, his thoughts were interrupted by three short blasts from a loud, deep whistle, emanating from a curious craft that was indicating its intention to dock. He had read about this remarkable vessel but had been too busy to take a ride. It was a large steamboat with a single smokestack and a side paddle wheel. The wheel churned the water strongly; that had been the objection to the first successful one, the *Charlotte Dundas,* in 1802. The boat had pulled barges successfully but had generated such a forceful tide that it had threatened to overwhelm the banks of the Scottish canal on which it operated.

This one looked to be a British copy of the American vessel, *New Orleans*: 148 feet long, 32 feet wide, and of 360 tons burden. Robert Fulton, designer of the *New Orleans*, maintained that his design was capable of a dependable speed of eight knots.

The engine of this steamboat, christened the *Queen Charlotte*, was an altered Watt and Boulton, brought from England, but the boat itself had been assembled at a small local dockyard the year before. Its creator, Zephram Cochrane, was a shirt tail relative of the Scottish Earl of Dundonald; a prolific inventor whose creations had all proven unprofitable. Cochrane had invested his life savings in the vessel and had sought to convince the Hapsburg emperor that it could be of great use in a war. The abdication of Bonaparte in April had smashed his hopes and brought bankruptcy.

A nephew of the Earl of Clancarty, James Trench, had purchased the *Queen* for a song. He was man with a bent for science who fancied expensive curios. He had hired a Scottish mechanic named Angus Montgomery to operate it. Montgomery was a man of low birth but high technical genius; there was no broken machine that he could not fix. Montgomery loved his work and earned a respectable profit by turning the vessel into an amusement ride. He offered three-hour sightseeing cruises of the Danube, three times daily, powerful men and fashionable women being his main customers. Ice on the Danube would end those trips in a few weeks, but this evening the river was free and clear.

On impulse, he hailed Montgomery. "I say, Mr. Montgomery, could I trouble you for a brief ride? I shall pay whatever fee you care to name."

The edge of the boat had almost touched the dock, but the mooring lines had not been extended.

Montgomery assessed the man standing on the dock. His navy-blue boat cloak spoke of Saville Row, his accent belonged to the Court of St. James, and his authoritative voice and bearing proclaimed a soldier of considerable service. No reason not to make some extra profit by doubling his usual fee. "How far do you want to go?"

"Just a short hop to the Klugstrasse. I am bound for *Les Ambassadeurs,* which is but half a block from the water's edge."

So, the man is a gambler, thought Montgomery, *probably has plenty of cash on his person.* "It will cost you two shillings, sir." A handsome fee for a ride that would only take a few minutes.

"I accept," said Pennywhistle with delight. The maritime future was steam, not sail, despite the loud protestations of hidebound admirals who refused to acknowledge change.

"Come aboard, then."

Pennywhistle leaped the foot gap between boat and dock easily. He shook Montgomery's hand vigorously. "Could you grant me a quick tour of your remarkable vessel?"

The word "remarkable" had a noticeable effect on Montgomery. He beamed with pride. He had might not have built the vessel, but with the modifications that he had made, he was definitely a midwife. "It would be my pleasure, sir."

The tour was short but informative. It excited Pennywhistle's childlike awe of innovation and was a relief from thinking about matters of death and conspiracy.

His passenger's reactions pleased Montgomery. Most gentlemen had no interest in things mechanical, but this one had a keen eye for detail and peppered him with lots of perceptive questions. They were on the order of, "does your engine have an enlarged condenser; do the pistons have special protective coatings; what are the revolutions per minute of the sidewheel?" He answered them patiently like a

Attaché Extraordinaire

father being asked to speak about the triumphs of a son. The gentleman deserved a reward.

In the wheelhouse, Montgomery inquired, "Would you like to take the helm, sir?"

"I would, indeed," responded Pennywhistle.

The ten minutes that followed were ones of sublime delight. *The Queen* was nimble and responded quickly to Pennywhistle's hands. He felt the joy of command, but unlike a sailing ship, there were no orders to shout about setting sails because the wind was of as little moment as the tears of a dove. While time and tide might wait for no man, a man often waited on their pleasure. A trip across the Strait of Dover, a mere 21 miles, might take as little as five hours, but one could easily wait a whole day for a favorable wind. The steady *chug chug chug* of the *Queen*'s engine was a reassuring heartbeat that made the vessel seem alive. The inky smoke arising from her chimney seemed a shadowy hand waving goodbye to the age of sail. It was not often that one got not only to ride the wave of the future but to direct its course as well.

He sighed slightly as the Klugstrasse was reached. He did not wish the magical voyage to stop and longed to steam on into the starry night until the requirements of duty were distant memories. But all good things had to come to an end. He thanked Montgomery profusely and gave him a two-shilling tip. He left him a happy man and had an odd presentiment that both Montgomery and his vessel would play a significant role in his life.

What lay ahead was much less pleasant: Wilson. He conducted a mental review of what he wanted to say as he walked the half block to the club. He felt the old anger rising, not just for Wilson's letting the side down at Trafalgar, but because Wilson had been the main cause of the suicide of his dear cousin. They had been engaged and Wilson had cruelly jilted her. The shock had been too much for Caroline and she had sought release at the end of a pistol. At one point, he had seriously contemplated killing Wilson.

He reminded himself that forgiveness was a quality of angels and should be practiced at every opportunity. He was as far from an angel as coal was from a diamond, yet he was also a man of practical reason. It was greatly in the interest of his mission to do a little fence mending, even if it meant stifling his pride.

Les Ambassadeurs was housed in a white and gold square of three stories that was an odd pastiche of architectural styles: a body that was Palladian, a central dome that appeared stolen from Samarkand, and pagoda like entrance festooned with dragons, straight from the Court of Kublai Khan. The mix was meant to distinguish it from the neighboring structures, advertising the exotic adventures within. As he rapped the door knocker, in the shape of a fenghuang, the Chinese version of the phoenix, he thought the owners had succeeded admirably.

The doors opened portentously, and a tall man with a grave face greeted him, though it was more of an assessment than a welcome. He was not just the club's major domo but its chief sentinel. He determined Pennywhistle was a gentleman by his attire and bearing and invited him into a small entrance hall but no further. "I have not seen you before and must ask, are you a member?" He held up a small circular tray.

"No, I am not, but I shall consider it, if I am pleased by what transpires tonight." He placed his calling card on the tray.

Attaché Extraordinaire

The major domo glanced quickly at the card and a nod of his eyes indicated that he had noted Pennywhistle's title and diplomatic status.

"I am looking for a member with whom I have important business. He told me to meet him here. Mr. Peter Wilson."

The name acted like magic on the sentinel and his face became less judgmental, though it stopped short of friendly. "Yes, Mr. Wilson is a frequent visitor, and he is in attendance this evening. A player of great skill, I must say."

"Would you see that he gets my card?"

"I shall do so at once, Sir Thomas. In the meantime, please take a seat and make yourself comfortable."

Pennywhistle did so and amused himself by thinking of the shock his card would cause Wilson. Of course, it was just possible Wilson would choose to not receive him because he knew Pennywhistle disapproved of gambling, not because it was wicked but because it was foolish. Still, his curiosity would be piqued at Pennywhistle's presence in the city's chief den of upper-class, card-playing iniquity. Wilson was an opportunist and Pennywhistle's diplomatic status might give him information about card players yet to be fleeced, who resided at the embassy.

"I would have had to see it to believe it," said a familiar voice with a mellifluous baritone. "The great Thomas Pennywhistle condescending to meet a black sheep from his past and in a hotbed of vice. I understand you have a title now. Whose boots did you kiss to get it?"

Pennywhistle ignored the sarcasm, rose slowly from the settee, and pasted a welcoming smile on his face. He extended his hand which Wilson accepted tentatively and shook the same way. "I understand you have prospered since we last met," remarked Pennywhistle with false good cheer, "and that your unique gifts have found a proper home."

Wilson was four years older than Pennywhistle and looked much as he remembered him from *Bellerophon*. Six feet tall, well proportioned, with flaxen hair and a handsome face marred only by a small purplish birthmark. The lines in the face had deepened a bit and the cheeks were not quite as firm, but he wore the same peculiar half smile that suggested he had sold his soul and won it back by besting Satan in a game of whist. He was dressed fashionably in buff and blue, yet, it was tastefully understated: a contrast to the dandyism that was rife among many attendees of the Congress.

"It is a good thing you do not play cards. You have two tells. You move your right foot ever so slightly and your left shoulder droops a fraction of an inch. You have reservations about this meeting. You are not here to discuss old times," observed Wilson. "You never did anything casual but always had a greater purpose in mind. What is it tonight?"

Pennywhistle blinked in surprise, having forgotten just how observant Wilson was. There was no point in subterfuge. A *quid pro quo* would work far better. "I wish to let bygones be bygones and focus on the future. I need information, and I can direct several players your way in return. Let us just say these players have more money than skill." Pennywhistle disliked doing this but there were two aristocratic sprigs at the embassy who were itching to squander their fortunes. They would find a way to do it anyway and it made sense to direct their actions toward the furtherance of a patriotic goal.

"Guiding minnows to the shark, my, my." Wilson flashed a cynical grin. "Is that a blemish I see on your spotless heart and a cloud gathered round your saintly conscience? The archangels must have fainted, now that their chief acolyte has strayed from the straight and narrow."

"You have to break eggs to create an omelet."

"Speaking in clichés and acting as a Greek bearing gifts?" Wilson chuckled. "I should be suspicious if it were any other man than yourself. Very well then, I am always seeking new opportunities. There is a small café adjoining the bar area, where we can discuss it in privacy. The bar serves all manner of entertaining drinks, but as I recall, the one thing you and I have in common is retaining a clear head in a tight situation. The café serves excellent coffee and with Viennese cream it is a delight that even a man with your... uh... temperament might appreciate."

Pennywhistle followed Wilson through the main gambling salon to the café. It was early but the club was already crowded. The players were noisy, though expensively dressed, apparently shedding their aristocratic reserve when confronted with the prospect of a hot wager. The air was charged with tension and tobacco smoke, and the smell of alcohol was strong enough that Pennywhistle feared the lighting of additional pipes might provoke an explosion. It was an all-male crowd though, curiously, the bartenders were females, dressed in attire that seemed borrowed from a Turkish Seraglio. They were certainly stunning to look at and Pennywhistle guessed they were skilled at other things than mixing drinks.

Wilson ordered coffee with cream for the two of them and they seated themselves in a small alcove shielded from the noise of the main room. Pennywhistle took a tentative sip of his coffee. He liked his thick and black and this had a toffee color and a finer consistency. To his surprise, his tongue returned a verdict of "delicious."

Wilson noted his smile. "Well, well, well, how things have changed! The monk with a hair shirt actually enjoying the sensuality of taste."

"I have never reckoned it a crime to enjoy a good cup of coffee." He gave a wry half smile. "Besides, we monks need the alertness it provokes to discharge our devotions properly. Speaking of devotions, that is why I have come to talk to you this evening. These devotions are of a patriotic rather than divine nature."

"You? Appealing to my patriotism? That's rich. I thought you had always reckoned me a conscienceless bounder who cared more for cash than king."

"I believe all men have the capacity for change" said Pennywhistle, calmly refusing to be baited. "I think you are a complicated man Wilson, but I sense deep down that you would welcome a chance to atone for your conduct at Trafalgar."

Wilson scowled and snarled a response. "I did my duty; maybe not well, but I did it. Saved your life, though you would never have believed me if I had told you after the battle, since you and the men had christened me a coward."

"You saved my life?" said Pennywhistle with sarcasm mixed with skepticism. "I should be eager to hear the tale."

Wilson paused thoughtfully. "You once said on *Bellerophon* that things supposedly obvious are not always what they seem. You placed me next to Dale and Higgins because you did not trust me. When the French boarded, one of the matelots tossed a grenade that I caught in my gloved hand. I was only a few paces away from you and had an opportunity to throw it at your chest and put an end to your constant hectoring. Instead, I tossed it overboard. A second later, I was hit by a spent round and knocked unconscious. No one saw the bruise, and all assumed that I had passed out from fear."

"Well, you did not exactly save my life, but you certainly made a choice that I applaud. It does put matters in a different light and tells me my estimation that you would welcome a chance to do your country service is not mistaken."

"My resignation was the best service I could render my country. I was the wrong man in the wrong place at the wrong time. My destiny lies in places like the club we are presently in."

"I have come to understand that. Courage is… let us just say, not your close friend. That makes you neither bad nor evil. Now that some of the bad blood between us is dissipated, can we do business?"

"We can. What do you need to know?"

"I am looking for information about this man." Pennywhistle took out a folded sheet of paper on which he had drawn a good likeness of von Gilsa's face "Do you know him?"

Wilson chuckled wryly. "Von Gilsa. Oh yes, I do know him and enjoy playing with him. He is a stupid believer in the magic of luck and trusts in things like winning streaks and talismans to bring him success. I have nicknamed him "Soddy" because he is a vice admiral of the narrow seas."

"Ah," said Pennywhistle in understanding. Soddy meant sodomite.

"He often brings a teen aged boy with him as that talisman, although he maintains the fiction that the boy is an aide de camp."

Pennywhistle nodded. A man with such exotic tastes could be a severe embarrassment to his employer. Sodomy was no longer a crime on the Continent as it was in Britain, but it still carried a considerable degree of opprobrium in the mind of the average person.

Pennywhistle did not understand a romantic affinity between men, but he had occasionally encountered officers practicing it during his military service. The practitioners had been discreet, and it had not intruded upon the performance of their duties. While he found the oppression of such men distasteful, he had just been handed a weapon that he could not afford to ignore.

"When does he usually come to the club?"

"Usually twice a week, after ten on Thursdays and Friday's. But what business could you possibly have with that kind of man? You are the straightest of arrows, while he is a bent twig."

Pennywhistle steepled his hands. "Let's just say it involves affairs of state. I need to know more about his employer, who poses a danger to the crown."

Wilson barked a laugh suffused with cynical understanding. "So, you wish to compromise him through his bedroom tastes? Well, I never thought I would see the day when the upright Pennywhistle became a blackmailer. And I am the moral reprobate?"

Pennywhistle's face turned hard. "Seneca was right when he said '*necessitas non habet leges.*' Sometimes one must set aside his moral sensibilities in pursuit of a greater good. I may not like it, but I do what needs to be done."

Wilson responded with surprising compassion. "I am a man of the world and am not judging you as you judged me. It is good to see that you are human after all."

"All too human, I fear. "

"Undoubtedly, and yet your actions have brought you a knighthood. That is not something I am ever likely to obtain, though I am well on my way to amassing a fortune. I look forward to the day I shall not have to seek out bad players and put up with women on the make."

Pennywhistle noticed Wilson still wore the ring with the blood ruby that his cousin had given him. His face turned earnest and inquisitive. "Speaking of women, satisfy my curiosity. Did you ever care for my cousin, or was it all a sham?"

Wilson looked him hard in the eye. "I will not try to beguile you with a lilting description of the great width of my heart. I am not capable of a deep love for any woman but to the extent that I possess an acquaintance with that emotion, I did care for her. I will not deny that her fortune held allure, but her sweetness had a definite effect on my cynical outlook. She made me foolish, and I might even have followed through on the engagement, but for the fear of her father who saw my true nature. For the first and last time in my life, I panicked and fled. I was much saddened when she took her own life. I do not blame myself for it and yet, and yet..." His voice trailed off as his eyes grew glassy.

Pennywhistle almost felt sorry for him, since introspection was clearly as rare as it was painful for him. It was time for a change of tack. "I cannot say that I approve of you, but I understand you better. I would like to open a regular channel of communication between us, one that will be beneficial to us both. You encounter the great and mighty on a nightly basis. I gather that they talk incautiously after a few libations. You have perceptive ears and a good nose for sniffing out useful gossip. I should like to be privy to the highlights of that gossip, since it might help my superior, Lord Castlereagh. He would, of course, not acknowledge how he had obtained said information but would nonetheless use it to advance Britain's welfare. In return, certain discretionary funds might be made available to you, as well as additional names of men looking for a reliable fourth in games of whist played in private residences—very, very august residences."

"Now I have heard everything," chuckled Wilson. "You want me to become His Majesty's secret snitch? I do not think there is any such title on the diplomatic roster."

"This would all be off the books. A private understanding between you and me that would never be recorded on paper. Have I offended your delicate moral sensibilities?" said Pennywhistle sarcastically.

"By no means, it is just that you and I are more alike than I would ever have supposed. I am pleased that you trust me. I know you do not grant that lightly."

"I do trust you, but only to a certain point and only on very particular matters. Do not expect me to one day proclaim my undying friendship for you. We can be useful to each other and establish a *modus vivendi*; a détente, not a peace treaty."

"I can live with that. In fact, had you promised more, I should be deeply suspicious. Perhaps I could say we are the best of enemies. "

"Almost like the luck of the draw brought us together, but you and I know luck is a chimera. The next time von Gilsa comes to the club send word as fast as you can."

Chapter 12

Von Steinwehr was a light sleeper. Like a fireman, he was subconsciously alert for the next political blaze that would have to be put out at a moment's notice. The soft chimes of the bedroom clock announced it was just six. The heavy curtains kept the room warm, and outside the sky was still winter dark; he had a busy day ahead, but right now he was holding on to the last flickers of a pleasant dream. The bed was a heavy, dark, walnut affair, intricately carved with figures from Germanic mythology.

Next to him, his wife, Ingrid, pushed aside the heavy down comforter and abruptly sat straight up, as if she had heard a bugle blowing reveille. She blinked twice, rubbed her eyes to clear out the sleepy winkers, and shook her husband vigorously. "Klaus, Klaus! This is no day to sleep in! I have much to tell you."

Von Steinwehr sat up slowly, his mind sharpening with each small movement. "I am lucky I have my own personal rooster, even if she is female. Why don't you ring for tea? I could do with a large cup of Darjeeling."

Ingrid did so with an anticipatory smile. Like her husband, she considered a large cup of tea a *sine qua non* for a good start to a morning. She could never understand her sister's preference for coffee.

John Danielski

"My work yesterday went well, Klaus. I know you question my enthusiasm for amateur theatrics, but yesterday my experience in organizing plays paid off handsomely. My audience of one was completely convinced that I was who I claimed. She heeded my counsel and gave me not only the result I wanted but applause, in the form of many useful tidbits about herself and her husband." She paused and frowned in disapproval. "She was not at all what I expected. Given what you have told me of her husband, I expected a lady for all seasons, or alternatively a shy and naive blossom in his shadow. One who would be an ornament to her husband in every situation. Imagine my surprise when her first words to me were, "Call me Sammie Jo." Her voice managed to simultaneously mimic a Southern drawl and convey disdain for the same.

"Sammie Jo, Sammie Jo?" he ejaculated. "What sort of name is that? It does not even sound Christian. I cannot imagine you going along with such undue familiarity in a receiving line."

"She *is* American." This said with contempt.

"Ahhhhhh!" Her husband's voice indicated her former nationality explained everything. Americans were blunt, forward, understood nothing of tradition, and had no fluency in languages. He himself spoke German, French, English, and Latin.

Ingrid continued. "I see you wonder how she came to be the wife of a man of achievement and pedigree. I can explain. She is a woman of extraordinary beauty. She radiates a magnetism that seems to beckon to the basest desires of men. The sensual challenge of her voice, the spark in her eyes, and the swaying of her hips remind even me of a cat in heat, and I am a woman." She sniffed. "Think of her as a woman with ambition, a would-be Empress Theodora, sleeping her way to the top. From what you have told me of Alexander, he will pounce on her like a cat on a canary, should they ever meet."

"Oh, they will. There is a grand ball New Year's Eve at the Razoumovsky Palace to which her husband and my employer are both invited." He sighed. "I have counseled Alexander again and again that his bedding of unvetted women is a grave security risk, but my admonitions have had the opposite effect. He revels in his reputation as the great stud of the Congress and welcomes any chance to further it."

"She is untutored, unmannered, and un-housebroken, but she carries herself with a certain country charm that Alexander will find appealing."

Ingrid stopping talking when the tea arrived. Her lady's maid had been with her for many years and understood from her mistress's expression that she was deep in discussion with her husband and did not want to be fussed over. She quietly laid out the implements and sweets on the large silver tray, poured the tea, and departed swiftly.

Ingrid and Klaus sipped their tea and took leisurely bites of peach strudel. They were enjoying the taste and using the interval to give their minds time to think.

"I think, husband, we have your opponent and his wife in the ideal situation. His lady has signed the lease and I am going to assist her in providing staff. I have selected three reliable informants that I will ensure are hired. Americans are as ignorant about staffing an establishment as they are about knowing the difference between a flunkey and a footman. She was visibly delighted with the safe and shall use it to hold... should I call it 'the book of our destiny'? I showed her the combination. I estimate it will take several days for the Pennywhistles to settle in and for their new staff to become acquainted with the details of their duties. Once we have their report, we can determine the optimal time to strike. If you have a chance to speak with Pennywhistle in a social capacity, it might give you an opportunity to anticipate any countermeasures."

"An excellent plan. I do regret that you will not be able to attend the ball, lest Lady Pennywhistle realize you are a countess, not a realtor. She might be puzzled and mention it to her husband, and I do not wish our name to come to his attention outside the political arena. There is, however, a possibility that the book may reside at the embassy, but I may have a way to find that out. Because of von Gilsa's bungling, I have reached the conclusion that Pennywhistle would not carry it on his person."

"I do wish my cousin possessed more skill, but he always made me laugh as a child. I grew up in a grim household, and his visits cheered me. That is why I have argued so hard for you to retain his services."

"We all need someone or something that alleviates our gloom, as you do for me. But could you tell me, dear, a few more details about the gossip you gleaned from this... er... Sammie Jo? I have a hard time saying that name. I have a certain idea of her husband's character from his actions, but I should like a more intimate portrait, painted by the brush of a loved one. The meeting of the International River Committee is at two o'clock this afternoon. I shall be there as the Czar's chief representative. Pennywhistle's name is on the roster as Castlereagh's man. It will be our first meeting and I want the advantage of being able to interpret his actions and words by the light of reason and logic. Knowledge is power, and never more so than when you come face-to-face with an opponent who has cost you a great deal of time and an inordinate amount of trouble."

Attaché Extraordinaire

"And sleepless nights," remarked Ingrid, "that have robbed me of repose as well. Sammie Jo prattled on and on about her husband. She is obviously smitten by him. This may take several hours."

"Proceed. I would leave no stone unturned."

***

Two hours later and four miles away, a fully dressed Sammie Jo shook her husband awake. He was stretched out in the elaborately appointed Rococo bed that intimidated her. "C'mon, you old sleepyhead, day's a wastin'. You got in pretty late; you looked tired, tore up, and like you had a flight of cawing crows swirling round in your head. If I didn't know better, I would have said you were a wastrel, back from a bender. 'Course, you smelled like a pot of coffee, not a bottle of Scotch. That thunderhead on your brow told me you didn't want to talk, so I kept quiet. Just got you bedded down as quick as I could, figuring you'd let me in on your demons this a.m. I got a lot to tell you, as well. Signed a lease yesterday!"

Pennywhistle's instinct was to pull the pillow over his head and go back to sleep, but his wife was right. He had an important meeting this afternoon and wanted to prepare. He had read five lengthy papers on the key issues, but wanted to study them one more time to be sure. He felt uneasy from his talk with Wilson the previous night. He had left thinking that they had come to a *rapprochement*, but his dreams had warned him that he might have been played.

Pennywhistle reluctantly sat up; the pain nipped at his wound like an ill-trained pup. He focused on the cheer and excitement of his wife's voice, and his mood brightened a little. "Not much to tell about my evening. I met an old acquaintance. Actually, an old enemy. I thought we had mended fences, but now I am not so sure. I shall tell you more as I learn more. Your signing a lease is a much happier occurrence. Please tell me all about your day."

And Sammie Jo did. For the next hour, she talked so rapidly that she barely stopped to suck in air. She gushed and cooed, laughed and clapped her hands, sighing in remembered awe and shivering in delight. She proclaimed herself "happier than a pup with two tails to wag." Her eyes became twin suns full of joy and hope. She was a little girl, given not just a pony but the whole stable. Her enthusiasm bumped his mood back up to its usual pragmatic equanimity.

Her husband's approval pleased Sammie Jo. He had trusted her with a major responsibility, and she had not disappointed: it was a significant milestone in her evolution from country girl to lady of consequence. But she had been rippling on like a woodpecker drilling a tree and had completely neglected to give him information that he needed for his mission. He had indulged her, and she wanted to return the favor by assisting his career, particularly when the well-being of her new-found country was at stake.

"Now, much as I like our new stompin' grounds, Sugar Plum, something was wrong with the realtor, like a cake pretending to be a pie. I wonder if she was working for the man behind the attacks on you. She was definitely looking me over, trying to get me to let my stupid tongue run wild so she could scout you through me. She thought she had me squatting with my spurs on. Well, two can play at that game. I gave her what she wanted. Course, I might have altered a fact or two. Or three. Hell, I even threw in one big old whopper the size of a Maryland pine tree, a right good hornswoggle. Acting dumber than a sack of rocks has advantages with Europeans who think God should have consulted them before he made the world."

Attaché Extraordinaire

Pennywhistle laughed. The "realtor" probably took appearances at face value, while Sammie Jo saw beyond them. "Please, Hawkeye, give me the full particulars about this woman and her conduct. My opponent has switched tactics. Guile and deception seem to have replaced violence and directness."

Sammie Jo remembered her husband's classifications of discourse: fact was verifiable information divorced from emotion, opinion was fact supported by experience, ignorance was opinion in the absence of fact, and stupidity was opinion that ignored facts in favor of comforting falsehoods. Her talk became as perceptive as it was coldly unemotional. The country girl was gone, replaced by a hard woman who would have made a fine intelligence operative.

Sammie Jo described the negotiations with the realtor, including the instructions for the workings of the safe, emphasizing that she couldn't quite explain the odd hunch that had come over her, but both were warriors enough to appreciate the value of intuition. "I also followed your instructions and hired an actor to impersonate you. It took visits to three theatres, but I found a right good copy of you. He don't speak much English, though. He called about an hour ago, so Lady Leith and I got him kitted up, gave him the map of the random stops you wanted him to make, and sent him on his way. Johnny will be following him and will report back on who is tailing him. I dressed Johnny like an apprentice, and he is so small that no one will take any notice of him."

"I now have a *doppelgänger*!" Pennywhistle chuckled. "While I am studying papers in the embassy, my opponent will believe I am walking about and will waste efforts on having me followed."

John Danielski

"Here is where I went you one better, Sugar Plum. Lady Leith and I will be meeting this Stottler bi—... uh... woman around noon, to discuss staffing arrangements. When she leaves, she will be followed by a maid of Lady Leith's. This maid's mother was from Hanover, and she speaks some German. It will be interesting to see if the realtor heads for a home or the Amelienburg. I am betting on the second."

"Well done, my dear. You never cease to amaze me. My opponent counted on one foe. He never planned for two."

Chapter 13

Johnny was normally ashamed of the time that he had spent as a street urchin in Plymouth. With his parents dead and the master printer cruel to his apprentices, he had broken his indenture when that master had sought to commit uncleanness with him. As a runaway apprentice, he had been relentlessly pursued by the authorities and fallen in with the notorious Hopkins Gang in Plymouth: youthful pickpockets led by a clever man who fancied himself a cross between Fra Diavolo and Dick Turpin.

Now he was grateful for his street sense and ability to vanish into a crowd, because he had a chance to repay a small part of his debt to Pennywhistle by following a man who was himself following a man hired to be Pennywhistle's double. His schooling on how to read a mark's character, assess his wealth, and relieve him of his valuables would come in very handy today. He had precise instructions from Lady Pennywhistle, but she, like her husband, respected initiative and he hoped he would have a chance to exceed his briefing.

He had talked briefly with Herr Heinrich Lippe, the actor hired to impersonate Pennywhistle, wanting to get an idea of his route and stops. Johnny had christened him *der ritter*, the German equivalent of knight. Herr Lippe spoke little English, but the Earl Grosvenor had served as a translator at Lady

Leith's request. Something romantic was going on between those two, which pleased Johnny; they had both treated him more like a relative than a servant.

Like a bouncing tennis ball, the weather fluctuated daily. While the previous day had been marked by flurries, the temperature this morning was in the high forties on the Fahrenheit scale. It was sufficiently warm that great coats and cloaks were nowhere in evidence. Johnny's mark was dressed in a double-breasted tailcoat that was the gray of sleet and a broad-brimmed round hat of the same color. His trousers were the grey of pebbles on an ocean beach. It was a rig designed to proclaim the wearer a gentleman yet attract no attention in a crowd.

In marked contrast, *der ritter* was dressed in an outfit chosen to attract attention—something the man he was impersonating would never have done. This would make his tail's task considerably easier. The doppelgänger wore a copper-colored tailcoat cinched two inches above the waist, revealing the bottom edge of a *café-au-lait* silk waistcoat covered in a floral print of tiny roses. The breeches were bottle green, the stockings white silk, and the shoes capped with silver buckles. His top hat was black and exceptionally tall.

Der ritter's perambulation was leisurely. The British Embassy was close to both Metternich's palace and not far from the Amelienburg. The Burggarten that was the actor's first stop was still being landscaped; the area had been devastated by Bonaparte's troops in 1809. The crowds were heavy this morning due to the good weather, and *der ritter's* tail would have been hard to follow for a set of eyes less practiced than Johnny's. The actor's tail maintained a distance of half a block, and Johnny stayed the same distance astern his own mark.

Attaché Extraordinaire

The actor was a personable fellow, and he spoke pleasantly to two well-dressed gentlemen in the park—diplomats by their attire. Though he had never met them, he behaved as though they were old friends. He told them he was new to the city and wished to know if either could recommend a likely spot for a good dinner. He dutifully wrote their recommendations in a small notebook.

His minder scribbled his own observations in a notebook of his own. He carefully noted the faces and dress of Pennywhistle's contacts. It was possible his master would know who they were.

Johnny crouched behind the topiary sculpture of a stag and watched everything with satisfaction. He knew how to read people, and *der ritter's* tail had been thoroughly gammoned.

The actor's next stop was a pond at the Ressel Park, several blocks away. He repeated the same procedure he had used at the Burgarten. His minder dutifully recorded the meeting.

Der ritter's third port of call was the lake at the Stadpark. There was another encounter, seemingly with an affable stranger, and his minder scribbled more notes.

Johnny watched it all, realizing the meets could be seen two ways, depending on your penchant for suspicion. An ordinary man would see the day as the late morning stroll of a gentleman who simply liked parks with all their attendant trees, shrubbery, topiary work, statues, and fountains. A man trained to look for something sinister would see it as an operative, meeting a series of cut outs in public venues.

Der ritter's final stop was the Arenberg Park—much smaller than the other three and left in a wild state, preserving Nature's landscaping rather than celebrating the carefully engineered geometric designs of man. The actor's dramatic flair asserted itself. He took out a pocketknife and carved four Norse runes on a low hanging tree branch. He then cut three small boughs from a shrub in front of it. The gap left by the boughs formed a triangle that pointed toward the branch with the runes. Johnny realized it would look like the marker for a dead drop, with the runes functioning as a message for someone with the right codebook.

Der ritter left the park immediately after, followed by his minder. Johnny stayed put, trusting his instincts. It was only a few blocks to the embassy and no further stops were planned. The actor's minder had to follow and would not have time to dutifully record the runes. He would return.

Sure enough, the minder hove in view thirty minutes later and positioned himself to transcribe the runes with Germanic thoroughness.

Johnny's mark exited the park and hailed the Viennese equivalent of a London hansom cab. Most urchins would have given up at that point, but Johnny was nimble enough to shift position. Carriage and cab traffic was heavy because of the unseasonably fine weather and movement on the roadways was slow. Drivers' attentions were focused ahead, with no thought to what lay astern, searching for an opening that would allow them to move forward. Johnny leaped aboard a large carriage with an empty luggage platform at its rear, directly behind the carriage that was bearing away the man he followed. His drab clothing gave him a rudimentary camouflage. He kept his eyes fixed on the cab ahead.

Traffic wound through Vienna's twisting streets like a sluggish snake. Johnny switched carriages from time to time as they changed course. He had to be more and more careful as the traffic stream thinned and afforded less cover. Finally, the park of a great palace loomed ahead. He recognized it as

Attaché Extraordinaire

the Amelienburg Wing of the Hofburg Palace from embassy gossip. This was his mark's final destination.

Johnny made a leap of faith that translated into physical action. He jumped aboard a faster moving vehicle that was approaching the palace. He wanted to arrive ahead of his target and find a good observation post. He noticed a spare coach boy's uniform, folded and lashed to the luggage on the back board: it proved to be a good fit and a suitable disguise.

Five minutes later he jumped off in front of the main gate to the Amelienburg Park. He walked purposefully through, as if seeking the carriage house to report for duty. A few palace staff personnel passed by but paid no attention to a stable boy. He positioned himself fifty yards from the entrance, sheltering behind the topiary work of a lion rampant. He calculated the time necessary for a quick dash across the foot path and spied a suitable hiding spot on the opposite side, behind another topiary sculpture, that of a tiger.

He mentally rehearsed his upcoming actions. His feet would have to be fast, his movements deft, his fingers nimble. The consequences of failure would be disastrous. If he were taken for a thief, he could very well end the day in prison. Yet he feared the loss of his own liberty less than disappointing Pennywhistle.

He stilled his breathing and focused his thoughts, just as he imagined Pennywhistle did before battle. He watched, waited, and reminded himself that once his mark felt himself safe, his precautions and perceptions would be relaxed. Surprise was on his side, and, save for his failure with Pennywhistle, he was good at this nefarious art.

His patience was rewarded, as the man he had shadowed walked briskly through the iron gate. Johnny's mind focused on his target, and his will steeled. He drew a small knife, a gift from Gabriel. Its hilt settled into the palm of his hand as if it were a bird returned to its nest. No sweat from his palms marred its hold. His target was five yards away and the nearest person to him was a good twenty yards away. It was now or never!

Johnny became a brown blur of motion. He dashed behind his mark, reaching up and making a rapid slash at the right pocket of his coat. The force of gravity dropped the notebook into Johnny's outstretched hand. In seconds, he was sheltering under the blessed cover of the topiary tiger. His mark's stride continued unabated, and Johnny breathed a sigh of relief.

He rifled through the notebook but, as expected, it was in German. No matter. The Earl could translate it.

His mark stopped in front of a fountain featuring Poseidon and dolphins, though the mythological allusion was lost on Johnny. The man stopped and twiddled his fingers along the seams of his trousers in impatience.

A woman appeared five minutes later, clad in the attire of a gentlewoman, though her face and carriage struck Johnny as anything but gentle. An animated conversation began. Johnny could hear the words but had no idea what they meant. He did catch the names "Von Gilsa" and "Stottler" as they addressed each other. From the ironic smile on the man's face when he said Stottler, Johnny apprehended the name was an alias.

He narrowly suppressed a loud laugh when he beheld Von Gilsa's horror at reaching into his pocket and discovering... nothing. Von Gilsa shouted a string of what Johnny guessed were the worst of German curse words and made hand gestures that would have done credit to an Italian street vendor. The woman berated him angrily. Johnny gathered that a *dummkopf* was the worst kind of fool.

Attaché Extraordinaire

He had seen enough. He made his way quickly through the gates and began eyeing transportation.

He thought he had spotted a suitable conveyance when a voice hailed him. He started in fear, and then relaxed as he realized it was English, not German, that he was hearing. The voice was friendly and familiar.

"I say, Johnny, what are you doing here? Thought you would have been busy at the residence."

The voice belonged to Lord Steven Thynne, mounted upon his huge sable stallion, Mandrake. Thynne wore an extravagantly plumed indigo hat and daringly cut crimson cape that flared as he turned, the very picture a gentleman of leisure with a taste for adventure.

Johnny melted in relief. "Lord Steven, I am most glad to see you! It is not my story to tell, but I have something tremendously important to show Sir Thomas!"

"Do you need a ride back to the embassy?" inquired Thynne with his usual stylish indifference.

"Like a fish needs water! How fast can you get me there?"

Thynne motioned him to leap aboard, and Johnny did so with alacrity.

"Let's find out. Hold on tight!"

He put the spurs to Mandrake and the horse became black lightning.

Chapter 14

The Committee Meeting on International Rivers was underway. The long mahogany table at which the Committee sat was dwarfed by the white and gold splendor of the large ballroom in which they had convened. Say what you would about the Habsburgs, they knew how to construct a palace that impressed the visitor with its artistry, even as it displayed the political power of the commissioning dynasty. The Hofburg Palace was the largest in Vienna, with 18 wings, 19 courtyards, and 2,550 rooms. The attention to detail in the marble sculpting of the fireplaces, the heraldic beasts that ornamented the door pediments, and the painted ceiling showcasing the Hapsburg triumph over the Turks during the Great Siege of 1683, was a visual metaphor for the complicated preparations each representative had made for today's session. The architecture conveyed a sense of expansive hospitality, with an undercurrent of warning: *Here is Power. Defy us at your peril.*

This was the family's winter residence. Ironically, because of overcrowding caused by the many official visitors, some lesser members of the family had to remain at the family's summer dwelling, the Schoenbrunn.

The representatives of Austria, Prussia, Russia, and France had each given an opening statement that summarized the aims of their nations in a general way. Those aims lacked

Attaché Extraordinaire

specifics because hammering out details was the goal of the Committee, and no one wanted to be hamstrung by a position that did not allow room for maneuvering. The language was courtly, each delivery courteous, and the voices overflowed with a genteel earnestness that was a product of good breeding. Yet raw power and ambition flowed through the room like a dark river just below a thin layer of ice.

The representatives and their aides had spoken informally outside the ballroom in the hour before the formal session, but that was merely well-dressed animals giving each other quick sniffs to get a general impression of their aggressive or submissive tendencies. One aide to the French representative wore a violet waist coat with embroidered silk bees—surprising, given that the color and insects were associated with Bonaparte. Was this mere fashion, or intended to imply a loyalty to the deposed tyrant?

The opening statements gave the diplomats a chance to assess how vague indications might translate into actual policies, as well as the thinking of their opponents. For opponents they were, despite all the grand talk about shared ideals, cooperative efforts, and international good fellowship. Some of these men could start an argument in an empty house. Shakespeare was right that the emptiest vessel usually made the loudest noise, but for now, they were behaving themselves.

Pennywhistle was the last to speak and his remarks were extemporized, based in part on his deep knowledge of the issues, and in part on how he read the attentiveness of his audience. His speech was also the shortest of the lot. Brevity was not only the soul of wit, but a way of distinguishing oneself, when dealing with men who took a great deal of time to say very little. He mentioned the idealism that underpinned the British perspective. He talked of the joys of peace, and how peace should be used in furtherance of unhindered commerce that would bring prosperity to every nation. He spoke of how free trade could prevent a reoccurrence of the terrible famines of the previous century, and how manufactured goods and labor-saving devices would increase the productivity of every nation. "The only commerce that must be ended is the vile one that traffics in human flesh." He concluded with the observation, "Europe must never again allow a man like Bonaparte to close the Continent to the bounty offered by the rest of the world. The Congress has a clear choice. Embrace a future of free trade and unhindered navigation and see Europe prosper, or return to medieval ways and watch Europe sink into want and mediocrity."

His words were met with expressions of studied neutrality, edged with cynicism.

Pennywhistle noticed that the Russian representative, a Colonel von Steinwehr, failed to suppress the brief smirk of a man who delights in telling a child that Father Christmas is not real.

Unlike Pennywhistle, who wore a buff tailcoat and navy-blue breeches that fit in well with the civilian attire of the other attendees, von Steinwehr had cloaked himself in a uniform, the apple-green tunic and lead-grey breeches of the Russian Imperial Guard. His broad chest bore an impressive array of medals.

So impressive was his size that he reminded Pennywhistle of an oak tree given human form. His heavily scarred face seemed designed to haunt a house or serve as a model for the bogeyman that parents threatened children with, when they would not go to bed on time.

Attaché Extraordinaire

Von Steinwehr read his opening speech from a sheaf of papers. Pennywhistle concluded that here was a careful man who wanted to make sure he omitted nothing, who left nothing to chance. His voice was at odds with his physique, resembling the notes played on a harp. His words flowed in a pleasing current of modulated charm; however, his message matched his frightening appearance.

Pennywhistle realized that here was an authoritarian who regarded the liberal goals of free trade, the end of slavery, the elimination of feudal dues, and the expansion of suffrage as inherently dangerous to the maintenance of established order. He clearly wanted to turn back the clock five hundred years, to a time when a word from the local lord could have a peasant banished or executed. He talked as if the French Revolution had never happened and appeared impervious to the lesson that had cost Louis XVI his head: if you suck the air from gasping peasants to fuel the fires of oppression long enough, those peasants will eventually set fires of their own that will incinerate every aristocrat who gets in their way. He obviously subscribed to the oxymoron of a benevolent despot and had no faith that man in his natural state might have a few good ideas about how he should be governed. He looked at the world through glasses ground to a diametrically different prescription from Pennywhistle's.

Then the committee chairman, Prince Karl von Auersperg, introduced the first item: control of the mouth of the River Scheldt. The Scheldt was the chief artery for Antwerp, which in turn was an *entrepot* port for the commerce of much of Northern Europe. It was also a dagger pointed at the heart of England, since its mouth was directly opposite the Thames estuary, only 120 miles away. The men in Whitehall wanted that mouth in neutral hands, best accomplished by creating a Kingdom of the Netherlands. As Pennywhistle listened, he suddenly realized that the Scheldt issue was the stalking horse for whether the Netherlands should be independent or controlled by others.

The French wanted retention of those territories of the North Sea Plain, which they had overrun in the 1790's.

The Prussians strongly opposed France possessing those lands, since they had covetous designs on the eastern edges of what had been the Dutch Republic. They had briefly invaded the Netherlands in 1787, seeking to restore the Stadholder, who was married to a Prussian princess. Prussia was positioning itself to become the leader of the German speaking peoples of Europe, replacing the Hapsburg Emperor. Dutch was not German but close enough that speakers of either language could get across basic meanings, if not hold steady conversations.

The Austrians opposed Prussian designs because they wanted to continue to be the leader of Europe's German speaking peoples. Until 1806 the formal subsidiary title of the Holy Roman Emperor had been "Emperor of the German Nation." Part of the Low Countries had been designated the Austrian Netherlands until 1789, but the radical reforms of the Emperor Joseph had provoked a revolt, resulting in the severing of formal relations between the Belgian provinces led by Brabant and the government in Vienna. The Austrians had ruthlessly crushed the revolt in 1790; those provinces did not want their former overlords back, and the Austrians had no wish to re-acquire the Brabant headache.

The Russians could be expected to back the Prussians. The Czar exercised great influence over King Frederick William III, who was a man of considerable intelligence but weak will. Alexander had no particular interest in the region, since his attentions were focused on Poland. Still, Pennywhistle was surprised to hear von Steinwehr say, "His Imperial Majesty has no official position on the disposition of the Netherlands at this time. He reserves the right to proclaim one, but he needs more information before arriving at a decision. As you know, his Imperial Majesty is not a man who makes decisions without the utmost reflection."

Pennywhistle nearly rolled his eyes at the last observation. The Czar was intelligent, but he often cancelled that out by listening to flatterers and trusting to impulse what should have been reserved for reason. And yet, the Russian position, or lack of it, gave him an opportunity. When it came to control of the Low Countries, the Austrians were aligned with Britain; they also disliked Russia meddling in the affairs of Europe. If the Russians could be brought round, it would be three to two for an independent Kingdom of The Netherlands.

"I might be in possession of new information that would help his Imperial Majesty make up his mind," said Pennywhistle confidently. He addressed his remarks to the Russian representative but spoke loudly enough for all to hear. The information had been gathered from Dutch bankers who were anxious not to have their country gobbled up by some large power. They had made it clear they would extend a very favorable loan policy to any nation that backed a restoration of the Netherlands independence. Until the French overran the Netherlands in 1795, Amsterdam had been Europe's financial center. That center had shifted to London, but Dutch bankers still wielded considerable economic power, and the Czar was always needing loans.

Von Steinwehr looked at Pennywhistle skeptically, but his expression shifted to guarded optimism a second later. "I should be most interested to hear what that information might be." He turned to von Auersperg. "*Herr Prinz*, might I request a half hour recess so I may confer with my esteemed colleague."

Pennywhistle sensed the Russian representative had a special issue he wanted resolved and might be willing to bargain to secure Pennywhistle's support. A *quid pro quo* was sometimes a serviceable bridge between men whose philosophies were fundamentally opposed.

"I shall be happy to grant your request, *Herr Kolonel*." Von Auersperg banged his gavel. "The meeting is in recess for thirty minutes." The committee dispersed quietly and left to seek the refreshments readied by legions of servants, hovering just outside the ballroom.

Von Steinwehr walked with surprising grace for such a large man, a cross between a dancer's step and that of an experienced swordsman. He approached Pennywhistle with his hand extended and an expression that was an odd compromise between friendliness and wariness. With his badly scarred face and strong features, it was hard for Pennywhistle to get a read on his intentions. And yet, the idea that he was willing to talk at all, offered hope.

Pennywhistle shook the proffered hand firmly, and von Steinwehr returned the grip with equal firmness. Pennywhistle sensed the man was holding back a strength that could have crushed his hand, perhaps an analogue for a strength of personality reined in to serve his purpose. Pennywhistle was a tall man by the standards of the time at 6'2, but von Steinwehr overtopped him by four inches. Whereas Pennywhistle had a lean, rangy build, the components of von Steinwehr's body were outsize in every respect: legs that were tree trunks, chest like a giant battering ram, and shoulders that seemed designed for Atlas's understudy.

Attaché Extraordinaire

Von Steinwehr spoke first, in the soothing tones expected of a diplomat. Pennywhistle suspected this was the result of practice rather than the man's native disposition. "Sir Thomas Pennywhistle! It is a pleasure to meet you. You have distinguished yourself in your chosen career, and I envy you the honor of being a participant of the greatest fleet action of the age. Allow me to offer my felicitations on your recent knighthood. The capture of Washington was a smart stroke, and I expect you had more to do with its planning and execution than is widely known. Might I ask, is this your first time in Vienna?"

"Yes, it is, Colonel von Steinwehr," replied Pennywhistle carefully, enunciating syllables with exactitude to maintain formality. "It is a delightful city, though I am just beginning to learn my way about." His opponent seemed to know an unsettling amount about his career. He had done his homework as well, and had unearthed a wealth of information on his fellow delegates, all except von Steinwehr. He could find no records of the man before 1812, when he had joined the Czar's service. It was if he had not existed at all before that date and had instead enjoyed a birth like Athena's, springing full blown from the head of Zeus.

It suggested to Pennywhistle that a deliberate and systematic effort had been made to expunge his past. Why would he do that? What was he hiding? Was he living a new identity because his old one had been riddled with disgrace and calumny? Whoever he really was, his face indicated a history of fighting. You did not become a chief aide to the Czar unless you had the experience and skills of a warrior, as well as the guile necessary to survive the intrigues and cabals that seemed as inherent in the Russian character as their love for vodka and florid poetry.

"It is indeed a beautiful setting for negotiations that may bring great good to the peoples of Europe," continued Pennywhistle. "I thank you for granting me a short audience. I believe your master will find the information I offer useful. I propose we seek out some champagne and find a quiet corner where we may talk freely and frankly."

"I am in agreement, Sir Thomas, and I know, down the hall, they have pastries to go with that champagne. Good food and good drink are the best accompaniments to good conversation."

A few minutes later, each had consumed half a strudel and reduced the contents of his champagne glass by a third. They ate and drank in silence, enjoying the small repast as if they were art aficionados contemplating the brush strokes of an Old Master. But the sensations of taste were secondary to the sensations of intuition. Each man was assessing the other, two titans pretending they were ordinary earthlings, using cues of posture and expression to gain an understanding of the other's character, strength of will, and future conduct. Both kept their faces impassive, but a scholar of human nature could discern the verdict each had reached about the other in subtle changes of expression registered on a second-by-second basis. That mutual verdict could be summed up in one word: formidable.

Pennywhistle broke the silence. "Let me get right to the point. It is well known that the Czar wishes to bring his nation fully into the 19th century and that he regrets that certain of its practices keep Russia bound to medieval times. I know he desires modernizations that include building roads, shipyards, and iron works, as well as turning swamps into pastures, hamlets into villages, and towns into cities. All of that will necessitate great expense, far beyond what the contents of His Imperial Majesty's purse can provide. I know your country has improved its tax farming efficiency, but in the end, your master will need massive loans to carry out his programs. I can help with that."

"How so?"

"I have had several extended discussions with a man who represents a consortium of Dutch bankers. An independent Kingdom of The Netherlands would be very good for their business. Alexander would have but to ask for any loan, no matter how large, if he would come out formally in support of a neutral Kingdom. And it so happens that a neutral Kingdom is the one thing Talleyrand would oppose with vehemence. Your master's contempt for Talleyrand is as vast as it is personal. This would be a way for your master to land a metaphorical punch to Talleyrand's nose."

Von Steinwehr gave a wintry smile. "The Czar would indeed relish a chance to vex Talleyrand. I would, of course, have to consult with him, but I can say with confidence that your proposal would find favor with him. But you are clearly a man of the world and so must realize that he will ask something in return."

"I should be surprised if he did not. Have you any idea what it might be?"

"I do. It is the restoration of a small state," his pleasant voice suddenly took on a hard edge, "viciously wiped from existence by the monster Bonaparte in 1806."

Pennywhistle inferred the "small state" was important to von Steinwehr personally.

"The name of the state is Reichenau. You probably will not have heard of it." His eyes took on the Other Worldly luster of a man visualizing a personal Paradise Lost. "It was a happy land of 38,000 souls on the banks of the Rhine, between Mannheim and Gemmersheim. It was blessed with good rulers and contented subjects until the cruel Corsican took a hammer to it." His face darkened to the shade of a thundercloud. "Corsicans! A race so ignominious that the Romans disdained to employ them as slaves."

"I have not only heard of Reichenau, *Herr Kolonel*; I stayed the night there. I had an opportunity to walk its streets and observe its architecture, customs, and people. I found all agreeable, but I had an extended conversation with the city's mayor that was... unsettling. It centered on stories about the previous ruler.

Von Steinwehr's eyes lit like twin volcanoes. "Just what did the mayor say?"

"He never mentioned the ruler by name, referring to him by the appellation his disaffected subjects used in private: "The Gorgon." Apparently, the original three sisters had a brother who was far worse. The mayor struck me as a man driven by the old notion that to speak a demon's actual name was to summon him from Tartarus. He informed me that the people viewed Napoleon, not as a conqueror, but as a liberator. I will spare you his litany of profanity about that ruler, but relate a story that gives insight into his autocratic character."

"A peasant and foul language," observed von Steinwehr with disdain, "are bonded like a mule and his harness."

"This ruler hated people talking against his governance. One of his chief magnates criticized his tax policy. He had that man hauled before him and berated him in front of his court. The grandee had the temerity to say, 'You would never cause your first noble to suffer death merely for the exercise of his tongue.' The Gorgon took that as a challenge and sentenced him to death the next day, allowing him a night in a dark cell to contemplate his misdeeds. Before the execution, the Gorgon attended a church service. The sermon delivered was about the necessity for mercy. It so moved the Gorgon that he shed tears. And yet, he had the execution carried out in a particularly cruel fashion. The noble was garroted in front of the court."

"That is indeed a disquieting story," huffed von Steinwehr, "but being a ruler is like holding a ravenous wolf by the ears. Such a tale sounds more the stuff of legend. That sort of yarn grows in each telling, becoming an amalgam of fantasy, folklore, and the dark resentments of ignorant peasants who cannot realize that their sovereign must consider greater matters than the welfare of a single serf... uh... citizen. It is unwise to pay too close attention to peasants who drink like fish, rut like goats, and live like pigs. Whatever small benefits might be gained by listening to them would be like using an ocean to drown a fly." He spoke in the manner of a wise parent dealing with wayward children. As he continued, a maniacal glee infiltrated his voice as the skin tightened on his cheeks, blood drained from his lips, and his eyes became the hooded ones of a cobra. "Spare the rod and spoil the child is a Biblical lesson rulers would do well to heed."

"Curious that you should quote The Good Book," Pennywhistle observed. "The Gorgon had a wife who was fond of Biblical admonitions. She was of a piece with her husband and was referred to as Hela by the locals. I am sure you recall that the Norse Goddess Hela is the basis for Hell's name. She had a split face that was half beautiful woman and half rotting corpse."

"Disgraceful, disgraceful! To refer to any woman of distinguished pedigree that way!" Von Steinwehr shook his head in disgust. "Peasants treat women shamefully, as little better than brood mares. I have always believed that a woman of quality can be a man's equal partner."

"I agree, but I would use the word quality to refer to character rather than a caprice of birth. A woman of quality may just as well come from a cabin as a castle. My own wife has humble origins but in terms of character, she possesses a splendid pedigree."

"An idyllic sentiment, Sir Thomas, but a dangerous one. Peasants most certainly are not like us. As the Bard warned, 'untune the string, remove but degree, and hark, what discord follows.' It is up to people like us to make sure the string stays tuned."

Pennywhistle felt that limiting the rights of the majority robbed a country of a great reserve of talent. There was no such thing as an enlightened despot, since their power was undergirded by the rod von Steinwehr held in such high regard. His defense of hereditary privilege tracked with his support for autocracy, but the forcefulness behind his response seemed a product of personal animus rather than disinterested principle. There had to be a direct, highly personal connection with Reichenau.

Then a speculation hit him so forcefully that he barely stopped a violent shudder. His stomach capsized, his innards dropped to his knees, and icicles corkscrewed up his spine. A powerful image strutted across his consciousness—the Gorgon of which the mayor spoke. He pictured it as shark-faced demon with rot seeping through its bones, centipedes crawling its cheeks, and maggots dancing on its fingertips; a walking decay who spread it to every man he encountered. Given von Steinwehr's size and face, he could see why peasants would give him such a nasty nickname. If he were that despised ruler, it would explain why Pennywhistle could find almost no information on him. It would also account for why von Steinwehr was willing to make a large concession in return for

Attaché Extraordinaire

a small one. He did not just want the reinstatement of Reichenau on the map; he wanted to be reinstalled as its ruler!

Pennywhistle suddenly understood everything. This was the man who had been trying to eliminate him since London. The translation of the letters would give his master leverage over Castlereagh, possibly enough to restore an anachronism to life. Such an outcome would certainly motivate a Gorgon to kill.

Having the official backing of the Congress would mean much more than the backing of medieval tradition. It might well grant von Steinwehr unlimited license. The reference to the rod chilled him; that license might be a license to kill.

He would also want his seat back on the *Reichstag*, the anachronistic Imperial Assembly under nominal Austrian control. In permanent session in Regensburg, it consisted of three colleges: 9 electors, 34 princes, and 51 free cities. It would probably survive the Congress and would give a ruler a platform to spread his pernicious ideas to other parts of Germany.

Of course, he could be wrong. He needed to find out a great deal more to confirm or negate his suspicions. He would never accuse a man of something that would damn him to perdition, if he were less than certain. And yet, his instincts had never played him false, and they had sharpened since his brief excursion to "The Other Side."

Von Steinwehr had continued speaking, but Pennywhistle only heard every other sentence. Then von Steinwehr mentioned a book that caught his attention, because the author's name was familiar.

"I suspect that tale was put about by a malicious Frenchman named du Teil, who wrote a number of books about governance that were drivel and cant. He was a close advisor to that rascal Talleyrand, but has since left the conference." There was the tiniest edge of rage in his voice, like a child denied a toy to which he felt entitled. "I would ask you to put aside unfounded rumor and consider a practical basis for the restoration of Reichenau. An independent Reichenau would be in line with Lord Castlereagh's desire to ring France with buffer states. Allow me to suggest we consult with our principals this evening and meet here tomorrow at the same time to share our results. I feel certain they will be agreeable."

"That seems a sensible course of action," offered Pennywhistle. He searched his memory for the name du Teil. Of course! He had left the Congress because he had left the earth. He was one of the victims of the serial killer stalking Vienna, the one the papers had termed the Edelweiss Executioner for his practice of leaving those flowers at the scene of his crimes. Du Teil's death now seemed anything but random, the product not of unhinged madness but calculated purpose.

"We can indeed meet here tomorrow. I hear the bell summoning us back to the meeting. Let us shake on our agreement," said Pennywhistle, putting false hope into his voice. Under the best of circumstances, it would be hard to sell Castlereagh on the restoration of a small state that was a medieval relic. Castlereagh favored the consolidation of small German entities into greater ones. He decided he would merely ask permission to dangle the prize, to keep the negotiations ongoing.

Both shook hands vigorously. As they walked back to the ballroom, Pennywhistle wondered where he could get hold of du Teil's books. Castlereagh was a bibliophile and would know. For now, a long afternoon of sophistical windiness awaited.

Attaché Extraordinaire

He speculated on where von Steinwehr might be keeping the letters, if they were indeed in his possession, and began to consider ways to find out.

Chapter 15

The shadows of early evening descended slowly on the four-story Palladian wing of the Auersperg Palace that fronted on the Josepfgasse. The temperature was dropping rapidly and a light snow had begun to fall. Newly hired servants moved rapidly in and out of the rear entrances, bringing in what few belongings they had, so they could settle in for the next three months.

"Allow me to tell you what is expected of a princely house in this city," said Lady Leith to Sammie Jo.

Sammie Jo felt exasperated; there was no end to what she was required to learn as a newly minted aristocrat. At the same time, she appreciated Lady Leith's consideration and composed herself to listen.

"The lady of the house needs two chambermaids, a manservant, a washerwoman, an extra girl, two parlor maids, a porter, a messenger, and two extra servants. The man of the house needs a secretary, two *valets de chambre*, a lackey, a huntsman, messengers, footmen, and two general servants. "

Sammie Jo made a face. "Jesus, Margaret. Back home, one person did a ton of things. Servants were as rare as virgins in whorehouses."

"And here servants are as common as fleas on a dog's coat," offered Lady Leith. "For the general service of the house, there needs to be a butler, underbutler, porter, two charwomen, two houseboys, and a gatekeeper. The kitchen requires a head cook, confectioner, pastry cook, roasts-cook plus an assortment of kitchen boys, kitchen porters, washers-up and scullery maids. The stables should be looked after by a master of the horses, a riding master, two coachmen, two postillions, two outriders, two grooms and four stable lads."

"Paint me green and call me a cucumber!" exclaimed Sammie Jo, "That's not a house, that's a city! I don't even know what most of those titles even mean. What the hell is *valet de chambre* anyway?"

"Don't fret, Sammie Jo," said Lady Leith in a calming voice. "I know you and Tom are independent sorts and prefer things simpler, so we can eliminate a lot of those positions. A *valet de chambre* is a dresser. Usually they work in pairs; one chooses and lays out his master's attire then the other dresses him. "

"I declare, Margaret, staffing a home is like trying to remember if you have gotten every last animal on the Ark," said Sammie Jo crossly. "When Tom and I moved in with you, I stepped into a place already up and running. I never really thought how tough it would be to assemble a staff from the ground up. And it's all made a sight harder when the new people don't speak English. I don't like the idea of keeping that translator Frau Stottler recommended at my heels every waking moment. How many have we hired today, Margaret? We have been as busy as beavers building a dam, and I have lost track."

"Thirty, to be precise," replied Lady Leith. "The minimum necessary for the proper staffing of the residence of a man of consequence. It is particularly important to have every task performed properly because of where we are. This is the largest assemblage of powerful and titled people that Europe has ever seen, and newcomers are subjected to the keen eyes of people eager to find fault with either staffing or protocol. It is up to us to make sure this house is faultless in appearance and the conduct of its servants beyond reproach. Don't forget, after you have gotten settled in, you will be expected to throw a grand party, to socially proclaim the arrival and importance of your husband. I will help you prepare the invitations. I want to make sure that party is seen as an event only to be missed in the event of Judgement Day."

"If it ain't ants, it's bedbugs!" exclaimed Sammie Jo as she shook her head slowly. "I am glad that Stottler woman is gone. She is like a hemorrhoid: a pain in the butt when she comes down, and a relief when she goes up. How soon do you think your lady's maid will return from tailing that German bi— woman?"

"It's been two hours, so I expect her return momentarily," replied Lady Leith. "And I think your suspicions of Stottler are very well founded."

"Did you hear all the information that Stottler woman was trying to coax out of me in between interviews?" huffed Sammie Jo, putting her hands on her hips as if they would give vent to her spleen. "What was my husband like: habits, hobbies, likes and dislikes. I thought she would never stop. It was supposed to be friendly gossip, but I felt like I was being interviewed instead of interviewing servants. What really clinched it were all those questions about his schedule, his hours of duty, his usual comings and goings. That is just the kind of information you would need if you wanted to steal something and make sure the man of the house was absent."

"Hmm, quite so, Sammie Jo. We not only followed most of her recommendations on servant candidates, we let her participate in making up the duty schedule. I assume that a few are her lackeys, put there to keep track of us."

"I hate the idea of spies in my own house, but they may grow careless, since they have no idea that we believe any of them to be anything other than exactly what they seem."

There was a quick rapping on the morning room's door. "Enter," said Lady Leith. Chivers did so and narrowly stopped herself from breaking into a run. She reminded Lady Leith of a child, eager to show her new puppy to a visiting relative. "You were right, my lady, that woman went to the Amelienberg but she took her time getting there. She stopped every once-in-a-while to check behind her and walked in a zigzag pattern sometimes. Twice she circled back to where she had been earlier. I got the idea she thought she was being followed, though she never got a look at me. It seemed to me that maybe this was not her first time being tracked."

"*Quod erat demonstrum*," exclaimed Lady Leith.

Sammie Jo shot her an exasperated glance. "That dead language again!"

"It means that we have proven what we expected to prove."

There was a second knock on the door.

"Enter, said Lady Leith. "You may go, Chivers. You have my thanks for your conduct today."

"Thank you, my lady." Chivers gave a quick curtsey and departed.

Johnny was just as excited as Chivers had been, but his boyish exuberance overwhelmed any sense of decorum. He closed the distance to Lady Leith and Sammie Jo with five bouncing leaps.

"You look like a horse on his way to oats and grain, Johnny," said Sammie Jo with amusement.

John Danielski

"I have real important news, real important!"

"Calm down, Johnny, and slowly tell us what it is, "said Lady Leith.

"Well, my ladies, I followed that actor who was pretending to be Sir Thomas. Sure enough, someone started to follow him. He scribbled a lot of things in a small notebook; I stole that book!" said Johnny in triumph, though his face frowned a second later. "I know stealing isn't right according to the Good Book, but I figured the stuff in the little book might be useful to Sir Thomas."

"Do you have the book with you now?" asked Sammie Jo.

"No, my lady, I took it to the embassy and the Third Secretary has it, to be given to your husband upon his return. Lord Steven gave me a lift on Mandrake and when we got to the embassy, he translated it because he studied at Heidelberg. We fell in with Sir Thomas's friend, Mr. Higgins, who is the Third Secretary and talked with him for a whole hour! He said, from my description, the man following the actor was the same man who had followed the Dutch servant who ran off a few days ago. Mr. Higgins said it was possible that the Hollander did not run off at all but was the victim..." Johnny paused for dramatic emphasis. "...*of foul play!*" His eyes were saucers and he waited to see the effect of his words.

"Those varmints don't care nothing about killing an underling. It's like swatting a fly to them." Sammie Jo huffed acidly, completely forgetting ladylike deportment.

"And I got the name of the man following the actor: Von Gilsa. He met a woman, and I got her name too."

"Was it Stottler?"

"Amazing! How did you know?" chirped Johnny.

"Let's just say our paths have crossed, Johnny. Was she about five feet four, strongly built but not fat, blue-eyed, red hair with a touch of grey and a face that..." Sammie Jo struggled to come up with the right description.

"A face that you would not want to start an argument with? That's her, and she has a tongue to match. She gave that von Gilsa fellow a tongue lashing that would peel paint!"

"Did they meet at the Amelienberg?" inquired Sammie Jo.

"Yes," said Johnny with surprise. "She went right in after the meet and the guards didn't pay her any mind. Do you have a crystal ball somewhere, my lady?"

"No, Johnny," laughed Sammie Jo. "Wish I had one right now, though. I am just putting two and two together. Well, more like putting a whole passel of twos and twos together."

"One other thing, my lady. The way von Gilsa used this woman's name. It was sort of in jest, like it wasn't her real name, but one that you would use upon a stage."

"That does not surprise me, Johnny. I think the real Frau Stottler is no longer in the city. Realtors do not frequent Hapsburg Palaces. Once I find out her real name, a lot of questions will be answered."

***

Deborah Dale was a slender woman of middling height who attracted people because of her intelligence and character rather than her beauty and attire. She was enjoying her second marriage. It was good that her nine-year-old son finally had his father, and happily, the two were much alike. She had thought Andrew Dale killed at Trafalgar, and had moved to London in her grief, bringing her printing press with her. Before her husband died in 1804, he had started a paper in Portsmouth to keep track of ships arrivals and departures and had left the day to day running of it to her. Her paper in London had evolved into a voice for men of consequence, who represented the new wealth of industry that was unrepresented in Parliament. When Dale showed up on her doorstep, after having lost track of her for many years, she had nearly fainted. They had married a month later. Dale encouraged her to keep her press going.

She had just finished meeting with Gustave Schurz, editor of *Weiner Zietung,* Vienna's oldest and most respected newspaper. His English was good if heavily accented. The conversation had been productive, but it had gone in a direction that scared her—and she did not scare easily. She had heard that a serial killer had been stalking Vienna. Indeed, much of Europe had heard of this monster, but she had never gotten any details. Until now. Schurz knew more about him than any man in the city and had given him his nickname, "The Edelweiss Executioner". As she walked, she recalled the conversation, and the evening air suddenly grew chillier.

"I know this may sound odd, Mrs. Dale, but I believe the Edelweiss Executioner to be sane." Schurz was a stout, middle-aged man who spoke in the hushed tones of a discreet banker advising a client about a secret account. "He may be a monster, but not the kind of monster found in fairy tales. Those creatures kill everything in their path, because it is in their nature. There is no rational planning behind the horrors they commit. Whoever carried out these awful crimes acted with deliberation. They were meant to seem the spontaneous acts of a madman, but they were executed with cold logic. They serve some hidden purpose. That he left flowers behind showed he had a sense of theatre, albeit a horrible one. He clearly relished the recognition of his atrocities."

"Have you any clue to his identity or why the murders seem to have stopped?" Deborah inquired earnestly. These were the questions her readers in London wanted answered.

Attaché Extraordinaire

Schurz removed his glasses, leaned his elbows on his desk, and compulsively clenched and unclenched his hands. "I have no answer for the second one except to say it is likely that he considers his dark purpose accomplished. That the murders have stopped reinforces my belief that the man is, at his core, rational. A madman driven by compulsions far beyond his control cannot simply stop. He must yield to them until he dies or until someone kills him. He would be as addicted to killing as an opium fiend is firmly hooked on his pipe. As to your first question, I have an idea, but at this point it is just speculation, and I would never consider printing it."

Deborah nodded.

"A suspect was offered up by a member of the Russian legation. The alleged culprit being a certain Captain Emil von Danniken, a hussar in the Emperor Francis's service. He had a reputation as a hothead in gambling dens, a habitual fighter of duels and a bedroom brawler, but had never spread his depredations beyond those arenas. The evidence against him was purely circumstantial, but the people of Vienna were eager to believe anything that might identify the terror stalking their streets. He disappeared before any legal action against him could be taken. He came from a prominent family, and it is my belief they are sheltering him at one of their more remote estates in Italy.

"The man who shouted *J'accuse!* posed as the city's savior and acquired considerable heroic cachet. Yet, I think his identification of von Daniken was clever misdirection, like a man who commits a murder, then plants the murder weapon on someone else. He alerts the authorities and claims credit for the resolution of a problem that he caused.

"So terrified have been the few eyewitnesses that their minds have worked hard to make them forget what they saw.

All they can agree upon was that he was a giant of a man with a face full of scars. Von Daniken, however, was short and had the face of an Adonis. Witnesses also agree the killer was dressed like a gentleman, though no one seems able to recall anything specific about the colors or cut of his attire. That fits von Daniken's accuser, but I have nothing else to connect him with the murders. As far as I can tell, he is a diplomat in good standing, who goes about his business with prudence and performs his duties with exceptional competence. It is not much to go on, but I trust my hunches. I am continuing my investigations."

"What is his name?"

"If I tell you, I must have your solemn promise that you will tell no one. I do not mind if you give your readers a general description, but you must not mention anything about a connection to the diplomatic corps or Czar Alexander. On your honor, do you promise not to print his name unless suitable evidence arises to confirm my suspicion?"

"I do. Back in London, I am often trusted with confidential information by gentlemen of repute." Even as she spoke the words, a shard of doubt started a fissure of irresolution. She had no intention of sharing the name with her readers, but wondered if Sir Thomas should know. He was the sponsor of her trip here, and as a diplomat deciding the fate of Europe, that information might be of importance, especially if the killer was a fellow diplomat. She was a patriotic Briton, after all, and if there was any man who could keep a secret, it was Sir Thomas Pennywhistle.

"Please, Herr Schurz. Favor me with a name."

"Klaus von Steinwehr."

Chapter 16

Pennywhistle decided on an early evening walk because his mind was in turmoil and that always ramped up his back pain from merely annoying to the degree where he seriously considered a laudanum ball. He thought he had his man, but he had to be sure. The crisp air of early evening and the swirling light snow cooled his fevered conjectures, reminding him that there was always time to be appreciative of beauty. Vienna was a lovely city and contemplation of its domes, towers, and the bright colors of its palaces, opera houses, and riding academies calmed his eagerness to jump to conclusions.

A voice from behind interrupted his musings, and he frowned when he heard it. "Might I offer you a lift, Sir Thomas? Seems rather a cold evening to be proceeding on foot." It was a mocking voice of pretended good cheer. Wilson!

He turned and saw an expensive looking flame-red landau halted five yards behind him, drawn by two well-matched grey horses. A liveried driver beckoned him. Another servant dismounted and opened its right door. The door was emblazoned with a coat of arms. Pennywhistle remembered that, though Wilson had been orphaned early, he was no foundling. His forebears had been distinguished for their bravery in a way that their descendant would never match.

John Danielski

He accepted the invitation because Wilson probably had new information. In exchange, Pennywhistle would alert Wilson to the arrival of another gambler to be fleeced. The man Pennywhistle had in mind was known as an annoying fop of substantial wealth and small prudence. Upon arriving in Vienna, this nephew of the Duke of Portland had confirmed his reputation by loudly demanding to be told where a bracing game of chance might be found.

As Pennywhistle settled into the luxurious Corinthian leather seat, the servant shut the door and Wilson signaled the driver to proceed.

"I thank you for the ride," said Pennywhistle with amused wariness. "How did you know I would be here?"

"We gamblers have multiple sources of information. In this case, it was a certain aide to the Prussian Minster. I play with him regularly, and when I asked him if your name were on the roster of those who would be-in-attendance at his next meeting, he replied in the affirmative. Then it simply became a matter of waiting. We gamblers are patient men."

"I presume you have information?"

"I do, and I think you will find it to your liking. I played cards with von Gilsa last night. He brought one of his "boys" with him for luck. As the evening wore on, his tongue became loose as he drank more and more wine. Turns out his "aide" has been casting about for a more generous patron and so von Gilsa is looking to replace him as his inamorato. He is meeting that replacement tonight at a Molly House. My driver has the address, and I can get you there. I thought you might want to have a heart-to-heart talk with von Gilsa. But you will have to exert caution. When he is sober, he takes precautions that his unusual... tastes remain concealed."

Attaché Extraordinaire

"You once told me part of being a successful gambler was timing, Wilson. Waiting until your opponent was off balance before delivering the *coup de grace*. I believe you have come at a providential time."

As the carriage ride progressed, Pennywhistle described the Duke of Portland's nephew to Wilson, who smiled with lupine glee at the prospect of a gullible mark: vain, arrogant, overconfident, supremely sure of his skill with cards. Such men were easy pickings in a game of whist.

Wilson dropped Pennywhistle a quarter block from The Adventurers' Club— an unintentionally amusing name for a Molly House—after suggesting a concealed location where Pennywhistle could have a clear view of its front entrance. Wilson's information proved reliable; Pennywhistle had only waited ten minutes before his target and his new "friend" emerged from the club, looking as if they had enjoyed an alcoholic celebration and were now in search of a private celebration of a very different kind.

Pennywhistle walked briskly toward them, pulling his wide-brimmed hat down low to conceal his face. The happy couple laughed and talked animatedly and heard nothing of his approach.

He put the bark of command into his voice, speaking in French because von Gilsa knew that tongue as well as he. "Von Gilsa! Turn around, you and your friend. Very slowly, make no untoward moves." He thought he sounded a convincing highwayman executing a robbery.

Both men did as he ordered. Pennywhistle quickly closed the distance to arm's length. His fiery eyes bored into von Gilsa's stunned face. "Tell your friend to be gone. Now! This is between... men. Boys who belong in school should not be playing dangerous games that they do not understand."

The face of von Gilsa's friend became suffused with terror. Even before von Gilsa uttered a word, the boy about-faced and commenced running with the speed of a hare chased by a hound.

"We need to talk," Pennywhistle continued in a quieter voice. "That I am standing here should alert you that your clandestine efforts against me are at an end. I am not a man who holds grudges, but I do have a long memory. I am not interested in you at all, but greatly interested in the name of the man you work for. Give it to me and this encounter will be short. Withhold it, and I shall make sure everyone in the city knows of your peculiar appetites. I should think that would wreck your reputation permanently, and I would guess that your employer would be vexed that someone in his service had brought disgrace upon his cause. He might even take out that anger in unpleasant, even fatal ways."

Von Gilsa started, then jerked back a step. His face reflected confusion, terror, and an active imagination. Pennywhistle guessed he was weighing outcomes, deciding which one posed the least risk and realizing that none of the outcomes was promising.

Von Gilsa said nothing for a full ten seconds. Pennywhistle realized that the horror of his options had frozen the man into immobility. In animal terms, the fight or flee responses were cancelling each other out. He needed a prod.

Pennywhistle tested the conclusion he had reached at the committee meeting. "You are the lackey of Klaus von Steinwehr."

The horror that washed over von Gilsa's face answered Pennywhistle's speculations far better than any spoken word. But it also provoked an unexpected reaction.

Attaché Extraordinaire

Von Gilsa's hand flew to his pocket. Even before he drew out its contents, Pennywhistle guessed it was a pistol, probably a short-range gambler's weapon of last resort.

Pennywhistle reacted with the experienced reflexes of the combat soldier and swiveled sideways to present the smallest possible target. The distance was so close that the advancing von Gilsa could not fully extend his arm. The pistol was just coming up to the point when Pennywhistle's right hand shot out, grabbing the wrist holding the weapon, forcing the muzzle of the pistol down towards von Gilsa's own groin, the one target no man would fire at. But the terror-stricken von Gilsa had steeled himself to drastic action, and his hand obeyed his mind's blind instruction.

The weapon discharged. Von Gilsa's groin bloomed with blood and the man emitted an unearthly squeal. Shocked and horrified, Pennywhistle stepped back. Von Gilsa slumped to the cobblestones of the street, dropping the pistol to clutch at his wound, a grip that loosened as he slipped into unconsciousness.

Pennywhistle's medically trained eye noted that the flow of blood was inordinate. The bullet must have also torn a femoral artery. Damn and blast! He had only intended to interrogate the man! What sort of fear did von Steinwehr instill in his servants? There was nothing he could do to save the man's life now, not with so much loss of blood, and dead men yield no information. But it was hard to feel much sympathy for the dying man's departure, because this was the same man who had tried to murder him five times. A spasm of pain reminded him of the second attempt. The abused wound to his back also reminded him that he was supposed to be resting, not getting into deadly street frays. Damn! He might have to have recourse this night to the laudanum after all, yet he had a horror of addiction to the stuff.

He wondered how von Steinwehr would react to the death of his minion. He would likely have the news by tomorrow morning. Pennywhistle would have a chance to observe the man's reactions firsthand tomorrow afternoon, when the International Rivers Committee resumed its deliberations. He might prod von Steinwehr with a few veiled remarks.

Nasty as the encounter with von Gilsa had been, it had clarified one matter. He was certain of his opponent now.

Chapter 17

"Come to bed, Klaus, it is after midnight," Ingrid said plaintively. "Our three daughters are sleeping soundly, and you need to spend more time in that restorative state. Surely the rest of those missives and memoranda can wait until tomorrow morning. You have been working since you came home, and overwork aggravates your mania."

"Perhaps, but overwork will be my lot when I am restored as ruler of Reichenau," said von Steinwehr with weary pride.

"A sublime misery?"

"A concomitant of power. I will join you in bed in half an hour. I must finish this proposal to Alexander. He likes communiques in writing."

"What is the subject?"

"Control of the Low Countries. The British want them neutral and would be grateful for Russian support. Control of the River Scheldt is a big issue for the British, but a small one for Alexander. Alexander has proposed the restoration of our country to Castlereagh but has not pushed it forcefully enough. I need more leverage! I must have that codebook." He was about to curse, but the words petered out into a long sigh of exasperation. "The Congress is fragments of different canvases scattered on a floor, Ingrid. All originally belonged to different paintings that were the creations of single artists, but

204

now those pieces must be stitched together to create a hybrid work that forms a coherent vision. Each artist wants that vision to conform to his political wisdom... or, " he sneered, "what I deem a lack thereof. It is like people who have never seen a horse trying to assemble one out of fragmented animal oddments."

"Like asking an Arab to draw a polar bear?" inquired Ingrid.

Klaus grunted a short laugh. "Just so, my dear." Then his eyes hollowed as his voice took on an edge of despair. "We have wagered so much of our fortune on Reichenau's recovery, particularly the expense of the Via Vindabona attack, that we shall have to begin economizing in the next month if matters do not swiftly turn in our favor. We have gone far out on a limb in our quest. I worry that my outbursts of mania have caused me to make foolish decisions that have sawed heavily on that branch."

"Great endeavors demand great risk, Klaus."

"I fear that the blood that I have shed has made me a black, devious outlaw, unlike the man that you married, and utterly divorced from the idealist who graduated Heidelberg. Though untouched by sloth and gluttony, I know the rest of The Seven Deadly Sins far too well; lust, in my case, being for power rather than flesh. For a man who embraced the enlightened hopes of Goethe, my conduct marks me as an outcast. I dread that I am become a scheming, bullying Dr. Faust, betraying the Gretchen of my ideals. The scars of battle on my face mirror the ones on my soul."

"No, no, no!" exclaimed Ingrid, as she made a sweeping motion with her right hand; a symbolic broom sweeping away any dust motes of doubt. "You were most handsome when you were young, Klaus, but it was the unlined, naive face of callow, untested youth. What you see as disfigurements, I see as escutcheons of honor. You were a book of half-filled pages, now you are one imprinted with a rich story, blessed with many heroic highlights. Yet it is a story without an ending, and I wish to help you write the one that you deserve."

"My father despised the fluctuations in my moods, Ingrid, as if they were a physical weakness," Klaus observed, with pain marbled with asperity. "He called me a hunchback of disposition, despite my athletic gifts. He said dogs barked at my approach because they instinctively know a man's character. I fear that it is the *game* of power I relish rather than the prize it will bring me."

His eyes became geysers about to erupt.

Ingrid gripped his forearm strongly in reassurance, and the incipient mania subsided.

"My dark energy draws people to me and makes them complicit in my crimes. I may be a cancer whose aura infects others and transforms them into reflections of myself. And yet, I would wish to be remembered as an enlightened sovereign who ruled with a firm but benign hand. Is it possible to become addicted to high risk?"

Ingrid's countenance and voice became that stern one of a Greek Fate telling a mortal that his self-prediction of his future was dead wrong. "I beg you, dear husband, do not weave a shroud of self-hatred. You have not polluted me; rather, your poetry of power has helped me become more of what I already was. No man reaches sovereign status without some unease of the soul. You are no monster; the real monster was Bonaparte, who stole your legacy like a thief in the night. I hear the depressive aspect of the mania in your voice, but know that it will pass. As the moon reminds me, whatever phase you are in, you are still whole. When you rule, you will have chances to atone for your imagined misdeeds by favoring your subjects with the wisdom that lies at your core. The pieces are falling into place for the recovery of the codebook."

"And does Lady Pennywhistle follow your recommendations?"

"To the letter. It is no exaggeration to say she is putty in my hands. I will see that her household is arranged conveniently to allow a break in—or rather, a breech from within."

"What additional conclusions have you formed about Lady Pennywhistle's character?"

"She is not quite as I first thought, though she still seems more suited to being a serving wench than a chatelaine. She could make a fortune as a courtesan and is exactly the type to bewitch the Czar. Men can be such fools! I am so glad to be married to a man who can see that superficial beauty is of less moment than character and strength of will."

"All cats are grey in the dark, Ingrid. I love our time in the boudoir, but it is moments like this, discussing matters of destiny and greatness, that make me most grateful we are husband and wife. We complement and enrich each other. I am a man with few equals, but you are one. You are someone with whom I can not only share my dreams, but also rely upon to help me translate them into action."

"That would make me blush if I were younger, Klaus. I should add in addition to being crude, Lady Pennywhistle has a temperament that reminds me of the animal from her homeland, the porcupine."

"Not a bag of fluff and flounce?"

"She is as far from Marie Antoinette as burlap is from silk."

There was a sudden and violent pounding on the door of the study. Klaus and Ingrid looked at each other in puzzlement. Their servants were well bred and discreet.

Attaché Extraordinaire

Klaus answered the door and was met with the frightened face of their butler, Hoffman. "There is a man downstairs, *Herr Kolonel.* He says he has very urgent business with you. He looks like a fellow who would just as soon cut your throat as look at you."

"Do not fret, Hoffman, I know exactly who he is. I am surprised he would come to my residence, and at such a late hour. His business with me must indeed be urgent. That will be all, Hoffman." The butler vanished so discreetly that it was as if he had never been there.

"Something is wrong, Ingrid. I told Kappel to never come to the palace. He obviously had to drop my name to gain entrance and that forms a connection I do not want known. Come with me, Ingrid; you might as well hear what he has to say."

The two walked deliberately down the stairs, rather than by the leaps and bounds the excitement demanded. It was important to maintain dignity when speaking with one's inferiors.

"Von Gilsa is dead! Dead!" The hawk-faced tall man in the blue cloak spoke the words as if he were telling of end of an Olympian who was never supposed to die.

"Oh, no," exclaimed Ingrid as tears started to her eyes.

"Calm down, Kappel. Compose yourself. How did it happen?"

"I do not know, *Herr Kolonel.* I was notified an hour ago. I maintain a network of street urchins whom I use as informants; one of them brought the news. I took care of the body. As near as I could tell, he was shot at close range with his own pistol."

"Any idea of motive?"

"Yes. He was found behind the Adventurer's Club."

"Isn't that..."

"Yes, Ingrid, it is," said Klaus with disgust. "I had no idea he had such perverted tastes."

"I think it was a lover's quarrel gone wrong, *Herr Kolonel*. No valuables were taken."

"Perhaps you are correct, Kappel. Did he have any papers on his person when you found him? Anything either official or unofficial that might tie him to me?"

"Nothing, *Herr Kolonel*, I searched him thoroughly."

"At least he maintained one kind of discretion to the end. What is the name of the undertaker? I shall see to his final arrangements. I want him buried and forgotten as fast as possible."

"Rudemacher and Sons, on the Wilhelmstrasse."

"You did right to come here, Kappel, but do not ever do so again. For now, you are dismissed."

As the door slammed, Klaus turned to Ingrid with a troubled look on his face. "I should have anticipated something like this. He was so eager to redeem himself from the bungled attempts on Pennywhistle that he probably tried too hard and did something fatally foolish." He rubbed his chin in thought. "The angry lover explanation may be entirely too convenient."

"What do you mean, Klaus?" She angrily wiped her tears away. She would miss the laughter her cousin had so easily provoked, and she was furious that his proclivities had led to this outcome.

"Though Kappel said he searched the body, if the man who killed him was not a wronged lover, it is quite possible that the killer had already removed anything of value."

"Who do you think might have killed him, Klaus?"

Attaché Extraordinaire

"I am not sure. The man had plenty of enemies. I thought he worked for me exclusively, but he may have been tempted to freelance. My mind keeps coming back to one conclusion: his death had something to do with Pennywhistle. I say that because he followed Pennywhistle one day and the next night, he turns up dead. I wonder if his surveillance was not as well disguised as he believed it was. I could not see any connection among the stops that Pennywhistle made. I am beginning to believe he knew he was being tailed and made his movements completely random. I am sometimes so eager to discern patterns where there are none that I become ripe for self-deception."

"How sure are you of this, Klaus?"

"Not certain at all. It is more a nagging voice than a logical deduction. In my meeting with him today, I got the idea that he is a man who has a tremendous curiosity and indulges it freely. After multiple attempts on his life, I should be surprised if he were not making discreet inquiries about the power behind those attacks. He will certainly expect another attempt to gain his codebook. I am glad that you have persuaded me that it is more easily obtained by guile than violence."

"A ship must tack and pursue an indirect course when the wind no longer comes from astern."

"Agreed. He is intelligent and determined. He will eventually discover my identity. We must make sure we possess the book and have translated the letters before that occurs. I look forward to seeing him at the meeting tomorrow. I should like to ask a few subtle questions about his peregrinations yesterday."

"Do not do so, husband. Trust me, Klaus. He will not see what we have planned coming. We will soon have all the information we need."

Chapter 18

"If I might trouble you for a few words, Sir Thomas, I should be most grateful." Deborah was waiting outside of Pennywhistle's office when he appeared at the stroke of eleven. She had found him to be as punctual as he was principled.

"I have a busy schedule today, starting with a meeting with Lord Castlereagh at half past the hour," replied Pennywhistle briskly but with a pleasant undercurrent in his voice. "However, I can spare a few minutes for the woman who has made an old friend very happy."

He saw a look of concern in her face, as if she were waging a private war over a deep moral principle. He knew her to be a serious woman as well as an intelligent one. "I gather this call concerns something related to affairs of state, else you would not have come to my office. Your appearance could not have come at a more opportune time. I had a favor to ask of you, one you may be uniquely qualified to carry out." He opened the door wide and beckoned her enter. "Please sit down and make yourself comfortable." She did so and he followed suit by settling into the red chair, which he pulled from behind his desk.

He fixed what he hoped was a comforting smile on his face. "Now, what matter has caused you such concern?"

"Well, Sir Thomas, you know that we in the newspaper trade sometimes obtain information that must be handled with care. If misused, it could damage reputations, upset the public order, or result in a prosecution for libel. But sometimes the safety of the public outweighs the strictures of confidentiality. I hate to break my solemn word, but it is possible that my information might forestall the return of a monster. I thought if there is anyone who would know what to do with that information, it would be you."

"I am honored that you hold me in such high regard. You say it could prevent the return of a monster?"

Deborah nodded.

Pennywhistle's eyebrows knitted as he steepled his hands in thought. His eyes brightened as his mind suddenly apprehended what she was about to reveal. "Would this have anything to do with the Edelweiss Executioner?"

"Yes, Sir Thomas!" Deborah gasped in astonishment. "How could you know?"

"I have been doing a little investigating myself, and I would welcome additional information. Please tell me what you know."

"I had a long talk with Herr Gustave Schurz yesterday. He is the publisher of Vienna's oldest and most respected newspaper. He has been following the marauding of this killer since the first murder. He believes the killer is a man named Klaus von Steinwehr. He is—

"A colonel in the Russian Service and a principal aide to Czar Alexander."

Deborah blinked in surprise.

"I have met the man. Indeed, I will be dealing with him at a committee meeting this afternoon. What you have told me is less a surprise than a confirmation of a hypothesis that I had already formed. However, your source is impeccable, and I am in your debt. I assure you that your patriotism and concern are not misplaced. This man needs to be stopped. I do not like to act unless I am sure, and now I am."

Deborah beamed with a mixture of relief and pride that she had done the right thing despite her doubts. "I should add, Sir Thomas, that Herr Schurz believes his motive was a cold one: to enhance his diplomatic standing by unbalancing the city, then posing as its savior by identifying a false killer. That accused killer fled before he could be arrested."

"That agrees with what I know of the man. And now I must ask you a favor," replied Pennywhistle. "I need the name of a local printer. We have not been long in the city, but I know you as a dedicated correspondent who establishes contacts relating to every aspect of your trade. That you have gained the confidence of Herr Schurz tells me that my estimation is correct. Perhaps he will know a man who can provide what I need."

"You say you need a printer, Sir Thomas, but you could use the man who prints all of the embassy stationary. I gather you are looking for someone with special abilities."

"Let us just say what I contemplate may help to stop von Steinwehr. I need a printer who can prepare a copy of a short volume and do so quickly. I am prepared to pay him handsomely for his trouble. I will make some alterations in one part of the manuscript, so the new book will not be an exact copy. In fact, since the volume I have in mind is forty years old, I need the copy to look suitably aged and dog-eared. I am not sure how that can be accomplished, yet art forgers do such things regularly to cozen unwary buyers into believing a reproduction is the work of an Old Master. I know I am asking much, since this task requires discretion, speed, and a very particular set of skills that are uncommon to find in a single man. And yet, I have great confidence in you."

"I am proud that you do, Sir Thomas, and I shall devote the entire day to finding that printer. Would tomorrow morning at this time be soon enough for the receipt of that information?"

"That is better than I hoped. I am lucky to have such an ally."

"Well then, Sir Thomas, I shall tarry no further. I thank you again for believing in me."

She favored him with a quick curtsey, and he returned the courtliest of bows. As soon as she shut the door, he sank back into his seat, immersed in deep thought. Newspaper people averred that you needed two trustworthy sources before running a story. He had those, plus a wealth of circumstantial and deduced evidence.

He took out the notebook that Johnny had pilfered, then a second one, containing Thynne's translation of its contents. Mostly it was just quick observations of various surveillances, which merely confirmed what he already knew. There were several references about reporting back to "The Big Man." It was a common enough appellation for a superior, yet was well suited to von Steinwehr's uncommon size.

It annoyed Pennywhistle that he had to stand on the defensive. But now that he had a name and a confirmation of the man's conduct, character, and future intentions, he could spike the guns of the enemy. A false codebook would render any translation of the damning letters a fangless confusion.

There was a knock at the door. Three measured raps; a military cadence. "Come!"

The door opened and in walked a Royal Marine Sergeant Major in full uniform. He had never seen the man before and wondered what he was doing at the embassy. The Sergeant

Attaché Extraordinaire

Major snapped to attention and saluted. Though Pennywhistle's attire was a civilian mantle of blue and grey, he nonetheless returned the salute. "To what do I owe the pleasure of this unexpected visit, Sarn't Major...?"

"Owens, Sir Thomas. Rhys Owens. I thought I should report to you since, as the naval attaché, you are my commanding officer in this venue. My officer, Captain Llewelyn, died on route, so I am now leading a group of 25 NCOs from the Royal Marines, 95th, and 52nd Regiments. We are here at Lord Castlereagh's behest. He informed London that he had many requests from foreign generals for demonstrations of the methods and tactics of British Light infantry. We are The Admiralty's and Horse Guards' joint answer."

"It is a pleasure to meet you, Sarn't Major, your face looks like it has seen some hard... uh... felt the sting of battle."

"It has, Sir Thomas. I am a Trafalgar man, like you."

"What ship? I was on *Bellerophon.*"

"The *Tonnant.* We were right ahead of you in line!"

"Where will you be staying?"

"On the grounds of an old abbey with plenty of space to pitch tents and practice drill."

"I am glad to have you here, Sarn't Major. Some of these foreign generals have a habit of underestimating British martial skill and fighting prowess. I expect that you and yours will dispel their misconceptions."

"Thank you, Sir Thomas. That is a kind and generous thing to say. I can see you are a busy man, sir, so I won't continue to distract you from your duties." He snapped to attention and saluted.

Pennywhistle returned the salute, acknowledging that Owens was dismissed.

Owens departed briskly, and Pennywhistle resumed his cogitations, his gaze resting pensively on the door. He had a strange feeling that the cadre of NCOs might prove exceptionally useful in the days ahead. If the cold war between him and von Steinwehr turned hot, he needed trained men available, upon whom he could absolutely depend.

He carefully reviewed his notes for his meeting with Castlereagh, now ten minutes away. Yesterday, Pennywhistle had asked Lord Castlereagh if he had a certain book in his library, *The Enlightened State,* by Baron du Teil. Castlereagh had replied that he did, but had not himself read it. Pennywhistle had borrowed the book and spent the night pouring over its contents, which confirmed his worst suspicions about von Steinwehr's nature. He had identified the man who controlled the letters, and now had a clear idea of how his nemesis intended to use them.

He had to be careful not to let duty slide into vendetta. Battles in a war were so much simpler than the one he was currently fighting: your enemy wore uniforms and were out in the open; their motives and your objectives were both clearly understood. Bonaparte had it right when he had said, "Better an open enemy than an uncertain ally." For the sake of national diplomacy, Pennywhistle and von Steinwehr must behave publicly as allies. Their secret warfare involving blackmail, the codebook, and the letters had to be kept strictly *sub rosa.*

In Vienna, the pen was often mightier than the sword. Words were weapons, and you might discover you had fought a battle only after it was done. Yesterday's friend might be tomorrow's enemy, and vice versa. At today's meeting, von Steinwehr would pretend to be his friend, and it would be wise to return the favor.

Chapter 19

Moving day for any great household was always an ordeal and the frown on the face of Peg-Leg Grimsby indicated that he disapproved of the way the proceedings were unfolding. These Germans had odd ways of doing things, though they moved smartly enough. They barely spoke, but at times they would burst into song, or they hummed when they worked, which disconcerted Grimsby. They rolled cloths instead of folding them. The maids, footmen, and other assorted servants could follow orders but lacked the polish and initiative of first-rate servants, and Baumann, the elfin man who served as the translator, spoke passable English but seemed to have trouble with its idioms. None of them were the pick of the litter, because servants were in high demand, and the grandees attending the Congress had snapped up the good ones, months ago. It galled Grimsby that these second rate make-dos would be paid what he considered extortionate wages.

Furthermore, several of the newly hired household raised his hackles. The under-butler, Knyphausen, seemed shifty. Wolfram, the coachman, bothered him in a way he could not explain. Krueger, the chief parlor maid, kept casting moon eyes in his direction; she was pretty enough, but he never mixed business with pleasure, and he thought her forwardness was bad form.

John Danielski

He was used to managing Lady Leith's London residence and bore the formal title of chief steward; superior to a butler, yet he sometimes carried out those functions in addition to his greater responsibilities. The new home—no, that wasn't quite right, it was an entire wing of a palace—had once belonged to friends of Prince Eugen of Savoy. It had been rented fully furnished, so the task of moving was less onerous than usual. Still, there was plenty of personal baggage to put in place. In addition, Lady Leith had informed him that it would be necessary to throw a grand ball within a few weeks to proclaim their arrival.

He was not the only person who was unsettled. That Stottler woman had come back, ostensibly to help, though more likely to snoop, and it was clear Lady Pennywhistle did not like her. He observed them talking across the hall, and though their tones were pleasant, their body language reminded him of two boxers circling, preparatory to taking jabs at each other.

"Why don't we just schedule a party next week and get it over with," grumped Sammie Jo. "I want to get that folderol out of the way as soon as possible and get on with living a normal life. Or as normal as possible in this city with all these struttin', prancin' diplomats who make peacocks seem pea hens."

"Lady Pennywhistle, that would be most unwise," replied Stottler condescendingly. "Every day next week is subscribed by balls scheduled weeks ago. You would not want to be in competition with royalty and the greatest nobles on the Continent. You desire these people as supporters, not rivals. Your husband comes from a good family and you... well, let us just say the Pennywhistles may be seen as *arrivistes*. You must do everything in your power to ensure that society sees you in

Attaché Extraordinaire

a favorable light. It is a wife's duty to make her husband look good."

Sammie Jo bristled at the disdain dripping from Stottler's cool voice and wanted to unleash a fusillade of her favorite expletives. She clapped irons on her worst instincts. "Well, Frau Stottler, where I come from, we care a lot more about how a man acts than how he dresses and talks. This Congress is not just about the Old Order, it's about change. It's about time the Old World acknowledged that the New World has a good idea or two."

She placed her hands on her hips as her eyes lit with inspiration. "Maybe we should make the arrival announcement a huntin' party instead of ball! I hear tell that hunting parties are popular with the nobility. We'd need to find a hunting ground, but perhaps," here she switched to a flattering, wheedling tone, "you could help with that, since you know so much. I am right good with a rifle. Where I grew up huntin' was a job, not a sport. I don't need whole regiments of helpers following me around, neither. I can manage my gun and powder all on my own!"

Stottler saw the confidence in Sammie Jo's eyes and knew she was telling the truth. She had underestimated the woman. By focusing on her lack of manners and refined deportment, she had missed a core ruthlessness. She was formidable, not in the sense members of the Congress looked for in a lady, but in the manner the ancient Germans would have understood. She might be ill at ease at a Viennese ball but was suited to the Teutoberg Forest, where the Germans had wiped out a Roman Army.

An inspiration struck Stottler, one that would give her a chance to test her conjectures. "There is a hunting party in two days that you might enjoy, my lady. It is sponsored by the

Baroness de Krudener, who enjoys the Czar's ear. It is exclusively for women, though, of course, there will be men present to provide support. I helped The Baroness find lodgings and she was most grateful for my advice. I believe I could secure you an invitation. Would that be of interest?'

Sammie Jo blinked in surprise. "I would like that fine, Frau Stottler; could be a heap of fun. Cooped up in these palaces, I miss the outdoors right fierce. 'Course, the way I hunt and shoot might be a little different."

"I am sure the ladies will enjoy seeing how an American woman hunts. It might also give you the chance to meet them in a setting where the manners will be much relaxed and your... uh... spontaneity will add to the charms of the hunt."

"It sounds right fine, Frau Stottler. I am much obliged." Sammie Jo gushed the words: playing the part of a rustic, grateful for a nod from the local lord.

"It is my pleasure, Lady Pennywhistle. I wish to make you welcome in my city and return the favor you have granted me by accepting my services. Finding a home for a prominent member of the British Embassy will not go unnoticed by future clients. Speaking of servants, how is the under butler I recommended working out?"

"Well, Grimsby tells me he needs a little seasoning, but some old-fashioned Marine discipline will lick him into shape." Grimsby had really told her that he deemed his loyalty uncertain.

"I am glad to hear that, my lady. And the coachman and maid I recommended, are they working out?"

"So far so good, though I won't really know until a week or so has gone past."

Curious about her inquiries, thought Sammie Jo. The coachman would be in a position to know when they were going out, the maid to snoop in drawers. "Do you suppose the Baroness would assist in letting me know when it would be a good time to schedule our own hunt?"

"She would be the perfect person. If you made a good impression, she will also convince others that your event must simply not be missed."

"That would be wonderful!" said Sammie Jo with pretended enthusiasm. "You know, Frau Stottler, I could jaw with you all day, but I got to get a movin' with this here household. Experience is the best teacher, and I got a lot to learn."

Stottler gave a dainty, false smile. "I quite understand. I will call upon you again when I have secured the invitation. For now, I bid you adieu and will take my leave."

The two exchanged insincere curtseys.

As soon as Stottler departed, Lady Leith approached. "I hope you do not mind that I did some inadvertent eavesdropping. The extraordinary acoustics of this place amplify even whispers."

"Glad you did, Margaret. Did you think she was as full of shit as I did? Sorry about the language but I can't think of no better word."

"She is a very practiced dissembler. Yet now that we know her real identity, everything she has said follows a consistent logic."

"I think I know the identities of at least three of the three spies she planted. We can spoon feed them the information we want them to have."

"Give them a play of a kind, Sammie Jo?"

"Yup, so she hears what she wants to hear and thinks she's pulling the strings. Let her think she is clever enough to order around another man's dog."

"She may have done you a favor, though. The acquaintance and patronage of the Baroness de Krudener would be remarkable. Since she has the confidence of the Czar, she might prove a source of useful backdoor information for Tom." Lady Leith chuckled. "For a little old country girl, you have developed a fascination with intrigue that would do credit to Talleyrand."

"Well, it's plumb useful to know whether you've gotten or been got. And you can't roll with the pigs and not get covered in mud."

"But these are elegantly dressed, well-mannered pigs."

"Maybe, but silk waistcoats and polite chitter chatter don't change the story, though I allow that words can change a halo into a noose right quick."

"That hunt should prove interesting. I would like to tag along."

"Honored to have you, Margaret."

"I am guessing the game will be stags, Sammie Jo, since early December is the height of the rutting season. The deer will be active, and the stags will be foolish."

"What kind of weapons will be used?"

"Most hunters have custom-made shotguns and rifles, the products of gunsmiths who charge high prices for their work. Not just good weapons, but works of art, sporting all manner of gold and silver inlays in the shapes of beasts, flowers, and arabesques. Nevertheless, they will be short and lightweight, designed to be carried on horseback by women who love to ride."

Sammie Jo chuckled wryly. "Well, that's to be expected when you hunt for sport and your supply of powder and shot is unlimited. I always had to conserve my supply of both. I came to depend upon my skill one fall, when the harvest failed: it was so dry that trees had to bribe dogs to piss on them. A missed shot meant I went hungry. An empty stomach is a damn powerful reason to become good at your craft. My weapon ain't a gun for amateurs: its beauty is in its simplicity. It is well-balanced, comes easy to the point, and I calibrated the sights myself. But in the end, it ain't the gun, it's the shooter. There is nothing like experience, and that don't come from shooting at paper targets or animals that don't have nowhere to run. Real skill comes from practice, like nailing a running buck with a quick shot at twilight."

Lady Leith chuckled. "Why, if I did not know better, Sammie Jo, I would say you sounded like a snob: an aristocrat of the gun."

Sammi Jo smiled sardonically. "Maybe that's so, Margaret. But I tell you this: after all we've been through together, The Widowmaker is my trusted friend with a will of her own."

"You see The Widowmaker as a living entity?"

"I do, and one that don't like men disrespecting her owner."

"This hunt will be interesting."

"Yup, and a welcome change from me always being the student. This time a backward little hick from Maryland will provide a lesson in how shootin' should be done."

Lady Leith smiled. There was nothing "little" about Sammie Jo. "And we shall appear in sartorial splendour. I will be astonished if there is any lady as well dressed as you on the hunt. I have the utmost confidence in our *haute couture.*"

Chapter 20

At the same time Sammie Jo was discussing a future hunt with Lady Leith, Pennywhistle was conferring about the future of Reichenau with Lord Castlereagh. The embassy study was quiet as a tomb, save for the ticking of the tall case clock and the thoughtful voices of two seated men, occasionally pausing to slowly sip Bushmills. The chairs in which they sat were supremely comfortable; allied to the whiskey, they facilitated frank and direct conversation.

"It is strange that the Czar should make such a fuss about a mere pumpernickel principality," said Castlereagh pensively. "Why he would be willing to put his prestige behind the restoration of an anachronism is a mystery, unless..." He paused as his eyes bored into Pennywhistle's, "...unless your conjectures are correct. The aide I glimpsed answers to your description of von Steinwehr. I agree that Alexander's bargaining and von Steinwehr's words at the meeting of your committee indicate that the German has the Clarke Letters. That Alexander did not press me harder also tells us that von Steinwehr only knows a fraction of what is in the letters but believes even that small portion of their revelations will cause me to abandon a well-considered position."

"What it means, my lord, is that you should stall for time," said Pennywhistle earnestly. "At this point, the leverage of the letters is more a possibility than a reality. You should treat the

Attaché Extraordinaire

Clarke threat as a ranging shot, not the opening salvo of the battle. There is no need to abandon your opposition to the restoration of robber baron states, but dropping a few hints to Alexander that an exception might be made as a personal favor... well, that could be advantageous to my mission."

Castlereagh rose from his chair and began to pace. His countenance was no longer that of a scholarly contemplative but that of a man with a thorny problem that he had yet to solve. Pennywhistle realized he was seeing a passionate side of his superior that was usually under tight control. Something important was coming. Pennywhistle leaned forward in his chair attentively.

"The situation with Alexander grows more complicated daily. Like all stubborn men, he is inclined to dig in his heels if pushed too hard." Castlereagh's velvety voice betrayed an undercurrent of anxiety. "These publicly feted alliances are, in truth, tenuous at best. A formal alliance with Prussia would give Russia tremendous influence over Central Europe—very dangerous to the balance of power. More and more small nations would fall under Russia's aegis. Whether we realize it or not, alliances are forming that will resemble the opposing sides of a game of chess."

He shook his head slowly twice, a combination of disapproval and alarm. "I have spoken with Metternich, who shares my concerns. I have also taken the liberty of asking Talleyrand to assist in opposing Alexander, if events move to a critical juncture. Even though the matter of the Low Countries is a point of contention, Talleyrand understands the greatest danger to France is Russia, and Alexander has a personal animus towards him. The agnostic Talleyrand relishes intriguing against a man who sees himself as the Messianic savior of Europe. It's messy and dangerous brinkmanship. The last thing I want is a war among those pledged to a Continental peace." He sank back into his chair in temporary emotional exhaustion, sighing deeply, as if he had just expelled a dangerous mental poison.

"Personalities outweighing logic," observed Pennywhistle, leaning back in his chair to digest Castlereagh's revelations. "The Achilles heel of man is his own contradictory nature. We wish to be enlightened men of principle, or at least pragmatic realists, yet our passions will not be denied. I am coming to see that diplomacy is guided as much by personalities as by principles. The degree to which a diplomat possesses health, intelligence, charm, and industry counts for just as much as the merits of his programs. Vanity, ineptitude, misunderstanding, and inadequate command of a foreign language can bury even the most meritorious ideas."

Castlereagh nodded in pleased relief that a colleague understood the concerns that often kept him awake long into the night. "Confusing, isn't it? Man is at once the most calculating and emotional of God's creatures. These developments make a resolution of the Reichenau issue even more critical, since it seems to constitute an *idée fixe* for the Czar. Is there any possibility that this von Steinwehr fellow might be open to... let us say, other possibilities? Perhaps a lifetime annuity, secretly paid out through third parties? The Rothschilds have discreet connections with the bankers in Amsterdam, Berne, and Geneva. We could make that annuity substantial enough to excite the interest of any reasonable man."

"The key words that you used, my lord, are 'reasonable man'. Von Steinwehr is not reasonable, but a fanatic. Might I explain?"

"Please do, Sir Thomas."

Attaché Extraordinaire

"My lord, before our meeting, I familiarized myself with the contents of that little volume you lent me, *The Enlightened State.*"

"I wish I had been able to read it, Sir Thomas, but such are the demands of this job; I have never been able to find the time."

"I quite understand, my lord. The book contained many references to von Steinwehr, though never naming him explicitly. Added to what I know, it enabled me to assemble a portrait of the man. One quote hammers at my memory: 'Reichenau was the worst of Rhineland's petty tyrannies, its ruler a despot of the most arrogant and unfeeling disposition, regarding his subjects as little better than cattle of a particularly stupid variety.'"

Castlereagh frowned. "That is exactly the kind of state and man I should prefer to see banished from the map of Europe."

"That quote is in complete agreement with the impression I formed of the man during the committee meeting. This is not about money; this is about what he sees as his destiny. He seeks power, not fortune, the kind of man who will end up either on a throne or a scaffold. He is brilliant, but as you have discovered, brilliance sometimes breeds arrogance and contempt for lesser beings."

Castlereagh nodded. "So, he believes himself a man of reason, but is in truth his opposite?"

"Indeed, my lord. A despot is often a strange mixture of arrogance and self-pity, at once powerful and brittle. Hard working and driven by an almost supernatural energy, he is contemptuous of others who lack his zeal. Such a man views terror and virtue as allies, not enemies: terror rescuing virtue from impotency. He sees himself through a peculiar mirror of his own devising. It is the reverse of the carnival mirrors used at county fairs, which render a bizarrely distorted image; the despot's mirror transforms his reflection into something approaching normality, though all others see the man as abnormal. His advisors will be opportunists, acting as a Greek Chorus to confirm his false image of himself as an outsized savior, half human, half divine. Exactly how Bonaparte represented himself when he seized the Emperor's crown from the Pope's hands and placed it on his own head. It is ironic that von Steinwehr hates and despises Napoleon, when in fact they have a great many characteristics in common."

"Would you say that he would employ that same mirror in his dealings with his subjects if Reichenau were restored?"

"He would, my lord. He would see himself as a benevolent father charged with giving a stern upbringing to wild children too long allowed to roam free. What you and I would label rank cruelty, he would view as benign discipline. He would violate traditions and ancient laws. He would believe he needed to break the letter of the laws to be true to their spirit. He would imagine himself a bringer of order when he would, in fact, be a destroyer."

"A true force of nihilism," responded Castlereagh, his voice a mixture of perplexity and contempt.

"Such men may temporarily modify their behavior," resumed Pennywhistle, his voice acidic, "but their cores do not change. For the Congress, he has become a changeling, adopting the cover of the diplomat. He appears a reasonable, direct gentleman, distinguished by a long record of military service. What remains unspoken is that that service may have given him opportunities to indulge his darker impulses. He uses the tonalities and timbre of his voice as expertly as Mozart played the piano, persuading his peers that he is a man of principle with whom they may share their deepest confidences. The peculiar combination of his physical appearance, which is of a man accustomed violence, with a voice that promises he is a man of peace, has an odd effect on audiences, whether they be diplomats or underlings, or, I suspect, his own countrymen. He signals listeners to indulge in vice while giving it the name of virtue, a dangerous wolf sending feral messages to domesticated dogs: 'Give into the beast within and know the savage pleasure of the hunt and the even greater satisfaction of the kill.'"

"A predator playing a peacemaker."

"Yes, my lord, and infectious as a plague. Might I favor you with my prescription for future actions?"

"Please do, Sir Thomas."

"This man cannot be reasoned with or diverted from his goal that burns at the core of his being. In his mind, the Universal Order of Things was put out of joint by Bonaparte. He hates Bonaparte, and yet, like the Corsican, he is a great believer in the power of Destiny. He will scheme, dissemble, bully, and even kill in pursuit of his. He will fight hard, well, and cleverly against any blocks to his goal, defiant to the end. I suspect that he believes he is only truly alive when he rules, and he wants a second chance to do so."

"You only live twice?" observed Castlereagh.

"Well put, my lord. So, we need to play a double game. We publicly pretend that we are taken in by his 'I am a reasonable man' charade."

"But privately proceed according to the truth?"

"Yes, my lord. He will believe our play-acting because all fanatics see themselves as clever and persuasive; he will trust that has posturing has had the intended effect. The authoritarian mind compels its owner to believe the propaganda it has created, which blind and deafen him to the contrary evidence of his own eyes and ears. And I may have a sop to drop in his path that will apparently give him exactly what he needs."

"Am I correct in assuming that this sop might be a near facsimile of something we discussed earlier?"

"You are, my lord. I see von Steinwehr as a larger-than-life figure, straight out of Shakespeare."

"I am a great admirer of the Bard. Who might that figure be?"

"Richard III."

Castlereagh blinked in surprise. "I thought you would say Macbeth, considering the man's career as a soldier."

"I see him as twisted within, as Richard was twisted without. Both Macbeth and Richard were driven by ambition, and both were murderers. And here I will share one detail I withheld previously, because the resulting scandal would publicly humiliate his master, Czar Alexander, who is not a man who would react well to humiliation. The Czar is already a loose cannon."

"And that detail is..."

"I have sound evidence to conclude that von Steinwehr is the Edelweiss Executioner."

Castlereagh's face turned white, and he abruptly sank back in his chair, barely able to catch his breath. His words came out as a whisper, "Monstrous! Inhuman!"

"Exactly, my lord. Richard and von Steinwehr killed for different reasons on the surface, but their goals were the same. They were both after power. Richard murdered children when he believed they obstructed his path to the throne. Von Steinwehr killed civil servants who possessed particular information that blocked his path to again be the *Landgrave* of Reichenau."

Attaché Extraordinaire

"You think von Steinwehr has the potential to be a villain of the same order as Richard?"

"He would be far worse, but the key word is *potential*. If we act with intelligence and dispatch, that potential will never become reality. He has likely made a promise to Alexander with regard to translating the Clarke Letters, and it is my job to make sure he cannot fulfill that promise."

"Do you think Alexander knows of the depredations his aide has carried out in private?"

"I do not. Though the Russian court is given to intrigue and extra-judicial murder, it is done with a degree of discretion. I doubt even Alexander would countenance such monstrous deeds."

"This information puts an entirely different cast upon matters," said Castlereagh gravely. "I have always tried to put the welfare of future generations first in my thoughts. This man must be stopped. Whilst dissembling is an offense against my nature, murder is an even greater one. I can mislead Alexander sufficiently to give cover to what you must do. My one question is, can you put a stop to this terrible maniac?"

"I will do whatever it takes, my lord. Whatever it takes."

"My lasting wish is for swords to be beaten into plow shares, but this looks to be a problem solvable only by the harsh application of a sharp blade," said Castlereagh, as a surge of emotion energized his normally phlegmatic face. He rose from his chair and extended his hand. "Good luck to you, Sir Thomas. I admire your steadfastness, but would not wish your task on anyone."

Pennywhistle departed, intent upon his next action. His subconscious was far more concerned with honesty than politeness, and it demanded that he forget the name von

John Danielski

Steinwehr and substitute the peasant's designation of "the Gorgon". He should call a monster by his right name.

He had wondered if his mission was one of justice or vengeance. He had never considered a third possibility: pest control. Hunting a powerful fiend was dangerous. Beowulf defeated Grendel and Grendel's dam, and even slew the dragon, but the dragon's bite killed him. Was von Steinwehr Grendel or the dragon? The answer did not really matter. Pennywhistle was a patriot with a job to do. He had a monster to slay.

Chapter 21

"This ain't at all what I expected, Margaret," huffed Sammie Jo. "This hunt is more like a mounted ball. It's a fashion show! Guess these folks need fancy clothes to go with their fancy guns. Course, my own outfit ain't exactly inconspicuous." Sammie Jo's outfit drew inspiration from a Spanish riding habit, but she had modified it to suit her New World outlook. Her honey blond hair was bound in a bun, under a black bolero hat. Her blue double-breasted Spencer jacket featured large brass buttons and was tail-less, tight-fitting, and cinched at the waist; her jade silk blouse featured a large jabot, above which she wore a crimson scarf. Her wide legged, black harem pantaloons allowed easy movement but appeared as a skirt, when standing. Her tall boots resembled those worn by Wellington. The weather was warm enough to obviate the need for the blue boat cloak she kept furled in her saddlebag.

Sammie Jo had also brought along what she called her "Three Wise Men": the bullwhip, hunting knife, and tomahawk, which were her backup weapons, when a rifle was impractical. It made no sense, to her way of thinking, to go on any kind of hunt unprepared.

Lady Leith smiled and replied, "The cut of the clothing and the colors call attention to their owners in a deliberate display of power and wealth."

Sammie Jo wrinkled her nose. "When I hunted stags back in the Chesapeake, I used to carry a pouch with dirt that deer had pissed on. It attracted the bucks. Here the smell of perfume is so strong that I feel like I am drowning. I am surprised it don't make the partridges fall out of the trees. The stink is going to play havoc with the noses of the tracking dogs." She sniffed again, this time in derision. "And I think riding sidesaddle is plum stupid, and I ain't stupid. But Margaret, I do wonder if some of this hunting isn't a way for women to get back at men they're mad at."

"How so?" inquired a puzzled Lady Leith.

"Well, we are females hunting a male animal. And not just any animal, but a large stag with a huge pair of antlers. I know the antlers are the big object, since they will go up on a wall. To me, it's like posting a pair of men's balls."

Lady Leith suppressed a giggle. "I never thought of it that way, but being permitted our own hunt is certainly a kind of freedom. But what lies before you is not as much about hunting as it is a display of status. Hunting is a way to establish social circles. It is also a substitute for warfare, with stags being the enemy, dogs the soldiers, the huntsmen and their retinue serving as noncommissioned officers; and today, we ladies are the officers. Many of the important men here began their day with a hunt, only transacting business in the afternoon.

"That don't make no sense, Margaret. Instead of being all hot and bothered about pedigree, a hunt should be... well... about putting meat on the table."

Attaché Extraordinaire

"When aristocrats hunt, Sammie Jo, their objectives are to take trophies, and their hosts do not want them to go home empty handed. There was a boar hunt two weeks before we arrived. Twenty large stands were constructed forming an amphitheater. Then six hundred animals were rounded up and released, a few at a time. Each monarch had a gun and numerous assistants to help in loading. Everyone fired according to rank, czars and emperors first, then kings, princes, dukes, field marshals, all the way down to lowly knights. Neither skill nor risk was involved, and no staying power was required."

"That's awful. What is the point to mere slaughter? Shooting like that kills the spirit of a real hunter! Speaking of spirit, this horse of mine don't seem to have none, and yours don't seem a whole lot better. "

"The baroness was not sure if we could ride and specified exceptionally gentle mounts."

"My ride seems half awake. Does she have a name?"

"It's Beatrice. Mine is Laura," said Margaret. "I think the Baroness likes Dante and Petrarch."

Sammie Jo whispered in her horse's ear. "Now Bea, you just follow my lead and we'll get on real fine. I'm afixin' to ride you a lot faster than any one's ever done but you're going to find it's a lot of fun."

The horse gave a short snuffle which Sammie Jo took as approval.

"This place don't seem like any hunting grounds I know," remarked Sammie Jo as she craned her head in a slow arc. "The trails are so wide that they look like avenues. I see lots of benches, a fancy stone bridge, and even a couple of fake ruined temples. Even the trees look like... well... like they did not grow here naturally. And their bases are clean, not surrounded by any undergrowth. It's more like a giant weeded garden than a real forest."

"You are correct, Sammie Jo, these are not hunting grounds but a hunting park, carefully landscaped by designers. Their philosophy translates into making a game park look natural but easily accessible, a compromise between the unruliness of nature and the formality of art. That means a wilderness devoid of real inconvenience and danger. Roman mythology is popular, so the temples are an homage to that. This park covers twenty thousand acres, with five hunting lodges that are in truth rustic palaces, eight hundred miles of roads substantial enough to accommodate carriages, and twenty fountains that are disguised as bubbling springs. Those temples are for lovers."

"Lovers?"

"Yes, these hunts are famous as trysting places. Young people may slip away from the hunt and meet in secret rendezvous, knowing they will be safe from chaperones, nature giving them the shelter to act naturally. A surprising number of babies are conceived thusly."

The planning for this hunt had begun three weeks before. The planning ensured that many disparate elements, both human and animal, arrived in the right place at the right time. While not as elaborate as the great hunt Lady Leith had described, this hunt was nevertheless as orchestrated as human engineering could render an encounter with wild animals in a natural, albeit cultivated, setting.

Now eighty women on horseback waited expectantly, each accompanied by several hounds and male servants. Their riding habits were more costumes than practical attire and came in a rainbow of colors, scarlet and hunter green being favorites. Specific shades proclaimed affiliation with some great house.

The upper parts of their habits resembled military uniforms, wide at the shoulders, cinched at the waist, with flowing tails, faced with buttons of silver or gold and elaborate piping on the collars, cuffs, and buttonholes. Their skirts were wide, voluminous, and granted easy movement. Velvet, satin, and silk were the preferred materials. Half of the skirts were of similar color to the tops of their habits, the rest were in colors that boldly contrasted with them. They flowed luxuriously over the sides of saddles.

Headgear was extravagant. Some women wore tall bonnets festooned with peacock and ostrich feathers. Others wore low crowned, wide-brimmed hats decorated with roses and posies. Some wore elaborate tricorn hats trimmed in gold and emblazoned with riotously colored, oversized cockades. A few fashion rebels wore men's top hats in colors contrasting with their habits. Some were shaped to showcase an elaborate hair style beneath. Many had arisen early, so their hairdressers would have plenty of time to work their magic.

Their horses were small, sleek, and had been specially bred for hunting. The dogs for a stag hunt had been selected for endurance rather than speed and were larger and stronger than the greyhounds used to hunt smaller game.

Ingrid von Steinwehr observed the conversation between Lady Leith and Sammie Jo through her pocket spyglass. Lady Leith looked like she belonged in this privileged assembly; Lady Pennywhistle did not. Ingrid guessed Lady Pennywhistle's attire would appeal to men, and she had to concede the practicality of pantaloons. But you had to be willing to scandalize people by refusing to ride sidesaddle. Americans had no proper manners!

The long rifle that protruded from Lady Pennywhistle's saddle was two inches short of five feet long, which struck Ingrid as unwieldy and difficult to fire from horseback. Perhaps it was an American rifle of the type that had killed so many British officers in the American War of Independence. The owners of such weapons were famous for their sharpshooting, and she wondered if Lady Pennywhistle was an heir to that tradition.

Ingrid maintained a fifty-yard distance from her targets, taking care that she never strayed close enough for either woman to discover that she was no realtor. Just to be sure, she wore a thin veil suspended from her hat. Observing her prey in a setting that resembled her natural habitat was proving revealing. Though Ingrid was still certain that it was Sammie Jo's sexual allure that had ensnared Sir Thomas, it was gradually dawning on her that Lady Pennywhistle had other gifts as well.

The Baroness de Krudener was the official sponsor of the hunt, but it was her secretary and sister Katrina, who had delivered the invitation to Sammie Jo and Lady Leith. Ingrid saw Katrina chatting pleasantly with her targets; she was acting as their translator and liaison to the hunt. Katrina was in her middle twenties, blessed with a pretty face and trim figure, yet her reputation for forthright speech, bordering on the outspoken, attracted few male admirers. She was the sort of woman men sought out when seeking sisterly advice but avoided when seeking wifely submissiveness.

"A glass of champagne, madame?" A livered servant from the House of Esterhazy offered Ingrid a perfectly chilled glass bursting with bubbles. "Thank you. Your timing is excellent." Ingrid put down her spyglass and grasped the flute shaped vessel in her hand, briefly allowing the bubbles to tweak her nostrils. The first sip was ambrosia and the perfect accompaniment to the hunt. She found it peculiar, indeed, that Lady Pennywhistle was refusing a glass. Americans had no appreciation for the refinements of life.

"I declare, Margaret, I feel like I am stuck in a tar pit. When is this damn hunt going to start? Some of the riders are looking pretty well lubricated, and I'm guessing they aren't all just sipping champagne." She inclined her head towards several women who were passing around a flask. "I wonder if they will be able to stay upright when the hunt starts," mocked Sammie Jo.

"Hunts always lose a few to drunken brushes with tree branches, but drink is part of the fun," replied Lady Leith. "To not have alcoholic inspiration would seem a cruel inhospitality to them."

"That tells me they ain't serious about this at all. I always kept a clear head when I went after a buck."

"They aren't serious, Sammie Jo. A stag, when caught, may well be left to the dogs, since it's only the antlers they want."

Sammie Jo shook her head vigorously. "That don't seem right at all. I like dogs but it ain't proper to feed them steak when a heap of people are one step away from starving. I ain't never forgot what it is like to have a hungry belly."

"There are a few lords who do allow the kill to be given to their servants or to the poor, but most think it encourages them to expect such donations on a regular basis. Lords also worry that peasants might develop a taste for venison and become poachers. Don't sneer, Sammie Jo, poachers are a serious problem. Not only will they hunt off season, when the animals need time to give birth and raise their young, they kill for profit more than for food, and they will shoot men as readily as they shoot foxes. In the German states, poachers are not individuals operating alone, but organized gangs who offer armed resistance to authorities sent to disperse them. One group in Bavaria put to ignominious flight a group of soldiers sent to root them out."

"I noticed something about the common folk here. How short they are. Is that because they don't eat a lot of meat?"

"It is, Sammie Jo. America is heavily wooded, with plenty of game available to the poorest folk if they care to hunt. We in England have sometimes been able to recognize Yankees from afar because they are usually two or three inches taller than their English counterparts."

Tutatuta tah! Tutatuta tah! The Master of the Hunt's horn sounded. All conversation ceased and champagne glasses were handed back to servants. "They are about to release the stags," said Lady Leith.

"Stags?" responded Sammie Jo in puzzlement. "I thought there would be only one."

"Plenty of people want trophies." Lady Leith unfurled her spyglass and pointed it at the top of a hill, where the stags were being held in a pen. "It looks like there are ten, and all appear prime specimens." Each red deer was between five to seven years of age years in age, from seven to eight feet in length and three and half to four feet in height. Weights varied between four and five hundred pounds. All had magnificently large antlers.

"Now remember, Sammie Jo, don't dash ahead of the rest of us like I know you want to. Let the deer get a respectable lead and allow the trackers do their jobs. When the trackers signal that the hounds should be released, let the dogs do their job as well. That task is to harry the stag, slow it down, and if possible, drag it to the ground. The task of us in saddles is to finish the beasts off with our guns. However, some hunts

Attaché Extraordinaire

prefer the spectacle of death rather than the infliction of it. That may happen today, since the Baroness is more a voyeur of carnage than one to cause it by her own hand. In such a case, the chief huntsman cuts the exhausted stag's tendons so he cannot flee and slits the stag's throat The dogs contend for its entrails, the lead tracking dog gets the head, and the chief huntsman's assistant holds aloft the antlers."

"Hell, Margaret, where is the satisfaction in that? Letting others do all the work and then feeling happy because you watched something noble die in agony? That's twisted! And they think I am uncivilized? I may have trouble remembering the right glass or the right eatin'iron, but my heart knows a lot more about what is right and wrong than people who don't appear to have ever done an honest day's work."

She continued with a barely suppressed anger. "Hunting should be a test of skill, where the animal has at least a chance of survival. Where I come from, the Piscataway Indians say a prayer over the body of a slain beast and offer thanks to his soul for having given up his body for their welfare. I never done that, but I always had respect for the beasts I hunted. This hunt is like putting a turtle on top of a fence post: you know it don't belong there, you know it did not get there by accident, and you know that sooner or later, it's going to fall off." She shook her head in disgust. "Margaret, do any of these stags ever run out of the park, break away from the usual paths?"

"Once in a great while, and it causes the gamesmen distress, since it offends their plans for a well-managed hunt. It would be like an orchestra having one member playing off a different score. Should that happen, the Master of the Hunt would dispatch his best trained representatives to bring it down."

Sammie Jo smiled ferally. "A rogue deer. I like the sound of it. That's the kind of challenge that makes hunting worthwhile."

"Remember your husband, Sammie Jo. You are under a microscope today, since no other diplomat is married to an American. Your beauty, height, and attire have already made an impression. That you husband is British strikes many as particularly odd, since your nation and his are still at war. The Baroness has influence with the Czar, and you must never, ever, outpace her." Lady Leith pointed her out.

"She looks like an old witch who stole some fancy clothes and decided to use a horse instead of a broomstick. Kind of fat, too. Those dogs around her look as groomed as the horses."

To Sammie Jo's surprise, their translator, Katrina, smirked; amused rather than offended at Sammie Jo's characterization of her sister.

Katrina spoke pleasantly, "Her dogs are quite famous in hunting circles, Lady Pennywhistle. She once had a group portrait of them done that hangs in the entrance hall of her Vienna residence. Bonne, Nonne, Blonde, Folle, Mitte, and Tane are their names."

"Dogs having their portraits painted! Talk about barking up the wrong tree!"

Ta Tah Ta Tah Ta Tah! A second horn sounded, and the gates of the stag corral flew open. Its captives raced madly down the hill, rightly understanding they were in the run of their lives.

Sammie Jo tightened her grip on the reins. It was only with difficulty that she prevented herself from putting the riding crop to her horse, waiting for the baroness to take the lead.

Attaché Extraordinaire

The stags raced off in multiple directions, taking the artificial roadways in the interest of putting as much distance between themselves and their pursuers as fast as possible.

Sammie Jo thought them magnificent and wished they could remain living monuments to nature's grace. If they had to die, it should at least be quick and done in the service of giving people a decent meal. She wasn't going to let any pack of dogs rip them to shreds. Protocol be damned! She would finish any cornered animal near her with a clean shot to the head.

The huntsmen on the hill waited ten minutes for the stags to get a decent lead. They then released a pack of hounds for each animal. A hundred hounds dashed gleefully down the hill, barking in savage delight. Sammie Jo looked in astonishment at the dogs clustered round the riders close to her. They were just window dressing, pampered canine princes. The real work would be done by the packs careening down the hill.

Her impatience to get moving was mirrored by the ladies around her.

"We must wait for the huntsman's next horn, Sammie Jo," cautioned Lady Leith.

"Ta! Ta! Ta! Ta! Ta! Ta!

"Does that mean we can finally get moving?"

"It does, but follow the pace of the Baroness."

"Hallelujah and Heaven's Hope! Finally!"

The Baroness led the hunt with a brisk trot. It had no urgency and seemed more fitted to a sight-seeing expedition. There was definite excitement in the expressions and postures of the ladies following, but the pace was controlled and disciplined, as if a reel had been turned into a stately minuet.

The riders increased their pace as a different horn sounded, one indicating that the dogs had cornered a stag.

More than a few riders took quick gulps from flasks of brandy, using alcohol to add to the building excitement. One middle aged, matronly looking lady had her flask knocked from her grip as she collided with the branch of a pine tree. The impact swept her out of the saddle like a giant hand. She sprawled on the ground, unconscious and devoid of any dignity.

A different horn riff caused the women to use their crops to push their mounts to a gallop. A kill was imminent! No one wanted to miss the fun.

Sammie Jo, realizing she was too far behind to use her rifle, slackened her pace until the colorful assemblage had disappeared round a bend. Dogs barked, horns sounded, and shouts of triumph echoed, but Sammie Jo's face fell. She halted Beatrice and Lady Leith did the same with Laura.

"I killed plenty of bucks, but don't want to watch a bunch of perfumed bitches drool while one dies. I will sit this death out."

"I don't blame you, Sammie Jo."

"You know Margaret, I could do with a drink about now, to make me forget where I am. You have that hip flask with you?"

"I do. I brought it to revive any ladies who might have become faint from the sight of the blood."

"I ain't going to faint, but the callousness of them ladies makes me want to puke."

Lady Leith handed Sammie Jo the flask. She was about to take her first sip when her peripheral vision detected movement in the woods, two hundred and fifty yards away. Her hunter's instincts went on high alert. Something was out there, and it was big.

Attaché Extraordinaire

She put a finger to her lips. "Dismount real slow and easy, Margaret, then get behind Laura and use her as a shield. We need to stay downwind."

Lady Leith looked puzzled.

"Trust me," Sammie Jo whispered.

Lady Leith obeyed. The forest was Sammie Jo's kingdom. She was as at home here as she was out of place in a drawing room.

Sammie Jo dismounted with an easy grace and slowly slid her rifle from the saddle. She placed herself behind Beatrice, whose docile nature now proved an advantage. She forced herself to recall a stag's instincts. Patience was called for. Let the beast believe he faced no threat. Stay put, let him come to her.

She breathed slowly and deeply, calming herself and focusing her concentration. She had often used hides in the forests of Maryland, and the two horses functioned as an improvised one. One minute stretched to five before the first movement. The rustling became louder and louder as a titan moved slowly through the woods. The ladies of the hunt had been so focused on protocol and so reliant on others that they had ridden blindly past something that lurked at their side.

Suddenly, he emerged into the open, and he was the finest buck Sammie Jo had ever seen: truly a king of the forest. He rotated his head slowly to allow his eyes and ears to detect any danger. He sniffed the air cautiously, and Sammie Jo was glad that she was crude enough never to wear perfume on a hunt.

Lady Leith looked at her with disapproval mixed with admiration. What she believed Sammie Jo was about to do contradicted the traditions of the hunt and yet, watching a craftsman about her work was mesmerizing. She held her breath.

The stag stood motionless for a minute; his large frame silhouetted against the late morning sun. While Sammie Jo scoffed at the idea of dogs being immortalized on canvas, she could see where an artist might find this magnificent beast a captivating subject.

Satisfied he was safe; the beast began to slowly move in a direction that would take him out of the hunting park. Sammie Jo eased herself round Beatrice's nose and dropped to one knee, wanting to present the smallest possible outline. She trusted the beast would focus on the horse and dismiss the unmoving woman as an unimportant object. She brought The Widowmaker to her shoulder and lined up her sights on the stag's head. She breathed in and out slowly and readied herself to take the shot. She had him.

Then she stopped. She did not need the food and did not need to add to the orgy of killing. This animal was true to his nature while most of those on the hunt were betraying their humanity. Why not spare him?

She started to put the rifle down when she heard a loud baying of hounds not far off and closing fast. She knew from their cry that they had acquired the stag's scent. The stag heard their howls and began to run.

The hounds were close and the outcome inevitable. *No! God damn it. They would not have him.*

Lady Leith looked at her with an expression that said, "Are you sure?"

Sammie Jo gave a quick nod and brought The Widowmaker to her shoulder. She saw the first few dogs emerge from the wood and dash onto the plain. This would have to be a quick shot. The stag had broken into a flat out run. The distance was two hundred and seventy-five yards and opening fast. She held her breath and set the rear of the weapon's double set triggers. She lined up the sights on his head, held her breath, then let it out at the bottom of a slow exhale. She flicked the first trigger with a feather light touch.

Her aim was true. The round entered just below the stag's right eye. His bounding legs went suddenly limp, and his body fell lifelessly to the earth.

The dogs quickened their pace. She reloaded with lightning speed. She surveyed the onrushing pack, looking for the pack leader. The second she found him, she squeezed the trigger. The shot penetrated the beast's heart and the canine tide ground to a halt, the bewildered animals circling and sniffing their fallen leader.

She had stopped the pack; now she needed to drive it off. She had probably killed an extremely valuable dog, but did not care. She quickly identified the canine second in command. She reloaded, fired, and the animal gave a short howl as a bullet passed through his left ear. The pack bayed in fear, lamentation, and confusion, and swiftly took off running in the opposite direction.

Lady Leith sighed. "I know why you did what you did, and a part of me sympathizes, but it was a major social *faux pas*."

"Well, at least nobody saw it, Margaret."

But someone had seen it; two persons, in fact. Ingrid had followed the two and viewed the entire episode through her spyglass. She was appalled, but fascinated. Lady Pennywhistle might be an idiot about protocol, but she was a brilliant shot.

Their translator, Katrina de Krudener, rode up and Lady Leith cringed. Sammie Jo remained defiant.

"That was remarkable! Remarkable!" gushed Katrina with admiration. "Most women shoot like near-sighted old men who have broken their glasses. If the baroness finds out, she will be angry." She laughed. "Wonderful! That you have spoiled part of her hunt pleases me immensely; I hate the woman. She has never lost a chance to advance herself at my expense."

Sammie Jo smiled tentatively at the speaker.

"We shall have to dispose of the stag's carcass," said Lady Leith. She paused thoughtfully. "The Mekhitarist Monastery lies at the edge of this park. The monks are well known for their efforts to aid the poor, and a message sent to their abbot accompanied by a few coins would likely cause him to send a wagon to retrieve the stag. The meat would be distributed to the needy this very evening."

Katrina was delighted with this plan. "Even better! A stag will go unaccounted for and a lady who has been promised a trophy will go home empty handed and irate. My sister will be livid!"

Only Sammie Jo's keen ears heard the click of hammers pulled to full cock. She swiveled her head slowly toward the source of the sounds.

Eight men clad in forest green trousers, waistcoats, and hats advanced from the edge of the woods. They had probably been lurking there since the start of the hunt, unnoticed because they blended in with their surroundings. They were dressed as jaegers, German for hunters, the equivalent of gamekeepers found on English estates. But there was something wrong with the picture. The men looked predatory and furtive, not stalwart and reliable. Hunters they might be, but these men hunted outside of the law.

Poachers! thought Sammie Jo. They had probably been looking to scavenge from the hunt and had now spotted something far superior to leftovers. And she herself had conveniently driven off the dogs that would have kept the poachers at bay, or at least summoned help.

Attaché Extraordinaire

The men emerged onto the plain and stalked toward the three women. They kept their rifles leveled. Sammie Jo assumed they were loaded, just as she assumed they were experienced marksmen.

Sammie Jo knew men and knew predators. She wondered if they could be reasoned with or bribed. She had something they wanted—and she would be fine with giving it up to them. Except, she saw in their eyes that they wanted something more than game. The cruel, lustful glint in seven sets of eyes told her why they had chosen to follow this particular hunt. They were here to scavenge women as well as game. The prospect of the forced sexual conquest of a great lady was probably as important a prize as the meat of a giant stag.

The man who was their apparent leader walked in front. He was tall and gaunt, with a face that spoke of a hard life and an enjoyment of sadism. He favored Sammie Jo with a sneering smile. He looked the type who liked his women terrified and squealing. For such types, the sex act was not one of passion but one of conquest. That they would be forcing themselves on ladies of high social status would make the coupling even more delicious.

Sammie Jo was not terrified but angered. Like her husband she hated bullies, and rapists were several rungs lower on the scale of human detritus than ordinary bullies.

She contemplated how fast she could reload her rifle, then stopped herself. That simply was not practical. The jaeger leader expected a kitten, but not one with a whip and wiles. Pretending to quiver and cringe, she took her cloak from the saddle and threw in around her shoulders, hoping to convey the impression she was using it to suppress chills.

She shot a glance at Margaret and saw awareness, not fear. Aristocrat she might be, but her core was as tough as Sammie

Jo's. A second quick glance directed her way signaled, *Get ready.*

Margaret edged close to Sammie Jo and cowered, feigning fear. Under cover of the cloak, Sammie Jo unobtrusively passed Lady Leith The Widowmaker, never taking her eyes off the lead jaeger. Using the horses and Sammie Jo's body as a shield, Margaret began reloading the long rifle. Katrina was crying, which distracted the poachers. Several of them jeered at her, obscenely telling what they planned to do.

Sammie Jo removed two items from her saddle and hid them inside the pockets of her cloak. Then in a timid manner she moved to Katrina's side, as if anxious to comfort her. Katrina turned to her a face the color of new milk.

"I need you to translate, Katrina. Trust me, I will get us out of this."

Katrina gasped. Strangely, she did trust Lady Pennywhistle. Color began to return to her cheeks.

From her cover behind the trees, Ingrid wondered what Lady Pennywhistle was up to. With a sudden insight, she guessed it had nothing to do with surrender.

Sammie Jo hesitantly walked forward, like a fearful person trying to protect her even more fearful friends. She made an entreating gesture with her hands, five yards from the lead jaeger.

He faced her full on, and a smirk distorted his mouth.

"Good sir," she said in a voice that groveled, "I have no quarrel with you." Katrina translated, careful to convey the accompanying emotion in her own tone of voice. "We have something that you want: a great stag. Take it with our compliments and allow us to depart in peace." The tremor in her voice conveyed that rape was the ultimate horror, that a woman would give up anything to prevent it from happening.

Attaché Extraordinaire

Katrina translated, and the jägermeister's smirk changed to a leer. His men were exchanging crude remarks and even cruder gestures, their weapons now dangling by shoulder straps, arguing over which man would take which woman, and bragging about how many times he would possess her before passing her on.

"We will take what we want. You offer me nothing."

Katerina translated, and Sammie Jo pasted a look of abject terror on her face even as her soul blazed with fire and her mind turned icy.

"Please good sir. I have a purse of coins. Come forward, take it, and turn away from impure thoughts. Then carve up the beast and depart happy men." Yes, her time spent among ladies of quality meant she could occasionally exactly mimic their speech.

The unexpected prospect of *specie* changed the lead jaeger's smile from one of lust to one of avarice. "I accept your gift," he said as he advanced on Sammie Jo.

Sammie Jo began groping in her cloak, as if reaching for a purse, making a quick, barely perceptible motion with her head to Margaret, who understood perfectly. The jaeger was about to receive a gift all right, just not the one he expected.

A yard distant from the tall lady, his world changed in a flash. The woman's expression turned from one of fear to the smile Satan radiates just as he seizes a man's soul. With one hand she threw back her cloak, revealing a bull whip gripped in the other. She took a step back to position herself, and the whip cut through the air to wrap around his wrist. Excruciating pain caused him to drop the rifle with a loud cry. She swiftly unfurled it from his wrist and then snapped it firmly around his neck. His breath was instantly cut off, and he felt a terrible mounting pressure in his head.

John Danielski

The tall woman pulled him toward her. The man's eyes bulged. He tried to pull away, but each jerk of resistance diminished his strength.

Three of the jaegers groped for weapons, while the others stared, bewildered and astonished. They were ambushers and scavengers, unused to facing armed and determined resistance. Katrina shrieked. Grimly, Margaret raised The Widowmaker. She was one against three, and this was about to go very badly for Sammie Jo, but she would do what she could. Two poachers leveled their guns at Sammie Jo, while the third advanced with knife, drawn to sever the deadly whip.

Margaret shot one man in the head, despair gripping her heart as the other man fired his weapon at short range. Miraculously, his shot went wild, and a second miracle occurred as a shot fired from an unknown source burst through the chest of a second. Margaret did not have time to solve the mystery of the twin miracles; she was reloading as fast as she could. There were still six poachers to deal with.

Katrina was tired of being frightened. The other women were fighting back; she could too. Thankfully, these ladies' horses were trained to stay quiet, even in the presence of gunfire. She dashed to the side of her own horse and seized her 32-inch, lightweight rifle, and fired a shot that hit one man in the chest. He arched his back in agony, dropping his blade before he fell to the bloody ground.

Sammie Jo dropped the whip and grabbed her hunting knife from inside the cloak. She plunged it into the jägermeister's throat. Blood jetted from the carotid artery as she withdrew the knife. He clutched the wound, gurgled horribly, and slowly collapsed.

Attaché Extraordinaire

Lady Leith coolly fired The Widowmaker and her shot pierced the chest of a nasty looking jaeger with a long nose and pointed chin.

The standing poachers were sizing up the situation. They saw two women shielded by horses, busily reloading guns, and a tall woman who had just killed their leader groping in her cloak, no doubt for yet another weapon. Anger warred with an emotion they had never felt before during an ambush: fear. Stepping back to put distance between themselves and the three furies, they raised their guns, even as the two women did the same. Four guns discharged.

The men hesitated; deep down, they did not want to shoot women, and their shots missed. Lady Leith aimed carefully with no hesitation. Her bullet struck one man in the left shoulder. Katrina's shot went wild; she had never fired at a man until a minute ago and the horror of the situation rattled her. She stood dazed, and the rifle fell from her nervous fingers.

The three remaining men turned to run as fast as their legs could carry them to the cover of the forest. Sammie Jo's knife sailed through the air, impaling the one slowed by the shoulder wound.

Rather than reload, Lady Leith moved to Katrina's side. As far as she was concerned, the fight was over, and they'd won.

But Sammie Jo's dander was up. Not one of these varmints would keep on breathing if she had any say in the outcome. There was a brief, protesting wail from that part of her that wanted to be a lady, silenced by cold logic. All the poachers had been well dressed, which meant they had money enough to buy bread, and they still chose to do this instead. Any survivors would go right back to doing what they had tried to do today, maybe even persuading others to join them.

Tomahawk in hand, she strode forward, her feral gaze intent. One of the skunks seemed hampered by a gimpy leg. Him first, but she'd have to close the distance.

Sammie Jo started running, her long legs quickly bearing her to within the optimal 15-foot range. A high-pitched, keening yell of the kind made by Piscataway Indians of Maryland caused her prey to look back in terror, then redouble his efforts to escape. A straight arm throw, and her tomahawk imbedded itself between his shoulder blades. He went down.

But the eighth poacher had put himself safely beyond reach of any thrown blade.

Cursing, Sammie Jo ran back towards the clearing as fast as she could, yelling to Margaret to ready The Widowmaker. Lady Leith paused in her ministrations to Katrina, and by the time Sammie Jo, red faced and wild-eyed, was reaching a long arm out for her rifle, the gun was ready in Margaret's outstretched hand. "Here. You'll need your best friend to complete the job."

If the forest had not been thinned for aristocratic hunts, the shot would have been impossible. As it was, the trees were so spaced that Sammie Jo could see the fleeing man in the distance. He was fast, but she was faster. She ran to higher ground for the advantage of line of sight, braced her legs wide apart, aimed carefully, and gently squeezed the trigger.

Clack. Whoosh. Bang!

It was a head shot, and it felled him.

Walking now, Sammie Jo covered the 150 yards through the trees to make sure. There was no doubt he was dead. Flies were already gathering and settling on the bloody mess that had been his skull. With a scowl, she retrieved her tomahawk and knife, and then made her way back through the trees to where Margaret and Katrina stood waiting.

Attaché Extraordinaire

Lady Leith walked over, wearing an expression of embarrassment. "And to think I envisioned a refined event that would be a further advancement of your social education."

Sammie Jo shook her head and flashed a sardonic half-smile. "Well, it surely did expand my education. Turning a blood sport into a blood bath has made me see that for all of Europe's civilized ways, they got their share of varmits, too, just better organized and better dressed than the ones back home. I cannot think when I have felt less a lady, but I sure do feel alive."

Her face assumed a philosophical cast. "Mind you, I ain't never relished killing for its own sake, but sending these human termites to the bone orchard has made the world a little safer, and ain't that what this here Congress is supposed to be about? That stag over yonder means a few less people will go hungry tonight, and that gives his death a lot more meaning than if he'd died for the amusement of a passel of over fed ladies. Animals only kill when they have to, and never betray their own kind; if humans acted so, there would not even be a need for this Congress." She took a deep breath to end her excursion into moralizing, and then rubbed her chin, as she turned her attention to more practical matters. "Do you think those monks you mentioned could take care of the bodies, if we sent a few extra coins their way?"

"Hmm, probably, if we promise to pay for proper Christian burials and add a little extra for their building fund."

Katrina came over to stand beside them, a look of shock on her face. She was trembling. "I cannot believe I just shot a man."

"I'm glad you did," said Sammie Jo in a calming voice. "I know you think killin' ain't right, but it's different when you do so to save lives. You will probably have a few sleepless nights, but those will pass as you come to realize you did the right thing. But it might be best if your sister is left with a mystery and never finds out what happened here, or the role you played."

"Indeed not, Lady Pennywhistle. However much I might like the Baroness to die of embarrassment, my fortune is tied to hers."

"Since we have fought together, I think we can drop the formality. Seems fittin' you should call me by my rightful name rather than a title I got by marriage. I'm plain old Sammie Jo."

"Sammie Jo it is then," said Katrina with a surprised smile.

"I think we had best get moving," cautioned Lady Leith. "We need to get the monks here as fast as possible."

Sammie Jo and Lady Leith quickly mounted their horses.

"How long do you figure it will take to get to the monastery, if we push these nags of ours, Margaret?" inquired Sammie Jo.

"A quarter hour at the gallop."

"I hope old Bea don't up and die on me," said Sammie Jo ruefully.

Now that they had all calmed down, Lady Leith remembered something. "But Katrina, Sammie Jo, there was someone else here. There had to have been. The first time I fired, there were two men aiming guns at you, Sammie Jo. Both men died. I'm a good shot, but not that good. Who was the individual who fired the shot that none of us did?"

All three women scanned the woods around the clearing, but there was no sign of any other person.

"Too bad, I would have liked to have shaken her hand. I hope, Katrina, that whoever it was don't make trouble for you with your sister or anyone else. But time's a wastin'. I will race

Attaché Extraordinaire

you, Margaret. You too, Katrina. Last one to the monastery is a rotten egg." She laughed heartily, expelling residual tension. When she slapped Beatrice with her riding crop, the startled animal took off with a speed for which Sammie Jo had hardly given her credit.

***

Ingrid stepped out from the circle of pines in which she had concealed herself and her horse. There were several such dense plantings of pine trees, designed to serve as hides for hunters. She was proud of her shot. Lady Pennywhistle might be an enemy, but Ingrid hated presumptuous peasants.

She was still trying to comprehend the massacre she had witnessed; the actions of a female tornado had made bad men reap a Biblical whirlwind. Lady Pennywhistle was more than an oversexed kitten, she was a lioness of Olympian ferocity. Much as it galled her, she admired what her opponent had just done. While she could never count Lady Pennywhistle a friend, it would be hard to see her as a complete enemy. And yet, that lady's conduct and character confirmed her as a truly formidable obstacle to the restoration of Reichenau. She reminded herself that Lady Pennywhistle should not be seen as a person, but a problem to be eliminated. The concerns of the mighty trumped the lives of lesser beings, who simply did not understand the exigencies of sovereigns. Small people had to be pushed aside so big ones could rule. Lady Pennywhistle and her husband were small people.

Chapter 22

Katarina Friederike Wilhelmine Benigna von Biron was a ravishing beauty with blonde hair and brown eyes. The 33-year-old hailed from the Baltic area referred to as Lithuania. She held the rank of princess of that locale, but she preferred to use a subsidiary title derived from a family estate near Berlin. The Duchess of Sagan was gifted with a superb mind, reinforced by an iron will. Nicknamed "the Cleopatra of Courland", she spoke six languages fluently, managed her properties personally, conducted a salon that attracted the most enlightened thinkers, and gave dinner parties famous for the quality of food and guests. Her laughter was infectious, yet an invisible cloud of sadness hovered over her; as if she held within some deep, melancholy secret.

Though her fortune was one of the largest in Europe, she was burning through it rapidly by entertaining frequently and lavishly, striving to surpass the woman across the courtyard of the Palm Palace, her hated rival, The Russian Princess Bagration, the widow of a hero of Borodino. Both were considered arbiters of taste and fashion; both had captivatingly expressive eyes, but Sagan had a bigger heart. She was involved with many charities, had founded a hospital

Attaché Extraordinaire

for wounded soldiers, and had even acted as a midwife to an unmarried servant girl who had unexpectedly given birth.

Twice divorced, she had complained, "I am ruining myself with husbands."

Tonight's dinner party was smaller than the usual biweekly affair, as Sagan was attempting to economize. Dinner consisted of three courses rather than the usual four and featured only a single violinist playing in the background instead of a string quartet. Turkey, which was cheaper than goose, was served as the main course. The guest list had been trimmed to a mere 20. It included her former lover, Prince Alfred von Windischgratz, but not her current *amour*, Prince Metternich.

Sagan sensed her guests' surprise at the absence of Metternich, but they were too well mannered to comment or inquire. Dinner passed with less than the usual witty repartee because Alfred dominated the conversation, his booming voice interrupting every time someone tried to change the subject—which was the heroic role he had played at the Battle of Leipzig. Boasting was typical behavior for the 31-year-old colonel of hussars. Alfred was impulsive, dashing, and forceful, handsome and accustomed to speaking to military subordinates who hung on his every word. He was utterly oblivious to the looks of boredom and irritation on the faces of his dinner companions.

Sagan had invited Alfred on impulse, after he sent word that he had just arrived in the city. She was curious to see how he had changed in the four years since their *liaison* had ended, but was not intending to rekindle their bedroom fire. She cared for Metternich but had become chagrinned at his inability to fulfill a promise that mattered greatly to her. Metternich was everything Alfred was not: educated, charming, considerate, handsome in a refined way. He could discourse on many subjects with wisdom and insight. The 41-year-old was a seasoned diplomat, and one of the most respected and effective negotiators at the Congress.

While her other guests lingered over their dessert of *clafoutis aux cerises*, savouring each mouthful of cherries, custard, and chocolate, Alfred pitched into his like a starved ranker, ploughing through the exquisite confection as if it was an enemy to be finished off. Sagan frowned slightly; she had forgotten his manners were those of the barracks. Metternich's manners were as polished as his speech, and right now, she wished he were occupying his usual spot.

Alfred wolfed down the last bite of dessert whilst the rest of her guests were only halfway through theirs. He then astonished them by reaching under the table and flourishing a cylindrical object, brown, long, and large. It was something that Sagan's guests had heard about but never seen: a cigar. Cigars were manufactured in Spain; they had been spread to Britain and the Low Countries by soldiers returning from the Peninsular War but had not yet made an appearance in Vienna. Alfred had discovered them in Brussels, the city of his birth.

He astonished Sagan's guests even more when he pulled a clipping device and a flint and striker from his pocket. Without so much as a by your leave, he leisurely snipped the cigar, lit it, took a long, slow drag, and exhaled the smoke, as if he were experiencing a heavenly pleasure. After a short pause, he took four quick puffs, then blew smoke rings into the air. The rings slowly wafted down the length of the table.

Many of Sagan's guests gasped, and several vigorously waved their hands to chase the smoke away. Murmurs of disapproval followed. "It isn't done." "Was he raised in a barn?" "Barbaric!" "He's no better than a Turk!" "That smell is spoiling my dessert!"

In a haze of tobacco bliss, Alfred acted as if he were deaf. One comment got through, however. The Countess Zichy exclaimed loudly, "I would like to try one."

Alfred smiled warmly. "Where are my manners?" he said, with a complete lack of irony. "Of course, Countess! I have brought an entire box and I have enough for every guest."

The Countess had an adventurous streak, and her bold request had the effect of transforming disapproval to curiosity. Some at the table had used snuff, but cigars were an exotic novelty—and aristocrats loved exotic novelties.

For the women, smoking a cigar could be a quick dash into *risque* territory, a titillating thought to well-bred women who normally prided themselves on their gentility. The men did not want to be outdone, and though Alfred was boorish, he radiated raw masculinity.

Alfred put his cigar down on his dessert plate and brought forth the cigar box. He rose from the table and sauntered over to Zichy. He bowed, then clipped off the end of a cigar and presented it to her. She took it tentatively and rolled it in her hand several times, examining its texture as she rallied her nerve. She put the cigar in her mouth. Alfred lit it and said, "You do not have to inhale. Let the smoke come to you."

The Countess took a quick puff, then jerked the cigar out and coughed loudly for a few seconds.

"Try it again," urged Alfred. "You will get the hang of it."

The Countess's face took on a look of determination and she followed Alfred's advice. This time she did not cough, and her eyes widened as the effects of nicotine took hold. She took three more puffs. "I could get used to this," she told a pleased Alfred.

Emboldened by her support, Alfred said loudly, "Would anyone else care to try one?"

Everyone's hand went up, although Sagan was the last to do so and raised hers tentatively. Cigar smoking suddenly seemed a fashionable activity.

Alfred moved clockwise around the table, and by the end of his perambulation every guest had a lighted cigar. Two men and two women turned shades of green and fled the table, seeking a receptacle for the contents of their stomachs, to return later with pale faces and watering eyes. The rest puffed contentedly, and the room filled with smoke.

"It's a warm evening," said Sagan cheerfully. "Why don't we all step on the balcony to finish?"

Murmurs of agreement arose, and Sagan led the way to the second-floor balcony, which was large enough to accommodate the orchestra that she regularly hired for important events. There was little conversation as each guest enjoyed his own private reverie with tobacco.

Alfred moved within whispering distance of his hostess. "Cigars are sensual. Their very shape sends a clear message. Don't you agree, Wilhemine?"

"Perhaps not sensual, Alfred, but undeniably relaxing. I have been under a strain today, and this is lightening my burden."

"There is an even better way, Wilhelmine. It might be good to relive old times." He smiled slyly.

Sagan regarded him cynically. He was an opportunist, and his conversation was as devoid of wit as it was forgettable. But he had a point. Alfred had always done his best talking with the long appendage beneath his legs. She was angry with Metternich, and quick, fiery sex with Alfred would be a change of pace from the sensual love making which Metternich favored.

She looked deep into his eyes and saw hot embers. His intent gaze caused a tingling in her loins.

"You are a rogue, Alfred," she said coolly. "But a very attractive rogue."

She thought back to when they had met. He had commented on a large ruby ring she had bought the day before, and when he kissed her hand, he curled his tongue around the ruby, implying what pleasures he could offer a lady. When she jerked back her hand, the ruby came unexpectedly loose, and Alfred had accidentally swallowed it. Chastened, he returned the ruby two days later, and laughter over the incident had sparked a romance.

Now she looked him up and down, as if appraising a prize bull, and decided what he offered was exactly what she needed. "Very well, but only for tonight. Let us both be discreet for the remainder of the evening, so my guests will have no cause to suspect our forthcoming rendezvous."

"I am discretion itself," said Alfred.

Alfred did not understand the meaning of the word; throughout the rest of the night he cast lustful eyes in her direction. She kept her face pleasantly neutral and did not return his ocular advances. Unlike Alfred, her guests were not stupid, and from their expressions, she saw that many had inferred that Alfred would be staying the night.

It was with relief that she said goodbye to her second-to-last guest at midnight. The instant the guest exited the entrance hall, Alfred sprang into action. He spoke no words but simply seized her, sweeping her off her feet and carrying her as if she had fainted. In truth, she was not far from swooning. He swiftly carried her up two flights of stairs to the master bedroom. She had no idea how he knew the location, but it was quite possible this was not the first time he had visited the Palm Palace on an assignation, and bedroom placements were standard throughout.

He threw her on the bed and her excitement mounted. He did not undress her but ripped off her skirts, kissing her hard and deep as he did. Her expensive blue silk dress was destroyed, but she did not care. He swiftly divested himself of his ornate hussar uniform and jumped on top of her. There were no words, only growls, grunts, and moans of pleasure. His hands and tongue roamed her body freely, and the heady sensations they provoked banished all her worries. When he entered her, his thrusts were fast and violent. She nearly passed out when the release came, yet she felt marvelously alive and refreshed. She was in a mood to talk, but Alfred rolled off with the contented smile of a cow and dropped off to sleep. A moment later, he was loudly snoring.

Her joy soured to frustration. Metternich would have talked with her. After staring at the ceiling for a period, she realized sleep would not come; her worries returned, doubled. Her heart ached and tears formed in her eyes.

She thought of little Vava, taken from her at birth. She had gotten pregnant at age 18 by a famous Swedish cavalryman, Count Gustave von Armfelt, when he was a guest at one of her mother's castles. Von Armfelt was also her mother's lover, and when she discovered the two of them *in flagrante delicto*, she had banished the Swede and beaten Wilhelmine. When Wilhelmine had turned up pregnant, her mother exiled her to the estate of Sagan and put out the story that she was recovering from a bad carriage accident. The birth of Adelaine Gustava, the child's formal name, had been beset by difficulties. The baby had survived, but Wilhelmine could never again have children.

She had bonded strongly with the child, but after two weeks her mother gave Vava to von Armfelt, who sent his illegitimate daughter to an estate in the Grand Duchy of Finland, controlled by the Russians. That had been many years ago. Vava was fourteen now, and not a day went by that Sagan did not try to picture what she looked like. Her efforts to wrest custody from von Armfelt had been expensive and unsuccessful. She herself had been married off to a nobleman she barely knew within a month of Vava's departure, her mother eager to chase away any whiff of scandal. Her husband had had but one talent, spending her fortune as quickly as he could.

Metternich had promised to pressure Alexander into obtaining custody, but the Austrian had been unsuccessful. Though Sagan cared for Metternich, that promise was the chief reason she had been his lover for the past year. But she had grown angry that his efforts had enjoyed no success. It should not have surprised her, since Alexander was Metternich's bitter enemy.

It was time to take a step she should have taken a long time ago. She would speak to the Czar next week, at the Four Elements Ball, to which they were both invited. Once that decision was made, her tension dissipated. She yawned, stretched, and drifted off into a deep, restorative sleep, unaware that a footman named Schazenbach, a spy for von Hager, had been listening outside the door and had heard the bedroom encounter.

The next morning, seated at her boudoir table, Sagan whispered her doubts out loud. God, what have I done?" An inner voice answered the question in a way she did not like. "You know what you love; you know what you need."

Her doubts deepened into misgivings when Alfred sent for his belongings and laid claim to her second-best bedroom. There would be no way to conceal this turn of events from Metternich. But then, Metternich had already failed her. Her eyes squeezed shut, and two glistening tears dropped onto her lap.

Chapter 23

By the second hour of the River Committee meeting, Pennywhistle's moods fluctuated between boredom and annoyance, punctuated at irregular intervals with stabs of back pain. Boredom because the members had been speechifying, substituting florid phrases for actionable specifics. Annoyance because not until they had finished their thundering perorations could a recess be called and the real business commence: discussing particulars one-on-one with individual members.

He was also unsettled by Sammie Jo's revelations about the hunting party. She had certainly done the world, and womankind in particular, a favor, and he was not in the least surprised that she had ruthlessly dealt with the despoilers. Nevertheless, he shuddered to think how infamy would attach to her if the extraordinary incident became common knowledge. Thank God she'd had the presence of mind to summon the Mekhitarist Monks. There had been no corpses to give rise to gossip and scandal.

He and Sammie Jo both wondered who had fired the anonymous shot from the woods, but speculation was pointless. Clearly, that person was also keeping quiet.

A laudanum ball beckoned seductively, but that was exactly the reason not to take one; opium promised pleasant oblivion but turned a mind to mush. It had transformed the poet Samuel Taylor Coleridge into an erratic eccentric and had likely contributed to Lord Byron's scandalous behavior.

The person he most wanted to speak with had arrived late. That struck him as odd, since von Steinwehr usually was as punctual as himself. Pennywhistle was already planning how to assassinate the man, but that would have to be set aside until he accomplished his mission for the crown to retrieve the Clarke Letters. He reminded himself that von Steinwehr was a murderer many times over, and he would be administering the same sentence a judge would hand down, if von Steinwehr's crimes ever made it to a court of law.

Strangely, the prospect of killing his brother's murderer held less appeal after Castlereagh had granted him official permission. Pennywhistle had killed before, but that had been in battle or part of his military duties. The initial desire for revenge had modulated as he came to realize that extralegal killing was at loggerheads with the legacy his brother had left behind. Peter had been a man of wisdom and persuasion, waging his wars with guile and words so that others did not have to fight with cannons and muskets. Peter had saved lives by preventing conflicts, whereas generals expended lives in battle.

The brothers had been estranged for many years. Thomas had been convinced that Peter was driven purely by avarice, repelled by his brother's public charade, which functioned as a cover for his travels and clandestine activities on behalf of the Crown. Peter would disappear for weeks at a time, purportedly to evaluate the potential profitability of new strikes at his copper mines. It was only after his murder that Pennywhistle realized how completely wrong he had been about his elder sibling. The demeanour of the profit-minded entrepreneur had been a very effective cloak for the valuable work he performed

Attaché Extraordinaire

for the government in secret, solving thorny diplomatic problems by unconventional means. Pennywhistle realized that his current assignment resembled his brother's work in that, if he accomplished the task, he could claim no public credit; but if he failed, Castlereagh would not hesitate to use him as a public scapegoat.

There was another issue that vexed him. Extralegal murder coarsened a man, even as it burdened his soul. Since his excursion to the Other Side, his guilt over past mistakes had vanished, as had his occasional tremors from too many battles. He had no wish to start acquiring a fresh set of either. But it seemed inevitable that, were von Steinwehr ever restored to Reichenau, he would kill again and again, with the impunity conferred by a ball and scepter.

Faced with an opponent like von Steinwehr, Peter Pennywhistle would have worked behind the scenes to rob him of his credibility and destroy his reputation to prevent his restoration. That method appealed to Pennywhistle, yet doing so would involve severing the Gorgon's affiliation with the Czar, potentially provoking Alexander's wrath, which would spill over into his negotiations with Castlereagh. No, von Steinwehr would have to be decommissioned with discretion, in such a way that no whisper of blame would fall on Castlereagh.

Pennywhistle's ears perked up at the absence of sound. Schildmann, the Austrian representative, had finally concluded his speech. Pennywhistle could now approach von Steinwehr with a reply to Alexander's asking price for backing the neutrality of the Scheldt Estuary. It would take all his reserve energy to negotiate with Von Steinwehr. He had had little sleep the two previous nights because he was playing ghost writer, forging an alternative table of *The Little Code*

Breaker and Pocket Cryptographer. Only the tenth decryption table could translate the Clarke Letters. It was difficult creating a convincing forgery that would not generate a message of mere gibberish. It had to give a translation that conveyed meaning, yet gave rise to misdirection, confusion, and uncertainty.

What he really needed was for von Steinwehr to reveal where the Clarke Letters were kept. After von Steinwehr stole the codebook, he would begin decryption promptly, but with luck, it would take a few days before he realized he had been outfoxed. He would have to lay the letters alongside the codebook for decryption. Once von Steinwehr and the letters were in the same room, Pennywhistle could accomplish both his missions.

Realistically, however, Pennywhistle presumed the place of translation would be hard to find and heavily guarded. Von Steinwehr would never do it at the Amelienberg, a palace riddled with secret passages, where servants—and spies —were in and out at all hours of the day and night. Castlereagh had warned him that the Russian delegation was thoroughly penetrated by Austrian spies. So, von Steinwehr would need a secure, private residence; but where?

Then it hit him, and he nearly clapped himself on the forehead for his stupidity. He had been so focused on Reichenau as a chess piece in the game that he had forgotten that von Steinwehr would have found a country residence after being ousted from his palace. Nobles always had subsidiary inheritances of small castles or elaborate hunting lodges.

There would also need to be access to Vienna: it could not be too far distant. The Danube was the fastest avenue of conveyance, so von Steinwehr's place was probably built along its banks. Those banks were flat in the city, but there were bluffs ten miles upriver, where castles commanded spectacular views, reliable water supplies, and defensibility. Yet, many of the castles were in ruins after decades of neglect— or worse, the forced billeting of Napoleon's troops. Vienna had been overrun twice, in 1805 and 1809.

There might be a way to find out the location of von Steinwehr's aerie in the next few minutes. He would just have to play to von Steinwehr's vanity, which was as outsized as his height.

Von Auersperg had just gaveled a recess. Pennywhistle rose from his chair and walked briskly over to von Steinwehr. *"Herr Kolonel,* I wonder if we might recommence our very pleasant earlier talk about... boundaries, in more private surroundings."

"Of course, Sir Thomas. I have news from my principal, and I suspect you have information from you own that you wish to convey."

Both men exited the room, stopped briefly to collect glasses of champagne, and proceeded to a small study that had been recently designated as a conference room. They each sank down in a green leather wingback chair and sipped champagne pensively. Each seemed to be waiting for the other to commence the conversation, neither wanting to appear too eager or to lose the advantage of mystery.

Pennywhistle broke the ice.

"It seems rather a shame to begin with bad news, given this excellent champagne, yet I am resolved to speak it, so we may move past it and proceed to more felicitous subjects. To be blunt, Lord Castlereagh cannot support the restoration of Reichenau at this time. Mind you, he does not rule it out," Pennywhistle lied, "but certain assurances would have to be made before he could be moved to your point of view."

"What might those assurances be?"

"Alexander's support for ending the slave trade, the restoration of the city of Krakow as a free republic, and a reduction in the indemnity for the late wars that will be charged to France."

Von Steinwehr frowned. He had hoped the Scheldt issue was of sufficient importance to force Castlereagh's hand on Reichenau. "I am disappointed to hear of Lord Castlereagh's position on Reichenau, but reassured to hear he is not beyond persuasion. Czar Alexander would be agreeable to releasing Krakow from his hold, if Lord Castlereagh agreed to return Ragusa to the Austrians."

That made sense and was certainly an offer of parity. Ragusa was a strategic port. "Lord Castlereagh would be agreeable to that if Czar Alexander would relinquish his claims on Malta as well."

"He would be willing to grant your nation free and unfettered control of that island."

"Then we are in agreement on that point. What of the others?"

"Support for ending the slave trade, however, could be problematic, Sir Thomas. Though it does not affect him directly, The Czar has a reasonable concern that interfering with Africa's slave markets might excite a yearning for freedom on the parts of Russian serfs. As you probably know, serfs are bound to estates by law. The Czar does not wish those laws to be challenged or questioned."

Here Pennywhistle had to exercise restraint. He did not approve of the way serfs were regarded as slaves in all but name. "That is understandable, *Herr Kolonel*. And yet, since the Czar has no Caribbean colonies, dare I hope that his position on the slave issue is not inviolable?"

Attaché Extraordinaire

"He might be moved, Sir Thomas, if there is a *quid pro quo*."

"Then that is an area for further discussion at a later time. If Czar Alexander can make his preferences known, I am confident that a way can be found forward on this point as well."

Pennywhistle realized that the subjects were moving far beyond the stated purview of the committee. It occurred to him that he was being used as a backchannel to Castlereagh. Such a development had advantages, in that sovereigns and foreign ministers had a dignity and prestige to maintain that sometimes limited frank discussion. Far better that any open disagreements or even shouting matches be limited to underlings, so that the face of the Congress would be seen as one of unity and harmony.

Von Steinwehr continued. "I am curious as to why Lord Castlereagh is concerned with reducing the French indemnity. I thought Britain and France were mortal enemies. The wars France started devastated Europe; they should pay the costs of repairing what they have broken.'

"Lord Castlereagh looks to the future, not the past. Burdening France with an enormous debt would result in the levying of heavy taxes, of the kind that could provoke desperate peasants into revolt. A prosperous France is a safe France. It is also easier for a thriving nation to make reparations than for a financially devastated one. I know the Czar is pleased that the royal line of the Bourbons has been restored to power, but he must know Louis's grip on the French throne is tenuous. Financial instability would further weaken that grip."

"That is a good argument, and the Czar might be willing to reduce his demand for reparations. But bear in mind that

Russia was invaded by Napoleon's troops and suffered far more in the way of losses than your high-minded Castlereagh can imagine or comprehend. The indemnities would have to render reparation to Russia."

"The Czar is a reasonable man," Pennywhistle said politely. "And your own arguments are cogent. Russia did, indeed, suffer depredations and losses such as Britain has not known in centuries. So, I will speak to Lord Castlereagh on the Czar's behalf in this matter. On to our third point, then. May Lord Castlereagh rely upon the Czar's preliminary support for a neutral Scheldt?

"You may, so long as you in turn continue to keep the matter of Reichenau front and center with your principal."

"I shall continue to call the matter to his attention until a satisfactory resolution has been reached." It was an honest enough commitment, though Castlereagh was never going to change his mind. "On, then, to more pleasant matters! I hope my wife will have a chance to meet your lady at the Razoumovsky Ball on New Year's Eve."

"Alas, no. My wife has taken ill and her physician has confined her to bed for an extended period."

"I am distressed to hear that." On the contrary, Pennywhistle was delighted. This was a prime opportunity to make a solicitous sounding inquiry. "Do you think a spot of country air would speed her recovery?"

"Kreigshammer always brightens her spirits, but she knows I need her counsel, even if it is delivered from bed. Since I cannot leave the city, she chooses to remain here. I am sure Lady Pennywhistle would do the same if she were in my wife's situation."

Attaché Extraordinaire

Pennywhistle nodded and rejoiced inwardly. He had the name of an estate! Now it was time to present his opponent with an open back door.

"Injuries of mine were recently aggravated and compel me to take a rest. Unfortunately, embassy business is brisk, so I shall not be able to take a brief holiday until a week from Friday."

Von Steinwehr's eyes flickered briefly. Had that bungler von Gilsa at least partially succeeded? More interestingly, did this mean that it was Pennywhistle himself who had dispatched von Gilsa?

Pennywhistle noted the reaction. He continued pleasantly, "My wife wants to do a bit of sightseeing, and so we have decided to take an afternoon cruise on Mr. Montgomery's excellent steamboat, a week from Friday. I find sketching a relaxing activity, one that will not hamper my recovery. I shall pursue my quiet interest while my wife enjoys the social life aboard." After a few more polite words, he excused himself.

His back was aching abominably. Pennywhistle went in search of a breath of fresh air and refreshment. He was not a main attraction at these events, which meant that he could absent himself from most of the side shows.

As for von Steinwehr, he could barely contain his excitement. The perfect opportunity to search for what he needed had just dropped into his lap. He already knew that Pennywhistle did not carry the code book upon his person. The city of Vienna was plagued by an epidemic of pickpockets, many of them highly skilled. No man of Pennywhistle's carefulness would risk the theft of so valuable an item; the book would be secured in the safest place he could command. The only question was whether the code book was kept in Pennywhistle's residence or at the embassy; he would have to arrange to have both places searched. Either way, he knew the exact day to act, and once the cypher was in his hands, he would be able to translate the damning letters in full and leverage all his demands. The universe was about to be set right.

Chapter 24

The next day, the weather continued its war between autumn and winter. Morning had dawned cold and snowy, whereas on the previous day temperatures in the low fifties had spawned a thaw that created small rivers on the cobblestones. That water had refrozen, and getting about required short, mincing steps to avoid becoming a speeding horizontal projectile.

Lady Leith and Earl Grosvenor leaned against each other for balance as well as affection. They were shopping for supplemental furniture for Pennywhistle's new residence. Since the furniture was needed immediately, they chose to visit the city's second-hand shops, rather than commission pieces from cabinet makers..

The term 'second hand' was correct yet misleading. The Congress had flooded Vienna with a vast array of wealthy people who were keeping the cabinet makers busy. The clientele was eager to display the styles deemed the most *au courant,* causing a rash of sell offs of recent constructions and fine pieces of workmanship. Those with discerning eyes could purchase very high-quality furniture for very reasonable prices.

Lady Leith knew what she wanted, but she did not know the city, and her knowledge of German was spotty. The Earl knew the city well and his command of German was superb. The Earl was happy to assist because he planned to make the outing as much a sightseeing tour of a city he loved as a shopping expedition. He had developed a great affection for Lady Leith, which surprised him. He had never really recovered from the death of his wife in childbirth. The murder of his beloved son at Peter Pennywhistle's side had created a seal round his heart as tight as a pauper's budget.

Until he had met Margaret, the only emotions he had allowed himself were grief, anger, and a thirst for vengeance. She had reawakened the gentle aspects of his character, and the rogue in the mirror that he saw each morning had gradually changed into a fellow that he liked and for whom there was hope. He was tired of being alone and knew she felt the same way.

They came from similar backgrounds, had equally distinguished pedigrees and social standing, and lived conservatively. At their age, potential children were not an issue, and matters of inheritance had been settled long ago.

Among the better classes, marriage was often a matter of the joining of estates and pedigree, where love played almost no role. He could cast all of that aside and instead follow the calling of his heart. A proposal would be precipitate, and he did not want to frighten Margaret away. This morning he sought "an understanding," and was looking for the right moment to broach the subject.

"I say, Margaret, that shop up ahead, Schindler's, lists a fine selection of desks in its newspaper advertisement. Since a man's desk generally houses items dear to him, why don't we begin our search here."

"A fine idea, Robert. Tom has very particular tastes in such matters, so I shall make a thorough survey of the items available before reaching a decision. I know he prefers English design, but since French furnishings are all the rage, perhaps we can introduce a little variety into his life. I was thinking of a desk with many compartments but limited gilt and filigree work."

"Grace and functionality in one package?"

"Exactly."

As they entered the store, Grosvenor caught a passing reflection of a man behind them in the store's front window. He had seen that face twice, earlier this morning-- once at the Café Central where they had had their morning repast and once when they had stopped to purchase a newspaper. The man's attire had attracted Grosvenor's attention; it was colorful, dandyish, and stood out like a beacon against the slowly falling snow. Seeing a strange face three times meant only one thing: they were being followed.

He had no idea who the man was. By his dress it was unlikely he was a footpad, but he might be connected to the shadowy figure who was Pennywhistle's nemesis—the man who had murdered his son Algernon.

He said nothing to Margaret as they entered the shop, but the protective side of his nature had been triggered. He would do nothing for the time being but keep a weather eye cocked to see how long their tail persisted.

Herr Schindler was a friendly gnome of a man in his mid-sixties, with little English but sprightly enthusiasm. He recognized that his customers were highborn. When Grosvenor announced that they were looking for a desk, one designed for a diplomat whose correspondence was extensive, Herr Schindler exclaimed that he had three possibilities, all formerly owned by diplomats.

John Danielski

He sensed a bond between the two customers, though the lack of rings indicated that they were not married. *Widowed people,* he thought. He and his current wife were very happy, and both had been widowed before marriage.

What followed next reminded Grosvenor of the old English folktale of *Goldilocks and the Three Bears.* The first desk was too small. It was in the Louis XIV style and had plenty of nooks and crannies but insufficient leg room for a man as tall as Pennywhistle.

The second was too large. It was a massive rococo entity in the Louis XVI style, festooned with lots of gilt and ornate mythological carvings but apparently built for a committee rather than one man.

The third was just right. It was an 8-foot-tall mahogany desk and bookcase combination, topped with a split pediment. A small statue of Minerva, Goddess of Wisdom, stood in the center of the pediment. The three foot wide desk portion featured a slant top and the bookcase had two large, vertical doors. The piece was in the Chippendale style practiced by the cabinetmakers in Philadelphia and was what Americans called a secretary. It had belonged to Thomas Jefferson during his time in Paris; he had tasked Parisian cabinet makers to create something that reminded him of home.

Lady Leith thought that owning a desk that had once belonged to an American president would gratify Pennywhistle's sense of history, but the statue of Minerva was the deciding factor in her decision. She knew of Pennywhistle's fascination with the sage Seneca and the Rome of the Julio-Claudians, making this piece the perfect choice. Roman tastes were enjoying a resurgence, as artifacts buried by Vesuvius found their way back into modern European commerce. Tom even wore his hair short and cropped, "*a la Titus,*" a style copied from 2nd century statues. His concessions to modernity were the sideburns that extended to his jawline, framing his face.

Once the sale had been concluded and arrangements made for delivery, Grosvenor asked Schindler if he had a quiet space where he and the lady might confer about additional purchases. Schindler provided a small alcove at the store front, shielded by tall bookcases from the main area.

Once they were secluded, the Earl said quietly, "Margaret, we are being followed. I wanted to make certain, and so did not tell you earlier. The fellow has been watching us the whole time we have been in here." He nodded to the bow window." Look across the street, at the corner of that three-story grey building. Do you see the occasional spark of sunlight?"

Margaret nodded.

"It is a reflection off his telescope. He is astonishingly bad at his job," he remarked critically. "Perhaps his presence has to do with what you have been telling me about the new staff at our residence."

"You mean, that several of them seem to be spies?"

"Yes, I think he represents an additional precaution on the part of their employer. It would make sense that their master would want to discover our habits and schedules. Are you up for a little play acting?"

"I think so, Robert. What do you have in mind?"

"I have a surprise that I was saving for later. Something... ah... hum... romantic. But now I see a way it may also serve an end we both wish, outfoxing the informants in the house."

"Romantic? I am intrigued, Robert, most intrigued."

"Ah. Then let us give him a show. He will not hear our words, but his glass will permit him to observe our actions, so we must exaggerate our expressions and gestures. To complete this bit of theatre, the deliverance of a kiss is required."

"And would that kiss be theatre or a true expression of deeper feelings?"

Grosvenor blushed as Lady Leith suppressed the sort of smile you would give an awkward schoolboy speaking to his first potential sweetheart. It was plain to her that his feelings were sincere, but that it had been a very long time since his heart had been touched and he did not want his manner to appear abrupt or inept.

"It cannot have escaped your notice that I admire you."

"I may be old, but I am far from blind. I was wondering when you would give voice to your thoughts. I am surprised it has taken this long. Let me assure you your feelings will not go unrequited."

Grosvenor let out a long sigh of relief. "I was afraid you would think me impetuous."

"At our age, impetuosity is a good thing."

"Then let me give you a demonstration! But first, we must position ourselves in front of the window. I would ask you to follow my lead."

"If it is the kind of lead I expect, I shall do so eagerly."

"What the spies must be able to tell their master is that *no one of consequence* will be in our residence from late morning to early afternoon on Friday. Then his minions can, like the mice in the proverb, play while the cat is away."

"That is ingenious, Robert. Let him sniff the gravy and tell his master that he can soon chew the meat."

Once he was certain that the observing glass was fixed on them, Grosvenor took Lady Leith's hands in his, drew her close, and shared a kiss with her which in any place but Vienna would have been considered scandalous.

She reciprocated warmly, not wanting the kiss to end.

Attaché Extraordinaire

When Robert drew back, he gasped, "I trust we have conveyed the first part of the message. Now for the surprise."

He reached into his coat and produced two tickets. He flourished them slowly, trusting that the time, place, and nature of the event would be noted through the glass of their unwanted observer, then announced, making sure to mouth the words distinctly, "I thought it would be a splendid idea if you and I could sightsee on the Danube by steamboat. With Tom and his wife, we could make up a foursome." *Sotto voce,* he murmured, "If you would be so kind as to act delighted in the manner of *Le Comedie Francaise?*"

Lady Leith threw up her hands in a gesture of exaggerated delight and exclaimed, "How wonderful! Oh, Robert, you think of *everything!*" This time they embraced, and the kiss they exchanged was deeper.

Across the street, their tail, the cynical Gabriel Fouché, nephew of Napoleon's chief of police, received the exact message Grosvenor intended to send. He was something of a libertine himself; von Steinwehr had used him to seduce Talleyrand's niece. Sexual conquest he understood, romance not at all. He was puzzled and slightly repelled by what he saw. Older folk were supposed to be long past such carryings on. If they did marry, he guessed they would spend their honeymoon just getting out of the carriage. No matter, he had what his master wanted and the faster he reported his results, the quicker would be the reward.

Grosvenor held Lady Leith close as he waited for the glint of the telescope to disappear from his peripheral vision. When it did, he kissed her hand and a smile illuminated his face like the noonday sun. "I was going to ask if we have an understanding, Margaret, but I believe I have received my answer."

John Danielski

Lady Leith giggled like a schoolgirl. "You would not be mistaken, Robert."

Chapter 25

The Four Elements Ball was proving the social event of what was already an extraordinary season. The crowded dance floor hosted at least three hundred celebrants clad in attire that was as expensive as it was colorful. All the ladies wore tiaras with gemstones that represented the colors of a chosen element: rubies and topazes for fire; sapphires and emeralds for water, with a few tiaras of moonstones or diamonds for the ladies who chose the vaporous or solid phases of the element; sapphires and diamonds for air. The Earth element was least represented, as it was deemed the least glamorous.

Princess Esterhazy, however, had decided that Earth took precedence, since all treasures come from it. Her tiara blazed with rare brown diamonds, and her dress was sewn with chocolate opals and threads of gold and silver. Countess Zichy had hit upon the novel concept of a dress that mimicked an erupting volcano, with swirls of brown and black silk for the skirt, red silk embracing her *décolletage,* and more red silk to simulate rivulets of lava that emphasized her curves.

The military men wore full dress uniforms in a variety of splendid colors.

Spectators crowded the Corinthian-columned white and gold balcony. four thousand candles illuminated the room, their dancing lights glinting off the jewels worn by the women and the ornate epaulettes, medals, and orders of chivalry worn by the men.

Count Razoumovsky had lent the services of his orchestra, one of the largest and most experienced in a city famous for its music, and the ball had opened with a polonaise. This slow-moving dance was more of a stately procession. It was intended to allow the participants to show off their splendid gowns, uniforms, and civilian habiliments, as well as to give the spectators plenty of opportunity to view royalty, aristocratic *demi-mondes*, and distinguished soldiers. The charged atmosphere radiated romance and intrigue. A minuet followed, and then a quadrille, cotillion, and ecossaise, an energetic dance in which couples faced each other in two parallel lines.

Metternich had come alone and watched from the spectator's gallery. Sure enough, Sagan was dancing with von Wildeschgratz. He scowled in jealousy, but his heart whispered that he had to speak to her.

There was an intermission of fifteen minutes after the ecossaise, to allow the dancers to recover their breath and for participants to prepare for the Four Elements Ceremony. Metternich spotted Alexander, surrounded by a circle of women doting on his every word. He sneered, knowing that the women were attracted by crude power, rather than any elegance of deportment or actual intelligence of speech. He knew that Alexander cared nothing for the women he bedded. They were simply shiny objects to be collected and then discarded when he grew bored. He wondered if Alexander knew that his wife, the Czarina Elizabeth, was sleeping with his chief advisor on the Polish Question, Adam Krzytowski. He probably did, but simply did not care.

A quirk of acoustics allowed him to overhear a snippet of Alexander's conversation. "So, madam, I am sorry your husband is away on a diplomatic mission, but might I be his stand in tonight when the ball ends?" That was brazen, even for Alexander, but effective; the woman nodded her head and smiled. Other women in the circle looked disappointed.

Bagration was present, of course, surrounded by a crowd of male admirers. She had once been Metternich's lover, and he suspected that her child, Klementina, was his own. She had let it be known that she would be interested in welcoming him back to her life, but he had no interest in any woman but Sagan. Bagration was beautiful, but she bestowed her bedroom favors freely, and her most recent bedmate had been his hated rival, the Czar. Her dress certainly lived up to her nickname of "The Naked Angel", being more a negligee than a frock: low cut, clinging, and of an expensive fabric so sheer that viewers had no doubt as to the nature of her charms.

Talleyrand had not danced at all, which was unsurprising for a man with a club foot. He spent the time talking with key figures when they were not engaged in dancing. He was likely building support for the preservation of Saxony.

Talleyrand's niece had danced mostly with the handsome Count Clam-Martinez, who had once saved Bonaparte's life. From the joy on her face, Metternich thought a relationship might be developing.

Charles Stewart, Castlereagh's wayward younger brother, was living up to his reputation as the colorful rogue of the Conference. He was talking loudly and making extravagant gestures. A crowd of men near him laughed raucously at what was likely a crude joke. Metternich considered him annoying but realized he served a purpose. Charles could float ideas that his reserved brother could never be seen to articulate and which Castlereagh could deny if they proved unpopular.

Charles also served as conduit, to funnel ideas to his brother that foreign diplomats were unwilling to present officially.

Two heralds blew trumpets, proclaiming the start of the Four Elements Ceremony. Dancers moved to the edges of the ballroom, leaving the center clear. A procession of forty eight women entered.

Twelve women representing air were attired in sky blue dresses with wispy wings attached to the back, meant to depict winds. Twelve women representing fire came next, dressed in crimson satin with sashes of ruby red round their waists and headdresses of scarlet and gold, adorned with gold jewelry. Each carried a small torch. The twelve posing as water succeeded them, wearing green dresses accented with coral. All had seashells entwined in their hair.

The best, in Metternich's opinion, came last. This delegation represented earth, led by Sagan. She, like her band, was dressed in brown velvet, her impressive breasts barely concealed by diamonds. She wore an elaborate circular headdress that featured white roses, posies, and garlands interspersed with even more diamonds.

The group promenaded the circuit of the ballroom floor as the orchestra performed "*Spring*" from Vivaldi's *The Four Seasons*. Metternich surveyed Sagan closely during its ten-minute playing time. She walked with queenly dignity, a faerie sovereign surveying her court and seeing all men as supplicants. He certainly considered himself one and wondered when he would have a chance to plead his case in private. He noted von Windischgratz and Alexander eyeing her with lust; his blood boiled as his heart ached.

When "*Spring*" finished, the parading Four Elements were back where they started. Sagan stepped out in front and confidently recited a poem from memory... in English! It was

Attaché Extraordinaire

intended to showcase her mastery of languages, although only half of the crowd possessed enough English to fully understand her words. However, the rest could make out enough cognate words in French to get a general idea what she was saying.

"The fire, earth, and air did contest," she began,
"which was strongest, noblest, and best.
Who was of greatest use and mightiest force.
In placid terms they thought now to discourse,
That in due order each her turn should speak.
But enmity this amity did break."

Metternich noted Bagration staring at Sagan, daggers in her eyes.

"All would be chief, and all scorn'd to be under
Whence issu'd winds & rains, lightning & thunder.
The quaking earth did groan, the Sky lookt black
The Fire, the forced Air, in sunder crack;
The sea did threat the heav'ns, the heavn's the earth.
All looked like a Chaos or new birth.

Sagan's sister Dorothée mouthed the words silently in time with her sister. She, too, was a devotee of the works of Anne Bradstreet, the first published poet of the New World. It was typical of her sister to choose the work of a woman rather than a man.

"Fire broiled Earth, & scorched Earth it choaked
Both by their darings, water so provoked

John Danielski

> That roaring in it came, and with its source
> Soon made the Combatants abate their force.
> The rumbling hissing, puffing was so great
> The worlds confusion it did seem to threat.

Alexander's eyes sparkled in admiration, while von Wildeschgratz's revealed his puzzlement; he understood not a word of what she was saying.

> "Till gentle Air, Contention so abated
> That betwixt hot and cold, she arbitrated
> The others difference, being less did cease
> All storms now laid, and they in perfect peace
> That Fire should first begin, the rest consent,
> The noblest and most active Element."

The women representing fire bobbed their torches up and down.

"Wonderful!" shouted Stewart drunkenly. He began clapping violently, and it was infectious. The crowd joined him enthusiastically, clearly delighting Sagan. Metternich was surprised that she did not curtsy in acknowledgement. The promenaders dispersed, mingling with the crowd. Sagan headed toward a punch bowl, alone. Metternich dashed down the stairs, hoping to intercept her before she was overwhelmed by well-wishers and admirers.

Alas, by the time he reached the floor, he was too late. She had not, in fact, been headed toward the punchbowl but toward the Czar, who stood close to it. Metternich moved through the crowd, trying to get within earshot without either of the two detecting his presence.

Attaché Extraordinaire

Sagan ignored the ladies crowded round Alexander and strode boldly up to him, disregarding their expressions that told her she was unwelcome. Her own expression suggested she was a woman on a mission. Metternich fervently hoped he was wrong about what she intended, and what price she was willing to pay.

"Your Imperial Majesty, might I have a word with you?"

"Of course, Duchess, I always have time to speak with a woman of discernment. A most impressive performance, by the way."

The women standing near him frowned.

The orchestra conductor rang a small bell, signaling that the waltz, an intimate dance which was proving the hit of the season, would begin in two minutes. It was time for people to find partners.

"Perhaps we may have that word while we dance," suggested Alexander. He gave a grand, courtly bow.

"I should be honored and delighted, Your Imperial Majesty," Sagan murmured as she curtseyed.

Alexander took her arm and moved onto the dance floor. All eyes followed them, none more closely than Metternich's. He felt a tap on his shoulder. Turning, he found Bagration had come up behind him so quietly he had not noticed her approach.

"Klemens, would you honor me with this dance?"

"You are being very forward this evening, Catherine, but I accept," said Metternich with a diplomatic smile.

"One has to be, since you have repeatedly declined invitations to attend my salon."

"Need I remind you, I have been busy."

John Danielski

"Surely not so busy as to spare a few moments for the mother of your child. She is doing well, by the way. Very precocious, as I imagine you were, at six."

Metternich's eyebrows arched. "I am pleased for you, but surprised by your assurance, and that you waited so long to inform me. Do you expect support or acknowledgment?"

"Of course not, but since she looks and acts so much like you, I thought perhaps you and I might explore the possibilities of getting reacquainted."

"You seem to have been become acquainted with a variety of men of late. You will forgive me if I choose not to join the queue."

Bagration spoke pleasantly, but there was the hint of a scowl in her voice. "Don't play the moralist, Klemens, it does not suit you. Let us make this dance a start." She took Metternich's hand and led him onto the dance floor.

The music commenced and a sea of couples began a series of sensual, slow revolves, proceeding counterclockwise. Each man held his partner's hand and waist with an intimacy that had shocked many when the waltz had first been introduced to Vienna a decade before.

Alexander completed four circles with Sagan before he spoke. "So, Duchess, what is it you wish to say?"

Metternich guided his dance with Bagration close to Alexander's with Sagan. Each couple saw the other.

"There is a matter of great importance to me that I wish resolved. I could use your help getting custody of my daughter."

"I would be happy to give it, but with the recent death of her father, her situation is... complicated. I will grant you an audience so I can explain in detail."

Attaché Extraordinaire

Metternich was stunned. He had thought Vava's father long dead! How much else had Sagan not told him?

Sagan smiled in relief. "Your Imperial Majesty is very kind. I am at your disposal."

"Shall we make it tomorrow at 11, at your apartments in the Palm Palace?" said Alexander, purposely raising his voice so Metternich would hear.

"Perfect," replied Sagan.

Metternich frowned. Eleven had been the usual time for his morning *tete-a-tete* with Sagan, up until a week ago. Alexander was aware of this and had chosen the time to spite him.

Metternich completed the rest of the dance with lead feet and a heavy heart. His earlier resolve to speak with Sagan had deserted him. In return for helping with Vava, Alexander would no doubt gain entrance to Sagan's bed and probably demand that she break things off, once and for all, with Metternich. The Czar was just that petty.

When the dance ended, the sad look on Metternich's face was not lost on Bagration.

"You should not waste your time courting such a worthless woman," Bagration observed coldly. "Why chase after someone who no longer wants you when you have someone in front of you who wants you very much?"

Metternich looked her straight in the eye. "I desire something more substantial than what you offer. I know you were with Alexander two nights ago, and that the commitment you pretend to offer would not last a week. You may flirt with fidelity, but in the end, you will always revert to your true nature, and that involves multiple lovers. I do not judge you, but I do understand you."

Metternich felt tears forming in his eyes as he viewed Sagan talking with Alexander.

"I must go, Catherine. It was a mistake to come. I face mountains of work and I must not waste time on foolish dancing. I wish you a pleasant night." He bowed curtly, about faced, and exited the ballroom.

Bagration sighed angrily. *Damn the man*, she thought. *Why won't he listen? My darling Klementina already has a fortune, but that is no substitute for a father. She deserves happiness.*

In a rare moment of self-reflection she wondered, *Is this about my daughter or about me? Do I want Metternich simply because I cannot have him?*

Alexander came up behind Bagration and tapped her on the shoulder. She turned around to confront a wolfish smile.

"He is not worth your efforts, Catherine. But if you really want him, consider substituting the stick for the carrot. You might remind Metternich that you possess many secrets about Austria; acquired in your salons and your boudoir. Secrets that you could broadcast if you were of a mind to do so."

Bagration looked surprised.

"Whether you succeed with that stick does not affect our arrangement, Catherine. I am perfectly content with our casual encounters."

Bagration cast a demure look at Alexander, but there was steel in her voice when she said, "I also am content with our arrangement, but that would change if you become involved with Sagan."

"Jealousy ill becomes you, Catherine, but you are getting ahead of yourself. I merely seek to be a gracious sovereign; helping a subject with a problem. I assure you, I have no other designs."

Attaché Extraordinaire

"You forget, I know you, Alexander. You like trophies. However, your point about the stick is well taken, and I shall consider it."

Dorothée noted her sister's talk with Alexander and wondered what she was up to. Her sister had seemed satisfied with von Windeschgratz, though he was her inferior to her in every way. She also knew of her sister's deep involvement with Metternich; she guessed his departure had involved wounded feelings. Dorothée surmised her sister wanted something from Alexander. She would inform Talleyrand tomorrow.

She also spotted von Windeschgratz conversing animatedly with Stewart. He had not danced the waltz but had spent the time talking and laughing with a variety of ladies who swooned over his uniform and physique, if not his conversation. Stewart and von Windeschgratz seemed to be having a fine time: two minds without a single thought. Not surprising, since they were both cavalrymen, and shared similar passions.

Four trumpets sounded, announcing that the supper, served buffet style, was ready.

Though the supper offered ices, broths, sweets, and innumerable delicacies, neither Sagan nor Bagration displayed much of an appetite. Both had agendas and both were making plans on just how to carry them out.

By the time a deeply distraught Metternich had reached the Hofsburg, he, too, had an agenda. He would win Sagan back, no matter the cost. That cost might involve not just stopping a rival but eliminating him forever. He would challenge Alexander to a duel.

Chapter 26

No home or palace of note was complete without a music room. Some were string quartet size while others could house a full orchestra. The wing of the von Auersperg Palace that the Pennywhistles rented featured one with green and gold filigreed walls hung with 15-foot tapestries, each showcasing one of the seasons. The most prominent feature of the room was a 7-foot-long grand piano weighing twelve hundred pounds. It produced tones worthy of Beethoven, though it was currently being played by claws instead of hands. Plymouth danced merrily upon its keys in rhythm with Gabriel's trumpet and Johnny's recorder. The music room doubled as Plymouth's playground. The high ceiling gave him plenty of room for flight.

Parrots are intelligent creatures with a well-developed sense of curiosity, so the room was equipped with balls, small ladders, hanging wicker baskets, and various sorts of puzzles that Johnny and Gabriel had collected on several shopping expeditions. Plymouth's favorite amusement was a large wooden maze with three-foot high walls, six feet by nine feet. A century old, it had started life as a landscape architect's 1/100th scale model for the puzzle garden built at von Auersperg's country estate, which featured both a central solution and a back exit, primarily for use by the gardeners.

Attaché Extraordinaire

Johnny had discovered it in a basement room off the kitchens. Intrigued by the chance to test Plymouth's intelligence, Pennywhistle and Sammie Jo had moved it to the music room. Each time Plymouth had successfully navigated a portion, avoiding the lures of blind turns, Johnny had rewarded him with a cashew, the bird loving the challenge. Within a week Plymouth had mastered the maze, and walking it soon became his favorite activity—after dancing.

Gabriel had discovered Bach, thanks to the Earl, and Pennywhistle had purchased some of Bach's early compositions for Gabriel, since he read music as well as the printed word. Johnny did not read music, but he had a good sense of harmony and supplied a pleasing, intuitive counterpoint on his recorder. Today the measured, mathematical cadences of Bach's *Allegro ma non Tanto* filled the music room. Gabriel reluctantly lowered his trumpet when the tall case clock at the corner of the room struck two. "I could play for hours, Johnny, but Sir Thomas asked me to exercise Spartan this afternoon, since he will be away. I figure you'd want to tag along and help out. You've been doing right fine riding mares, and I think today just might be the day that you move up to a stallion. Spartan is real forgiving to new riders, not an ornery bone in his body."

"I would love to ride Spartan, Gabriel!"

"Then we best be about our business. I think Plymouth will be fine with his toys for a couple of hours."

As if in agreement, Plymouth flew down from the piano, landing in front of the labyrinth and marching in slow circles. "Dark, dark!" he squawked.

"What does that mean?" asked Gabriel.

"He wants the storage cloth thrown over the top. It's more challenging that way."

"That's a mighty clever bird."

"Truly, he is, Gabriel."

Johnny picked up the tarp, laid it over the top of the labyrinth, placed a small tray of cashews at the back exit of the labyrinth for a reward, then bent down and spoke fondly to Plymouth. "We will be leaving now, Plymouth. Behave yourself!" He handed Plymouth a cashew, which the bird took in a claw and devoured. Johnny pointed at the labyrinth. "You know where to find more!"

"I do! I do!"

Johnny rose and smiled. "Now let's do some riding. I want you to show me that Lippizaner Piroutte move from the Spanish Riding School."

"My pleasure, Johnny, but it's going to take a while to master, just like it took Plymouth a while to solve the maze." The bird, hearing his name, flew to Gabriel's shoulder and affectionately nibbled his hair, accompanying his two friends towards the door to see them off.

After Gabriel and Johnny left, a sudden gust of wind hit the French doors to the balcony. It should have had no effect, as the doors were usually secured with a box lock. But today that gust opened a gap. A second blast followed, blowing the doors wide open, admitting not just cold.

Medusa, von Steinwehr's peregrine falcon, blazed through the opening, emitting a shrill cry.

Plymouth heard, glanced up, and knew he was the peregrine's target. While the falcon was not much larger in size, it was a predator, while Plymouth was a peaceable beast who consumed nuts and berries. The entrance to the labyrinth and safety lay only steps away, but his instinct told him he would not reach it in time.

Just as the peregrine's talons extended to catch and break Plymouth's back, Medusa was set upon by three angry ravens. The ravens attacked because they were defending a nest on the balcony, which Medusa had threatened in passing. She recovered and soared to the top of the room, prepared to do battle. While the hawk and ravens swirled in a mad farrago, Plymouth darted inside the maze.

The ravens shrieked as they whirled, swirled, and pecked at the interloper. Their numbers, and their large size, would have driven off most falcons, but Medusa was a Valkenswaard variant, and they never yielded. She turned tighter and faster than her opponents. She counter-attacked viciously, breaking one bird's neck and ripping a gash along the wing of a second, causing the third to squawk and retreat in terror, closely followed by the wounded second.

Medusa resumed her search for her quarry and landed in front of the labyrinth. She sensed Plymouth was inside, but the labyrinth confused her. She hesitated, and then tentatively entered. It was dark, but she had excellent night vision, unlike a parrot, and she could hear a rustling ahead of her. She stalked five more paces, then halted when she came to the first bend. The path split in two directions, and she was uncertain which to take. She *craaaed* her frustration.

Hearing his enemy behind him in the maze and scenting the harsh odor of a predator, Plymouth exited quietly, ignoring the cashews.

Plymouth had the advantage of knowing the room. He had explored the space thoroughly, particularly from above, and he knew a secret which might provide him a defense. He silently took flight and landed atop the large tapestry depicting winter.

John Danielski

The heavy woolen tapestry was suspended from the wall by three cords, all badly frayed; this tapestry, the oldest, was over 100 years old, and the casual servants had not had the tapestries cleaned nor mended. It was impossible for anyone on the ground to know that it was just a matter of time before the cords gave way. Plymouth just had to help them along.

He surveyed the labyrinth below and reasoned that the fallen tapestry would cover its entrance. He began vigorously pecking away at the cord that was the most threadbare. It gave way and the tapestry sagged. Frantic pecking at the second cord severed it next. The drag on the third cord increased. Plymouth alighted on that portion of the tapestry and waited.

Medusa was backing out of the labyrinth, wary of what she sensed was a trap. Plymouth saw her tail feathers and pecked madly, literally for dear life.

Medusa looked up, but by the time she saw the threat, the heavy tapestry was already descending. The cloth cascade half-crushed the majestic falcon, and its smothering weight suffocated her.

Plymouth waited, then descended on the tapestry. He walked around for a bit, making sure that what lay under was truly dead. Satisfied that he had pulled the wool over his enemy's eyes, he flew to the labyrinth's exit to claim his reward. Cashews had never tasted so good.

Pennywhistle arrived home unexpectedly; he had forgotten an important document. A presentiment of something wrong gripped him and intuitively guided him to the music room, mere minutes after the avian battle had ended. The fallen tapestry surprised him, but the rapidity with which Plymouth flew to his shoulder and clung to it in deep agitation surprised him even more. A dead raven added to the puzzlement.

Attaché Extraordinaire

"Look, look!" squawked Plymouth, inclining his head toward the tapestry.

Pennywhistle wondered what secret the heavy wool hid and bent down to find out. Pulling it back, he was astonished to find a dead falcon. He examined it closely; it looked familiar. Then it came to him: he had seen it on *Speedwell*! The bird was a minion of von Steinwehr's, but why on earth was she here? He could not have been a target, nor could the code book. Plymouth? His eyebrows shot skyward. Was his opponent so petty that he dispatched one pet to finish off another? A proxy war?

He rubbed his chin in thought, and then walked over to the French doors to shut them. He paused, musing. During winter, they were kept latched. He checked the mechanism, and it was sound. No wind could have opened the way to the falcon. There must have been human agency, and he knew with absolute assurance that neither Gabriel not Johnny would have imperiled the beloved bird by opening the French doors to cold draughts.

***

Ten hours later, von Steinwehr stared forlornly into the starry sky, willing his beloved Medusa to return. He had sent a message with very specific directions to one of his agents, taking advantage of Pennywhistle's absence and the windy day.

His wife stepped onto the balcony and spoke in a voice of compassion mixed with anger. "She is not coming back, and all the wishing in the world will not cause her to reappear. You were out of your mind to send her. It's the mania, isn't it?"

"I know I should not have done it, but I felt I had to take something from him that he cared for! He is so smugly self-composed that I wanted him to feel the pain of loss, even if only in a small way. I wanted to give him a taste of the pain that I feel every day, over the loss of Reichenau. You told me how much everyone in that household loved that parrot, and so…"

"I did not tell you so that you could give him a foretaste of our plans, you fool!" she hissed.

Von Steinwehr's startled face became that of a child slapped by a mother who never hit anyone.

Ingrid's tones gentled and she put her arm around her husband. "Come to bed, Klaus. This phase will pass. You need sleep so your reason will awaken. Nothing more can we do this night. Trust me!"

"I do, always."

She took him by the hand and gently eased him onto their wide bed. She stroked his forehead and whispered, "Sleep, sleep, sleep."

His eyes flickered, and obediently he passed from waking into the Kingdom of Morpheus.

Chapter 27

Pennywhistle's nerves sang an electric protest as goosebumps pebbled his arms. His shoulder muscles bunched, and needles of pain made his back feel like a pincushion. He clasped and unclasped his hands compulsively; what he was about to do was a terrible risk. He was about to put the codebook, which he had safeguarded with his life and honor, for which his brother had sacrificed his own life, into the hands of a stranger.

It came down to how much he trusted Deborah, and if Deborah's faith in Herr Schurz was well founded or misplaced. His instincts approved, but his mind warned him that the next step was still a grave risk.

The printer he was about to meet had requested advance information about Pennywhistle, which Deborah had supplied. He apparently wanted to be certain that any information he shared with Pennywhistle, an accredited diplomat, would not be passed on to either Imperial authorities or officials of the city government.

Schurz had said this man was good at handling special printing and painting jobs that required the utmost discretion. Pennywhistle took that to mean he was a practiced forger whose skills were good enough to attract a steady stream of clients but whose prudence ensured that both his name and theirs remained hidden from authorities. He probably ran a legitimate shop most of the time and was willing to take a step to the other side, if a client offered sufficient remuneration. The man went by the name of "Schmidt." No Herr attached, and no first name. This was a man who valued his anonymity.

Schmidt's studio lay three miles from Pennywhistle's new residence. That he would refer to it as a studio rather than a shop told Pennywhistle that he considered himself something of an artist. Pennywhistle acted as if he were being followed, though it was problematic, given his precautions. He'd had one of the house-servants dressed as himself enter Lady Leith's carriage, which then moved off in a direction opposite from Pennywhistle's real destination. He hoped that any tail would follow that carriage for hours. Then Gabriel had taken the secondary carriage out, ostensibly to go shopping, and Pennywhistle, dressed inconspicuously in civilian clothes, had entered the carriage from a side street. Even so, he instructed Gabriel to take a circuitous route to Schmidt's studio, doubling back occasionally to see if he had been followed. It tripled the time necessary to reach Schmidt, but he felt safer for doing so.

He carried the codebook in an inside buttoned flap of his buff watch coat. He carried two pocket pistols and wore a short colichemarde sword. He was prepared to kill if anything went wrong.

Schmidt's studio was in a dingy warehouse district on the Danube River; well away from the grander buildings of the city. It was marked with a small, heavily weathered sign, Transworld Exports. Superficially, that designation was so vague that it could mean whatever a passerby took it to mean. Pennywhistle took it as a hidden bit of artistic hubris; the man behind the sign created products exported to many types of clients, inhabiting many different worlds.

Attaché Extraordinaire

He alighted twenty yards from the entrance, checking the street carefully to make sure there were no minders disguised as street urchins. Satisfied he was alone, he told Gabriel to move the carriage to a nearby alley but hold himself ready to move at a moment's notice.

He pounded on the studio door three times. He heard footsteps, locks being opened, and the sound of a pistol being full cocked. The door swung partly open, a chain restraining it, and a face peeked through the opening. Pennywhistle was confronted by a man who was his own age, surprisingly handsome, with grey eyes that reflected both suspicion and the dreamy conjectures of a born artist.

The eyes scanned him, and then relaxed. "You match the description given me, Sir Thomas. I hope my precautions have not upset you, but I have survived by being very, very careful." He removed the chain and opened the door fully. "Please come in, Sir Thomas."

"Thank you. Your wariness reassures me, Schmidt. I can see that what I was told about you was also correct."

Pennywhistle entered and was shown up a long flight of stairs leading to a large room, brightly lit from three large skylights. It was a factory of a kind, a combination atelier, print shop, and cookery. In addition to easels, canvases, and myriad jars of exotic ingredients from which could be created every color of the rainbow and dozens more, the room had a printing press and row upon row of type trays, containing many fonts which Pennywhistle had never seen. There were large stocks of printing paper of various types, quality, and age. Two large ovens stood in the corner, but they were clearly not for baking bread.

A long bench at the back of the room contained at least 100 bottles of ink in varied colors, as well as numerous pens and brushes varying from coarse to superfine. Just what you'd expect from a practiced forger.

But all of that only briefly commanded Pennywhistle's attention. Three partly finished paintings on easels caused him to blink hard. They were of a blind old man, a laughing young man in armor, and an aged cleric with a long, aesthetic face. One appeared to be a Rembrandt, one a Hals, and one an El Greco. Each was painted in the exact style of an old Master. Pennywhistle would likely have been completely duped by the finished products if he had seen them in an art gallery. He wondered why he was being allowed to view them.

"One picture is worth a thousand words, Sir Thomas. Rather than prate on and on about my skill, I thought I would simply show you. I plan on charging a considerable price for my services, and I deemed it likely that you would forego tedious and time-consuming negotiations if you saw a manifestation of my talents. My business may sometimes flirt with the strict definition of honesty, but I would have lost my livelihood long ago if I did not have a well-deserved reputation for brilliance and delivering promised goods on time."

"You are indeed a master, though it seems rather sad that you have chosen to be known for copying the talents of others rather than establishing a reputation of your own. I am certain that your unique style, whatever it is, would find much favor."

"Perhaps, but I have no wish to spend years as a starving artist. People would only pay a pittance for my work, while the great and mighty are willing to pay small fortunes for the works of men whose artistic merits they only dimly understand. Most of my clients buy these paintings, not because they love the artist's visions, but because they have been told that possession an of Old Master is prestigious. My work is sufficiently lucrative that I can retire into private life when the Congress is done. And then I shall paint as I will. As it happens, I enjoy working in the style of the Old Masters, depicting nature, men, women, and the realms of allegory as they would have, had they possessed my vision. When viewers praise what they see on the walls of my clients, they praise me and my work, and I take satisfaction in that."

"I agree it is regrettable that artists of merit rarely enjoy prominence and remuneration in their lifetimes. Now about my book..."

"Please, Sir Thomas, bring it over to my work bench and let me examine it. It will take me a few minutes to give you a preliminary assessment."

Pennywhistle did as Schmidt asked. Schmidt bade him alight in an uncomfortable chair while he sat down behind his workbench. He accepted the volume as carefully as if he were handling a new-born babe. He looked at the cover and rotated the book several times. He thumbed through the pages, stopping now and then to utter an *Ah* or an *Ooh*.

He put the book down on the table and took out a large magnifying glass. He went through the slim volume page by page, his grey eyes lighting up as he did so. This was a man who enjoyed his work.

The process took thirty minutes. Pennywhistle said nothing, not wanting to disturb his concentration. The delay reassured him. This was a careful man who would work hard to get things right.

Pennywhistle withdrew from a pocket a sheet of paper over which he had labored many hours. It contained the altered tenth decryption table, the one that would render the Clarke Letters confusing and useless. "There is one more detail to the job I need done. Can you substitute this chart for the one on page eighty nine?"

Schmidt took the page and studied it, then compared its chart to the original. He placed the paper beside the book, then looked up with a smile of satisfaction on his face. "I can make the copy with the substitution, but it will take two weeks."

"I must have it sooner than that. Money is no object."

"Four hundred Thalers will get it done in one week."

"Done," Pennywhistle said resignedly, knowing he had been extorted. "You could buy a Caravaggio for that, but then, why would you, when you could create one yourself?"

"I prefer your JMW Turner, Sir Thomas. He is an artist in transition and fascinating to watch, moving from the short, precise brush strokes of the traditional artist to broad, sweeping ones. He is less concerned with accuracy than creating an impression of the mood a scene evokes."

Pennywhistle nodded at the mention of his favorite artist. "So, you consider his work a kind of..." Pennywhistle searched for a suitable word... "impressionism?"

"A fine characterization, Sir Thomas: Turner maybe the herald of a new era in art. The works of such a man are harder to duplicate than those of artists long dead whose styles are necessarily fixed."

Schmidt scrutinized the first few pages of the code book, then said, "This book was originally printed in Amsterdam forty years ago. Its font style is little used today, but I have the type."

Pennywhistle recalled that Amsterdam was the greatest printing center on the Continent. Obscure and outré works were a specialty.

"The paper can be matched from my stocks. To age the book suitably, it will have to be thrice baked in one of my ovens. The cover will have to be reconstructed by hand.

Attaché Extraordinaire

Weights on certain pages will give the book the unevenness that you would expect from an old volume. I will add some wormholes and page tears."

"You are indeed thorough."

"When you have to fool czars and kings, you pay attention to little touches."

"I cannot tell you why this book is important, though I am sure a perceptive man like yourself may hazard a few guesses from its title."

"I find guessing to be a dangerous indulgence, Sir Thomas. In my line of work, the less I know the better. I prefer to focus on the product, not the content. Now I must ask you for the first half of my payment. The second I shall require upon delivery."

Pennywhistle extracted a leather pouch from his watch coat and carefully doled out ten gold Napoleons, untraceable to the embassy accounts. He handed them to Schmidt, who beamed. "Art may satisfy the soul, Sir Thomas, but it does not put food upon the table."

"I must ask that when you are not working on my book, you must keep it under lock and key."

"I can guarantee you that. I will close my studio until you return."

"I shall call upon you in one week at," Pennywhistle opened his Blancpain, "9 am."

"That will do. Now I think a celebration is in order. I realize champagne is traditional, but in my line of work I need a clear head and a steady hand. Do you prefer coffee or tea? I have several varieties of both, though I prefer Brazilian coffee."

Pennywhistle smiled. "Brazilian coffee is my favorite."

John Danielski

"One thing occurs to me. Given the title of the book, men using it might be under considerable pressure. I think assorted sweat stains might increase the degree of verisimilitude. What do you think?"

Pennywhistle chuckled. "An excellent touch."

"I understand much about human nature, Sir Thomas. It is why I am so successful. When recreating a painting it is wise to give the client a less than perfect copy. They expect that the work has made many journeys, rather than the single one from the creator's studio. It is also why most of my copies are never signed. Rembrandt signed only about half of his paintings. The lack of a signature also obviates the legal charge of fraud. A man may believe what he wishes about a newly acquired trophy in the absence of definitive proof."

"I am guessing that you wish you could sign your own name to the copy of my volume."

"I do, Sir Thomas, for this will be a work of art. But my vanity is gratified by the fact that my works hang in the halls of nobles and royalty. I do not know for what purpose you intend my copy of your book, but I understand it will serve some important purpose, and that is in itself a reward."

<h1 style="text-align:center">Chapter 28</h1>

Four hours after his visit to Schmidt, Pennywhistle was hunched over his embassy desk, swotting his way through several mountains of paper. He might be on a special mission for the Prince Regent, but he was still a senior civil servant. As His Britannic Majesty's Naval Attaché, he faced a steady stream of petitioners, some official, but most merchants with a complaint. The official ones generally wanted clarification about the Royal Navy's view on a particular aspect of maritime law, often involving trade with their nation. The rest sought some private relief, usually compensation for ships they believed had been unjustly seized as prizes. The papers seemed to have a life of their own, gifted with the power of reproduction. Just as one pile was dealt with, another magically appeared to take its place.

The pain in his back was particularly bad this morning, and the vision of a laudanum ball danced in his head. His physician had prescribed laudanum in London, but after three days' use, Pennywhistle found his thinking occluded, his perceptions dulled, and his sleep disrupted. Laudanum was derived from the Indian continent's export of opium, and doctors prescribed it for its pain-dulling properties. He fought the temptation, reminding himself that the meditation he had learned as a boy was a far safer alternative. It did not banish the pain so much as render it irrelevant. It was with relief that he heard a discreet rapping on his door, the distinctive cadence of his secretary Trevor Bracknell.

"Excuse me, Sir Thomas, but you have a visitor. Big, rather frightening chap who says he is a representative of the Czar. He was most insistent that he see you."

Von Steinwehr? thought Pennywhistle. *What the blazes was he doing at the embassy?* Either he had some new proposal that had just flown off the Czar's desk or he was here to appraise his opponent in his den.

It occurred to Pennywhistle that this visit could not have come at a better time. This would be an opportunity to be "accidentally indiscreet" and give von Steinwehr clues to the codebook's whereabouts.

The splendid desk that Lady Leith had purchased for him contained plenty of secret panels in which important documents could be secured. Von Steinwehr fancied himself a clever man, and so he was. By now he surely knew that the code book was not kept in the safe; he must be wondering if it were stashed at the embassy, and he might be using the visit as an opportunity to look for likely hiding places.

"Show him in, Bracknell."

"Very good, Sir Thomas."

The two shook hands strongly and Pennywhistle again experienced the man's overwhelming physical presence.

In previous encounters, Pennywhistle had only seen the man in full military attire with a panoply of medals marching across his chest. Von Steinwehr probably felt that he had already impressed others with his military prowess and now deemed a uniform unnecessary. He was dressed in conservative civilian attire that minimized his size and alarming exterior: a black silk stock around his neck, sapphire-blue tailcoat, azure waistcoat, midnight-blue breeches, and white silk stockings above black pumps with gold buckles. The ensemble was superbly tailored.

"Please sit down, *Herr Kolonel*. I gather you have something important to discuss and such matters are best entertained in settings of comfort." He advanced a few paces and threw several logs on the waning fire. It was a cold day in Vienna and the upturn in heat caused both to turn their hands toward the ornate marble fireplace.

Pennywhistle returned to his seat and rang a servant's bell. "I know that it only just past midday, but as we British say, the sun is always over the yardarm someplace. Would you prefer sherry or schnapps?"

Von Steinwehr barked a small laugh. "Schnapps would be most welcome. I am surprised that you have it on hand. Its taste is a little strong for British palettes.

"I admit, I find it overbearing."

An underbutler appeared, clad in the Royal Livery of the House of Hanover. "May I get you something, Sir Thomas?"

"Yes, Bates. A sherry for me, and schnapps for my guest."

"Very good, Sir Thomas."

Bates disappeared, and Von Steinwehr asked, "Do you find your work interesting, Major Pennywhistle?"

Pennywhistle's rank as a knight took precedence over his military rank; Von Steinwehr knew this and so was being deliberately provocative. But good form dictated that Pennywhistle ignore the jibe. "Yes, interesting and satisfying. It gives me a chance to do some good for people who have no other recourse."

Bates returned and handed one glass from the silver tray to von Steinwehr, then traversed a short span of Persian rug to deliver the sherry to Pennywhistle, who said, "Thank you, Bates, that will be all."

Bates bowed and was gone.

Von Steinwehr took a sip of his drink as Pennywhistle brought the sherry to his lips.

"The schnapps is very good, Sir Thomas. The Embassy cellars are better stocked than I had guessed. But then, the British always seem to hold something in reserve."

Pennywhistle finished his sip and put the sherry down. "We try to make our intentions plain, but our customary reserve sometimes causes others to underestimate us." He looked around the room, allowing his face to show concern. "I apologize for the clutter in my office. It is simply too small, but the embassy has no further room for expansion. I shall be moving my office to my residence tomorrow, along with my files. There I will have more space, and if any further meetings are required of me, my guests will not be so cramped."

He sighed, as if in exasperation. "My new desk is also larger, and much better suited to the tasks at hand." He waved towards his desk, where papers were piled in tall stacks. "I will at last have the means of organizing my correspondence." He took in the glint of speculation that appeared in von Steinwehr's eyes.

Von Steinwehr raised the schnapps glass, using the action to conceal his face as he studied Pennywhistle's workspace.

The mahogany campaign desk was typical of those favored by British officers in the field. The piece came in three parts: two side chests upon which rested a wide top covered in heavy green cloth; easily disassembled for relocations. The side chests contained drawers, and possibly concealed compartments; von Steinwehr speculated that if the codebook were, indeed, kept at the embassy, it was most likely to be

Attaché Extraordinaire

found in one of the two chests. However, he could not rule out the possibility that the insufferable Lord Castlereagh had it in his keeping, where it would be much harder to get to.

Most of the desk top was covered with piles of paper, all neatly stacked and arranged in such a way that suggested the documents had been prioritized according to urgency. The stack nearest Pennywhistle's quill pen, gold inkpot, and embassy stationary was probably the most pressing, the one farthest away the least. Logical and efficient, but that did not tell von Steinwehr anything about his opponent that he did not already know. The front of the desk was more interesting. Prominently displayed were two mastless ship models, their sterns serving as bookends for a large folio size volume bound in expensive polished calfskin.

He surmised the ships were 1/48 scale British Admiralty models; such models preceded construction of the actual vessel. One was a ship-of-the-line, the other a frigate. The lettering on their sterns proclaimed them *Bellerophon* and *Active*. He gathered they were ships on which Pennywhistle had served. As the British Naval Attaché, displaying symbols of the Royal Navy's dominance of the seas sent a clear message to any foreign gentlemen with whom he had business. The folio encased by the bookends was volume one of Diderot's *Encyclopédie, ou Dictionnaire Raisonné des Sciences, des Arts, et des Métiers*. The thirty-five-volume encyclopedia, originally published between 1751 and 1773, was *de rigueur* for the thinking man's library. The set was the world's first methodical effort to present the entire scope of human learning through reason, intellectual discourse, and the scientific method. He recalled the volume he was looking at contained a great deal of information on naval affairs. Exactly the kind of book a man like Pennywhistle would consult regularly.

John Danielski

To the left of the book ends stood a bronze bust that surprised von Steinwehr. It was of Napoleon.

Was Pennywhistle a secret admirer? That would be strange, given his career. More likely the sculpture served to remind him that one of Castlereagh's goals was to create a Europe where such a usurper could never come anywhere near a throne.

Pennywhistle noticed his opponent's examination and answered the unasked question. "Bonaparte kept a bust of Nelson in his office at the Tuileries to school him that you could admire certain aspects of a man, even as you had to do everything in your power to oppose the cause for which he fought. Bonaparte is an object lesson in the dangers of genius divorced from the virtue of moderation; and yet, a careful study of his military methods has improved my strategic thinking. You and I share a desire, *Herr Kolonel,* to see justice done, by repairing the harm that he caused. We may have differing prescriptions about how that should be accomplished, but in the end, we both wish for the same thing."

To Pennywhistle's consternation, von Steinwehr's eyes took on a reddish tint, and he seemed to swell visibly in his chair. "I wear a red carnation in my boutonniere as a *memento mori;* symbolizing the blood my family has spilt opposing the Corsican Ogre. He has brought only misery to my fortune, honor, and Fatherland. I wish there were a way I could transfer that misery to every member of his repugnant clan whom he placed on thrones or married off to royalty."

"Many others feel as you do, *Herr Kolonel,* but for this Congress to be fruitful, its participants ought to move beyond a desire for vengeance." With a pang, Pennywhistle realized the hypocrisy in his words; the actions he contemplated against von Steinwehr had a great deal to do with vengeance.

Attaché Extraordinaire

Von Steinwehr's eyes challenged Pennywhistle with the intensity of drawn steel. "There are those who would say you are right, Sir Thomas; and yet, hatred is a powerful energy which, transmuted, may accomplish great things."

Pennywhistle forced a bland, diplomatic smile onto his face. "And now, *Herr Kolonel*, what is this urgent matter that has caused you to call upon me before the committee meeting?"

Von Steinwehr returned a malicious, ironic smile, that of a dark creature that had just lured a maiden into a fatal embrace. "It is very happy news. I thought you should know. The Czar informed me several hours ago that Talleyrand is now agreeable to Reichenau's restoration. One of his underlings delivered a formal note to that effect this morning."

Pennywhistle's studied Stoicism vanished for a few brief seconds, but he kept his face neutral, save for a twitch of his lower lip. He felt like a Presbyterian being told that John Knox had been a secret atheist. "I confess I am stun... ah... uh... surprised. This is an unexpected development. Have you any idea what brought about his change of mind?"

Von Steinwehr knew exactly how Talleyrand had been persuaded: blackmail. Fouché, who was in Von Steinwehr's pocket, had been sleeping with Talleyrand's niece, and their pillow talk had unearthed some very entertaining, and damaging, information. He replied, "I could not say. Talleyrand wears many faces, and no man sees them all."

Pennywhistle's alarm took the form of a sharp jab of pain in his back. Talleyrand's vote, added to Alexander's and Metternich's, meant that von Steinwehr was four fifths of the way home. Frederick William of Prussia would likely follow Alexander's lead, now that France and Austria were on board.

"Sadly, I must tell you, *Herr Kolonel*, the position of Lord Castlereagh with regard to Reichenau has not changed. I have spoken to him several times on the matter." Pennywhistle hoped the allusion to his master's obstinacy might make the translation of the letters more urgent.

"That is regrettable, but I am in hopes that your principal will see reason. "I have brought a proposal that I think may find favor with him."

"I should be most interested to hear that proposal," lied Pennywhistle. Castlereagh was firm in his policy of banishing diplomatic relics. It was of a piece with his opposition to slavery, and the people of Reichenau had been slaves in all but name.

"I know the British are concerned with free and open navigation on Europe's rivers. What I propose is a compromise. Rather than eliminating tolls, I suggest they be reduced in number, and that the amount to be paid be made uniform throughout Europe. That would reduce confusion among the bargemen and eliminate many of the delays. I would inaugurate a Toll Federation of Europe and make it a permanent governing body that included representatives of all the key nations of Europe. It would be like a smaller version of your own Parliament, but tasked with only one responsibility."

Pennywhistle knew the fight to make all of Europe's rivers toll free was an uphill battle. Von Steinwehr's idea had merit, but the price was too high. Still, his job was not to conclude the negotiations but keep them going.

"I think your proposal has merit. You speak of reducing the number of tolls. Would that mean developing, shall we call them, toll hubs? Places where tolls for a given area could be paid in one lump sum, which would later be distributed to the regional landowners?"

Attaché Extraordinaire

"That is precisely what I had in mind. Reichenau would be one of three hubs on the Rhine, as well as home to the Toll Federation Assembly."

"Reichenau is geographically well placed to serve that function," said Pennywhistle, with false thoughtfulness. Inwardly he was deeply alarmed. *Making Reichenau the headquarters of such a federation would put his small country on the map in a metaphorical sense as well as the literal. The arrangement would grant him political power and access to enormous financial resources*, thought Pennywhistle. "I can promise nothing, *Herr Kolonel*, but I shall present your ideas to Lord Castlereagh tomorrow morning.

"I can ask no more, Sir Thomas. The chiming of your case clock reminds me that we are both due at the committee meeting shortly. May I offer you a lift in my carriage?"

"IIow kind! Of course." It would have been boorish to refuse, yet it was ironic, since each man knew the other was a mortal enemy. Politics not only made strange bedfellows, it made for strange carriage mates.

Chapter 29

Franz von Hager entered Metternich's Office at the Chancellery with an anxious look on his face. He came every morning at 10 a.m. to deliver a verbal intelligence briefing, accompanied by a written report. He had performed the same function for the Emperor Francis an hour before. Each man read his reports carefully and asked perceptive questions. While the Emperor was concerned with the general safety of his realm, he also enjoyed scurrilous and salacious gossip.

Metternich had a different focus. He was only concerned with personal details if they offered insights into the mind of an opponent or allowed him to anticipate their possible courses of action. His sharp features, perceptive eyes, and expressive mouth worked in concert with his erudite charm, easygoing amiability, and graceful manners, to make him just as welcome in a salon as a conference room. All of that acted as a mask for an inner self that was cold, calculating, and understanding that knowledge was power. He hated the chaos wrought by the wars with Napoleon, and knowing more secrets than your opposite numbers was a good way to prevent their recurrence.

Von Hager handed his report to Metternich. "I should warn you, *Herr Chancellor*, that there is a certain item which may cause you personal distress."

Attaché Extraordinaire

"I appreciate the warning, *Herr Baron,* but I find it is always better to know the truth, no matter how painful, rather than stumble through life acting on illusions. Please sit down while I read."

"I know that is your philosophy, *Herr Chancellor*, so I placed the bad news at the beginning of the report."

Metternich seated himself and took a sip of his morning tea. His eyes moved quickly across the report; he was famous for his reading speed and ability to digest a large amount of information in a short time. His pleasant expression vanished. Shock, anger, and sadness followed in quick succession. He threw down the report and his eyes bored into von Hager's. "Is this true? Could this not just be malicious rumor? The Duchess has many enemies eager to blacken her reputation."

"I have received the same information from three sources. They are all reliable, but I interviewed them again this morning just to be sure. I am truly saddened to bring this news to your attention."

Metternich pasted a look of composure on his face that he knew was less than convincing. His heart had just been pierced, as if by a dagger, and that was a hard thing to conceal. "You did right to bring it to my attention, *Herr Baron,* but let us forego the rest of this briefing while I consider the best way to deal with this news."

"Of course, *Herr Chancellor*. Just send word when you need me. I shall hold myself at your beck and call."

"Thank you, *Herr Baron*. For now, you are dismissed."

Von Hager had just closed the door when Metternich felt tears well up in his eyes. His beloved Wilhemine had betrayed him! And with a stupid, foolish hussar! His intuition told him that Alexander had purposely placed the hussar in her path.

John Danielski

He could hardly believe it, yet the warning signs had all been there. She had been unavailable the past week for their usual 11 o'clock meeting at the Palm Palace, where they sipped hot chocolate and discussed politics. She had not responded for the same period to the letters he sent on a daily basis. The last time they had spoken, she had been distant, even cold. Clearly, she was frustrated by his inability to persuade Alexander to secure custody of her lost daughter, Vava.

He had to win her back! He had to! He decided to write a letter explaining the depth of his feelings. He had written the Duchess more than three hundred times over the past year, but this one would have special urgency. He settled himself into his writing desk, selected his finest writing paper and goose quill pen, and began to write fervently.

> *You have made me drunk with happiness, my dearest Wilhelmine. I love you! I love you a hundred times more than my life! I do not live, I shall not live, except for you.*
>
> *Word has reached me of your congress with Alfred. You have done me greater harm than can ever be compensated by the whole universe. You have broken the springs of my soul and endangered my existence at a moment when my life is bound up with questions that will decide the fate of whole generations. Do not forsake me and our future. I give you my most sacred word I will get your daughter back. We must meet, so our hearts can again beat as one.*

He continued to write for the next half hour, desperately trying to bring order to a disordered heart. A lifelong philanderer was not supposed to fall in love. He had cared for many of the women in his past, but living without them had never posed a problem. Now the prospect of life without Wilhelmine wrenched his very soul and jeopardized the clear-headed thinking that was the cornerstone of his life.

When he could think of nothing more to say, he folded the long letter and applied the wax seal of the Chancellor of

Attaché Extraordinaire

Austria. He summoned a messenger and instructed him, in no uncertain terms, that the letter needed to be delivered to the Palm Palace as soon as possible.

There was a knock on the door soon after his messenger left. "Come," he said, still in the grip of melancholy. The door opened and he could not have been more surprised. It was the Emperor Francis himself. Normally, Metternich went to the office of the Emperor, not the other way round. Even more surprising was what the Emperor carried: his violin and a sheaf of music.

Metternich shot from his chair and stood to attention. "Your Apostolic Majesty, this is indeed an unexpected pleasure. To what do I owe the honor?"

Francis smiled kindly. "This is not an official visit. I read von Hager's report and thought you could use the company of a friend. Music always soothes my spirits in sad times and this morning I received a composition for violin, cello, and piano, written by Beethoven himself. It has never been performed and I thought you and I might have a go at it. Since the piano's role is minor, we may creditably perform without its presence."

Metternich bowed. "It would be an honor and a privilege." He brought two chairs and two music stands from a corner of the room and positioned them to the side of his desk.

The Emperor handed him a copy of the composition and his eyes skimmed it briefly. "This will be challenging to play, Your Apostolic Majesty."

"Yes, but very beautiful. Now why don't you fetch your cello, and we can begin."

Metternich did just that, and at the first stroke of his bow, he felt his tension start to dissipate. There was no better medicine for a wounded heart than creating lovely music.

For the next hour, two of the most powerful men in Europe forgot the affairs of state and dedicated themselves to bringing joy to everyone within earshot. Staff and servants crowded close to the office door, delighted to hear a duet by two exceptionally talented musicians.

Talleyrand was, at that moment, enjoying a leisurely bath at the Kaunitz Palace. He generally rose late and took his time about his morning toilette. Early rising and hurried actions were suited only to farm laborers.

The copper bathtub in which he relaxed was large, tall sided, and filled with perfumed hot water. His aged manservant, Le Beau, scrubbed his back with lemon scented soap. The steam from the bath water warmed Talleyrand's face, fresh from the daily application of herbs and cucumber slices. Two valets hovered in the background ready to powder his hair, perfume his feet, and dress him in silk stockings, breeches, and shirt. A third valet near his closet would help him choose a coat for the day. Talleyrand slowly sipped chamomile tea.

In public, he was the picture of aristocratic detachment, most famously when gambling, blue eyes half closed as if wearied by ennui and lips perpetually on the verge of a smile. It was the countenance of man who had survived the French Revolution and the Napoleonic Wars, unimpressed by either threat to his life or equanimity.

He turned thoughtful as he reviewed his schedule for the day ahead. He had just begun to muse on the Saxon question when Dorothée, his niece by marriage, entered the room carrying a portable writing desk, quills, and stationary. She took up her accustomed position in a chair four feet from the tub. She was the one person in whom he reposed perfect trust and confidence.

Mindful that her mother had once been Talleyrand's lover, she did not share his bed but was intimate with him in every other way. She served as his sounding board and secretary, writing his letters as he dictated them and suggesting the best ways to translate his ideas into the written word. She never hesitated to tell him when he was wrong, though she always did so with charm and grace.

"You may go," said Talleyrand to the servants. "I shall summon you around noon. Until then, you are free to visit the kitchens." Talleyrand might be a throwback to the *Ancien Regime* but he treated his servants well. He had the best kitchens in Vienna and even the lesser fare from them was delightful.

The servants bowed, mumbled acknowledgements, and departed.

Dorothée spoke. "I had a visit from a friend this morning. She was a guest at my sister's dinner party last night and brought news that I think you will want to hear."

"The Duchess has fine dinners, but my food is better. What news did she bring?"

"Prince Alfred von Windeschgratz has returned to the city and was present at the dinner. Metternich was not."

"Ah, Prince Alfred. A strutting fellow with good looks and a head full of mush."

"He appears to have taken up residence at the Palm Palace."

Talleyrand calmly sipped his tea. "Metternich must be greatly upset. For a man who plays his cards close to the chest, his relationship with Sagan is shockingly obvious. I am scheduled to meet with him at four to discuss the Saxon question and this tidbit of information is most useful. He will be off his game, and this may open him to persuasion, if I can play nurse to a wounded soldier of the heart. I want the King of Saxony to retain his crown, but Metternich has not made up his mind."

"His help would be most useful in opposing the Czar," replied Dorothée. "Do you suppose the Czar could be persuaded to forego his demand that Saxony be annihilated, and its land turned over to Prussia?"

Talleyrand sighed. "Alexander is like a spinning top that changes direction drunkenly, without any grace or decorum." He took another sip of tea. "Sagan's relationship with Prince Alfred suggests her bed might also be open to others. It is no secret that Alexander covets Sagan for himself, and bedding her would be a severe cut at Metternich; stealing something he holds dear."

Talleyrand finished his tea. "If Metternich is not receptive to my logical arguments for Saxony's preservation, an opportunity to strike back at the Czar will give him an emotional reason to support my position."

"Men can be such fools!" said Dorothée with asperity. "I am relieved that you have not allowed love or lust to rule *your* conduct."

"Both are expensive vanities that no wise diplomat should ever indulge, yet they can be useful weapons. My position is that, since love and lust are eternal verities, why not employ them for the good of France? And now Dorothée, why don't you give me a briefing on affairs of state that do not involve boors or boudoirs."

"I shall be happy to oblige, Uncle. After that, would you consider a game of chess?"

"A fine idea. Chess focuses my mind on the things that matter."

Alexander had just completed his usual morning hunt. He had bagged a large and wily stag and was well-pleased with himself. Von Steinwehr and two aides had accompanied him.

Von Steinwehr moved his horse close to Alexander's. "Your Imperial Majesty, something that concerns Metternich has come to my attention."

Alexander glowered. "That knave!"

"My information involves a vulnerability that I believe you might enjoy exploiting."

Alexander's expression changed to one of avid curiosity. "You mean we could damage him?"

"In a very personal way that might help you diplomatically."

"Please tell me more." The Czar's eyes glowed in anticipation.

"It is well known that Metternich is intimate with the Duchess of Sagan."

"Yes," replied Alexander with disgust. "Surprising that such a beautiful woman would make such a poor choice for a lover."

"It appears that she is no longer restricting her favors to Metternich. A young colonel of hussars has moved into her residence."

"Really? I thought the bond she had with Metternich was unbreakable."

"Apparently not."

"How did you discover this? Is your source reliable?"

"I do not like to reveal sources, but I will make an exception in this case. It is Dorothée, Talleyrand's niece and Sagan's sister."

"My God! I despise Talleyrand even more than Metternich. How did you manage it? I have met his niece and she does not seem the type to betray anyone."

"She had no idea of what she has done. She may be poised and brilliant but is unschooled in the ways of even casual couplings. One of my agents is a handsome fellow, for whom she has formed a romantic attachment. She and he had a quick assignation early this morning and her tongue flapped. She thinks my man is a starving artist whose talent the world has been too blind to appreciate."

"So," chuckled Alexander, "you believe Sagan is no longer off the market?"

"I do. This is an opportunity to humiliate Metternich in a public fashion. He is so head-over-heels in love with her that there is no telling what he will do if she breaks things off with him. His behavior may even become so erratic that you can persuade Francis to dismiss him from his service."

"Excellent, Colonel. I could not be more pleased. I will redouble my efforts to return Reichenau to you!"

"I also could not be more pleased, Your Imperial Majesty."

Chapter 30

"Awk! Awk! Awk! Odd! Odd! Odd!" Plymouth flapped his wings dramatically to attract attention. For added emphasis, he pecked at a nearly imperceptible hole to the right of a large green and gilt bookcase until Sammie Jo came over to investigate. He then paced back and forth on its top shelf three times, as if he were in deep thought about something he had discovered. He had been amusing himself by flying into rooms of the new residence and exploring their contents. The large library, containing regiments of books, was his latest port of call.

Sammie Jo moved closer, and as she did, the bird moved aside. She put her finger to the hole and felt something unexpected: a draught of air. Considering the high price to lease this residence, rot in the walls should not be an issue.

Then she looked at the hole closely. It was perfectly round, not ragged, something that had been deliberately cut. She ran her finger round the edges, which felt smooth and even. Why was it there? On impulse, she pounded the wall behind it. The noise returned was not the expected one of thick wood but the resonance of thin wood concealing a hollow space.

She ran her hand below the right edge of the bookcase, using touch rather than vision as her engine of exploration. After a minute, her fingers felt smooth wood. Then they

330

touched a small nub that was a tiny toggle switch. She pushed it hard.

Amidst a creaking that sounded like ship's timbers in a storm, the bookcase slowly swung aside as if it were a door. The crack was barely wide enough to admit a person, so she let go of the switch and manually helped the bookcase along. When the bookcase had reached a 90-degree angle, she heard the click of a locking latch.

Yawning before her was a passage leading God knows where. No mention of it had been made by Frau Stottler.

Sammie Jo was eager to explore, but thought it was always wise to do so in pairs, lest the unexpected ambush the solitary venturer. She stroked the parrot's head several times. "Good boy! Good boy."

The parrot jumped onto her shoulder and cooed. He stayed there as she walked quickly to summon Lady Leith.

"Margaret, I found something! Or rather, Plymouth did. A secret passage!"

Lady Leith rose from her writing desk, her face glowing with excitement. "Sounds like it needs exploring. We will need some candleholders. There is a candelabra in my bedroom which should work nicely."

They returned to the library a few minutes later, Sammie Jo bearing the candelabra with its six brightly burning spermaceti candles, imported from Nantucket Island.

Sammie Jo cautiously stepped across the threshold, followed by Lady Leith.

"What do you think it is, Margaret?"

"It's either to do with intrigue or love. It may have been a way to spy on secret negotiations, or a way for illicit lovers to visit each other's bedrooms without attracting notice. That opening you found is a spy hole. It could be used for detecting secret plots or for voyeurs wishing to watch lovers in congress. It is possible that in the early days of this house, this library might have been a bedroom."

Sammie Jo moved down the passage and panned the candelabra around. Lady Leith followed a pace behind. The clandestine corridor was four feet wide and had six feet of headroom. It was long, running the whole length of the floor, and had branches that connected to five rooms. A weak breeze fluttered down the passage, cooling the beads of excitement on Sammie Jo's brow.

Sammie Jo and Margaret walked slowly and in silence, closely inspecting the floor and walls as they proceeded. Plymouth remained on Sammie Jo's shoulder and offered a running commentary that varied as he passed judgement, "Good! Bad! Like!"

There were plenty of cobwebs, insects that skittered away, and the floorboards occasionally creaked. A mouse froze, examined them for a brief second and raced away. Sammie Jo would not have been surprised to see a witch's broom, a skeleton, or a black cat turn up. She did find a badly rusted dagger and the red remnants of what might have been a cloak.

"Don Juan," murmured Lady Leith.

"Who?" inquired Sammie Jo.

"Never mind."

One branch led to the home's largest guest suite. That was the first portion built of the residence and represented careful planning on the part of its initial owner. The Hapsburgs had visited many times; and this suite would have been given to Royal visitors. The door to this suite also had a peep hole. Whether pillow talk or talk of diplomacy, it would have been easy to use a royal visit as a source of useful information or even blackmail.

The other three branches lead to smaller guest bedrooms. Sammie Jo saw a pattern. When royals or high nobles visited, sometimes for a week at a time, they often brought large entourages. Observation of their doings might provide a wealth of information. The man who had built the residence was Count Heinrich von Auersperg, a general in the War of the Spanish Succession and a close friend of Prince Eugene of Savoy. Margaret had told her that he had a reputation, both as an intriguer and master swordsman of the boudoir. This secret passage fit that picture.

An idea hit Sammie Jo. Why not return the passage to its original function? She motioned Lady Leith to follow her back to the library.

When they had exited and Sammie Jo had sealed the corridor, she gave voice to her thoughts. "I was thinking, Margaret, we should move Tom's new desk here from his study and make the library his temporary office."

"I understand what you propose, Sammie Jo, and it's clever."

"You and I both believe the moles are the parlor maid, the underbutler, and the coachman's assistant. We know they are going to rifle through the desk. Let us put it in a place that can be watched, just like the hides I used to build to waylay deer. Tom thinks they will strike when we are gone tomorrow. Lord Steven might agree to conduct the surveillance and follow the miscreants once the deed is done. I suspect he would enjoy the work."

"That is a fine plan, Sammie Jo. The moles have been active. Three nights ago, at Tom's instruction, I placed tiny hairs across the safe's door. They are nearly invisible if you are not looking for them. When I came back in the morning, they had been displaced, indicating that the safe had been opened.

Attaché Extraordinaire

They are being thorough. As a test, I put my jewelry inside the next night, and all the pieces were present in the morning. Our thieves are being sufficiently well paid that they were not tempted by ordinary theft."

"You know, Margaret, maybe it ain't about the money, maybe it's about loyalty. Maybe von Steinwehr promised them something even more valuable than quick wealth."

"That makes perfect sense."

"The files and Tom should be along in a couple of hours," remarked Sammie Jo. "Why don't you arrange to get the desk and armoire moved while I pay a visit to Lord Steven. I am right curious to see them Lippizaner stallions he talks so much about. Bet they would be a heap more fun to ride than old Bea."

"And I," said Lady Leith, "will put Tom in the picture when he arrives."

"It's a good plan Margaret."

"It is, Sammie Jo, but as Tom is fond of saying, 'There is many a slip twixt the cup and the lip.' We must be careful not to think ourselves too clever."

***

At the Amelienberg, Ingrid reviewed the newest report from her chief mole. She frowned, then sighed in exasperation. It was disappointing, yet not unexpected. The codebook was not being kept in the safe at all. But then, after what her husband had told her after his last meeting with Pennywhistle, his new desk was a more likely hiding place. Her people would be able to search the desk at their leisure one week hence.

She was pleased that her husband trusted her to handle the entire planning of the theft that would seal their future. He had enough to worry about, securing official backing for

Reichenau's return. Four keys had turned in their locks and they were almost in possession of the element that would turn the final one. And it was she who would be performing the translation of the Clarke Letters at Kreigshammer. He had chosen the location for her safety, wanting to insulate her from any attempts to recover the book, and from prying Russian eyes.

Klaus had identified twelve letters of the alphabet. Once she had the codebook, she could render a complete translation of all twenty three Clarke Letters. Idly, Ingrid wondered if the letters were entirely in that bastard language, English, or if portions were written in French, or even Latin. No matter, she was fluent in four languages.

She put down the report and wondered about her opposite number, Lady Pennywhistle, or Sammie Jo, as she styled herself. She was far more than a country tart who had got lucky. Her actions during the hunting party showed her as dangerous and decisive. Much as it pained Ingrid to admit it, Lady Pennywhistle and Sir Thomas likely had a partnership much like her own with Klaus. Ingrid even felt a certain admiration for Lady Pennywhistle, but if that hunt had taught her anything about the woman, it was that she would pursue vengeance relentlessly. Pennywhistle had to die; he knew too much. Which meant Lady Pennywhistle also had to die.

Chapter 31

A week later in his new office, Pennywhistle carefully studied Schmidt's forgery, prior to secreting it away. Schimdt was indeed a master of his craft; the forgery of *"The Little Code Breaker and Pocket Cryptographer"* that Pennywhistle held in his hand, was indistinguishable from the original when placed side by side. The wormholes, assorted sweat stains, and worn edges were of a piece with the brown patina of the cover and would reassure anyone giving it a close inspection for authenticity. He expected von Steinwehr to do just that.

His new desk was imposing, honeycombed with hiding places. It had fifteen storage spaces, and the slant top could be locked when folded in. Three large, rectangular storage nooks with false backs stood upon four drawers with false bottoms. Their twins flanked a large square central storage box marked by two pilasters, with a door that could be locked. The central storage box had a compartment that could be pulled out. Its false bottom was accessed by pressing a hidden spring with a finger or penknife.

Pennywhistle checked again the line of sight between the desk and the hidden peephole. Satisfied that Thynne would have a clear view, he contemplated the likely conduct of the underbutler, based on Grimsby's evidence. He had said the man's temperament was mulish, but he was a quick study with very nimble hands.

The original codebook would be secreted in a hollowed-out volume of Diderot, indistinguishable from any of the hundreds of other books in the library.

It took Pennywhistle an hour to fill the desk with miscellaneous, important-looking documents of no great consequence. All of the false backs and bottoms received layers of paperwork that would take time to sift through.

He filled the desk's bookcase with small volumes on all manner of arcane subjects.

He chose the false bottom of the shelf below the central storage compartment for the resting place of the prize. He then locked the door to it and folded up the slant top. He locked that as well, and then pocketed the keys. He hoped the spies had enough skill to open the locks without damaging the magnificent desk.

There was a knock at the library door, in a cadence he recognized. "Enter!"

A very amused Thynne entered. "I know this is serious business, Tom, but I must say this spy stuff is rather fun. I brought food and wine with me in case this is a long wait." He held up a hamper with an insouciant air.

"Did anyone see you when you came in, Steven?"

"Johnny was on the lookout, and Sammie Jo let me in when no one else was about." Thynne looked about the room with interest, strolled over to the desk, and rapped on it. "Solid construction."

"Yes," replied Pennywhistle, "which means the spies will want to search for the book as soon as our foursome leaves, knowing that it will take them awhile to find the book's hiding place."

Attaché Extraordinaire

"Which one is the ringleader?

"Knyphausen, the underbutler; a tall, thin man with a face like old cauliflower. The other two are Wolfram and Krueger, the coachman and the parlor maid."

"I am ready for whatever comes," said Thynne cheerfully. "Now show me the passage."

Pennywhistle lit a nearby candelabra, walked a few paces, and pressed the hidden toggle switch. The door swung open — Pennywhistle had taken the time to clean and oil the mechanism, and Sammie Jo had swept the corridors—and the lock clicked.

"Ah," said Thynne as he stepped inside. "Looks like you have your own personal catacombs. How far does this passage run?"

"The length of the floor. There is a folding iron staircase that leads to the tradesman's entrance and loading dock. I gather that the builder wanted an escape hatch, a way for illicit lovers to flee quickly."

Thynne set down his basket and drew forth a checked tablecloth that he laid upon the cold stones. He uncorked a bottle of claret, then extracted a glass from the hamper and filled it. He withdrew a baguette, a cheese knife, and a small round of Gouda cheese, and placed them on the cloth. "No reason surveillance can't be civilized and comfortable."

"Let me complete the setting," said Pennywhistle, as he brought forward a wheeled mini-staircase, one used to reach books high up on shelves. "You may use this as your seat."

Thynne made himself as comfortable as the stepladder allowed, verified that he could sight the desk through the spy hole, then took a leisurely sip of claret. Pennywhistle placed the candelabra on the floor at a sufficient distance to provide illumination without betraying the peep hole, then pointed out the location of the toggle switch to open the passage from Thynne's side.

"You'd best be going Tom. I have everything I need. I know your wife and the others are eager to depart."

"Good luck! We should return in six or seven hours. If you are not back from tailing the thief at that time, I will wait here in the library."

"Got it. Now shut the door and be off with you. Remember, it's *pleasure*, not business!"

Pennywhistle closed the passage and headed toward the door. Steven was right. He should allow himself to enjoy the outing ahead. The scenery would be beautiful and the company delightful; he deserved a respite from all the long hours that he had been logging in His Majesty's service. Even so, the analytical part of his mind would not rest. He wanted this clandestine contest with von Steinwehr brought to a close, and viewing the fortified nest of his opponent would give him an advantage.

Forty five minutes after Pennywhistle's departure from the library, Thynne heard noises. He put down his wine glass and placed his eye close to the spy hole. The noises were of metal upon metal, as if a small pick and tension wrench were being applied to the library door's lock. The sounds continued for several minutes, and then the door opened slowly. Three people entered: two men and a blonde woman. Knyphausen really did have a face like an old cauliflower!

"Did you check the armoire yesterday, Krueger?" Knyphausen asked the woman.

"Yes, in the afternoon when I dusted. I opened the safe like always, but the contents were just the broaches, no book. Pretty broaches they were, too!"

"Don't talk like that, and don't be tempted!"

Attaché Extraordinaire

"I just looked. That's not a crime."

"Remember that what we stand to gain is worth more than baubles. When Reichenau is restored, we will have positions at court where we will rule others, rather than serve them."

"We serve a great man," said Wolfram in his gravelly voice. "It is a privilege! A privilege."

"Shut up," hissed Knyphausen. "We have a job to do. The less noise we make the better. We must be neat and leave no sign that we were here. With luck, it will be days before the loss of the book is noticed. By that time, we will be long gone."

"But won't that mark us as the culprits?" asked Krueger.

"So what? We shall be far away and amply rewarded."

Knyphausen led them to the desk, then applied himself to using the pick and tension wrench to open the top.

"*Scheisse!*" he exclaimed, when he saw the numerous compartments. "All right, Krueger, you take the contents on the right side, Wolfram you take those on the left, I will take what is in the center. Check for false backs and bottoms. Listen for a hollow sound when you knock. Remember, the book is small, thin, and will fit in a very shallow hiding place."

Thynne watched with fascination. He had never seen secret panels discovered before, and the thieves were thorough and systematic. He had just finished a second glass of wine when Knyphausen exclaimed, "I found it! I found it!"

"Are you sure?" said Wolfram.

Knyphausen paged quickly through the book. "Yes. There can be no doubt."

Thynne wondered who the forger was. The man would probably have a smile of satisfaction on his face if he could see how well his deception had succeeded.

"Replace everything quickly, but make sure we leave the desk as we found it. I will leave immediately and send for you shortly. Our master's wife will see to our needs."

Thynne watched as they tidied up. After they departed and relocked the library door, he tidied up, then opened the secret passage. It would take a few minutes for Knyphausen to ready a horse. He would allow his quarry a small lead before he saddled a horse from the stable and followed.

Chapter 32

The weather continued to act as unpredictably as a jilted lover. Yesterday had been freezing, but this early afternoon, the sun had chased away the scowling clouds and had bumped the temperature into the high forties. There were shards of ice floating in the Danube, but nothing that posed any danger to the *Queen Charlotte.*

"Relax, Tom," said Sammie Jo, "this is supposed to be a holiday. The views are beautiful, and I am enjoying my champagne. Why don't you take a sip of yours, instead of glowering at the glass like it was full of horse pee." Sammie Jo was in a merry mood and saw no reason why others around her should not share in it. "Remember, Tom, you're under jury rig, not full sail. Treat this voyage as a way to forget your pain for a while."

"You are right, my dear," sighed Pennywhistle. "We have ninety minutes before we reach the area where I believe Kreigshammer is located. I was not as clever as I thought. Montgomery said the name is actually not one of a particular castle, but a giant escarpment shaped like a war hammer, upon which three castles perch." He took a slow sip of champagne. "I intend to memorize the chief landmarks of each."

"Tom, enjoy means appreciate, it don't mean dissect. I mean, to dissect something you first have to kill it."

"I was just thinking, what if I had to make this journey at night? Which landmarks would I use for navigation?"

"Hold your horses, Tom! I understand you want to prepare, but right now you are radiating enough tension to make a pot of coffee nervous. I thought this might happen. You have been so focused on your mission that you forgot something you normally would have brought by instinct. I have a solution that might kill two birds with one stone. I took your sketch book along and some pencils. Drawing always relaxes you, and it would be a way to make a pictorial record of those landmarks."

A smile creased Pennywhistle's face. "You do know your man, and you have saved the day!" He kissed her warmly.

Sammie Jo snuggled into his embrace appreciatively, then gently pulled away, smiling into his face, to lead him over to the supplies. "Now make yourself comfortable and create some art. I won't disturb you. Margaret and Robert want me to meet a few people, so I will leave you to confer with your imagination."

Pennywhistle nodded absentmindedly. The feel of a pencil in his hand had already inaugurated a private journey. It was always thus. Shutting down some senses heightened and focused others. He felt the tension drain away, as if someone had inserted a tap into a rain barrel filled with murky water.

Soon a castle came into view, as the *Queen* rounded a large bend. He could deduce it was not the one he was looking for; it was a residence, not a fortress, yet it was scenic enough, and rendering its architectural contours was good practice. The castle stood five hundred feet above the river and three hundred yards back from its shore. Its outer walls encased a rectangular courtyard; one high tower reminded him of the Palazzo Publico in Sienna. The three others were shorter, capped with red tops shaped like muffin hats, the arrow slits replaced by large glass windows.

It was pretty to look at; its originally grim function had been erased, its owners wanting to turn something medieval into something Baroque. No sentinels were visible. It was calm, peaceful, and could have taken its place in a Constable painting; not the kind of eagle's aerie that von Steinwehr would choose for his lair.

Sammie Jo relished the running commentary of the Earl. He had cruised this section of the river on numerous occasions. He talked about the trees, plants, and animals of the region, knowing they interested Sammie Jo, who smiled as she listened. Her husband's discourse would have been all about the military possibilities of the river: how wide and deep it was, the speed and direction of its current, hidden sandbars and underwater obstructions, staging areas and landing points.

She glanced back at her husband. His forehead was creased, his brows knitted, his lips pursed. His eyes blazed with fierce concentration as his pencil stabbed and swept across the large sketchbook. He was finally enjoying himself!

Lady Leith noted Sammie Jo's pleased expression. Superficially, she and Tom were an odd couple, but on a deeper level, well matched. She wondered about second chances, whether she and Robert had a future. She had loved her first husband dearly and had never expected lightning to strike twice. And yet, maybe she did not need lightning but serenity, a calm presence she could trust, someone with whom she could speak her innermost thoughts without fear of criticism or ridicule. The hot blood of youth certainly had its joys, as watching Sammie Jo reminded her, but Scots whiskey mellowed and improved with age, yet still had a kick.

She believed life was like a river, with numerous eddies, flows, ripple effects. The events that had swept her together with Robert had dark beginnings, yet the currents might carry them on to bright places.

She had never been a mother but had strong maternal instincts, which she had lavished on Tom. Robert needed a little bit of mothering as well. He had been so angry, so bitter about the death of his son that he had been staggering through life, in a fury alternating with melancholia. Smiles had been strangers, laughter neither sought nor heard. Over the past weeks, her patience and willingness to listen had brought him out of his self-imposed shell. He walked with a happy confidence when with her, nattered on about subjects that interested him, and most amazingly, cracked wry jokes that revealed a singular wit.

"Margaret, Sammie Jo, did I ever tell you about the time that I went boar hunting in those hills?" Grosvenor pointed to a gigantic boulder balanced on four thinner ones; the formation resembled a pregnant hedgehog. "I ended up discovering a species of rodent, as well as a pot of coins once belonging to Suleiman the Magnificent!"

If Sammie Jo had heard that statement from anyone else, she would have expected a tall tale coming on. She had heard her share of whoppers, usually related by old geezers over a checkerboard and cracker barrel at the local trading post. In Europe, they were told by polished men with elegant clothes, manners, and speech — but they were still whoppers. The Earl was an exception, a born truth teller even if he fit the profile of European yarn spinners.

Attaché Extraordinaire

"Who was Suleiman the Magnificent?" inquired Sammie Jo. "Sounds like a pretty fancy foreigner."

"He was the Turkish Sultan who besieged Vienna in 1529. He was a most capable and curious ruler. He began the siege by..."

Pennywhistle looked up from his drawing briefly to see how his friends were managing. A gust of wind brought snippets of conversation to his ear. He smiled. Sammie Jo and Margaret were about to be treated to a history lesson. Nothing to worry about; they would be occupied for quite some time. The Earl was a treasure trove of information about the area. That might come in handy in the not very distant future.

The Danube narrowed, and he guessed this was the place where a giant chain had been suspended across the river in 1683, blocking the passage of Turkish vessels. A second castle came into view. This one fit what he would expect of von Steinwehr. It reminded him of a scaled down version of the great Krak des Chevaliers in Syria, one of the crown gems of Crusader Castles. Six square towers at regular intervals punctuated walls that were twenty feet high and probably ten feet thick. The escarpment spur it sat upon, eight hundred feet above the river, was bare, rough granite and afforded the castle defenders clear fields of fire.

He put down his pencil and sketchbook and unfurled the Ramsden. He panned it slowly over the castle, to look for avenues of approach. The ground sloped steeply and unevenly towards the rear of the structure, making an approach difficult for an armed body of men. He could find nothing that could be called a road, though he did discern one narrow path that might have been used by the castle's chief huntsman. The only road of note led up from a small landing on the river, and travelers could be brought under fire from the crenellated barbican at its end.

Through the glass he could now see that none of the buildings in the courtyard had roofs. It was a ruin, too far gone for it to be rehabilitated by von Steinwehr. And yet... He furled his Ramsden and began sketching the structure in detail. Castles in a given area of a certain period often shared the same designer. Any insights gained from this one might be usefully applied when he discovered his opponent's real lair.

That happened thirty minutes later. He knew instantly when he saw it. The castle sat atop a 500-foot bluff, shaped exactly like the head of an ancient Warhammer. A quarter of the castle was a ruin, but scaffolds atop parts of the walls told him it was undergoing extensive repair. The remainder of the castle looked in good shape: a mixture of menace and comfort. Colorful banners flew from the four buildings that had replaced the original keep.

One banner caught his eye, because the image on it recalled something from du Teil's book: a giant white tiger. Du Teil had related that a 17th century Graf of Reichenau had hosted an Indian maharajah taking the Grand Tour. The maharajah had been so pleased with their hospitality that he gifted them with an albino Bengal Tiger of nearly supernatural proportions. Von Steinwehr's great-grandfather had been so delighted with the unusual animal that he had incorporated it into his personal coat of arms.

The banner was certainly distinctive. Pennywhistle wondered if Czar Alexander knew about this fortress of his underling, probably staffed with a small private army. Possibly not. There was so much happening in Vienna that it would be easy to miss. Besides, since von Steinwehr functioned as the chief Russian intelligence officer, it would be easy for him to control the flow of information reaching the Czar. But the cost of maintaining guards and rebuilding a castle must be ruinous. Von Steinwehr had to be near the end of his resources and would need the restoration of Reichenau and its revenues very soon.

He unfurled his Ramsden and panned it slowly across Kreigshammer's structure. The walls were well maintained and bristled with twelve-pounder cannons on iron garrison carriages, fully stocked shot garlands arrayed next to them. Taking full advantage of the spyglass's magnification of twenty five, he examined the balls closely; not a speck of rust. These guns were meant for action, not show.

He counted six well-armed men patrolling the walls and did some quick mathematics. A man like von Steinwehr would hold most of his men in reserve. He estimated his opponent fielded fifty to seventy effectives. The reserves would emerge from hidden sally ports to stage deadly ambushes. Not so different from the "stall and hook" tactics that he himself favored.

The men patrolling the walls did not look to be new recruits; their hard faces, precise gestures, focus, and abstention from tobacco use told him a lot. Smoking was common among new recruits, even on duty. Smoking a pipe might seem harmless, but it reduced a sentinel's night vision. And while the average soldier was in his early twenties, most of these sentinels looked to be in their mid-thirties. They were probably combat-tested veterans of the Napoleonic Wars. They wore green coatees and white trousers, which could be mistaken for the uniform of any of the minor princes of Germany, except for one thing. Their black shakos featured a white tiger badge.

Pennywhistle surmised these men were well paid, though he suspected much of their loyalty sprang not from what they received as a salary but from the promise of the rewards that would be theirs when von Steinwehr was re-established as a ruler.

He sketched vigorously for the next twenty minutes, trying to capture the castle from various perspectives, so he could work out possible avenues of approach. With each passing minute, his despair grew. The surreptitious entry of even a single man into such a fortress would be difficult to manage. Finding a turncoat on the inside to assist would be even more difficult.

Then it hit him. He was thinking like a spy, not a soldier. What one man could not do, twenty five men could. He thought of the cadre of British NCOs visiting the city and realized that, with Castlereagh's tacit approval, he had a ready-made army of skilled veterans. He would not have to tell them why they were going, merely that the safety of the realm was in jeopardy.

He had to be certain the letters were destroyed, even if it meant—and here he grimaced—blowing up the entire castle. There was bound to be a large powder magazine to support the garrison, and every castle, no matter how well constructed, had weak points. That thought gave new life to his sketches, as he contemplated scaling ladders, grappling hooks— and explosions.

The Castle was well defended for most of its walled perimeter, but it had one spot that looked unguarded, because the approach featured five hundred feet of sheer rock, slanted at a ninety-degree angle to the river below. There looked to be a small landing at its base. Could a boat get close enough to land twenty five men? It would be tricky. Then the climb would be exceptionally dangerous, even for an experienced mountaineer. It would be even slower for armed men. But as he looked at the smokestack on the *Queen Charlotte*, it occurred to him that, with some ingenuity and steam power, there might just be a way. If one man could breech the wall, he could rig something to bring the rest up in short order.

But they might not be able to return the same way they came. He and his men might have to use the steep road leading down to the river from the main gate. Thank goodness the moat had long ago been filled in by a landscaping lord, concerned more with appearances than defensibility.

Brush in hand, Pennywhistle noticed an open storage shed just outside the castle walls. He unshipped his Ramsden for a better look. What he saw inside made him smile, two very large sleighs. Some sleighs at the Congress were large enough literally to accommodate small orchestras. The Hapsburgs liked music during their winter outings, and often several sleighs, containing musicians, followed the royal vehicle. Closer inspection also revealed racks of skis. That made sense; the Swedes had deployed Norwegian ski troops in several of their wars against the Russians, and scouts on skis had played a role in the campaign against Napoleon in 1813. Since then, the winter recreational use of skis had spread, because they were a fast and nearly silent mode of travel. Pennywhistle wondered if von Steinwehr had sent messages and instructions by skiers in his efforts to put *finis* to England's pursuit of the missing letters.

His gaze fixed on three wooden conveyances whose name he could not remember. He recalled that they had first been used as cargo sleds by British troops stationed in Canada during the Seven Years War. Bored by the long winters, soldiers had taken to riding empty ones downhill. The name came to him. Toboggans! Like skis, those conveyances would only work if there was ice or snow on the ground. The weather was warm and clear today, but it might yet turn cold and snowy. On the other hand, cold might create ice chunks in the Danube, which might prove an obstacle if he followed the plan forming in his mind.

He realized that he had filled up the last page in his sketch book, so he closed it and sighed in satisfaction. He had what he needed. A proper reconnaissance would have included a close inspection of the walls, but he had done the best that could be managed. He would show the sketches to his improvised army and have them memorize the details.

Seeing him close the book, Sammie Jo strolled over. "Did you get what you came for?" she asked. "You ain't paid attention to any of the scenery except castles."

"Yes, I did. It's not the answer I wanted, but it is an answer."

"Please, tell me the castle I am looking at is not von Steinwehr's."

"You already know the answer, Hawkeye."

"Lordy! How do you plan on getting in? That place looks like my idea of suicide, and I want you around for a while! You got a young' un on the way!"

"Calm down, Sammie Jo. I have the start of a plan that should work."

"*Should* work? That ain't good enough for me, not by a long shot."

"It will need some refinement, I grant you, but I believe I can work out the details. Didn't you once tell me that 'There ain't no horse that can't be broke'?"

"I also said, 'There ain't no rider can't be throwed'," retorted Sammie Jo, "And I aim to protect my investment. I'm coming with."

"Are you insane?"

"No more insane than you going in the first place."

Attaché Extraordinaire

"I absolutely forbid it. I forbid it!"

"Don't give me that." As Sammie Jo dug in her heels, her speech lapsed back to her broadest Maryland tones.' You married a partner, not an 'obedient wife.' If I'd been a milksop, you'd never even have looked at me. You leaving me behind now would be like me goin' huntin' without Widowmaker. I'm goin', and that's settled. I am willing to bet Margaret and Robert will want to go as well. This is personal to Robert, and the way Margaret is lookin' at him, she will not let him out of her sight. His cause is her cause."

Pennywhistle considered, then said, "You are correct. Very well, Sammie Jo. But I will ask you to stay on the boat when we do this; I don't want you trying to scale the wall. As it happens, there is a job that needs doing that I will assign to you."

"All right, but it better not be little stuff disguised as something important."

"The success of the entire enterprise depends on it."

"Good! Now let's get a glass of champagne."

***

At the time Pennywhistle and Sammie Jo were arguing, Thynne was completing the last leg of his surveillance. He had been wrong about Knyphausen heading to the Amelienburg. The man had, instead, proceeded to a seedy inn called the Hofbrau Hus. It looked the kind of place where you could just as easily get a knife in your back as a drink. Thynne was far too well dressed to enter without attracting the attention of patrons, who probably liked aristocrats as much as they liked the Plague, so he and Mandrake moved to an adjoining alley, where he could keep an eye on the front door. He unfurled his spyglass and waited.

Five minutes later, Knyphausen exited, accompanied by a much shorter man. Thynne looked closely at the short man. There was something familiar about his face. He had seen him before. But where? There was also something odd about the face, as if its features represented oddments from assorted masks. Was that makeup? Yes! He had it! It was a woman disguised as a man!

Now he knew. It was the woman Johnny had so exactly described, the one who'd met von Gilsa. That certainly tracked with the meeting unfolding before him. Knyphausen withdrew the book from a concealed pocket and handed it to the woman. In return, she handed him a purse of coins. Thynne wondered why the exchange was taking place outdoors, rather than indoors, and then realized that the inn was not the sort of place where you would let strangers glimpse anything valuable, such as a purse of coins. Out in the open, both parties could spot the approach of any interlopers.

The disguised woman looked through the book as if determined to ascertain its authenticity. When she got to the last page, she nodded in satisfaction. She patted the man's shoulder as if she were praising a dog for retrieving a pheasant. Judging from their expressions and gestures, Thynne got the impression that their association was one of long standing and today's meeting was not its end.

The next moment, Thynne got the shock of his life. The bonhomie was a false flag. There was a small pop, like a paper bag being exploded— the report of a muff pistol fired at very close range.

Knyphausen slowly folded to the ground, a look of complete surprise frozen on his face. The woman calmly bent down and retrieved the purse. She turned on her heel, marched a few paces, then mounted her horse. She moved off at a brisk trot, apparently subscribing to the axiom that dead men tell no tales.

Thynne followed her, at a distance. She rode to a park, where an exceptionally tall man on a horseback rode up to her. Both horses halted. Thynne got a good look at the man's face. It was an exceptionally ugly one that he would see in his dreams for many nights to come.

Chapter 33

The next morning, after a night of quiet celebration and fervent love-making, von Steinwehr retrieved the codebook from its hiding place and handed it to Ingrid. Smiling fondly at his wife, he asked, "How long do you think it will take you to crack the code?"

"I can do it in two days or less, once I have the proper decryption, but there is a problem."

"What is that?"

"The book has ten decryption tables. Only one of them is the proper one for our endeavors. I wish I could say I had a quick way to determine which one to use, but trial and error is the only way, and that takes time."

"How much time?"

"A minimum of a week, but probably longer. I might get lucky, but perseverance will be the best guarantor of success."

"I need to tell Alexander something, Ingrid, as soon as possible. He is not a patient man. I have given him sincere promises, but unless I deliver actionable information very soon, his attentions will all too likely shift away from Reichenau."

"Can you stall him?

"Difficult, but it can be managed. You know how mercurial he is."

Attaché Extraordinaire

"I will not let you down, Husband. The future of our family is riding on this."

"It occurs to me, Ingrid, that two heads are better than one. When you find the correct table, send word to me; I will join you and assist with the translating. I will miss your company, but you'll need to depart for Kreigshammer this morning. At Kreigshammer you can work undisturbed and protected."

"I think you are being overly cautious, Klaus."

"I think of it as being supremely prudent. I have one more suggestion to make. Hire the fastest packet boat you can find and engage her master for two weeks. You need a vessel that can return you to Vienna as swiftly as possible, once you have identified the proper table."

"I anticipated that, Husband. I did a little exploring of the docks yesterday morning and I got lucky. I found a captain who began operating a small steamboat last week and was cagerly seeking to acquire a regular clientele. He told me the *Eulenspiegel* is capable of 14 knots, making it the fastest thing on the river. It was designed as a mail delivery vessel rather than one intended for bulk goods, but can still carry four passengers.

"Is the captain trustworthy?"

"Greedy. Hard coin will keep his mouth shut and cause him to forget all that he sees and hears."

Klaus took Ingrid in his arms and kissed her passionately. "What would I ever do without you?"

"Worry not about that, Klaus. Think instead about the great things we will do *together* when we rule Reichenau."

***

"How long have you been up, Tom? Inquired a sleepy Sammie Jo. "It's just a little after eight."

"A couple of hours. The pain woke me up. I have been sitting here thinking and watching the street below our balcony. Not so much the people as the weather. I am hoping for cold and snow. It was clear when the sun came up, but I have detected some flurries in the distance."

Sammie Jo got out of bed, sat down next to him, and began massaging his back. "I know why the weather interests you. Do you think von Steinwehr has accepted the stolen codebook as authentic?"

"We shall know soon. Steven graciously consented to an all-night surveillance of the Amelienberg. He will send word as soon as he knows something. I have been thinking about what he told me yesterday, and I can only come to one conclusion: that von Steinwehr's wife is as great a fanatic as her husband and is involved up to her neck."

"Of course she is, Tom! I don't like her, but she is smart and aggressive. I watched her during the servant interviews. She likes power and takes jollification from ordering people about."

"Her willingness to commit murder tells me you are exactly right, Sammie Jo. I understand the use of a cut-out in espionage, but why would von Steinwehr send his own wife to collect the codebook? He could have used any number of his lesser minions. I believe she was sent because she was the best person to make an on-the-spot judgment about whether the codebook was real."

"You think she knows something about codes?" Sammie Jo brushed her hand quickly over her forehead and a startled look came over her face. "You think she is going to help translate the letters?"

Attaché Extraordinaire

"I do. I think von Steinwehr and his wife have a close partnership that is as effective as it is lethal. They work in tandem as we do, to different ends."

There was a knock on the door. Sammie Jo quickly threw on a robe to make herself presentable.

Pennywhistle answered the knock; the man on the threshold was the expected one.

"She is on the move, Tom," said Thynne directly. "I followed her to the docks, where she boarded a boat, a steam launch, in fact. She is on her way to Kreigshammer."

"The game is afoot, Steven."

"More like aboat, Tom."

***

A few miles away, The Foreign Secretary was discussing Reichenau with his wife as he finished a compote of stewed figs and apricots. Unlike his Continental counterparts, Lord Castlereagh believed in a full, hearty breakfast, being of the opinion that one could not decide the fate of Europe on a diet of croissants and strudel. To prepare for a long day, he had begun his breakfast with porridge, followed by two poached eggs, two rashers of bacon, two Cumberland sausages, a hash of lamb with pickled walnut, and a small portion of smoked haddock. Two slices of buttered toast with marmalade served as an accompaniment, as did a pot of tea. He ate slowly and appreciatively. A man of precise, orderly habits, he kept his waistline trim by eating like a potentate at breakfast, a prince at dinner, and a pauper at supper.

"Czar Alexander continues to press me on the matter of this small principality, Emily. I grow weary of deflecting his attention to other matters."

"What about Sir Thomas? How fares his mission?" asked Emily as she poured a second cup of tea. Her breakfast had been the same as his, with the addition of deviled kidneys.

"He is meeting with me later this morning to give me an idea of his progress. From the wording of his note, I deduce he is close to a solution, but his message stated that he might need additional support. He mentioned Sergeant Major Owens."

"Who is he, Robert? I don't recall the name."

"Welsh fellow who is leading the delegation of British NCOs. Their demonstrations of British light infantry tactics has been well received, particularly by the Prussians and Austrians. I have an idea what Sir Thomas wants him for. Indeed, I apprehend he may want the entire delegation."

"I thought his mission would be one of stealth, Robert. It sounds to me like his solution could be noisy and cause embarrassment."

"I hope there is quiet solution, but this matter of the Clarke Letters has been hanging fire too long and I want it resolved." Castlereagh sighed. "I have been avoiding Alexander for the last few days and I must frame an official response to his Reichenau entreaties. It is my hope that his secret leverage will have been removed by the time of the Razoumovsky Ball."

"I am so looking forward to that ball, Robert! I am having a special outfit made, but you shall not see it until the evening of the dance. You know it is to be a masked affair, as well as a costume ball?"

"I actually did not. One of my aides accepted the invitation and only informed me in a general way. I am blessed to have a wife who revels in social details."

"The social milieu of parties and pageantry represents my world, Robert, just as the negotiating table and the treaty

Attaché Extraordinaire

room signify yours. The choice of costume is supposed to reveal something of the nature of its wearer. The wearing of masks permits people to speak more freely than they ordinarily would. Considering the duplicity that characterizes so much of this conference, the ball may provide a window into minds that are usually opaque. I assure you that I will keep my eyes and ears open. I have chosen a costume for you that is in keeping with your dashing inner nature that you work so hard to conceal. Rather than endure your anticipated protests, I shall hand you your costume at the time I don my own, when it is far too late for you to object. I ask you to trust my judgment and... dare I say it... allow yourself to have fun! For one evening, acknowledge that the universe can be a place of delight. There will be so much dancing!"

"I know you love dancing; I wish I were better at it."

"You don't lack ability, you lack enthusiasm, Robert. You ought to cast aside your customary reserve."

He loved his wife's exuberance, though occasionally it got out of hand. She sometimes called a little too much attention to herself by the vigor with which she danced. In a slim young woman such enthusiasm might attract admiration, but in a middle-aged woman it could appear ridiculous. Nevertheless, he would not change a thing about his wife, and he did not care what judgements others passed.

"My dear, you are correct. I ought to improve my dancing. That is what the Congress is, after all, one great dance."

***

Deborah and Dale were also sharing breakfast. Dale's morning repast of choice, when not at sea, consisted of pork pie, baked beans, fried bread, and a pot of coffee. Deborah preferred eggs fried with onions, and she had taken a liking to

360

apple strudel baked with raisins, cardamom, and cinnamon. Like her husband, she preferred strong, black coffee to tea, which she sweetened with a spoonful of honey. One of her quiet sources of amusement was noticing how bees produced such distinctive tasting honey, depending on the season of year, climate, and local flowers. These differences made each day's coffee an adventure. But now her enjoyment was marred by concern, for her husband had just described his plans.

"Andrew, you are retired. I don't want you taking the risk. I lost you once; I do not want to lose you again. Besides, you have a son to think of. He looks up to you and is eager to absorb the instructions you wish to teach."

"Deborah, this is a matter of discharging obligations to an old friend. Sir Thomas needs my help. I remind you of the assistance he has afforded both my career and my finances. Indeed, if I had not remained close to him, I would never have found you again. If I shunned my obligation now, I would be a man unworthy of the admiration that our son so trustingly gives. I revel in the joys of marriage and civilian life as much as you do, but if I left a debt of honor unpaid, any triumphs in my new life would be ashes in my mouth."

"You make a point, Andrew," sighed Deborah. "What you say is true. But sometimes the truth hurts."

Chapter 34

Pennywhistle thought his head would explode if he had to endure another hour of paperwork. His back troubled him and he longed for one of Sammie Jo's massages. Just as the pain spiked, there was a discreet rapping on his library/ office door. It was his secretary, Bracknell.

"I regret to disturb you Sir Thomas, but there is a gentleman waiting to see you."

Pennywhistle sighed, "Another foreigner claiming we seized his ship illegally?"

"Oh no, Sir Thomas. This fellow is an Englishman, says you were shipmates of *Bellerophon*. His name is Mr. Peter Wilson."

Pennywhistle blinked in surprise. Why would Wilson come to his new office at his residence instead of sending word through the usual channels? They usually met under the streetlamp round the corner from *Les Ambassadeurs* if something was up. Wilson would not deviate from their routine unless he had a very good reason. Sardonic opportunist he might be, but he had provided a steady stream of information, and the weekly stipend Pennywhistle paid him had proven a good investment.

"Very well, Bracknell, show him in."

"Right, sir."

Bracknell vanished and a moment later Wilson stepped through the door. Gone was his customary shark's half smile, replaced with the look of a man told his bank was about to fail. Instead of a sarcastic greeting, he spoke in urgent tones. "Let me lock the door. I must be sure no one outside of this room hears a word of what I am about to say."

A puzzled Pennywhistle replied, "Go ahead. I am curious why you came here. If I did not know any better, I would say you are worried."

Wilson glanced furtively from side to side, as if he believed the walls literally had ears. He plopped down in the chair opposite Pennywhistle's desk, fidgeted briefly, then took a deep breath.

"I would offer you a coffee," said Pennywhistle in even tones, "but you already seem to have had quite a few cups. You look like a man who needs to get something off his chest. Now what is so important that it looks like cynicism is suddenly bad form?"

"I am here to stop a war. I know you think me a creature of convenience, not conscience; but war would not only be bad for Britain, it would irreparably damage the gambling trade."

"Stop a war? That's rather a fantastic conceit, yet I have never known you to engage in hyperbole."Wilson's face wore an expression of earnestness that he had never seen before.

"Do you think you are the only one who knows just how fragile is the alliance that has brought about this Congress? I hear rumblings over the tables every night about just how close the Congress is to exploding."

Attaché Extraordinaire

"Lord Castlereagh works hard to maintain the façade of amity among our allies," said Pennywhistle, "but cracks develop from time-to-time, and he expends a great deal of effort trying to paper over them. The last thing he needs is a giant fissure. That is what you are talking about, is it not, Wilson?"

"A rift the size of a canyon! Last night, I had a conversation with Metternich's chief aide, Count von Berlichingen. He is usually skilled at whist, but played badly yesterday evening. I sensed something eating at his soul, and considering whom he serves, I thought it might be profitable to find out what it was. Now, I am normally not the kind of chap to whom a fellow unburdens himself, but the Count was desperate, and I can summon a certain residual charm on occasion. I invited him back to my place and one drink soon became many. He is currently sleeping off his excesses at my residence."

Wilson rubbed his temples in anxiety. "Turns out he had spent the whole afternoon trying to convince Metternich not to fight a duel. He failed, and Metternich tasked him to act as his second and deliver the challenge. He had been unable to steel himself to the assignment because the duel's potential ripple effects terrified him. He came to the club, hoping that cards might calm him and cause a solution to materialize."

Pennywhistle's face reflected alarm as he remembered how a duel had nearly wrecked his own life. "My God, the Congress is no place for diplomats to fight duels!"

"You will be astonished when I tell you who the challenged party was supposed to have been."

"I am almost afraid to ask."

"Czar Alexander."

John Danielski

"God's death!" Pennywhistle burst out, appalled at the monstrous stupidity. "The Czar is just reckless enough to accept such a foolish challenge! Can you imagine what would happen if Alexander died? Or Metternich?" He shook his head in frustration. "Is the nature of dispute a matter of state, something with which Lord Castlereagh might be familiar and could help resolve?"

Alas, no. It is a case of *cherchez la femme*. And the woman in question is the exquisite Duchess Sagan, the famous *salonière*. Both men have taken an interest in her, and neither one will brook a rival for her attentions."

"Blast!" exclaimed Pennywhistle in a voice edged with contempt. "We Britons came to Vienna to repair the damage done by war, not start another one! At least the war just past brought down a tyrant. Starting a war for reasons of male vanity is as ridiculous as it is appalling. That Castlereagh's system of balance and equilibrium could be wrecked by unhinged passion makes me livid!"

Pennywhistle hated exposing his emotional inner nature and took a deep breath to calm himself. "Castlereagh had warned me about these two men competing for bedmates, boys coveting each other's toys; but this woman clearly has a deeper hold on Metternich's affections, and Alexander threatens that."

"The Count emphasized that Metternich is so madly in love with her that he has quite lost his reason. He writes long letters to her every day and has showered her with gifts."

"I am astonished. I had formed the idea that Metternich's only real love is for power and that he devotes himself single-mindedly to its pursuit. Two millennia ago, Seneca informed us that love has its own agenda, one that displaces all others. Metternich is living proof that he was right."

"My only interest in love is when it makes him sufficiently foolish to be a bad player at the whist table."

"You were right to come, Wilson. Metternich's madness could destroy everything the Congress has worked so hard to build. You say the Count is sleeping last night off at your place. Could you keep him there for another eight hours?"

"That won't be difficult. He has a poor head for alcohol, and I will feed him a few more drinks."

"Good. I need to bring this to Castlereagh's attention as fast as possible. He is presently engaged at the Hofburg, but if I summon my carriage directly, he should have the information within an hour."

Pennywhistle's expression turned thoughtful as he remembered that the Chinese character that stood for danger also stood for opportunity. Castlereagh knew from personal experience the awful cost of an important official fighting a duel and might be able to convey that to Metternich. In addition, Castlereagh's plans for a secret alliance to stop Alexander's plans in central Europe might furnish Metternich a far more damaging way to gain satisfaction.

"I assume you expect to be well paid for this information, Wilson?"

Wilson's cynical half smile returned, and his posture relaxed. "A thousand pounds will do nicely. A cheap price for stopping a war."

"How generous. For a moment there, I thought you had grown a conscience."

"No danger of that, but I have done my bit for king and country. I have placed a delicate matter in the hands of a man uniquely qualified to make it go away."

"Your attempt at flattery does not blind me to the fact that the fee you ask is exorbitant. My offer is seven hundred fifty pounds; take it or leave it."

Wilson smiled. "Done! I expected only five hundred pounds. You should sharpen your negotiating skills. I saw the decision in your eyes."

"You have tells, too, Wilson. I was prepared to offer fifteen hundred. Remember, payment contingent upon you keeping the Count out of the way."

Wilson frowned, beaten at his own game.

"You can see yourself out, Wilson."

Pennywhistle rose from his chair and headed to the door. Once on the other side, he summoned Bracknell. "Ready my carriage, immediately."

"Very good, Sir Thomas."

Pennywhistle had just been handed a powder keg. He hoped he and Castlereagh would be in time to stop the burning fuse.

Chapter 35

At the same moment that Pennywhistle's carriage ground to a halt in front of the Hofburg Palace, Metternich was walking disconsolately, back to his Chancellery Office. Castlereagh had said that he wanted to meet this evening to discuss the refinement of an earlier proposal, but for once Metternich's mind was uninterested.

Metternich had gone for a long walk to clear his head. The Czar should have received his challenge yesterday, and given Alexander's hot-headed nature, he wondered why he had not received an affirmative response. Count von Berlichingen, the aide sent to deliver the challenge, was the epitome of loyal reliability, but he had not shown up at the Chancellery today, and inquiries as to his whereabouts had turned up no information. Both his wife and his mistress were worried.

Metternich wondered if his aide had met with some misadventure, and he had spoken to von Hager, who had alerted his extensive spy networks. Thus far, they had unearthed no actionable leads.

Von Hager had also provided new information about von Armfelt that put the situation of Sagan and Vava in a very different light. Metternich had been stunned to learn at the Four Elements Ball that Vava's father, Count von Armfelt, had died in August, but he had never disowned his daughter; on the contrary, he had formally adopted her. He had become suspicious of Sagan's story and had requested von Hager to assemble a detailed dossier on the man.

Rather than being the wastrel adventurer Sagan had made him out to be, von Armfelt had enjoyed a long and distinguished career as a diplomat and soldier. Instead of being unknown to the Czar, as Alexander had let him believe, von Armfelt had been a trusted advisor. At the time of his death, he had been the de facto ruler of the Grand Duchy of Finland. The Czar would do nothing to distress the widow of an important supporter; particularly one whose influence, even after death, could keep an unruly area quiescent. The Czar had strung him along, probably amused by his earnest sincerity; knowing full well that what Metternich wanted was never going to happen.

Much as it distressed him, Metternich had arrived at the conclusion that von Armfelt had probably been a better father to Vava than Sagan would ever be a mother. According to von Hager, Vava had wanted for nothing in her childhood.

The trigger for Metternich's challenge had been a long letter that he had received from Sagan, formally breaking off their affair. Though he could almost feel her invisible tears on the pages, the words and phrasing sounded exactly like Alexander's speech. The letter was undoubtedly the price the Czar had demanded for securing custody of her young daughter. Despite Sagan's torrid affair with Prince Alfred, Metternich believed the Duchess still loved him. He felt Sagan was sacrificing their love to be reunited with her only child. He understood perfectly, since his own son and daughter were dear to him.

As he wearily plodded into the Chancellery, an aide approached. "Begging your pardon, *Mein Prinz*. Lord Castlereagh is waiting in the Chancellery study. I know you were planning to speak to him this evening, and I took the liberty of making him comfortable, but he seems agitated. I thought you would want to see him at the earliest possible moment."

Metternich sighed in exasperation. Though his mind was still focused on Sagan and Alexander, it was high time he returned to his duty. "Thank you, *Herr Baron*. You were right to act as you did."

Castlereagh rose when Metternich entered the study. Metternich was pleased to see his aide had provided Castlereagh with a cup of tea and a plate of strudel. Castlereagh extended his hand, which Metternich shook firmly. The normally unreadable countenance of Castlereagh was now easily read; he was a man with a problem that wanted swift resolution.

"Please be seated, Lord Castlereagh. I am told you have a proposal for me, and I should be most interested to hear it." Metternich seated himself in the chair behind the desk.

"Ahhh...hemmm." Castlereagh cleared his throat, a singularly uncharacteristic delaying tactic. Something was up, Metternich realized.

"Prince Metternich, the proposal I wished to present can wait. A trusted confidant brought critical news to me, mere moments ago. News that requires immediate action and so takes precedence. I do not know how to put this delicately, so..."

"Please speak frankly, Lord Castlereagh."

"It has been brought to my attention that you wish to challenge the Czar to a duel."

Metternich was stunned into silence, but quickly recovered. "How on earth could you know that?"

"Let us just say that a friend of a trusted subordinate is in close contact with the second you sent to deliver the challenge. That second is... well... indisposed."

"I have been worried about Count von Berlichingen all day! I did not think the British would stoop to such a dastardly act as kidnapping."

"I assure you, I have violated no diplomat protocols. The Count is safe, unharmed, and free to go where he will... though he is sufficiently in wine that he will not be on his feet any time soon."

"So, he did not deliver my challenge?" inquired Metternich, with an undercurrent of relief.

"He did not. The Count was so upset at being called on to deliver your challenge that he sought refuge in alcohol. My subordinate's friend rescued von Berlichingen from his own excesses and provided a discreet haven. The Count relieved his burdened mind before sleep took him, and that information was communicated to my subordinate."

Metternich's eyebrows arched in understanding. "That explains why Alexander has not responded."

"Might I suggest, Prince Metternich, that the intervention of alcohol and an understanding Englishman may have saved you from a grave mistake? I have been informed that there were very personal reasons for your issuing the challenge, which I will not even attempt to raise because I would never presume to tell you your duty." Castlereagh's grey eyes met Metternich's brown ones and sent a message: *I am on your side.*

"I know you are concerned about the fate of Europe, *Herr Chancellor.* You desire a lasting peace, as do I. The death or injury of Alexander would make that impossible. I offer a proposal that would further peace and at the same time put a halt to Alexander's ambitions in central Europe." Castlereagh paused, as if worried about revealing confidential information. He continued a few moments later, his determined face reflecting doubts resolved. "Stopping Alexander's territorial advances will cause him far more pain than thwarting his... romantic advances."

Metternich's eyebrows arched. There was no point in pretending. Castlereagh's intelligence service might be smaller than his own but it was more seasoned and subtle, so he spoke with unvarnished honesty. "Your sources have not misinformed you, Lord Castlereagh. I do wish the Czar dead and I would take delight if it were by my own hand. My romantic attachments are... a problem. However...," He sighed deeply, as if releasing a weight burdening his chest. "...my country comes first. And it makes much more sense to thwart Alexander diplomatically than personally." Metternich was silent for a long moment, then said, "Very well then, Lord Castlereagh, please favor me with your proposal."

"Alexander greatly desires the creation of a Polish kingdom under his indirect control," Castlereagh began.

"Yes," interrupted Metternich. "I told him that if he creates such a puppet kingdom, the Austrians will create one next door to oppose it. He flew into such a rage that I was not sure if I would leave the conference room by the door or by the window. I departed before we broached the subject of his opposition to the continued existence of Saxony."

"He is a man of intemperate impulses," observed Castlereagh, "yet he understands power. He likes to get what he wants through bluster and bullying, but I suspect he would back down if faced with an actual war. Russia is still recovering from the losses inflicted by Napoleon's army."

"You had mentioned something last week about a secret alliance with France to oppose him in central Europe," said Metternich. "How has Talleyrand responded to your overtures?"

"He is in favor of a secret treaty of alliance, but he is concerned that the British do not have all their resources at hand, since the American War continues. I, too, have concerns about the distraction that war continues to pose," Lord Castlereagh replied. "A week ago, I sent urgent word to the negotiators in Ghent to discard earlier British demands and immediately seek a status quo *ante bellum*. The Americans are as tired of the war as we are. It is my devout hope that we will have news of a peace treaty before New Year's. Would you be willing to sign a formal agreement of alliance with France and Britain if the American War were concluded? Conclusion of the American war would free up a million pounds immediately. Consequently, England would then be able to finance 150,000 Austrian soldiers, in conjunction with a similar number from France, to act against Russia if Alexander refuses to see reason regarding Poland and Saxony."

"I will sign such an agreement, Lord Castlereagh, directly upon receiving your personal word that the American war has ceased. You propose a dangerous game of brinkmanship, but you have read Alexander correctly. Alexander treats women like provinces to be conquered, and I think that reflects his attitude toward all of Europe. He has played me for a fool in matters domestic, and I should be glad to return the favor in matters diplomatic."

"Do we have an *entante cordiale*, Prince Metternich?"

"We do, Lord Castlereagh. Have an *aide mémoire* drawn up to that effect, and have a messenger deliver it to the Chancellery. I believe that your associate may have saved the

Congress. Might I know who? I assure you, his name will be held in complete confidence.

"It is my naval attaché."

"Ah! Sir Thomas Pennywhistle," Metternich recited as his formidable memory kicked in. 'Bombproofed' Pennywhistle; a Briton with an American wife. Distinguished service in the Adriatic, Spain, and North America."

Castlereagh looked mildly amused. "All of that is public knowledge, and von Hager is thorough. I imagine you have a complete dossier on the man."

"I assume that your people have similar dossiers on Count von Berlichingen and myself."

"I make no comment," said Castlereagh, with an expression that said, *Of course.*

"I would like to meet so distinguished a soldier, particularly one who enjoys the Prince Regent's favor. Could you arrange a private meeting?"

"Sir Thomas is down the hall at this very moment, awaiting my return. I would count it a pleasure to introduce you."

Chapter 36

The Prater was the largest park in Vienna. Its vast greensward lined the south bank of the Danube. The Hauptalle, the wide, chestnut-lined avenue which ran through its center performed the same function as Rotten Row in London's Hyde Park, a destination where fashionable people on thoroughbreds came to see and be seen.

Unlike at Rotten Row, members of the Viennese lesser orders were welcomed, too, at the Prater, as long as their dress and conduct were respectable and their feet nimble enough to dodge horses sometimes ridden too fast. The park featured numerous Baroque gardens and its edges were decorated with pyramids of French cannon balls and cannon barrels captured in the last war. That was singularly appropriate today, because the former royal hunting ground was hosting a mock battle. A crowd of at least fifty thousand had assembled to watch the proceedings.

In addition to the expected generals and their aides crowding the domed reviewing stand, the park was ringed by the carriages of princes and nobles, who preferred to watch the imaginary carnage from the comfort of an enclosed cab. Legions of servants kept the carriages supplied with a steady stream of food and drink. Scores of young ladies of fashion dressed in sable furs had abandoned their carriages and

Attaché Extraordinaire

paraded around extravagantly, apparently hoping to attract the attention of future husbands.

A horde of common folk had formed to the rear of the carriages. Though their view was partly obstructed, they nevertheless appeared excited at the prospect of a bloodless battle. Dozens of bands played stirring marches and street vendors sold lots of beer, pretzels, and strudels. Jugglers, acrobats, mimes, puppeteers, folk dancers, and clowns added to the exuberance and spectacle of the event. There were sword swallowers, fire-eaters, and several novelty shows. One featured an opera-singing dwarf, another showcased a four-year-old violin prodigy, while a third promised "an African Venus": a native of Senegal who performed exotic dances.

Animal acts were popular; one featured a monkey, an owl, and a shark while another's star attraction was "Bruno, the Counting Horse."

A leather-lunged barker in front of a large tent loudly advertised a production depicting the burning of Moscow with "over a thousand moving figures!"

A giant hot-air balloon of gold rose slowly above the whole, simulating the sun and emblazoned with the Royal Arms of the sovereigns of Austria, Russia, and Prussia.

The battle was billed as a demonstration of British light infantry skills with their Prussian equivalents serving as opponents. As the British Naval Attaché, Pennywhistle was expected to attend, since some of the demonstrators were marines. He would also have preferred to observe the battle from the high ground a few hundred yards away, but instead made his way to his designated position on the reviewing stand.

Pennywhistle also would have preferred to watch the event incognito, in civilian clothing, but because of his official position, he felt compelled to wear his dress uniform. That consisted of a plumed black chapeau de bras, worn in a fore and aft rig, and a double-breasted scarlet coat with gold buttons and short swallow tails. The left side of the coat was donated by The Order of the Bath: an eight-pointed silver star with a circular red and gold center that featured three crowns and the motto *tria juncta in uno*. A gold epaulette graced each shoulder, a single white star in the center of each denoting his rank of major. A crescent-shaped gold gorget emblazoned with arms of King George hung suspended from a ribbon round his neck and the waist of his blue breeches was encircled by a crimson sash. Silk stockings and highly blacked Hessian boots completed the outfit.

He accepted the obligatory glass of champagne handed him by some general's aide and spent the next few minutes passing the time with an Austrian colonel who was curious about why the English liked fox hunts, something unknown on the Continent. The colonel could not understand why the English wasted effort on an animal the Austrians considered vermin. Since Pennywhistle disliked the sport, his ability to explain its popularity was limited.

"I'm looking forward to seeing British infantry in action." boomed a familiar but unwelcome voice from behind. "I have fought with or against many of the nations of Europe, but I have never encountered the British on the field of battle."

Pennywhistle pasted on a diplomatic smile as he turned to face von Steinwehr. The German sported an enormous blue and black shako with a massive Russian eagle in the center. His double-breasted, Prussian blue tailcoat featured huge gold epaulettes as well as a large medallion that Pennywhistle identified as the Russian Imperial Order of St. Ann, curiously similar in shape and heraldry to his own Order of the Bath. Von Steinwehr's bone white breeches fitted so tightly that you could almost see the formidable muscles flex beneath. His cavalry boots featured enormous heels that made a tall man seem a giant. Pennywhistle wondered why von Steinwehr had not worn his Imperial Guard uniform again. Perhaps he wanted to let others know that he was important enough to hold commissions in multiple Russian regiments.

"I am sure you will learn some valuable lessons today, *Herr Kolonel*. Though if the Congress has the outcome that we all hope for, it may be many years before you can apply them."

"Perhaps, Sir Thomas, but professional soldiers rarely remained unemployed for long. For men like us, there will always be another war to fight."

Pennywhistle disliked the implication that he was of a kind with the German, and so uttered the non-committal word the English favored when they found something offensive but did not wish to disagree openly. "Quite."

"I think that since man's flawed nature precludes the banishment of war, one should study the lessons of the war just completed, to secure victory in the one yet to be fought. That is why I have come today. I served with the Prussians in 1806, when Bonaparte smashed them at Auerstedt." Von Steinwehr frowned. "The rank and file fought bravely but were badly led by old barrack room generals with no aggressive spirit and tactics fifty years out of date. But the Prussians learned from their mistakes. The sweeping reforms of the past two years have resulted in a complete rebuilding of their army from the ground up. The part they played in the massive defeat of Bonaparte at Leipzig was impressive. I should be interested to see how those reforms fare against the tactics developed by men like your Wellington."

"Much as it pains me to admit it, you have a point, *Herr Kolonel*. If you desire peace, you should prepare for war.

Though I might wish otherwise, attempts to eradicate war will probably have as much success as a pan European movement to ban alcohol."

"Ha, ha, ha!" Von Steinwehr snorted a brittle laugh. "Given the German love for beer, that would take forever and a day."

"Germans without beer would be like birds without wings."

"Ha, ha! Yes! Such a Germany would share the fate of the wingless Dodo." Von Steinwehr's cold-as-death laugh stopped abruptly, and his expression turned judgmental. "But Germany will also suffer that creature's fate if its many states do not stop their squabbling. Germany must unite into a single, strong nation. For too long, powers like France, Austria, and even your country have used the principle of divide and conquer against the German people, resulting in a nearly unending series of wars. Since medieval times, Germany has been in the position of the Greek city states facing Rome. Peace in central Europe requires that Prussians, Saxons, Bavarians, Westphalians, and the rest understand that they have more in common with each other than the great powers who pretend to be their friends."

"Would that theoretical German state require stern, uncompromising leadership?" Pennywhistle could not resist baiting his nemesis.

"Absolutely! Steering a bold, new course always requires a firm hand on the tiller. Germany must unite or die. Or as Dr. Franklin observed, "we must all hang together or most assuredly we will hang separately. Recall the symbol of a Roman magistrate's power, Sir Thomas: the fasces. It was a bundle of tightly bound wooden rods with a projecting axe blade. The rods represented a magistrate's ability to sentence a man to be caned and the axe his ability to order a beheading. Bound together the rods are strong and unbreakable.

Attaché Extraordinaire

Separated, an individual rod may be snapped over a man's knee."

"Do you think the fasces would be a good symbol for a new Germany, *Herr Kolonel*?"

"An excellent one, Sir Thomas."

A light infantry bugle announced the demonstration was about to begin. People put down their champagne glasses and pulled out their spyglasses. Aides took out notebooks and prepared to record any observations of their generals.

The umpires raced to take their positions. There were twenty five of them; one for every two participants. They were dressed in canary yellow jackets so they could be easily distinguished from the demonstrators. Umpires had the power to proclaim a man "killed," if they thought he would have been hit by a round or stabbed by a bayonet. They all carried short trumpets with which their verdicts could be announced. Both sides would be using cartridges without balls, and though bayonets were attached to weapons, blades would be sheathed in leather.

The British Marines wore black coachman's hats, swallow-tailed brick red coats, and grey trousers. Members of the 52nd were dressed similarly, though with black shakos and stiff white fabric "wings" protruding from their shoulders which marked them as light infantry. Members of the 95th wore the green jackets that had earned them the nickname "grasshoppers" and carried Baker rifles instead of Brown Bess muskets.

The Prussians wore shakos of black, tailcoats of Prussian blue, and trousers of charcoal grey. Most carried model 1809 Potsdam muskets that were copies of the French Charleville, but five were armed with jaeger rifles.

John Danielski

The British would attack; the Prussians defend. Victory would be signaled by the capture of a large red flag posted on a hill, a hundred yards to the rear of the Prussian position. The head umpire would blow a trumpet to signal when one side had won. Victory could be achieved before the capture of the flag, if the umpire declared more than 75% of one side's participants as casualties.

The Prussians had positioned themselves in a very loose order behind a line of topiary animals that included lions, tigers, and bears; all animals often featured on regimental standards. The jaegers knelt, but the musket men stood with a stiffness one would never have seen among British light infantry. Pennywhistle judged they intended a static defense rather than a fluid one.

That told him something about the Prussian outlook, which was likely not lost on the British NCOs. A static defense indicated that a commander had a limited faith in his men's ability to use their initiative. The Prussians had made significant progress since 1806 in relaxing their tactical rigidity, but authoritarian thinking still lurked in the background. Their light infantry would be expected to follow a predictable set of procedures drilled in by the constant use of the lash. If the enemy responded in ways predicted by the researchers on the Prussian General Staff, their light infantry would be formidable. However, if an emergency arose where the enemy improvised and refused to conform to predictions, the Prussians' thorough training could well work against them.

The light infantry training pioneered by William Stewart and Coote Manningham employed a different perspective, which came to be known as "The Shornecliffe System", named after the camp where training took place. Much of it sprang from lessons learned about woodland warfare in the American conflict of the last century. Stewart said its purpose was," to steal the life of an enemy while putting the individual shooter at minimum risk." The new system was fluid and adaptable, attracting sharp-witted, clever men who flourished in desperate situations. The Shornecliffe System put a premium on marksmanship, initiative, and teamwork. The lash was seldom used; men were induced to self-discipline because they were taught pride in themselves and their unit. Soldiers were encouraged to think for themselves in tight spots and to understand that even the best training could not cover every eventuality.

Teamwork meant that men operated in pairs, each man responsible for the safety of his mate. Two pairs could be used as part of chain-order firing. By the time the last man in a chain had fired, the first was reloaded and ready to fire again. It was a good way to maintain a flexible forward movement as well as keep the enemy under a steady hail of lead.

The menacing looseness in the way the British held themselves told the experienced observer that these were veterans who had honed their skills on numerous battlefields. The British were considerably older than their opponents, all in their thirties or early forties, while most of the Prussians looked to be in their late teens or early twenties. British faces were hard and furrowed with cynicism while Prussian ones were the rosy-cheeked, unlined ones of that you would expect of confident lads not long out of training camp. Years of experience had taught the British what their Prussian opponents did not suspect: regulations were the beginning of combat wisdom, not the end.

Pennywhistle observed von Steinwehr's face with his peripheral vision. To his surprise, his expression had turned scholarly, as if he had signed up for a university lecture delivered by professors with muskets and bayonets.

John Danielski

The British line moved slowly forward. It was divided into six four-man firing chains, with Sergeant Major Owens serving as the overall commander. There were considerable gaps, between the chains and within them. Firing commenced as soon as movement began and became a steady *pop, pop, crackle, crackle* rather than the thunder of traditional volleys. When each man reloaded, he knelt to present a smaller target; popping up only an instant before he was ready to fire.

The umpires declared four Prussians dead.

The Prussians fired a volley, but the umpires ruled only one Briton dead. The Prussian version of light infantry might have included some training in marksmanship, but firing at men constantly bobbing up and down had not been part of their instruction.

The five jaegers fired a volley a moment after their musket men. Pennywhistle thought it foolish for them to discharge all their weapons simultaneously because their rifles were notoriously slow to load.

The British kept up a continuous barrage.

The umpires declared three more Prussians dead, which visibly angered their commander. Yet he did not change his tactics. That mistake cost him his "life"; luckily, this was a game.

One member of the sixth firing chain had taken up a prone position at the base of a large marble statue of Hermes. His job was to carefully observe the enemy line and discover who was giving the orders. He spotted his target quickly and fired.

He was fortunate to have an umpire standing nearby who witnessed the whole thing. The umpire blew his trumpet, dashed across the field, and informed the Prussian commander. He swore mightily and stormed off, protesting the umpire's call.

Attaché Extraordinaire

Pennywhistle noted von Steinwehr shaking his head vigorously, disapproving the Prussian's childish protests as well as his ineptitude. Von Steinwehr's face showed that he, like Pennywhistle was calculating the arithmetic: eight Prussians down; only one Briton *h'ors de combat*. The mock battle was unfolding much like a real one, where the losing side frequently suffered casualties far more severe than the victor.

The British continued their steady, methodical advance. Three Royal Marines fell but that was a poor payment for Prussian marksmanship, considering the number of shots that had been fired. The British riposte to the Prussians eliminated four more Prussians.

Twelve Prussians gone to four British was a winning equation in Pennywhistle's mind. From the look of surprised approval on von Steinwehr's face, the German agreed.

Finally, a Prussian sergeant major showed initiative and began shouting for the men to advance. The loss of their leader had unsettled them, and they were desperate for someone to tell them what to do. The men responded slowly, and the line lurched uncertainly forward.

Von Steinwehr clapped his hands to his temples, as if driving an unpleasant sight from his head. The Prussians were showing initiative at exactly the wrong time.

Rather than meeting fire with fire, the British fell back with well calculated steps. The firing chains reversed their earlier procedures and retreated a few steps after each discharge. Four of the chains retired directly whence they had come, but two others moved off at right angles; one went left, one went right.

Flank chain one went down on their bellies, nestling in a small Italian garden. The second did the same in bed of ferns that had been imported from South America. They waited patiently and unafraid, knowing they were poor targets.

Pennywhistle saw the satisfaction in Owens's face through his Ramsden and smiled. He was feigning weakness, luring the Prussians in; making it look as if his men were part of some slowly spreading panic. His timing was impeccable; he was reading his opponents well.

The Prussians took the bait, speeding up their steps. They looked pleased that their earlier misfortune had only been temporary and that the draconian discipline for which their nation was famous was finally paying dividends. Though there were three feet between each man and his mate, the line advanced with a rigidity that mimicked the stances that you'd expect when soldiers marched shoulder-to-shoulder. The Prussians had learned nothing from the fluid movement of the men they now faced and reminded Pennywhistle of a line of advancing iron. Iron might be strong, but it could also be brittle, if required to bend quickly.

The British movements were easy and graceful, like thin wire bending into whatever configurations best suited the needs of the moment. They were the maneuvers of men who trusted their own judgment. They responded to orders instantly and expertly, but in the absence of them, each soldier became his own general.

The British retreat slowed almost imperceptibly, while the Prussian advance speeded up to the same degree. Pennywhistle noted small smiles on both sides—the Prussians because of what was happening and the British because of what was about to happen. The Prussians stopped and fired a volley rather than relying on the bayonet, as the British would have done at this stage of the battle.

Attaché Extraordinaire

Four British soldiers went down, though Pennywhistle observed that no umpire had told them to do so. They lay inert instead of exiting the field. The emboldened Prussians stepped carefully over them, not understanding that they were not out of the fight. The Prussians had just acquired the equivalent of brush fires in their rear.

A bugle sounded, followed by Owens bellowing, "Halt! Form line!" The British retreat stopped instantly. Four of the chains silently coalesced into a formal line of battle, the men standing shoulder to shoulder. British light infantry was versatile and equally skilled at performing the more traditional battlefield evolutions.

A second British bugle sounded. The flanking chains stood up but maintained their loose order.

The Prussian advance slowed to a crawl at the shock of a nearly beaten enemy showing that it was anything but. Pennywhistle saw Owens smile ferally, as he readied the decisive counterstroke. His ears heard von Steinwehr mutter *Das is goot! Das is goot!"*

A third British bulge blared out and the "dead" rose like the spawn of Lazarus. Nothing frightened soldiers more than the enemy appearing unexpectedly in their rear.

Owens's voice thundered out, "Shoulder arms! Make ready!" Weapons were brought to full cock.

"Present!" Weapons were leveled and each man carefully selected a target. "Fire!" A solid British sheet of flame blasted out, but it came from four directions, not one. The flanking chains and the group of "dead" men fired at the same instant. The umpires turned active and declared five Prussians dead, just one shy of the eighteen needed to secure victory.

A double envelopment was the dream of every commander, to do what Hannibal had done to the Romans at Cannae. The British had managed a quadruple.

"Reload in quick time." The British did so and fired a second volley in under twenty seconds. The umpires quickly declared two more Prussians dead. Nineteen Prussians gone meant the British had achieved a statistical victory, but rather than ending the contest the chief umpire decided to let it play out; not wanting to disappoint the crowd, which was loudly cheering the British. The stalled Prussian line wavered like a shimmering mirage in desert heat.

Pennywhistle knew what came next, as did von Steinwehr. His nemesis smiled like a grinning skull. He silently mouthed something in German that Pennywhistle guessed meant, "finish it, finish it."

"Charge bayonets! Advance at the quick step!" Bayonets sheathed in leather still inspired terror. Such was the psychological impact of cold steel, that men often broke before a single blade tasted blood. The British moved quickly forward, boxing in the Prussians.

At that point, the survival instinct took over, even though it was a mock battle. With most of his friends gone and nowhere to run, one soldier threw up his arms and shouted *"Mein Komerads, Ich Kapituliere! Ich Kapituliere!"* Panic was infectious. An instant later, the rest of the line shot their hands skyward, and their voices became a surrender chorus.

"Halt!" bellowed Owens. The British line stopped five paces from the quaking Prussians. "Stand at... ease!" The Prussians realized it was the action of men who knew they nothing to fear from their opponents.

Owens stepped forward, looking for a Prussian NCO who might speak for his men. He understood only a smattering of

Attaché Extraordinaire

German, but his bold advance made his intentions clear. A sergeant major stepped forward, snapped to rigid attention, and flashed a quick salute. He was the oldest man in the formation, although he was not more than twenty five.

A hush had fallen over the crowd. Surrender was always dramatic, even though this was a battle where no one had really died.

Owens returned the salute graciously, sensing he was confronting a good man trying to do his best to execute a disagreeable duty. *"Ich heise Sergeant Major Owens."* The Welshman extended his hand.

"Ich bin Vizefeldwebel Klinghofer." The Prussian accepted the invitation and shook Owens's hand firmly. He then took his sword from his scabbard and offered it to Owens, as the traditional token of surrender. *Ich biete Ihnen mein Schwert an, Sergeant Major.*

Owens acknowledged the gesture with a quick nod, then accepted the sword. He glanced over it, and then made a magnanimous decision. He handed the blade back. *"Danke, Herr Feldwebel, aber ich muss Sie bitten, Ihr Schwert zu behalten. Sie haben ehrenhaft gekämpft."*

Pennywhistle gathered he was saying. "Keep it with honor. You have fought well." It was the gallant thing to say, even if it was not true.

Von Steinwehr scowled. *"Nein, Nein!"*

A sergeant in scarlet approached Owens, proudly flourishing the coveted red flag. Owens accepted it and held it aloft, like Perseus displaying the head of Medusa. The umpire blew the trumpet, signifying the demonstration was over.

The crowd began clapping and cheering loudly. The response on the reviewing stands was more muted, but murmurs of approval and assorted nods told Pennywhistle the military mandarins were impressed by the conduct of the Britons.

Except for one man: von Steinwehr. He wore an expression that suggested the immediate extinction of the surviving Prussians would be the condign judgement of a good commander.

"What troubles you, *Herr Kolonel*? I thought the demonstration went well."

"The British performed admirably, Sir Thomas, far exceeding my expectations. The Prussians performed dismally, disgracefully. Rather than their leader being given back his sword, I would have had him shot. As Voltaire said about your nation, "*Dans ce pays-ci, il est bon de tuer de temps en temps un amiral pour encourager les autres,*" In fact, I might have gone one better. The Romans practiced decimation when a unit failed badly, executing every tenth man. It is regrettable that practice has fallen into disuse."

Pennywhistle suppressed his shock at his opponent's response, though it was consistent with what he knew about the man. "I would remind you, *Herr Kolonel*, that Voltaire was expressing sympathy for the man who was shot, Admiral Byng. He failed to relieve Minorca, not through want of courage, but because the fleet given him was too small."

"You are entirely too forgiving, Sir Thomas. Failure is failure and must be punished not excused. I have no patience with men who say I could have succeeded but I was not given enough men, supplies, support... well, you see what I mean. Being a soldier is about making do, not bleating for a perfect situation that will never occur."

"Allow me to offer an alternative to your perspective, *Herr Kolonel*. I am reminded of something St. Theresa of Avila once said about a conversation that she had with God while in deep meditation. "Why do you make me suffer so much when I am your most faithful servant?" She maintained the response from On-High was "to test your faith, so it may be strengthened." Her response was "with a perspective like that, it is no wonder you have so few earthly friends."

Von Steinwehr's face turned brutally cynical and his voice rippled with contempt. "I have no time for mystics and their silly, dreamy-eyed prattle. Give me practical, hard-headed men who can solve problems in this world rather than focusing on the one to come. I do not seek confidants, companions, or friends, but want subordinates I can trust. This saint you speak of makes one point of value. Soldiers must have faith in their commander and should understand that testing their abilities makes them both better men and better soldiers."

"Push men to the edge of the abyss and see if they leap it or fall in? Is that a fair extrapolation?"

"An excellent one, Sir Thomas. Battle is a blast furnace that separates iron from dross. I have been through many fires, both literal and metaphorical, and it is only because of my struggles that I have become the man talking to you today."

Pennywhistle realized that von Steinwehr saw himself as a good man toughened by his travails rather than as a monster who had been broken by them. His ambition and arrogance were so great that they had stripped him of any ability to view himself honestly. No villain ever perceived himself as one, and each thought he was misunderstood by a world too stupid to grasp his grand wisdom.

"I think there are two ways to handle men, *Herr Kolonel.* The old way is to treat them like spaniels trainable only by a liberal application of the stick. I prefer to appeal to their better natures. I want them to always do the right thing, even when no one is watching."

"An admirable intention, Sir Thomas, but misguided. Most men have no better natures, only deeply flawed ones. Most men are fools driven by rampaging emotions; rational thought is beyond them and should be a function of their betters. Left to their own devices, the rank and file of any society generally produce chaos and suffering for those around them. I stand for order, discipline, and the primacy of natural law."

"Have mercy and compassion any roles to play in your universe?" inquired Pennywhistle, barely keeping the sarcasm from his voice.

"Mercy and compassion are best exercised by a strong ruler with the power of action at his fingertips rather than a weak one with only the power of good intentions." His eyes burned with self-righteousness and his voice became that of a judge ordering a hanging. "Men must be taught boldly who is their master and made to follow him without question."

"Ah," said Pennywhistle blandly, and his eyes narrowed in understanding. "King before conscience."

It was always helpful to have your opponent tell you in his own words why he had to be stopped. Von Steinwehr had just shown him a mind that was a sack of rabid cats and a character that was fixed in stone. A bonfire burned because that was its nature. You could either extinguish it or get out of its way. "I respectfully disagree, *Herr Kolonel*. The actions performed by British soldiers today reflect my philosophy, and I think you will allow that they performed admirably."

"They did, but it may well be due to the stalwart character of your nation, rather than an easing of traditional training methods."

Attaché Extraordinaire

This argument was going nowhere. Trying to persuade a fanatic was as futile as trying to work out the value of pi to the last digit. Pennywhistle thanked his lucky stars when an Austrian major appeared. "Pardon the interruption, Sir Thomas, but my general would like to have a few words with you about the demonstration just ended. He is most impressed and has many questions."

"I should be delighted to answer them." He turned to von Steinwehr. "I should like to continue this chat, *Herr Kolonel,*" he lied," but duty calls. You know how it is." Right now, duty would be a pleasure; talking with von Steinwehr made him feel like King Lear shouting his thoughts on a blasted heath.

"I quite understand, Sir Thomas. I look forward to our next meeting."

It was a sentiment that Pennywhistle did not reciprocate.

Chapter 37

After the demonstration ended, refreshments were offered to the British by their Austrian hosts. The Prussians were marched off by their vexed sergeant major.

"You have not lost your touch, Owens. You put on a smart show," said Dale.

"As I live and breathe, if it isn't Andrew Dale! I had heard you'd wedded and retired. I figured you'd logged your time and wanted to collect your pension. And who is this fine-looking lad?"

"My son, Andrew. Andrew, this is my old friend, Sergeant Major Owens."

The nine-year old straightened like a soldier and offered his hand. "Very pleased to meet you, sir."

"And I you, young man. You look very much like your father."

"I am proud that I do, sir. Tell me, Sergeant Major, where did you and my father serve together?"

"In Spain. I met your father during the raid on Santander, though we both fought at Trafalgar in ships near each other. Do you intend to be a soldier or a Marine, Andrew?"

"I like listening to my father's stories, but a military life is not for me. I wish to publish my own newspaper someday!"

Attaché Extraordinaire

"His mother ran a newspaper back in London," interjected Dale. "She is in Vienna covering the Congress as the correspondent for several London papers."

"So, you tagged along for the ride?" inquired Owens playfully.

Dale's expression turned serious. "The reason I am here involves something I need to discuss with you." His eyes became hard. "In private."

"So, this reunion is not accidental."

"I am glad to see you, of course, Owens, but this call is not a social one." Dale reached into his pocket and handed his son some coins. "Why don't you go and buy yourself some lemonade and strudel, Andrew?"

"Thank you, Father!" He accepted the coins, made a quick bow in Owens's direction, and dashed off.

"A fine boy, Dale, but when I knew you in Spain, you never mentioned children."

"I did not know of him until a few months ago. I had intended to marry his mother after I returned from Trafalgar, but I was mistakenly listed as killed in action. She was so overcome by grief that she moved to London and left no forwarding address. I lost track of her for many years."

"You were lucky to find her again. Did she have something to do with your retirement?"

"She helped me achieve my dream of becoming an innkeeper, the sort of inn where retired and traveling military men can gather convivially to swap war stories and other lies. We bought the Black Robin Inn in Kent. "

"Congratulations! And now... you are here." The two men strolled away from the crowds until they came to a deserted stretch of the garden, far away from the tables of food and drink.

"I am getting back in harness one final time."

"That is curious. I don't see any battles on the horizon."

"This will be an expedition without uniforms or identifying badges, the kind of expedition that can be explained away if it succeeds and denied if it goes wrong. But it needs a trained cadre of men to succeed."

"Sounds intriguing, but my men are neither mercenaries nor auxiliaries."

"But the outcome affects the British Crown, and I expect Lord Castlereagh to give his tacit approval in the next few hours. You and your men will be paid in hard coin, but no receipts will ever be submitted."

"This grows more interesting by the moment, Dale. What details can you tell me?"

"Only the barest. Once the mission is approved, you would receive a briefing from my former commanding officer, the present British Naval Attaché."

"Sir Thomas Pennywhistle? Owens blinked in surprise. 'Bombproofed Pennywhistle'? I met him, and he impressed me. But I thought his job was purely diplomatic."

"The task is diplomatic but requires military support to accomplish. It will involve a river approach, scaling a cliff, and breeching the walls of a well defended fortress. And it will have to be done at night."

Owens frowned. "That's asking a lot."

"It is. All I can say is that enemies of the realm will be empowered if we fail."

"When you put it that way..."

"I do put it that way."

"I doubt any of my men will demur, once they understand the importance of the mission. The extra pay will be very welcome, though I doubt that will be the primary motivation for any of them. Why did Sir Thomas not say anything about this when I visited his office?"

"He was not yet sure whether or how the mission would proceed. Now he is. He also wanted to see your men in action. Your demonstration today was an audition. He saw the whole thing and was most impressed. That is why he sent me over here after the demonstration and not before."

Owen rubbed his mutton-chop whiskers, hiding a smile. "I am curious about how Sir Thomas got his nickname. There is a wild story about that, but I put it down to a tall tale told by men who had drunk too much grog. "

"I do not know what tale you heard, but I was present when he was dubbed 'Bombproofed'. I would not have believed what happened, if I had not seen it for myself."

"And what exactly did happen?"

"His horse stepped on an infernal device planted by the Americans. It blew the horse apart and threw him high into the air. When he landed, he was dead, as least so far as I could see. No breath, no pulse, and his eyes were fixed and staring. Then, out of the blue, he started breathing and came back to life."

Owens looked skeptical.

"Truly, he did. You and I have seen death, and we both know the tricks by which cowards fake their own demise. This was nothing like that. He sat up and started talking, just like he had only been taking a nap. The men were astonished, and some were fearful. He explained it away as an unusual but recognized medical event, which reassured the soldiers, but to me... well... it seemed a miracle. And whatever happened to him in those five minutes... changed him."

"Did it make him better or worse?"

"Better, though he was good man to start with. He became a lot calmer, and the tics and tremors he had been suffering from went away. He'd always tried to conceal them, but I had seen him after battles, when the shakes started. He listens better now, and sometimes just seems to know little things about people. I have seen him sense an event well before it happens. Mostly, he acts as if some giant weight had been lifted from his shoulders, like Atlas after he no longer had to hold up the world. I think that weight might have been guilt. He was a fine soldier, but the killing bothered him. He was always a man with a conscience. I would say his encounter with death just fine tuned it, like a good musician suddenly being given the gift of perfect pitch. I should add that he has a not-quite healed wound that causes him chronic pain."

"I have heard of such things in the tales from my homeland. So, how soon will this expedition take place, and what is the expected duration?"

"Within the next two weeks, but your men would have to be ready to move on a moment's notice. I do not expect the venture to last more than twelve hours. Do you have access to scaling ladders and grappling hooks.?"

"Yes, we do. Our training camp is located on the grounds of what was once an abbey. And, hmm, the walls and windows are suitable for practice under cover of darkness."

"When the time draws near, could you put it about that some of your men have come down with dysentery? I do not want to have any absences commented upon or set off warning bells."

"I can do that. Will we receive any artillery support?"

"Sorry, no. This will be a stealth assault. I should also warn you that the fortress is armed with twelve pounders, which your men will need to spike. Do any of your men have a fear of

Attaché Extraordinaire

heights? I have a good reason for asking. There may be a way for several men to approach the fortress in an unusual fashion."

"And what is that 'unusual fashion'?"

"From the air."

Pennywhistle met with Lord Castlereagh later in the afternoon and gave a description of the demonstration and a summary of his evolving plan.

"I wish I could have attended the demonstration," remarked Castlereagh, "but Alexander was particularly long-winded." He drummed his fingers on the table. "You say there is no other way?" inquired a worried Castlereagh.

"None, my lord. I have looked at the situation from a variety of angles. My plan is complicated and expensive, but I believe it has a reasonable chance of success. We will not only have surprise on our side, but science. Considering what is at stake, I think we must act."

"Very well. You have my approval. You may draw on the special funds of the embassy. How long will your preparations take?"

"It may take a week to set up."

"And you can find a hot air balloon?"

"I saw one at the Prater Park demonstration you missed."

"What about those other contraptions? What did you call them, parachutes? I have never heard of such devices".

"They have been used to divert and delight Parisian crowds. Madame Marie Blanchard, who called herself an aeronaut, used to thrill Bonaparte by jumping from a balloon at seven thousand feet, hurtling toward the ground, and then opening her parachute to float gracefully to earth."

"That must have been a sight to see! Is she still performing?"

"Sadly, no. On her final jump, her parachute failed to open fully. She crashed onto a roof and fell three stories to the cobblestones."

"And you propose to jump at night?" demanded a horrified Castlereagh.

"I see no other way. The fortress is too well guarded for subterfuge or direct assault to work."

"And your parachutes are based on the one this Parisian aeronaut used?"

"I plan to make one modification to prevent the disaster that killed Blanchard."

"I am glad to hear that! But you are still taking an enormous risk. And who is going to construct these contraptions? Will they be discreet?"

"There are merchants in the city who have the raw materials, and I will place orders in such a way as to disguise our intent, putting it out that the material is for clothing and covers. I will call on the skills of experienced seamstresses used to sewing regimental flags; they are generally made of silk. The final work shall be done by British seamstresses who only speak English and so cannot gossip with foreign spies. I will search out ladies known for their discretion and patriotism."

"What about the air guns?"

"They are virtually silent and about the size of a Baker Rifle. The Lewis and Clark Expedition in America impressed the Indians with a Viennese made air rifle, but the American government declined to purchase any further specimens for general use because they are expensive to manufacture. I was lucky to discover a cache of unissued ones in a warehouse. And

Attaché Extraordinaire

I know where I can lay my hands on a stock of Prussian Foot Artillery uniforms; not the ones for battle, but those used for everyday duties. Their dark color will blend in well with the night, and if seen, will point the finger at the Prussians, not the British."

"Von Hardenberg would have a hard time explaining how that came about," remarked Castlereagh," and that could be useful in driving a wedge between the Prussians and the Russians. Perhaps you could deliberately leave a cap or two behind. Have you spoken to Mr. Montgomery about the *Queen Charlotte*?"

"I have. We have an understanding. It takes an hour to raise steam if the boilers are cold, and I will allow time for that. I have not told him why I need his boat, but I have said there may be risks. I have also added that His Majesty's government would be very grateful and will remunerate handsomely the cost of any repairs. The one thing that constitutes a wild card is the weather, my lord. Too much ice in the river could pose a problem for the *Queen*'s hull, though she is stoutly built. However, Mr. Montgomery assures me that even if we are hit with bitterly cold weather, it would still take a few days for a body of water as large as the Danube to freeze solid. I should mention that I have also engaged the *Queen Charlotte* as a deception."

"I am not sure I understand, Sir Thomas."

"Steamboats are noisy and belch smoke. Night can conceal the smoke, but the sound is a problem. The solution is to make something extraordinary seem ordinary. For the twelve nights of Christmas, the *Queen Charlotte* will be a pleasure cruise vessel, with a band playing music for the merry-makers and a chorus singing German carols. The younger sister of Baroness de Krudener will be hosting the events, and she has already issued invitations to many of the aristocracy. I assure you, Lord Castlereagh, that these invitations will be highly sought after. The castle guards will come to regard the passage of the boat and the noise of the engine as routine. When we make our approach on New Year's Eve, the seventh of the twelve nights, my hope is that the guards, inured to the spectacle, will not sound the alarm. At the very least, it will buy us some time before they realize their mistake."

"This is complicated," sighed Castlereagh. "So many variables."

"True, my lord. Yet it is analogous to the diplomatic situation in Vienna, which you deal with on a daily basis."

Chapter 38

December 31st, the day of the Razoumovsky Ball, dawned fair and crisp. Sammie Jo arose early to make the final preparations with Lady Leith.

The memory of a conversation with her husband a week earlier came back to her. "The ironsmith I hired delivered the contraption I designed this morning. It will allow the steam engine to transfer its energy horizontally to the tow ropes. I have five seamstresses working non-stop to construct the parachutes, and they should have them ready the morning of the ball. I gave Owens's men a very detailed briefing. Those sketches I made on the *Queen Charlotte* came in very handy, and I thank you again for bringing my sketch book and pencils. I distributed a down payment to the men that left them smiling."

"So, we launch on the evening of the ball?"

"Yes, with such a large crowd, it should be easy for us to slip away, particularly since we are disguised and masked. I do not want to cheat you of an interesting evening, so we will disappear later, rather than sooner. Indeed, it is important that people know we were there so our alibi can be established, and it would take a seer to associate us with what comes later. In addition, by the time we depart at midnight, many of the guests will be in an alcoholic fog, providing additional cover."

"Dinner, dancing, and death. Land sakes, Tom. That is going to be some evening."

"A night to remember, indeed. But remember, I want you safe. You remain on the *Queen Charlotte* and—"

"I know, I know, supervise that contraption of yours. I have to admit it's an unexpected way to move men quick," said Sammie Jo. "But they are going to have to hold on real tight once the line begins to move upward. How did you think of it?"

"It's not new, just an improvement on an old idea. Ships towing boats and sails positioned by using ropes are routine to me. In this case, steam replaces men and wind power, supplying a much steadier and more powerful source of energy. Ship's blocks will facilitate the action, functioning as pulleys. I sent Dale to a local shipyard with a list of supplies. I am sure the rope weavers are laboring hard as we speak."

***

As Sammie Jo finished breakfast, she related that conversation to Lady Leith. "Tom has all bets covered."

"I agree, Sammie Jo. I thought you might want to know what to expect at the ball, to make your plans accordingly. I have asked my friend, Emily, the wife of Lord Castlereagh, to call upon us when the clock strikes ten. We saw each other frequently during the London season. Count Razoumovsky is the nephew of Lord Clanwilliam, who is visiting the city and is a good friend of Emily. She will have information that most will not. I should add that she is eager to meet you."

"Not sure what to make of that, Margaret. Eager as in 'wants to get to know me' or eager as in 'freak shows can be amusing'."

Attaché Extraordinaire

Margaret laughed. "She is genuinely curious about Americans, having never met one. She has heard a lot about you, particularly after what people observed at the hunt. I know she is tired of the pretense and pomposity of Vienna, where British people are sometimes regarded as uncivilized outsiders—one of the drawbacks of being an island nation. Do not worry about guarding your tongue; she likes spontaneity so I think she will like you. She also likes to dance, as you do. Though you move with much more instinctive grace than she."

There was a knocking on the breakfast room door.

"Enter."

It was Grimsby. "Sorry to disturb you, mi ladies." He handed Sammie Jo an embossed card on a silver tray. Sammie Jo examined it and nodded.

"I have taken the liberty of showing Lady Castlereagh to the morning room."

"Very good, Grimsby," said Sammie Jo. We will be there shortly. Will you please see she is served tea and... scones?" She looked at Lady Leith.

"Strudel would be better."

"Make that tea and strudel, Grimsby."

"Very good, milady." He was gone in a flash.

Sammie Jo felt dwarfed by the gilt and gold Louis XIV style morning room, a child asked to sit at the adult table. It seemed more fitted to a public building than a home and promoted a feeling of stately formality rather than easy-going conversation. It was intended to send a message of superiority and it succeeded admirably.

Lady Castlereagh was quietly sipping tea when Sammie Jo and Lady Leith entered. Sammie Jo was struck by her perfect ordinariness. She was neither pretty nor homely, though there was a certain sweetness about her face. She was slightly overweight and could have passed for the wife of a prosperous publican, if she had not been so well dressed.

She wore a day dress of floral and striped robin's egg blue brocade with a decorative muslin apron flecked with gold starbursts. A wide red sash crossed the high waist, and the skirt was box pleated in the back; probably fluffed out with a small pad hidden under the waistline. She had removed her bonnet of green silk, revealing a braided hair style that could best be termed "sensible."

"Emily, how delightful to see you!" said Lady Leith extending both hands in greeting. Lady Castlereagh gave a gentle smile and rose. She took Lady Leith's hands and planted two pecks on her cheeks. Sammie Jo recognized the *au courant* French form of greeting.

"Lady Castlereagh, may I present my good friend, and the wife of my godson, Lady Pennywhistle."

Sammie Jo gave the expected curtsey which was swiftly returned.

"Enchanted, Lady Castlereagh."

"I as well, Lady Pennywhistle."

Since she wanted to meet an American, Sammie Jo decided it was time for some homespun directness. "Please milady, let us not stand on ceremony. I would like you to become as good a friend to me as you are to Margaret, and I thought I might speed things along. My formal name is Samantha Josephine, but I go by Sammie Jo."

Lady Castlereagh blinked. "My! You are direct and don't waste time."

Sammie Jo wondered if her mouth had just acquired a foot.

Lady Castlereagh smiled, clarifying the intent of her words. "Thank goodness for that. I am so tired of people in this town who want me to be awed by their titles and reputations; neither willing to extend the hand of real friendship nor receive it in return. Please, Sammie Jo, call me Emily."

"Phew!" drawled Sammie Jo. "I know I have a lot to learn about polite society, but I have had some excellent teachers, chief among them, Margaret here. I am hoping I can add you to the good people who have helped me so much."

"I take that as a great compliment," replied Lady Castlereagh. "If I may return your directness, I should be very curious to hear about your background. I have heard rumors that you are an excellent shot and that you ran off a contingent of poachers during the hunt. If those things are true, you are a woman in the tradition of the courageous Roman women of old."

There was a flutter of wings and Plymouth soared through the air, alighting on Sammie Jo's right shoulder. "Pleased to meet you," he chirpcd.

Lady Castlereagh burst out laughing. "What a beautiful bird."

"His name is Plymouth, and like me, he has survived a lot of dings and dents. I know my way around a rifle pretty good and let's just say those folks I ran off... well they wanted to get to know me a lot better; in a biblical sense."

"Oh my," gasped Lady Castlereagh.

Sammie Jo chuckled. "Guns, knives, and bullwhips are more persuasive than words. Those bas—er, yokels won't be bothering any other ladies this side of eternity."

"Good for you," said Lady Castlereagh with real enthusiasm. "Some of the men here... they are so arrogant and contemptuous of our sex that they are just... well... "

"Pigs?" replied Sammie Jo with devils in her eyes.

"Ha, ha, ha! Exactly! You don't mince words! So refreshing. How did you get that way?"

Satisfied that the ice was well and truly broken, Sammie Jo decided Lady Castlereagh would not suffer an attack of the vapors if she dispensed with sugarcoating. "I will tell you my story, Emily. It weren't always pretty, because every trail has some puddles, but you don't learn much when things always go right. And what I say is, when you get to the end of your rope, tie a knot and hang on."

"I shall be riveted!"

Sammie Jo related that story over the next half hour. She told it like an American Canterbury Tale, peppering it with colorful figures of speech that told a listener that her account was one of down-to-earth honesty, untouched by even a hint of artifice. She succeeded in bridling her passion for colorful expletives, but did not bother to conceal the fact that she had killed men: they had, of course, been bad men.

Lady Castlereagh sipped her tea and nibbled her strudel compulsively as the excitement mounted. She seemed fascinated by her rough and tumble background as well as her fierce independence. Rather than being put off by them, her eyes expressed admiration. Sammie Jo guessed she was tired of snotty women skilled in aristocratic back biting, the kind of people guaranteed never to be there when you needed them, since they were always looking to latch on to someone deemed more fashionable, more connected, and more the talk of the town.

When Sammie Jo finished, Emily exclaimed, "My stars, what an astonishing tale! I do not believe I have ever spent a more interesting hour. I know you wish to improve your manners and I applaud you for it, but do not ever change your character. I can see now why your husband chose you."

Attaché Extraordinaire

"Thank you, Emily, but I'm plumb scared of embarrassing my husband at the ball. I would be very grateful if you could tell me what to expect and how to prepare for it. Life is a lot simpler when you plough around the stumps, but I can't see them for the weeds at this here Congress."

"It would be my pleasure, Sammie Jo." Emily smiled broadly; reveling in the chance to play teacher to a worthy neophyte. "If the count follows his usual practice, there will first be a generalized, informal gathering, followed by a grand, formal promenade. A large, multi-course meal will follow. My best advice is to take baby bites of whatever is offered. Alcohol of all kinds will be offered freely. Drink sparingly. I often accept one glass of wine, take a few sips, then hold it for the rest of the evening.

A concert comes next. That gives the guests time to digest their food. After the music, comes dancing. The waltz is popular, as is the polonaise. The minuet still has its followers and country dances attract many couples. Country dances can vary from slow to very fast. Pace yourself; dancing can wear you out quickly."

Sammie Jo smiled. "One of the benefits of spending all that time hunting in the backwoods is that I do not tire easily."

"Wonderful! I can dance for hours. I am not a fan of these parties, but the chance to dance compensates for any tedium imposed by them. After the dancing, comes *le tableau vivant*.

"What's that?"

"It is the re-creation of a famous painting, using scenery, actors, and actresses. It is elaborate, detailed, and accompanied by music. You will find them amusing. Past ones have included Raphael's *The School of Athens*, Rubens's *the Judgement of Paris,* and Rembrandt's *Night Watch*."

"My husband has mentioned the last two artists, but I ain't never heard tell of the first one."

"Next, comes storytelling. Ghost stories are all the rage. Strangely, Bonaparte started that tradition. If you know any good ones, you will acquire a following."

"I got a whole fund of scary stories, Emily. I think they will like "The Penmore Poltergeist," and "The Haunted Knee of the Great Woz.""

"Then there is a lottery. Each guest will be given a ticket upon entering. You may well go home with a jeweled ring, a set of porcelain, or a diamond encrusted snuff box."

Sammie Jo shook her head in wonderment. "It's not just a party, it's Christmas!"

"Showing expansive largesse adds to the prestige of party givers. The climax of the evening is a joust on the palace grounds."

"A joust? Did I hear that right? You mean something like knights did in the olden days?"

"I do, though this is more theatre than anything else. Still, people can get hurt, especially since some of the knights...well let us just say some of their courage is of the liquid variety."

"Knights drunk as skunks with lances," Sammie Jo laughed.

"Sometimes the joust becomes a comedy rather than a drama."

"I ain't never heard of this polonaise dance you mention. What are the steps like?"

"I would be happy to show you, Sammie Jo, but dancing with the woman is a very imperfect imitation of dancing with a man."

"I believe I can remedy that," interjected Lady Leith. "The Earl is a floor below us. There are few dance steps he does not know. I am certain he would be happy to be Sammie Jo's partner."

"What an excellent coincidence," burbled Lady Castlereagh.

"I can't wait to start," said Sammie Jo.

The next two hours passed quickly and with much joy.

Chapter 39

Ingrid von Steinwehr had been living something akin to the solitary life of a monk for the past ten days, though her motives were the very earthly ones of power, status, and revenge. It was an existence devoted to hard work, deep concentration, and a meticulous attention to detail. She had eaten little, slept less, and was developing an unnatural affinity for coffee. *The Little Code Breaker and Pocket Cryptographer* was proving a very tough nut to crack. The eureka moment she had worked so hard for had eluded her. Tomorrow was New Year's Day, but it looked like 1815 was not going to start with a solution.

She regretted she could not attend the Razoumovsky Ball as the Countess who she deserved to be.

Eliminating the first five decryption tables had been a painstaking and dreary process of guess, test, fail, start over, guess, test, fail and begin again. Her husband's earlier efforts had helped, but she had been unable to get beyond his twelve letters. For example, 1 indicated a "T," 8 an "E," and 9 an "A" A semicolon indicated that a letter was repeated twice. Twelve letters accounted for 80% of English words; yet without the other fourteen, the letters were useless.

The encrypted half of each letter was a basic transposition code, part of a family that the French called *petit chiffres*, or small cyphers. It was a system that was easy to use but difficult to break, because it was utterly random. You needed a table or chart to give the equivalencies between numbers and letters.

The numbers reminded her of looking at arrest warrants that detailed the crimes but did not identify the perpetrators. The crimes alluded to in the plain text were impressive. Bribery, jobbery, extortion, blackmail, theft, and sale of offices were mere hors d'oeuvres. The main courses included sodomy, pedophilia, and murder. It was strongly suggested that the names associated with them were among the highest in the land. She and her husband had always thought the British corrupt, and what lay within likely furnished proof.

The letters had originally been part of a secret correspondence, wherein Mrs. Clarke had tried to blackmail her former lover, The Duke of York. He was the second son of George III, and had been the Commander-in-Chief of the British Army. When news of the letters leaked, he had been forced to resign. A parliamentary inquiry had abruptly been halted when it became clear that some highly placed people might be implicated in the scandal. He was later reinstated as Commander-in-Chief, but these letters could cause a second removal.

The von Steinwehr goal would remain a chimera unless she could find the right key to turn the final lock. She felt the sixth table was the right key. She began to pace and mutter, her frustration rising with each step. She stopped and slammed her hand on the long table, swearing loudly as she did so. She hit the table so hard that two unwanted things happened. Her ink pot and coffee cup both tipped, pouring their contents onto the edge of the sixth decryption table.

"No, no, no!" She screamed. Had she just destroyed her future? She wiped the page as quickly as she could, scraping most of the muck off. The chart was left intact, but some liquid had seeped under the cover. She slammed the book shut and commenced wiping the cover vigorously.

As she did, the gold lettering of the title began to weep. She picked up her magnifying glass and examined the letters closely. The lettering seemed to have been applied recently, not forty years ago. The layer of cloth beneath looked different when wet and seemed new material, not old. Something did not add up.

She ran her fingers over the cover, playing a hunch. Sure enough, the cover's lower layers had been glued together, not sewn. Gluing covers was a recent innovation and unknown forty years ago.

She scowled as she apprehended why she had been unsuccessful. The book was a forgery!

She threw the book down in a rage. Her hard work had been a complete waste of time! She and her husband had been tricked by a very clever plan.

She plopped into her chair and forced herself to think. The real book was still out there. It was time for complete ruthlessness. If you wanted to get a man to surrender something important, strike at what he held most dear. Men were most vulnerable where their hearts were concerned.

The grudging respect she had developed for Lady Pennywhistle disappeared in a whirlpool of anger. She spat several curses and realized she wanted revenge. How dare that American upstart think she could block the plans of a European Countess!

It would have to be a straight swap. Lady Pennywhistle for the codebook. That way there would be no deception.

She poured herself another cup of coffee and wondered how the abduction could be arranged. There would be lots of people at the Razoumovsky Ball and many different types of entertainment. All of that could provide the perfect cover for a kidnapping. Since it was to be a masked, costume affair it would be possible to get very close to their target without exciting suspicions.

The problem was, Lady Pennywhistle was a fighter by nature and her struggles would attract lots of unwanted attention.

Then she remembered Herr Moldenhower, an apothecary in the city who had given her some very efficacious pills for her migraine headaches. He had told her he was working on something to help those plagued with insomnia. It was a mixture of chlorinated lime and ethanol: intended to replace laughing gas, whose useful effects had been chiefly employed for amusement. He said if a solution were applied to a cloth placed over a person's nose, unconsciousness would follow shortly after. He said it was dangerous, because he was uncertain of how much to use: too much could make the sleep permanent.

He struck Ingrid as a man whose sensibilities could be lulled into somnolence for the right amount of coin. She would administer the dose herself. She knew she didn't have to, but she wanted the satisfaction of seeing the upstart American hoyden put down by her betters.

She needed a costume for the evening. She knew what the peasants had said about her and ordinarily, it made her blood boil. She was no Hela, but tonight it would be the perfect disguise. She needed a false identity that would cause people to look away when she approached. An old sable ball gown could be pressed into service; she would add a few slashes and bloodstains. Her lady's maid was a clever artist and jack-of-all trades and could create a split face mask, part skull and part flesh, part beauty and part ugliness.

Hela was the daughter of Loki, the trickster God so using deception to snatch a human prize seemed appropriate. In addition, the idea of posing as a bringer of death had a certain appeal, as she thought of the ignorant serfs who had disdained her gifts. Her husband was already planning to go as Siegfried: Norse mythology was hugely popular because it was tied to rising German nationalism. A Norse Goddess was a perfect compliment. The clock on the wall struck ten: the ball would commence at eight o' clock. There was no time to lose.

She opened the door and barked, "Schumacher! Schumacher!" Her husband's chief aide appeared in under a minute. "Tell Captain von Geisel to get the launch ready. I must go to Vienna immediately."

"Yes madam, but remember, the boiler is cold."

"I know! I know! Be gone with you. There is not a minute to waste."

"Yes madam, yes, yes!" He said with an obsequiousness that she found annoying. She liked strong independent men, not well-mannered lackeys. And yet his presence reminded her that she and her husband were born to rule over such lesser beings.

"Heidi! Heidi!" She bellowed.

Her maid appeared quickly. "Yes Countess?"

"I have an important job for you. You have one hour to complete it."

She spent the hour the boiler took to heat working out the details of her plan. She told herself things could still work out as Destiny intended.

Attaché Extraordinaire

The hour flew by. Here was Schumacher. "The launch is ready, madam. Captain von Geisel says the weather is good and he can have you in Vienna within an hour."

"Excellent!"

"The mask is done, Countess," said Heidi who stood behind Schumacher. "Try it on."

Ingrid did so. "What do you think?" she said to Heidi and Schumacher.

"Horrible!" said Schumacher.

"A nightmare!" said Heidi.

"Perfect," chortled Ingrid.

***

"What do you think of my costume Tom?" inquired Sammie Jo.

Pennywhistle laughed. "It is not really a costume at all. It's your old working gear. It is not an imitation of you, it is you. Very amusing! At a ball where deception is in vogue, you are telling the truth. You are an American Valkyrie."

She was dressed in a brown fringed hunting shirt of heavy linen, buckskin trousers, low black boots, and a wide brimmed slouch hat that was the color of dust. It was an outfit designed to blend in with the forest and not attract attention. Yet because of its earth tones and lack of flamboyance, it would be a magnet for many eyes at the ball.

Her simple attire would distinguish her as Ben Franklin's did in Paris. Amidst the corrupt, overdressed fops at the Court of Louis XVI, he had attired himself as an honest American burgher, clad in brown homespun.

"Are you planning on taking The Widowmaker?"

"No, I ain't, but I am going to wear my bullwhip."

Pennywhistle chuckled. "I must have your promise that you will not use it on impudent men tonight."

Sammie Jo smiled back." Nah! My tongue can handle things. Now I want to show you your costume."

She rang for Grimsby who quickly returned with a clothing bag. "I based the measurements on your uniform. I hope they got things right.

Pennywhistle opened the bag hesitantly, as if it were a serpent about to strike. These silly impersonations annoyed him. However, once he saw its contents, he laughed.

"Really Sammie Jo, is that how you see me?"

"Yes, it is. Underneath your fancy clothes, fancy speech, and fancy manners this is who you really are."

"A Viking, just lacking a longship? I should never have thought it, but you may just be right. We will make an interesting couple: the Viking and the Valkyrie."

"One thing I know for sure, Tom."

"What is that?"

"Nobody in his right mind is going to try to fu—uh... tangle with us tonight."

***

Deep in the underground kitchens of the residence, Gabriel was completing preparations of a different kind. He slowly stirred a pot with a hot clear liquid that was a solution to a problem that Sir Thomas had not anticipated. Gabriel feared that though his solution would be accepted, he himself would be left behind. No, he would spring his surprise just before the Kreigshammer Expedition departed. Sir Thomas would then have no choice but to permit him to join in. He had no intention of staying behind. His gut feelings told him that he'd be needed.

Attaché Extraordinaire

He heard Johnny's voice from behind. "What are you brewing, Gabriel?"

"An old recipe. It cures canine fever."

"It smells good!"

"You are smelling ginger, oranges, and rosemary."

"When are we going riding?" A bright smile creased Johnny's face.

"Let's give it another five minutes."

"Being with the horses is the best part of my day."

"You have the makings of a jockey, Johnny, though I know you want to be something much more. Last time I saw my son, he was about your size." Gabriel's eyes dimmed with sudden tears. "You're built like him, and you speak plain and true like he did."

"I never knew you had a son!" said Johnny with astonishment. "What happened to him?"

Gabriel shook his head and sighed deeply. "I don't rightly know. Mastuh Tom sold him off to pay gambling debts. That was the worst day of my life. I was proud of my boy, just like your parents must have been proud of you."

Johnny sniffled. "They were. I miss them every day. I cursed the Lord powerful bad when Yellow Jack took them, but now I know that God did not desert me. Now I have a second family, with all of you."

Gabriel smiled. "That's true."

Shyly, Johnny asked, "Did you ever... curse God? When you lost your son?"

"I was powerful angry, but not with God. God gave us free will, and that means sometimes folk do selfish things, bad things. But I know, I *know*, that being free to choose how we live is how God meant us to be."

John Danielski

Johnny looked Gabriel straight in the eye. "Truth is, when Sir Thomas first introduced us, I was... well... a little bit scared."

"Why? I thought I looked old and harmless."

"I saw that soon enough, and I saw that Sir Thomas and Lady Pennywhistle respect you and trust you." The boy was quiet for a moment, remembering, and then he said, "When I was a street orphan, I figured out fast that I had to read people true if I was going to survive. And I saw that some people are mighty quick to judge you by how you look, or dress, or talk. That's why I like horses; they only care about what you are and how you treat them, not how you dress, or where your people are from."

"That's so," agreed Gabriel. "And if you understand that, you're a sight wiser than many grown-ups."

Johnny spoke earnestly. "You see me as English, but my folk were from Cornwall. We are Celts, like the people in Wales, or Ireland. We have our own language, though not many speak it nowadays. But we still have our songs. We love to sing." He took a deep breath and warbled a song in a language Gabriel had never heard before, but the melody...

"Hold on," said an astonished Gabriel, "that's an American song!" He joined in on the second verse, singing different words to the familiar music:

> "Oh, Shenandoah, I long to see you—
> Far away, you rolling river—
> Oh, Shenandoah, I'll not deceive you,
> Away, I'm bound away, across the wide Missouri."

Johnny smiled in delight, then explained, "Sailors from Cornwall sing that song when they are far from home. My mother told me that it's common practice for folk to borrow music and set new words to old songs,. She said many of the hymns we sang in church were written that way." Johnny scrunched up his eyes, which had tears in them. "Speaking our own language at home was how we remembered who we were."

Gabriel patted Johnny's shoulder with a warm hand. "I know what you mean. I talked with my friends in Gullah when we did not want old Tom to understand. It's the language I learned from my grandpappy, who was from the Gold Coast." He put down the ladle with which he had been stirring the pot. "I think this batch is about done. Let me get it bottled and we can do some ridin'."

Johnny sighed happily. "I could ride every hour of every day for the rest of my life."

"Spoken like a true horseman."

Chapter 40

A children's chorus arrayed on either side of the main entrance to the Razoumovsky Palace sang "Do You Know How Edelweiss is Grown?" It was a tune designed for piping, innocent voices—a deliberate contrast to the sophisticated music that would soon resonate throughout the structure.

Count Andrey Razoumovsky stood nearby and listened rapturously. A charming cosmopolite of sixty two years, the Count was a talented violinist and played in a string quartet. Enormous wealth inherited from two Czarinas had enabled him to fund an orchestra and become a patron of Haydn, Mozart, and now Beethoven, who had written "The Razoumovsky Quartet" in his honor. His palace was less a residence than a museum, because he collected illuminated manuscripts, sculptures by Michelangelo and Bernini, and paintings by Da Vinci, Raphael, Rubens, and Van Dyck.

Torches, spaced every two yards, illuminated the outside of the palace, as if it were a giant cake of white and gold. On the inside, sixteen thousand candles caused the structure to glow with a light out of a fairy tale. Larger torches lined the approach road that was choked with two hundred carriages, bearing four times as many guests. A steady stream of impatient guests had decided to walk, to gain entrance more quickly. Strings of red and gold paper lanterns, copied from those popular with Chinese emperors, filled the gaps between the torches and lent an exotic touch. Imperial carriages could be distinguished by their dark green color, with a yellow coat of arms. An army of servants in the Razoumovsky livery of green and gold stood ready to assist the guests.

Hidden below the palace were a series of giant kitchens that had been busy since dawn. Those ovens were a hell for servants but necessary to create a heaven for their betters above. Legions of cooks, undercooks, pastry chefs and their assistants operated as the equivalent of culinary armies, bent on the conquest of the discriminating palettes of the great and mighty. That elite could be harshly critical if their high standards were not met, their disapproval reflecting not just on the servants, but on the Great Man employing them.

Thirty six course dinners represented an equation fully as complex as any of the military campaigns of Napoleon. The first of many shipments that had begun arriving days before included 300 hams, 200 partridges, 300 pigeons, 200 turkeys, 150 pheasants, *48 boeuf a la mode,* 40 large boars, and 600 pickled and salted tongues. There would also be 300 liters of olla soup, 2500 assorted biscuits, and 1000 *Mandel-Wandel*: a unique Viennese pastry filled with almonds. Fruits of every kind would be freely available as would pies, cakes, gateaux, ices, and strudel.

Thousands of pieces of silverware received their final polishing, tablecloths were checked one last time for the proper amount of starch, and napkins were folded carefully into a variety of exotic shapes that would have done credit to Japanese origami.

Even among the elite, there were light fingers bent on souvenir-hunting. By tomorrow morning, probably 3,000 pieces of silver would have gone missing.

The wine cellars were stocked with thousands of bottles, and the sommeliers had made careful and varied selections. Some bottles cost as much as a civil servant's yearly salary. Wine consumption was prodigious: the British Embassy had gone through 10,000 bottles since October.

Liqueurs varying from sweet to tart would be served in ornate_Sèvres cups.

The Russians loved their vodka, the French their brandy, the British their rum, and Germans their schnapps. Enough of each was available to fuel an army of Cossacks, a mass of musketeers, a fleet of sailors, and an entire order of Teutonic knights.

Coffee and tea were provided to clear the palate. The beverages would be heated in large tubs then transferred to elaborate silver and gold samovars. They would be served in ornate_Sèvres cups. Almond milk, lemonade, and chocolate were also available.

The moon was full, bright, and cold. The temperature stood just below freezing and many great ladies wore furs of sable, mink, lynx, and even leopard. Razoumovsky had spent a fortune installing a new central heating system under the kitchens that was an improvement on the ancient Roman one of hypocausts. Heat rose from fires lit beneath a building and warmth flowed outward from vents installed throughout the structure. Tonight would be the first test of his new system. He wanted the ball to be as much a dazzling display of heat as it was of light.

"I never thought there would be a traffic jam like this at a ball," exclaimed Sammie Jo to her husband, as they sat in Lady Leith's coach. "This is almost as bad as the one we were in when we first arrived in London. It's just that the vehicles here are a lot prettier."

Attaché Extraordinaire

She turned to Lady Leith, seated across from her. She was dressed as the Greek Goddess Athena, the champion of the city named after her. "I never thought I'd say this, but your coach seems kind of shabby compared to some here. Mind you, I don't mean no offense, but it looks like some of these folks put all of their wealth into their rides."

Margaret smiled. "The truth never offends me. Whatever I am back home, here I am a small fish in a big pond. And yet I swim well and fast and so do you. I have a good idea of the currents and eddies we will face. We both have large, sharp teeth but it is a matter of knowing when and how to use them. Often, they are best suggested rather than shown, at other times a quick baring of them is preferable to their actual use. When you do use them, do so sparingly. You must think of more than taking a slice out of your opponent; you want to send a message that you are a force to be reckoned with, who is unwise to challenge. I think your attire, height, and bearing will send that message, even before you open your mouth."

"In other words, chose your battles wisely; do not fight everyone."

"Exactly."

"Speaking of battles, Margaret, I think your accompanying Sammie Jo to Kreigshammer is a very bad idea," worried Pennywhistle. "It puts you in danger when there is no earthly reason why that need be so."

"I have a vested interest in seeing things through. Remember, you recovered in my house after this blackguard tried to kill you. I have financed this expedition and I want to see it through. I want you, Sammie Jo, and the baby to have a safe life, and that cannot happen until this dastard is finished once and for all. Besides, Robert is going, and I want to share the danger with him."

"Yes, but he has seen the face of battle many times," observed Pennywhistle.

Grosvenor, dressed as the Roman Emperor Marcus Aurelius, squeezed Lady Leith's hand. "I wish you would stay behind as well Margaret, but I know better than to argue with you when you have made up your mind. Please, at least stay on the boat with Sammie Jo. You can help with the tram line, yet be safe. The memory of my murdered son demands I go."

"Are we still set to leave the ball at midnight?" asked Sammie Jo. She barely kept the anxiety out of her voice as she worried about her husband's partly healed back.

"Yes, Hawkeye. Dale is expecting us to be on the *Queen Charlotte* at 12:30. I doubt we will be missed with ten thousand people strolling about." He rubbed his chin. "Make that thirty thousand: I forgot to include the staff and servants."

"Ten thousand? Thirty thousand? I thought you said four thousand were invited to this party."

"True, but this party has attracted the attention of the city and the ticket takers are lovers of profit. It is not uncommon that once the ticket takers accept the golden invitations, they resell some of them to the crowds outside the gates. By crowds, I do not mean rabble; most are respectable burghers dressed in their Sunday finest. Of course, the scalpers wait until the party is well under way and the invited guests are focused on each other. It is one of the few chances for those of the middling orders to see how those of the greater ones live."

"Instead of money changers in the temple you have scalpers in a palace," chortled Sammie Jo. "Don't that beat all."

"I think the Gods of Fortune have been consulting with those of justice and favor our enterprise tonight,"

Attaché Extraordinaire

Pennywhistle continued. "Montgomery, Dale, and Owens likely have things well in hand. The temperature is right, and though there are substantial chunks of ice in the Danube, I checked with Montgomery earlier and he believes the Queen's hull can handle them. There is wind but it is blowing in the right direction. The moonlight is more problematic. It can be a beacon for us but also one for the enemy. Still, with the wind and clouds, it may be blotted out from time to time. We will just have to take our chances."

There was a discreet rapping on the door of the carriage by a liveried servant. Gabriel halted the slow-moving vehicle.

"My ladies and lords, forgive the irregularity," said the servant in uncertain English: he had likely seen the arms on the door and deduced this coach contained people from the British Embassy. "Would you mind dismounting here and following me to the main entrance? It is a cold night, and my master does not want his guests to remain long in their coaches. He is most proud of his new heating system and wishes all to enjoy it at the earliest possible moment."

"Of course," replied Pennywhistle. He whispered to Sammie Jo," the play begins, and I know our reviews will be excellent. Just be ready for the curtain call at midnight."

"A Greek Goddess, a Roman Emperor, an American Valkyrie, and a Viking. How can we not be a hit?" Sammie Jo whispered back.

"Awk, awk, me too, me too!" squawked Plymouth as he flapped his wings and then descended on Sammie Jo's shoulder.

Pennywhistle directed a wry smile toward his wife. "His emotions may be the most honest ones here tonight. The Viennese love exotic animals and Francis may want him for the Zoo."

The four pulled their cloaks tight as the servant opened the door. They alighted and began their walk to a unique type of rarified reality.

Peter Wilson had just purchased a scalped ticket, confident that he had just bought his way into a gambler's paradise. One Russian prince had lost two million rubles in a single night. While he might not find someone that extravagantly stupid, the old axiom applied on a giant scale:"A fool and his money are soon parted."

Three miles away, Dale and Owens were discussing a much harder and more dangerous reality with the men under their command. Their words were anything but subtle and their tones the opposite of courtly.

Chapter 41

"Let us go over things one last time," said Owens. "You all know your jobs, but in a complex enterprise such as this, there is no such thing as too much preparation. We must not only plan our own steps carefully, but we must account for the likely ones of our opponents as well."

Owens spread out a diagram of the castle's interior. "Remember, these plans the Earl secured from an architectural firm date from 1720, at the time when the castle was partly transformed from a medieval structure into one of the Baroque. It is not necessarily what the architect achieved; it is what he intended to achieve, since funds ran out before the work could be completed. Some quick improvisation maybe necessary."

The twenty-five NCOs assembled in a semi-circle stared intently at the large blueprint. They were dressed in the uniforms of the Prussian Foot Artillery: overcoats of iron grey, trousers of ash grey, and a brimless circular hat that vaguely resembled a beret. None wore any badge of rank, but each had a rectangular white strip on his right shoulder that could be used to distinguish him from a foe. For the task ahead, they would work in six four-man chains, the same ones that had performed in such an exemplary fashion at the Prater Park demonstration.

John Danielski

The large campfire highlighted the tension in their faces. They were all hard men in their mid-thirties to early forties and in the peak of condition. They were of middling stature, wiry rather than bulky, but had muscle in the right places. What mattered even more was that their mental muscles were nimble and experienced.

The risk of this enterprise was formidable, and the employment of new technology made the outcome even more problematic. There was a good chance it might be an utter failure, and an even better one that many of them would not come back alive. The men were being paid as if this were a Forlorn Hope, the name for the initial assault following the first wall breech during a siege—a nearly suicidal task, but if successful, guaranteed promotion to the survivors.

They had been told by Sir Thomas that the mission was critical to the safety of the realm. He had said only that their objective was a packet of 23 letters but provided no detail as to their contents. Being led by "Bombproofed" Pennywhistle was a singular honor, though the veterans were skeptical of the fantastic story of how he had acquired his nickname. Yet if even part of that tale was true, he was certainly lucky. They would need that tonight.

"Before we review our tasks, let us hear from Captain Thynne," said Owens, "And his assistant, Johnny," The ten-year-old grinned and waved; provoking scattered amusement as the men acknowledged a mascot. "These two have had the castle under observation for forty straight hours and will provide us with the most up to date intelligence. Proceed, Captain Thynne, we are all ears."

"Thank you, Sargeant Major," said Thynne, his usual cheerful indifference veined with a thread of excitement. "The guards change every four hours, much like the watches of a ship at sea. The first watch is eight to midnight and consists of

Attaché Extraordinaire

six men; one man is posted at the main gate, one on each of the four towers of the outer walls, and one guard maintains a roving patrol behind the cannons sandwiched in between the east and west towers." He pointed to their positions on Owen's map. "The five-hundred-foot cliff that most of you will ascend is unwatched. They trust their defense entirely to nature." Thynne looked at Johnny. "Now why don't you finish the briefing?"

Thynne saw looks of surprise among the men. "Johnny has been much more than an assistant; he has been my eyes and ears. There was a cleft in the walls too small for a man, but with a liberal application of grease, Johnny squeezed through."

"I was only inside for an hour," said Johnny excitedly," and just had time to scout the front part of the battlements. The map is fine but..." he carefully traced a line with his fingers, "... this part is wrong. The tower door here is bricked over. There is a whole new corridor about thirty yards to the right. I followed the corridor and when I emerged outside, I found a very long flight of stairs. I dashed up them to a landing. A new door to the tower had been left open slightly, so I went inside a room full of books—a study, I think. I smelled perfume, so I would guess a woman had been there. I saw an empty cup and a coffee pot. I figured she had stepped out to fetch a new pot. I spied a table with letters and quickly rifled through them, knowing I did not have much time. There were seven in all, but these letters were different from what my ma wrote to my aunt. The bottom halves looked to be nothing but numbers. I thought about bringing one back, but realized if I did, it might be missed and would alert the man who owns the place that an outsider had paid a call. I got the feeling that something important had been happening in the room. But it's just a feeling."

"I wonder if the numbers represent some sort of code," remarked Sergeant Miller, the group's explosives expert.

"Possible, but it does not change a thing about our mission," responded Owens.

"You showed good judgement in limiting the time of your visit, Johnny," said Thynne in an avuncular manner. "I passed your information to Sir Thomas. He believes what you saw may be exactly what he seeks."

Johnny beamed.

"However," Thynne's face expressed a caveat. "It is Sir Thomas's surmise that, judging from the number of letters you saw, his opponent may have split the full cache of letters into several smaller ones, secreted in different locations, not wishing to put all his eggs in one basket.

"Darn!" said Johnny.

"What would you say of the quality of their soldiery, Captain Thynne?" inquired Owens.

"I would call them competent rather than zealous. They do their duty but no more. Indeed, I observed some shorting their duties in the interest of convenience. I have no doubt they will fight, yet their movements are those of well-trained spaniels."

"Good, good," muttered Owens.

"What would you recommend as the best spot for the pitons anchoring the tram line?" inquired Dale.

"I should say here," said Thynne, pointing to the blueprint. "It has a clear view of the river below, plenty of space to assemble the men, and a curve in the wall that matches a curve in the terrain, making the spot immune to the spyglasses of the men in the towers."

Owens carefully performed a quick survey of the areas adjacent to that spot. "Yes, it is strategically well placed and a good point to anchor the balloon, as well. I like the fact that it is shielded from the guards, but," Owens frowned, "The chutes worry me. My men have practiced jumping off the high walls of the church here, but that's a lot different than jumping two thousand feet from a hot air balloon. The wind could carry them anywhere. Their targets will be hard to see, though tonight's moon may help."

Thynne smiled wryly." It won't be as difficult as that. The guards light large torches at the beginning of their watches, preferring the comfort of light to cursing the darkness. Additional evidence that, though these men are veterans, they willing to cut corners. The closeness of those torches to their faces impairs night vision and gives your men useful aiming points. The roving guard carries his musket slung over his shoulder with the torch in one hand. He will be like a lighted, moving dot."

"I do not like the risk to the chutists either, Owens," remarked Dale," but let me acquaint you with something Sir Thomas told me about Napoleon's famous Parisian aeronaut. She maintained that jumping is like pregnancy. You are much safer with the first one than subsequent ones."

"Maybe," said Miller, "but she is still dead."

"True," responded Dale," but the design flaw in her chute has been fixed. "Besides you are lucky, Miller. I don't think you have used up more than two or three of your nine lives."

Miller pulled a face.

"I trust the air guns have been checked thoroughly?" inquired Owens.

"Finished my last check an hour ago," responded Sergeant Rhodes, who was charged with managing the teams' guns. "These air guns require careful maintenance. I can see why they were never in common use. Even so, I like the idea of multiple shots, as well as no muzzle flash and a nearly silent report."

"I am unfamiliar with air guns," said Thynne. "Could you tell me more, Rhodes?"

Rhodes held up a weapon and became a drillmaster talking to a recruit. "The Girandoni rifle is a .46 caliber breech-loader, It's four feet long, weighs ten pounds, and is powered by a detachable air reservoir in the buttstock. When you pull the trigger, the falling hammer pushes a pin that unlocks a check valve in the reservoir and injects the right amount of air into the firing chamber. It has a 22-round tube-shaped magazine alongside the barrel." He traced his fingers along the magazine and demonstrated the loading procedure. "You elevate the barrel, press a transverse slider switch to activate a spring loader, and a ball is thrust into place. When you have expended your ammunition," he held up a cylindrical tube," you replenish the magazine with a reload tube. Only takes about ten seconds. You just open the front magazine cap and pour in the contents of the tube. Each man carries four reload tubes and two fully charged air reservoirs. The weapon can discharge its magazine within thirty seconds and has sufficient striking power that its ball can penetrate a one-inch-thick pine board at 100 yards."

Johnny chirped the commonsense question that civilians everywhere might ask. "If those guns are such wonder weapons, how come everybody does not use them?"

"Because they're prone to breakdowns, and few gunsmiths have the skill to make them." Rhodes answered patiently. "It takes fifteen hundred strokes of a hand pump to bring the air reservoir up to eight hundred pounds pressure per square inch, and even a small leak in the air reservoir renders the weapon inoperable. And the air reservoirs sometimes explode if exposed to bright sunlight for too long. So it has remained only a lethal novelty."

"We will always have cold steel," said Mallory, the edged weapon mandarin. "The Baker Rifle bayonets are a perfect compromise between a bayonet and a cutlass and will not be cumbersome to carry."

"I can spike the cannons in two minutes," injected "Spike" McAfee, famous for spiking Santander's main battery in ten minutes.

"I think it boils down to how fast we remove the guards," said Jones, a boxer who had spent time at the East India company's post in Canton. He had learned a variety of fighting arts there and was the resident unarmed combat expert. "Captain Thynne, did you see anyone you could identify as an officer of the day, someone who supervised both the changing of the guard and their general conduct?"

"I did not, replied Thynne, "and I found that strange. Perhaps our opponent trusts his men overmuch, or is simply short of the funds to hire the necessary complement of officers. British NCOs are famous for their initiative, and I could see them managing quite well without an officer."

Smiles blossomed among the men.

"Sir Thomas believes the men we face tonight are Prussians, probably veterans unwilling or unable to adapt to the onset of peace. But whatever their former service was, I remind you that they are now mere mercenaries. They fight for cash and coin while we fight for king and country."

The veterans nodded in agreement. Money came and went, but the only thing that lasted was a man's honor.

"A brief history lesson is in order. In 1806, the Prussian Army enjoyed the finest reputation in Europe: the leading military mandarins of the day reckoned them unbeatable. But reputation and reality are two different things. The Prussians rested on past glories and thought like garrison troops. Bonaparte's upstart Grande Armée destroyed the Prussians in six weeks, because he made sure his hard-marching troops had good shoes, good rations, and good wine, while his opponents fussed over the proper polishing of buttons, brass, and boots. Though the Prussians have made many impressive reforms since then, they still have far too great a fascination with pomp and pipeclay."

Thynne's expression turned introspective. "I understand the difference between a headquarters habitué and a fighting soldier because I have been both. When I served with the 1st Life Guards in London, the only battles I fought were those of high society—parties, cards, and women—always wanting be seen with the smart set and treating my military obligations as annoying afterthoughts. I think back on what I was and when I look at you, I feel ashamed. Then a curious stroke of fate saved me from the life of a commissioned wastrel: a bureaucrat mistook my name for that of a cousin with a distinguished battle record and assigned me to Wellington's Army in Spain. Being around real fighting men changed me and I determined to make something of myself. Three years as an Exploring Officer showed me that field work is as different from garrison duty as the heavens are from the earth."

Approving murmurs coursed through the crowd. Exploring officers were universally respected because their work was exceptionally dangerous. They operated in full uniform for weeks at a time, behind enemy lines, acting as Wellington's eyes and ears. All the listening veterans had met officers who loved the pomp and pageantry of rank but disdained the performance of their duties. It was rare for an officer to reveal so much about himself, particularly information that put him in an unflattering light. That it came from the second son of the wealthiest Marquis in England was astonishing.

Johnny blinked in surprise. He had just assumed heroes had always been heroic.

Thynne continued, again donning his mask of studied nonchalance that closed access to the serious soldier at his core. "I will grant you, the Prussians have learned much, but as the Prater demonstration showed, conservative habits die hard. My observation of their NCOs at that event told me that, while they are brave, they adapt slowly to unforeseen circumstances. They are good at obeying orders but require a clear-thinking officer to issue them. Absent that officer, every soldier must show initiative. The ones we will face have guarded a fixed position long enough that boredom has induced a degree of mental torpor and carelessness. We will use speed and surprise to make them fight a mobile battle, rather than the set piece one for which they are prepared. I would think that if the guards are silenced quickly, no alarm will be given; the men in the barracks will simply sleep the night away."

"However, if they do react," added Rhodes, "we have more than sufficient firepower to handle them."

"I agree," said Dale.

"I think we stand a fair chance of success," said Owens. "Yet we must allow for the possibility that things could go badly. That is where you come in Miller; you are our insurance."

"Understood." Miller pointed at the diagram. "I think the powder magazine is here. I know the room is labelled something entirely different, but it's the only place deep enough, large enough, and with thick enough walls to accommodate enough powder barrels for the garrison's guns and cannons. I can set the fuses for fifteen, twenty, or thirty minutes, but the shorter the time the less chance a stray guard will be able to snuff them out. One gigantic explosion and the castle becomes a pile of rubble."

"Remember, the explosives represent a contingency plan," cautioned Owens. "Sir Thomas wishes to avoid a big sound and light show, but if the letters in the study provide no clue as to the location of the rest..." he frowned, "well... the castle is large, our force is small, it will be dark, and time will be of the essence. Rendering the remainder of the letters unreachable may be the only way to be sure. But take no action until Sir Thomas sends the word."

Dale noted worried looks. Large explosions did not differentiate between friend and foe.

"Getting out, "continued Owens "should be much easier than getting in, if all goes according to plan."

The men smiled cynically, knowing that a plan that went off without a hitch was a rarity.

"You all know your exits," Owens added, "but if everything goes wrong, make for the main gate as fast as possible. Once outside, head for the rally point at the storage shed."

"Could you describe the contents in detail?" asked Benson, the fastest runner in the group.

Owens provided tips for the use of the conveyances within. He concluded by saying, "All of these things are a lot faster than Benson can run and conditions tonight are ripe for their use. Once the men on the tram line reach the parapets, the *Queen Charlotte* will circle round to the main landing, where she will stand ready to pick us up."

Owens looked at Thynne and Dale. "I can't think of anything else to add, can you?" Both shook their heads.

Dale faced the men. "Have you any final questions?"

Attaché Extraordinaire

"Just one Sergeant Major," said Dobson, an expert in ropes and knots." If any of us fall, will you see to it that our loved ones receive our compensation for this job, and that the full amount of our pensions are paid, even though some of us have a few years left to go before retirement?"

"Absolutely! Lord Castlereagh will see to it personally. Before we depart write your name and the name of the loved ones you want designated as your heirs on a piece of paper. Fold it up and give it to Captain Thynne. He will put them in a pouch and drop them off at the embassy. Some of you may have, well... several people other than wives you will want designated as your heirs. I am sure you all know the saying, wives and sweethearts, may they never meet."

Several men snickered.

"Take the next fifteen minutes to make your choices," continued Dale. "We will then perform a final equipment check and move out."

The men dispersed into smaller groups as they discussed their choices with their friends.

Johnny clapped his hands together and barely restrained himself from jumping up and down. "This is so exciting. I can't wait."

Dale looked at him grimly. "If you'd seen the fighting I have, you could wait forever."

Thynne took Dale aside and spoke in hushed tones. "What chance do you think they have?"

Dale sighed in frustration. "It may just be a waste of good men, but it must be tried. Still, war itself is a wild card, often changing the nature of the game right in the middle of it. Men sometimes do the most remarkable things, not despite the odds, but because of them. It is only when things are at their worst and most hopeless, that a man discovers the best of himself. If that best is very good, he may just prevail. As I see it, you can put your hope in God, chance, or your men. Tonight, I am banking on my men. And that is how I think of them: my men."

Chapter 42

Pennywhistle and company donned their masks as they approached the entrance to the Razoumovsky Palace. For him and his wife, the masks were black and covered the space between eyebrows and lips. His two friends had full face, flesh-toned coverings. Other guests sported masks of varied sizes, colors, and types; some representing copies of classical statuary, some those of theatrical comedy and tragedy, some creatures of myth and even a few mimicking animals like lions and tigers.

The masks gave varying degrees of disguise, which Pennywhistle decided was intentional. Some partygoers wanted complete secrecy and the freedom it brought; some wanted partial disguise so they would be recognized by their friends, while others wanted very little, daring people to recognize them. A great many wore no masks at all, clearly wanting to be seen.

Numerous people had stopped at a red, Turkish style tent pavilion, ten yards in front of the main gate. They all had exotic breeds of dogs on leashes. Those dogs were turned over to servants, who would manage their care for the duration of the ball.

"What the fuc... uh... blazes, Tom? Dogs at a ball?"

John Danielski

"It's all about appearance, Hawkeye. Dogs are the expected appurtenances of aristocrats. Their owners are proud of them and want to show them off, even if they cannot bring them inside. Visiting yiplomats, if you will."

Sammie Jo chuckled. "Driving hard bark-gains and making ruff agreements."

"Devoted to common scents, pees, and fleadom."

"Ding, ding, ding," Plymouth chirped the sound of a doorbell-pull.

The dogs commenced loud barking.

Pennywhistle presented the group's tickets to the doorman and a liveried footman escorted them inside. Once the palace threshold was crossed, everything changed for Sammie Jo and she gasped. "This makes the Prince Regent's Ball seem like a dance in a doll house." A blast of heat and light hit her, making winter summer. The crush of bodies and the mysterious new heating system had turned the air sensually warm. The light of sixteen thousand candles was reflected and amplified by hundreds of large mirrors. She had to shield her eyes for a moment until they adjusted to the many blazing suns. "Lordy Tom, every aristocrat in creation must be here."

"Lots! Lots!" Squawked Plymouth.

"I would guess three thousand," replied her husband, "and we still have a thousand to go. It will take another forty minutes or so for the rest to arrive and we are expected to use that time to mingle with the crowds. Women and men usually separate here, not to reunite until trumpeters signal the assembling of the grand promenade."

Pennywhistle noted two groups of men who interested him; none of them wore a mask. One included the Prussian Chancellor von Hardenberg and his chief assistant, the Ambassador von Humboldt. Von Humboldt was a scholarly man after his own heart who was the chief font of Prussian ideas. He had also founded the University of Berlin and was the brother of a famous explorer.

The other group included the King of Denmark. Pennywhistle wished to hear his views on the Saxony question.

"I will let Margaret take charge of you, Hawkeye, while the Earl and I try to discover if something is rotten in the state of Denmark."

Sammie Jo's eyes widened to the size of small moons as she drank in the variety of costumes. She recalled the poverty of her childhood and recoiled at the excess and extravagance. The amount of money invested in the costumes was probably more than the yearly budgets of some of the smaller states of Europe.

Pirates, janissaries, knights, hoplites, centurions, crusaders, and Cossacks were common among the men.

Women favored milkmaids, ballerinas, harlequins, romantic heroines, and adaptations of male military finery. Close-fitting hussar jackets with elaborate piping and tight trousers were particularly popular. Roman goddesses and figures from Greek and Norse mythology were well represented. Three women were dressed in their impressions of "Iroquois Princesses", unaware that Iroquois women never wore diamond necklaces.

Her husband liked the exotic world of *"The Thousand and One Arabian Nights."* She spotted one man she took to be Ali Baba and one woman she thought was Princess Scheherazade.

Lady Leith informed Sammie Jo that most of the people not wearing masks were social climbers. Their ostentatious attire was intended to call attention to their exposed faces and render them memorable.

John Danielski

The unmasked men were nearly all dressed in military attire that came in a rainbow of colors. Coats and breeches were tightly fitted to showcase broad chests and well-shaped thighs. Boots were so carefully blacked that they could act as mirrors.

Sammie Jo was astonished to see one man clad in a pink uniform. She thought the color feminine, but Lady Leith said that in Europe the color was perceived as masculine: the pink man was a colonel in a famous Austrian cavalry regiment.

The chests of the maskless men were covered with medals, medallions, and orders of various nations. They clinked and clanged softly as the men walked, almost like trumpeters announcing their presence. Her husband disliked wearing his Order of the Bath ribbon and medallion and was grateful that his costume forbade their use tonight.

While it was a costume ball, many women wore dresses that reflected current fashions rather than those of legend and history. Those dresses were crafted of the most expensive crepe, silk, satin, velvet, or damask. White was the most popular color, followed by light blue, pink, and yellow. The gowns were awash with frills, embroidery, and daring *décolletage.* Sleeves were either long and trimmed with lace or short and combined with long silk gloves. Most dresses were form fitting and many were of fabric thin enough that the blinding candlelight gave a very good idea of the figure that lay beneath.

The women sported broaches, bracelets, earrings, necklaces, and tiaras with diamonds, rubies, emeralds, sapphires, and pearls in settings of gold and silver; all reflected light brilliantly and made the promenading women seem like sparkling meteors.

Attaché Extraordinaire

Hairstyles reflected hours of skilled preparation. Many were based on ancient Roman statuary and featured arabesques of braids, curls, and ringlets which framed the face; the remainder of the hair tied at the back in a loose bun known as The Psyche Knot. Most styles allowed twin locks to touch the shoulders. The preferred color was blonde, though unlike Sammie Jo, many owed it to a bottle rather than heredity. Ribbons, flowers, jeweled pins, and tiaras complimented the coiffures.

The bulwark of social climbers parted like the Red Sea before Moses when a solitary woman strode majestically down the wide marble stairs. She walked like a queen and Sammie Jo was surprised to hear from Lady Leith that she was not one. She was, however, a princess.

Lady Leith whispered that she was the Princess Esterhazy; of a family whose wealth rivaled the Hapsburgs and whose artistic impulses had made them patrons of the composer Haydn. In her honor, the small string quartet at the base of the stairs began playing the melody of "The Surprise Symphony."

Sammie Jo decided the princess was attractive enough for a middle-aged woman who might once have been reckoned pretty. Couturiers, coiffeurs, and make up mavens had made the most of her remaining looks. Yet, it was her dress that commanded attention rather than the woman who wore it.

The reflected candlelight caused exquisite pain for those gazing upon Princess Esterhazy's dress, because it was less a garment than a field of diamonds set in black silk: the sparkles from bust line to hem rendered the silk barely visible.

"If I had not seen that dress, I could never have believed it existed," gasped Sammie Jo in a child-like whisper. "That is the kind of thing wars are fought over. Who would make such a thing and what would it cost?" She once again became a backwoods little girl confronted by fantastic things beyond her ken.

Lady Leith replied with equal wonderment. "The dress is unprecedented, even for this crowd. It is rumored to have cost six million livres, designed by Louis de Roy of Paris. The Princess apparently told him that she wanted to be the most stellar figure in the brightest galaxy imaginable. De Roy has succeeded brilliantly."

Sammie Jo's mouth fell open. "six million? Did I hear that right?"

"You did."

"Tom told me Napoleon on Elba only gets two million livres a year. And he is an Emperor!"

Lady Leith noticed a masked woman whom she recognized by her distinctive stride and overripe figure. She was dressed in a white, flowing outfit that mimicked those of ancient Rome. Lady Leith took her arm and escorted her to Sammie Jo.

"Emily is that you?" inquired Sammie Jo."

"It is, Sammie Jo." The voice was that of Lady Castlereagh.

"Emily! Emily," squawked Plymouth.

"What a wonderful bird," exclaimed Lady Castlereagh.

"What is that thing in your hair, Emily? It don't look like jewelry made for a woman."

"It isn't. It's my husband's Order of The Garter. He does not like to wear it, but I like its dazzle and color."

"You look like a statue from a Roman temple. Are you supposed to be a high priestess or something?"

"A Vestal Virgin. They were seven in number and important in Rome. They served twenty years, and when their

Attaché Extraordinaire

term was finished, they were much sought after as marriage partners."

Sammie Jo suppressed a chuckle. There were precious few virgins here tonight and most would be sought for their fortunes, not their virtue.

"Your outfit is turning heads, Sammie Jo," remarked Lady Castlereagh. "The simplicity of it is striking, but more than that, it makes you look dangerous. There are plenty of attractive women here, but not one looks like she could give a man a sharp contest in a fist fight."

"I think some are wondering if your bullwhip is for the boudoir," laughed Lady Leith.

A low buzz of conversation swelled in volume, sounding first like a flight of bees, then a swarm, then an entire hive.

The three women turned toward its source. Two unmasked women were arguing, and the argument was escalating—two queen bees competing for control of the hive. Both were beautiful, and each woman appeared to have fifteen or so supporters who were encouraging their principals, almost as if they were boxers trading blows. Both women's blue silk dresses featured sheer fabric, eye-catching *décolletage*, and diamond necklaces. One wore rubies in her earrings, while the other wore emeralds. Each had an upswept hair arrangement to accommodate a tiara replete with diamonds and classical figures rendered in silver.

"Those two ladies don't look like social climbers to me, Margaret. Their rigs look mighty expensive."

"They are already at the top of the social pyramid, Sammie Jo. The taller one is the Duchess Sagan, the shorter one is the Princess Bagration."

"Tom mentioned them," said Sammie Jo. "He told me they despise each other. Apparently he was right."

The three stopped two feet behind the group and listened. Sammie Jo only understood a few of the French words, but she understood the emotion in the voices perfectly. The green-eyed monster was on a rampage.

Lady Leith whispered a running translation to Sammie Jo.

"Why would Alexander want you when he has partaken of the delights of my boudoir? He is far too intelligent and discriminating to be taken in by your threadbare charms," observed Bagration, her voice dripping with venom.

"And yet, he danced with me several times at the Esterhazy's ball." replied Sagan in arctic tones. "I do not seem to recall he danced with you at all."

"He was simply being considerate. He knew I had injured my foot the previous day and that dancing would be painful."

"Your pain saved him embarrassment. Your dancing is as inelegant as your wit, and I know it often provokes snickers from bystanders."

"It takes one to know one. Several people asked me if you have club feet after seeing you dance."

"Your last salon was a frightful bore. The only thing worse than the conversation was the food. And the wine! It was as if someone had fermented the grapes in an outhouse. You really need to hire a new sommelier."

"Cat fight," whispered Sammie Jo to Lady Leith.

"And you need to hire a new couturier. Your dress is so gauche, so... last year."

"And your dress appears put together with couturier castoffs. Though it is the perfect accompaniment to a face whose features seem the discarded oddments of others."

"At least my dress fits. You appear poured into yours; a ten-pound sausage in a casing designed for five."

Attaché Extraordinaire

"And you remind me of a donkey pretending to be a thoroughbred."

"That is still a lot better than being a full-time bitch."

"Yaaaaaaaah!" The last cut was the one too many for Sagan. She jumped at Bagration and knocked off her tiara, then commenced pulling her hair. The on lookers were horrified, yet they neither averted their gaze nor tried to break up what just might become a knock-down, drag-out battle.

The princess responded with a kick to the shin, causing Sagan to release her hold and stumble backward.

Lady Castlereagh gasped. "Disgraceful. It simply isn't done. Their behavior shames every lady here tonight."

"Want me to put an end to it, Emily?" said Sammie Jo.

"Yes, of course. But how can you, you don't speak their language."

"Watch me!" A second later, a stab of brown shot through the air, accompanied by a loud crack. Sammie Jo's whip stopped a fraction of an inch from Sagan's upraised fist, causing her to leap backwards in shock. She snapped the whip back with one quick motion, then snapped it again at the foot of the Princess. The Princess also leaped back.

The fight crowd turned their eyes toward Sammie Jo, not quite believing what had happened. A bullwhip in expert hands was something you'd expected in a barn, not at a ball. That it was wielded by a woman was even more astonishing. Who was this woman of wonder?

Lady Leith took the opportunity to answer the unspoken question on the crowd's faces. She stepped forward and spoke in her most formal French. "My ladies, this is Lady Samantha Pennywhistle who has made the journey here all the way from America. What you just saw reflects her heartfelt desire to prevent two fine ladies from injuring each other."

The group of thirty looked at one another in puzzlement, then agreement. Lady Pennywhistle's unconventional action had indeed kept a small embarrassment from becoming a big one.

Sammie Jo saw the approval, stepped forward, and touched the brim of her hat in acknowledgment. "I'm right glad to meet y'all." She followed with an artless smile that bewitched because of its obvious sincerity.

A few in the crowd spoke English, but what they had just heard sounded very different from the accents of English people walking the streets of Vienna. They all made the correct assumption that her exotic costume was not a costume at all, but something with which she was very familiar.

They were curious about America and Americans, and what they had just seen lived up to their expectations. Americans were forceful and direct, if sometimes lacking manners. Lady Pennywhistle looked to be a woman of quality, but in a very different way from how they generally used the expression. She was worth getting to know.

One middle-aged woman in a plum-colored dress stepped forward. She spoke in heavily accented English. "A great pleasure to make your acquaintance Lady Pennywhistle. That was a remarkable demonstration. I am Marie, the Countess de Bleuchamp." She curtseyed.

Sammie Jo looked her straight in the eye and instead of returning her curtsey, extended her hand. "Right glad to meet you, Marie. Lady Pennywhistle's kind of formal. In America, we ain't much for titles. Call me Sammie Jo."

"I'm Plymouth, Plymouth." Proclaimed the parrot.

The startled countess shook her hand uncertainly. The direct gaze of the American was unsettling, suggesting its owner thought every woman as good as the next. And yet, it

Attaché Extraordinaire

was something of a relief. This was a woman who welcomed sincerity, not the play acting that infected every phase of the Congress. The Countess decided that if the diplomats practiced such honesty, the Congress would conclude faster, with happier results.

A line quickly formed of women eager to meet Sammie Jo. Plymouth allowed his head to be stroked and proved a great crowd-pleaser. Only Sagan and the Princess chose not to join. They realized they had made fools of themselves and slunk away in embarrassment. The American had stolen their thunder and turned the crowd's eyes away from them. They had no wish to appear as her supplicants.

Lady Leith happily translated for Sammie Jo. Even before Lady Leith's words reached their ears, the crowd delighted in Sammie Jo's emotions and gestures. They liked her combination of frontier toughness and breezy bluntness. Thirty minutes passed like thirty seconds.

Ten livered trumpeters blew loud blasts, announcing it was time to assemble for the grand promenade. Twenty equerries stood behind them, armed with long lists of guests and their place in the line to come. The protocol of rank had to be strictly observed.

The crowd became a bubbling, weaving mass as men and women sought their partners for the evening. Getting the guests into their proper position reminded one equerry of herding cats.

Sammie Jo talked with her husband as the line began to form. "Looks like we are pretty near the end. I guess we are just minnows in this pond."

"Perhaps, but you are still the prettiest minnow I know," replied Pennywhistle.

"If anyone else but you had said that I'd say it sounded pretty fishy."

A footman came up to the couple. "Sir Thomas, Lady Pennywhistle, come with me. Let's get you situated."

Sammie Jo wondered how they had been identified, but decided it was one of those secret things that experienced servants just seemed to know.

***

Owens and his men reached the dock where the *Queen Charlotte* was moored. Their gear had arrived by wagon, half an hour before, and Montgomery's assistants had just finished stowing it.

Montgomery's first mate checked the boiler and satisfied himself that it was sufficiently warmed up. The coaler had assured him that they had more than enough coal for double the length of the journey that they expected to make. Montgomery had not told his first mate why they were ferrying soldiers, but the mate figured they were about some clandestine business.

Another wagon pulled up next to the dock. It was the balloon owner, Herr Heilmann, come to deliver the balloon and review with Dale the instructions for its inflation and use. Dale had spent the previous day practicing with Heilmann in a field; taking off from a boat's deck would be trickier, but Dale was used to making necessary things happen under difficult circumstances. Heilmann would have preferred to inflate and operate the balloon himself, but this enterprise looked to be dangerous, and so he would remain uninvolved. All that really mattered was that the renter had paid in full and had offered no objections to the exorbitant deposit he demanded.

Attaché Extraordinaire

The arrival of the balloon excited no attention among the few civilians who observed it. Katrina de Krudener had put out the story that the *Queen Charlotte* would not be fulfilling its reputation as a party boat for sophisticates on New Year's Eve, because everyone who was anyone would be at the Razoumovsky Ball. She had said that this night the boat would serve as a platform for a *feu de joie* of musketry, capped off by fireworks that would be visible from the Razoumovsky Palace.

Dale checked his watch, able to see the hands under the bright moonlight. Eight o clock. Just four and a half hours to go.

Chapter 43

Von Steinwehr and Ingrid had appropriated the office of the palace archivist as their headquarters for the evening; its lock had been easily picked, it was centrally located, and it contained architect's plans of the palace. Ingrid unfurled the master blueprint and used her fingers to trace the couple's expected movements.

"Our disgusting masks and costumes have worked well, Klaus; since no one wishes to look at us, we have become the human equivalent of wallpaper."

"I have secured the loan of Boris, Alexander's chief bodyguard," replied Klaus. "He will prove useful if Pennywhistle gets in the way. I told him to meet you at the entrance to Cloak Room B in twenty minutes. I made him repeat, 'no killing.'"

Ingrid shuddered. "That thing makes my skin crawl. If he fell into a pool of piranhas, it is the fish that would be in danger."

"Admittedly, he is tough and stupid, but his hulking appearance will also cause people to look away. He will be dressed as a harlequin—amusing, given his true nature." Von Steinwehr reached into his pocket and unfurled what looked like an official report. "Some good news has arrived, Ingrid. This is from a mining engineer who has discovered Reichenau contains substantial deposits of iron ore and coal. If exploited, they could turn our country into a center of industry."

"Excellent, Klaus! It would make us much less dependent on river tolls. Perhaps one day our land will lead a united Germany in a second industrial revolution that would put Britain's to shame. But husband, are you sure Sir Thomas will act as we wish him to?"

"My ransom note is simple and direct. If Pennywhistle is the man that I believe him to be, he will have discovered my lair and concluded that Kreigshammer is impregnable."

"Will you surrender Lady Pennywhistle when you have the codebook? She and her husband will be perpetual thorns in our sides, should we let them live."

"It depends, Ingrid. I judge Pennywhistle a man of his word and he must be satisfied that I will keep mine. Cold logic will prevail when he realizes his cause is untenable and he will cut his losses. Besides, the death of a well-placed diplomat might provoke unwanted official inquiries." Von Steinwehr drew in a deep, contemplative breath. "But I may be wrong. He has an unusual regard for justice. If he persists after the trade is concluded, he will be killed. I plan to offer proof of my resolve."

"What proof is that, Klaus?"

"An earlobe with Lady Pennywhistle's earring attached to the ransom note."

"Why not the entire ear?"

"That would be barbaric, and we most certainly are not barbarians."

Von Steinwehr and Ingrid wiped perspiration from their brows because the new heating system was working efficiently. Just a little too efficiently.

John Danielski

***

A vent in a cloak room was starting to change to an orange color, though the wallpaper surrounding it was green. If a man had put his fingers to the vent, he would have burned in seconds. The wallpaper was highly flammable, as were the expensive cloaks hanging from long rows of ebony pegs.

Metz, the servant in charge of the room, was an older man, content with his lot in life and the last man to make a fuss about anything. He was drinking from a purloined bottle of expensive chardonnay and wondering what banquet leftovers would be his. His eyes had turned glassy, and his nose was sleepy. He neither noticed the vent color nor smelled the heating iron of the grate.

***

Pennywhistle and Sammie Jo moved slowly forward as the promenade line advanced toward the grand ballroom. The wide central staircase of marble was decorated with hundreds of red and white roses and led to upper galleries and balconies, which were draped in gold and red velvet. Those structures overlooked a huge parquet floor with regiments of chairs symmetrically arranged. The spillover that the grand ballroom could not accommodate would be funneled into a smaller, subsidiary ballroom.

Pennywhistle and Sammie Jo conversed quietly as the line moved in fits and starts; people were bumping and jostling other in their efforts to see or be seen. Despite the grand setting and splendid costumes, the procession had elements of low comedy.

"Who is that sad little lady near the front, Tom? She don't look like she wants to be here," Sammie Jo whispered.

455

Attaché Extraordinaire

"That's Marie Louise, Bonaparte's second wife. And you are right; she really does not want to be here."

"Damnation! Why is she not with her husband on Elba? Oh, wait, it's one of them political marriages, ain't it? Choice don't really figure in."

"I think love has developed between the two, to the great surprise of everyone who arranged the marriage. The marriage was meant to cement an alliance between Austria and France, since she is the daughter of Emperor Francis. They have a son who is nearly four years old, whom she adores. Bonaparte has not seen him since his infancy. I understand she has tried to write to him and he to her, but their letters have been intercepted. A lot of people at the Congress want to make sure the two never meet again."

"That is cruel!"

"Politics, Hawkeye. The daughters of royals may live in luxury, but often they are pawns, with the destinies of brood mares. Choice is seldom a consideration; marriages at this level are political alliances between nations. The best a woman in such a situation can hope for is that she does not actively hate the man she is required to marry."

"Her escort looks mighty handsome; his eyepatch is dashing. Who is he?"

"General von Neipperg, an Austrian cavalryman. He is supposed to keep her happy and make her forget her husband. In addition, she is to be given the Duchy of Parma in Italy. They hope to pack her off to that place with the general in tow."

"Happy," said Sammie Jo slyly, "you mean, not just in a ballroom but in the boudoir."

"Exactly. But I think it is a great mistake to keep her parted from her husband. Bonaparte is a restless man and reports are already surfacing that he is tired of Elba. I understand that Louis has defaulted on the annuity he agreed to pay him. I cannot believe that a man who ruled an empire of millions is content to rule one of twelve thousand. But my betters at the Congress have ignored the stirrings of trouble. Mark my words, we have not seen the last of him."

It took twenty minutes for Sammie Jo and Pennywhistle to reach their destination. In that time, Sammie Jo acquired an education in European royalty. Her husband pointed out the Russian Czar and Czarina, the Austrian Emperor and his wife, and the kings of Bavaria, Denmark, and Wurttemberg.

"The Czar ain't a bad lookin' fella, Tom, but the rest remind me of dog litters that are products of way too many generations of in breeding."

Pennywhistle stifled a laugh. "You are not far wrong! Mongrels are generally heartier than purebreds because Nature knows best. Many of the royals have intermarried so extensively that foreign relations are literal foreign relations. As for Alexander, he considers himself a lady killer *par excellence* and has an insatiable appetite for women. He will certainly spot you at the ball, ask for a dance, and then suggest something much more intimate."

"If I can handle two bitches, I can handle one bastard. And with him, I won't have to use a whip."

***

Metz grew drunker by the minute. The pleasant fog grew thicker, and the welcoming heat increased his relaxation. He failed to notice that the orange color of the vent had transitioned to amber.

Chapter 44

The promenade dispersed gradually after its most prestigious members reached the grand ballroom. The czars, emperors, kings, field marshals and dukes took their seats, eager to observe the arrivals of their inferiors and to pass judgment on attire, deportment, and beauty, or the want of any or all three. Sammie Jo felt like she and her husband were part of a cattle fair. Though the surroundings were elegant, they were still livestock on display. Plymouth, on Sammie Jo's shoulder, loved the attention.

As she passed the Czar and Czarina, she noted a pleased look on Alexander's face and a frown on his wife's. A general buzz rippled down the line of the seated dignitaries that kept steady pace with their progress, informing her that her earlier activities had become a topic of gossip. Her husband had been right, these people got plumb fired up over trifles.

It took ten minutes to traverse the three hundred feet of the ballroom's length, under intense scrutiny all the way. The room was nearly as wide as it was long. It had tall windows spaced ten feet apart, filled with acres of glass. The spaces between the windows were covered with large mirrors. The room had a ceiling of sixty feet, decorated with paintings of scenes she did not understand, likely from Greek and Roman mythology. Elaborate crystal chandeliers provided lighting that was nearly as bright as midday.

"How are we doing, Tom?" she whispered.

"Very well, Hawkeye. Our audience seems to appreciate Vikings and Valkyries. Tomorrow, many will be suffering the ill effects of celebrating too intensely, but their memories of us will be clear."

When they reached the end of the room, each couple was handed off to an equerry, who explained their placement at the dinner, soon to be served. Because of the number of diners, there would be a series of smaller dinners rather than one grand one. Their equerry explained that the dinner would be served at twenty tables in five separate rooms: two hundred to a table with a hundred on either side, each allocated precisely eighteen inches per plate. The dining rooms were all named after Roman gods and goddesses associated with arts and feasts.

On their way to their assignment, Pennywhistle explained that placement corresponded to protocol. The Apollo Room included royalty, princes, dukes, electors, field marshals, and ambassadors of the greater powers. The Bacchus Room included generals, admirals, and nobles from viscounts to marquises. The Ceres Room included barons and important members of the diplomatic community. The Diana Room included knights, baronets, and cadet branches of the great families of several nations. The Egeria Room included the Congress's equivalent of the British 'Other Ranks,' though none could ever be called commoners.

"Where do we go?" inquired Sammie Jo.

"The Ceres Room. My appointment as Naval Attaché takes precedence over my Knighthood of the Bath."

Attaché Extraordinaire

The dining rooms were located a hundred yards from the Grand Ballroom. The largest, The Apollo Room, occupied the Palace's Hall of Ceremonies, a smaller copy of Versailles's Hall of Mirrors. The other rooms mimicked chambers found in Marie Antoinette's Trianon Palace.

Sammie Jo and Pennywhistle were seated with much ceremony by a fussy little man who seemed to have been constructed to worry himself sick over trifles.

The long mahogany table was covered in a tablecloth of red velvet. The centerpiece consisted of a pyramid of golden pineapple, an expensive, imported fruit that symbolized hospitality. A bowl of cherries from Sicily mixed with strawberries from England graced each place setting, with slivers of pineapple separating the two fruits. Each place setting featured a blue and gold porcelain plate decorated with the double headed Razoumovsky eagle. A formidable array of silverware resided on both sides of the plate.

"Remember," Pennywhistle whispered, "just start from the outside and work your way inward."

Each place setting had a napkin folded to conform to what she guessed where the shapes of miscellaneous cranes, each just a little different from its neighbor. A finger bowl filled with water stood next to each. Yet, it was not ordinary water and featured carbonated bubbles accented with a lemon peel. Each place setting had six glasses, one for water, one for a champagne toast, one for red wine, one for white, one for port, and one for a dessert wine.

"If I use every one of these glasses, Tom, I'll be drunk as a lord by the end of dinner."

"Just remember what Lady Castlereagh said: 'Tiny bites and small sips.' The guests will sample the evening's offerings so liberally that your abstemious conduct will not be noticed."

"How much should I talk? I don't think many here have more than a smattering of English."

"No one is expecting you to conduct a dinner table salon. Your facial expressions will count for much more than your words. Give the guests what they expect, and you will delight them. Just use the eight French phrases Lady Leith taught you and leave the rest to smiles and pantomime."

"Would you repeat those phrases one last time Tom? I want to come as close to your pronunciation as I can."

"Certainly. *'Oui, non, je m'appelle, tres bien, tout va bien, c'est magnifique, trop style, la vanche.'* The first three mean yes, no, and I call myself. From the tone of voice of those who address you, you will know when to deploy them. The second three mean roughly, very good, things are fine, that is marvelous. Again, use facial, posture, and tonal clues to tell you when to call them into battle. *Trop style* is used when you find something smart and stylish, and *la vanche* when you think something is out of this world."

"You are out of this world Tom. I know how lucky I am. I'd kiss you hard right here but... well...." Her voice trailed off.

"Just the thought of your kisses makes me smile, Hawkeye."

She sighed deeply. "This is one night I do wish I were better bred. I say foolish things. I only know one language and I don't speak that too well. I know people like to look at me, but I wonder if they are doing so because they wonder how a freak got into polite society. I hate embarrassing you, Tom."

Pennywhistle put a finger to her lips. "You once told me, the wilder the colt, the better the horse. I love you, Sammie Jo. I never feel the need to explain you to anyone."

Their conversation was ended by the loud popping of champagne corks. An army of servers appeared and began filling the water, champagne, and white wine glasses. Sammie Jo felt a breeze over her right shoulder as a waiter wielded two bottles and a carafe with the deft swiftness of a juggler. Her glasses were filled, even before she had a chance to decline the white wine.

Two other waiters appeared as the wine pourer vanished like a wraith. One plucked up the ornamental plate in front of Sammie Jo, replacing it with a small plate of fruit salad and vegetables: half of the plate held sliced grapes, peaches, and pears bathed in cream while the other half held peas, carrots, and parsnips wreathed in parsley. The boundary between the two was marked by slices of Seville oranges. The other waiter placed two bowls next to the salad plate. One bowl contained turtle soup, the other olla soup: a Spanish confection featuring chickpeas, bacon, chorizo, fennel, and hot chili peppers.

Pennywhistle whispered to Sammie Jo. "That is odd, combining two separate courses into one."

"What do you mean?"

"Usually, the soup comes before the salad, not alongside it. My guess is that they are trying to speed the dining along because there are so many entertainments to come. That probably accounts for why this dinner is a mixture of styles: à la Française and à la Russe.

"What does that mean?"

"*A la Française* means a meal served buffet style, laid out for the guests to help themselves. It is the older method." He gestured toward four long tables ten feet behind the diners, bearing hot platters featuring thirty types of meat in various cuts, twenty types of fowl, and fifty varieties of fish.

"The newer one is *à la Russe*—what you just experienced. Food is dispensed in courses with plates already filled. I like the older method. It breaks up the formality of the meal and gives guests who are not seated close to each other a chance to mingle and converse. When courses are served, you are supposed to only converse with the people across the table from you. This reduces the potential for good conversation."

"So, this really ain't the thirty six course dinner that the host boasted about."

"In terms of content, yes. In terms of presentation, no."

Sammie Jo noticed her tablemates starting their soup, so she picked up a round spoon and sampled the one with islands of turtle fat. "Like little ships going out to sea, I dip my spoon away from me." she whispered the rhyme Lady Leith had taught her. The soup was delicious. She took a second spoon and tried the olla soup, which proved equally delightful. She consumed both quickly, being careful to sip rather than slurp.

She ate only small portions of the salad, carefully pacing herself. She took a few sips of wine, but mainly confined her attentions to the water glass. In between bites, she fed Plymouth a steady stream of strawberries. There was surprisingly little conversation. The guests seated near to them were best described as "large people" and they had brought their formidable appetites with them. By the time she had finished the first course, most had already risen and walked to the buffet tables.

When she reached the tables, she gasped at the sheer variety of meats. While she was trying to decide whether to favor beef, poultry or fish, a woman about her age introduced herself as the Countess von Murrenberg; speaking French with a heavy German accent. Her pronunciation of French was even worse than the way Sammie Jo spoke the few words that she had acquired.

"Lady Pennywhistle, I presume?"

"*Oui. Je m'appelle Lady Pennywhistle.*"

Attaché Extraordinaire

"It is indeed a splendid party, is it not?"

"*Trop style!*"

"I admire your outfit. So unexpected and so dangerous. What do you think of my dress?"

"*C'est magnifique!*"

"Thank you. You should try the *Duck a l'orange.* I am informed it is delicious.

"*Tout va bien.*"

"I plan on also having roast trout, partridge, and ostrich. Have you eaten ostrich before?"

"*Non.*"

"It is so much better than kangaroo. It has a flavor like no other. You will want to save room for the many pastries here tonight. Those chocolate sponge cakes are incredible!"

"*Oui! La vanche!*"

Two other burbling women appeared and virtually abducted the Countess; they clearly knew about something she just had to see. Sammie Jo felt relieved; she had exhausted her supply of French.

Sammie Jo decided to enjoy the amazing variety of food, but she would limit herself to two bites of each. She picked the ostrich as well as roast beef, boiled boar, baked eelpout, fried shrimp, and something called *spatsburgunder,* which contained a meat she was unable to identify.

She returned to her table to find her husband had filled his plate entirely with roast beef, though he was just picking at it. He was engaged in an intense conversation with a grandee standing next to him, who bristled with aristocratic hauteur. From the man's intense tones and emphatic hand gestures, she judged the conversation was diplomatic business being done in a social setting.

The woman to her right was engaged in a life and death battle with a large pheasant. Sammie Jo decided to abandon a ladylike period of aesthetic contemplation and pitch into her food directly. It was, indeed, excellent and she allowed herself half a glass of champagne by way of accompaniment. Her husband had said, "Champagne goes well with any food," and he was right.

She had just finished her portion of ostrich when her husband's conversation partner stalked off, clearly displeased at the talk just ended.

"What was that all about? Who was he? You have hardly touched your food."

Her husband shook his head in exasperation. "The Marquis de Labrador, the Spanish Ambassador. I have listened to many insane ideas at this conference but the one I just heard takes the prize. Spain wants the Louisiana Purchase back."

"What the fu... uh... blazes?" gasped Sammie Jo.

"Labrador maintains that Bonaparte stole it from Spain then illegally sold it to the Americans. He is talking about taking away half of America's land!"

"I assume you told him to stick his thumb in his ear and go bowling. Very politely of course."

"I wanted to, but he proffered a carrot in return for the acceptance of his proposal. He offered to back Britain's championing of the abolition of the slave trade. Spain has proven the biggest obstacle to making that happen. He approached me because The Royal Navy would have to enforce that ban and I am, after all, the naval attaché. He felt it safer to float the idea with me than presenting it directly to Lord Castlereagh."

Sammie Jo frowned.

Attaché Extraordinaire

"Don't worry, Hawkeye. Britain will just have to offer him something else for his support. I wonder if he would settle for Trinidad?"

Sammie Jo tentatively put a sliver of pineapple in her mouth. Her eyes brightened in delight. She handed a sliver to her husband. "Try this, Sugar Plum. I guarantee it will make you forget the Marquis."

***

The Earl and Lady Leith were just finishing their meal in the Bacchus Room.

"I still wish you would remain in Vienna, Margaret. I do not like you putting yourself in danger."

"I understand, Robert, but I should be safe enough aboard the boat."

"Promise me you will stay there. Promise!"

"I promise." She brushed a hand over her mouth and murmured, "Unless something goes wrong."

The Earl was already plowing ahead. "This may not be the right place and time, but I want you to know how I feel, so I am going to ask you a question that I was saving until our return to London."

He reached into his pocket and extracted a small box that could contain only one thing.

"I wish I could get down on one knee, but this question is one of the heart, not the theatre. You saved me, brought me back from the darkest despair. I know in all the realms of the universe, there is no other woman like you. Margaret, will you marry me?"

"Oh, Robert! Yes!"

The Earl blinked in surprise. "Wonderful! That was easy!"

John Danielski

"Did you expect me to say no?"

"I thought you might say you needed time to think about it."

"At our age, time is something in short supply and we should take care never to waste it. I have been lonely since my husband died. I realize how much I have missed having a kind, thoughtful, intelligent man in my life; one who appreciates me just the way I am and finds my many eccentricities endearing rather than annoying."

***

"Report, Brunhilde!" Ingrid ordered, standing in the foyer leading to the dining rooms.

"Madame, Lady Pennywhistle is currently dining with her husband. I followed her to the dining room. My sister is waiting outside to resume the surveillance. As soon as the dance is done and people begin heading for the joust, I and my three sisters will meet you at the South Portico. That is where you want us, correct?"

"Yes. Boris will handle her husband. It is important that the crowd see her as a woman who has celebrated a little too extravagantly and view us as angels of mercy, escorting her home. There must be no suggestion that we are doing anything against her wishes."

"Yes, Madam, I understand. There will be no alarm. My sisters and I are most eager to become your ladies-in-waiting when the throne of Reichenau is restored to your husband."

"I know you will serve me well. You may even serve a queen one day!"

"Queen? I do not understand, Madame."

"Never mind. I think, however, that since I am so close to success, you may now call me Countess."

Attaché Extraordinaire

"Yes, Countess."

***

Sammie Jo put her husband back in festive mood by escorting him to the dessert table; the variety of pastries, ices, and sweets bewitched the salivary glands. Sammie Jo daringly put four pastries on her plate, realizing that it would be hard to keep up her policy of baby bites. She then added duplicate pastries to her husband's plate. They were *Pain à la Duchesse*, a long pastry roll filled with custard and topped with whipped crème that some had nicknamed an éclair, *pâte à choux*, a buttery tart with a center containing peaches, apricots, and orange marmalade topped with sugar shards, *marron glacé*, a candied and glazed chestnut, and a *petit pain a Carême*, a puff pastry that was creating a sensation in Vienna. Recently introduced by the famous Chef Marie Antoine Carême, its secret was a center that contained an exotic new flavoring, vanilla.

For many of the guests, especially the impromptu purchasers of scalped tickets, dinner was the high point of the evening. Satiated and content, those who had no interest in music or dancing began to depart in large numbers. Servants emptied out secondary and makeshift cloak rooms.

Metz, the main cloak hall servant, had fallen sound asleep, surrounded by the furs of the most exalted guests. They had been the first to arrive and would be the last to leave. The vent was glowing hotter and hotter. A stack of rags used for boot-blacking began to smolder.

Sammie Jo and Pennywhistle had just finished their last pastries when the sounds of the Razoumovsky Orchestra warming up reached their ears, a signal that the concert would soon begin. They rose and began a slow walk to the ballroom.

Chapter 45

The Grand Ballroom turned Grand Concert Hall filled gradually, as guests who had eaten too much took their time finding seats. Protocol played no part as each guest made his own decision about which seat promised the best acoustics.

Beethoven's entrance occasioned thunderous applause. He did not impress Sammie Jo. Or rather he did, but in the wrong way. He was only slightly taller than Napoleon and Razoumovsky's remark that "the world is too small for him," seemed to have things in reverse. His blunt face seemed more appropriate to that of a day laborer than a musical artiste. His clothing was of good quality, but he wore it with an indifference that suggested his usual appearance was one of disheveled absentmindedness. His surly expression reminded Sammie Jo of a man roused from a deep sleep against his will. Perhaps it was because he realized how out of place he was, even more a fish out of water than she was.

He was a tempest, flailing his arms extravagantly as he conducted the Razoumovsky Orchestra. The current offering, his Sixth Symphony, *The Pastorale*, was dedicated to the Count. Yet, his gestures were frequently out of synchronization with the music, as if he were conducting in 2/4 time whilst his orchestra was playing in 12/8 time. Sammie Jo noticed that many musicians were not paying any attention to the drama of his hands.

Attaché Extraordinaire

"How come his arm flapping don't have much to do with the music?" she whispered.

"He has lost most of his hearing," Pennywhistle murmured back. "He is basing his conducting on the vibrations of his podium caused by the instruments rather than their sound."

"A musician who can't hear. No wonder he is grumpy."

Sammie Jo noticed that most people had dispensed with their masks, so she decided to do so as well. The enjoyment of being incognito had a limited life span, probably because the many outsized personalities could hide their lights under a bushel for only so long.

Alexander observed Sammie Jo listening, and each second increased his mounting lust. He was amused by how she had put Sagan and Bagration in their places. Her use of a whip excited him: she would be a meteor in bed. He had to have her, tonight.

It never occurred to him that she might be deeply in love with her husband.

Pennywhistle listened to the music only intermittently. *The Pastorale* was lovely, but it did little to soothe his restless mind.

***

Ingrid was outside the Palace performing one last dosage check. She had borrowed one of the dogs from the Turkish pavilion by bribing his handler. The wolfhound was surprisingly docile and offered no resistance when she placed the chemically soaked cloth over his muzzle. His eyes fluttered, his lips quavered, his limbs buckled, and he collapsed. Five seconds. Good, though she would have preferred an instantaneous response. She checked his breathing—strong and steady. She had the dosage right.

***

Sammie Jo enjoyed the concert. There was long applause for Beethoven when the symphony finished, in which she joined. She hoped the dancing would burn off some of her nervous energy.

There was an extended interval as the audience rose from their chairs and legions of servants cleared the ballroom floor of chairs.

During the interval, a bedraggled messenger wearing a British courier's outfit entered the room. He looked like he had not slept for days, because of prolonged riding. His haggard appearance and anxious expression attracted plenty of curious stares. The messenger eyed the room until his gaze settled on Castlereagh, dressed as the Greek lawgiver, Solon. He walked quickly toward him. Castlereagh moved swiftly to meet him at the rear of the ballroom. The messenger handed Castlereagh a red dispatch case and smiled. He whispered to Castlereagh for a minute or so. Castlereagh rarely smiled, but now gave one that was pure joy.

Pennywhistle had followed this exchange, as had several people sitting nearby. But unlike them, he could read lips and understood the two words that Castlereagh mouthed silently with satisfaction, "Peace, peace!"

Pennywhistle breathed a sigh of relief because the messenger and dispatch case meant that The Treaty of Ghent had been signed. The American War was finally over.

Castlereagh and the courier left the room in a hurry. Castlereagh undoubtedly wanted to review the full particulars of the Treaty before making an official announcement.

Pennywhistle noted both Metternich and Talleyrand following Castlereagh's exit. They had likely guessed what knowledge the official dispatch case contained. Pennywhistle's gaze next alighted on Alexander, flirting with a woman. He had missed the entire episode and had no idea that the contents of the red case were about to make a great deal of difference in his dealings with the Congress.

The orchestra opened with a waltz conducted by the man who had written it: the Austrian Court *Kappelmeister,* Antonio Salieri. Yet, no one stepped immediately onto the dance floor. Sammie Jo guessed it had something to do with protocol, lesser beings waiting for greater ones to make the first move. That made little sense to her, since dancing was supposed to be a liberation from the concerns of the world. Someone had to make the first move. *Fuck protocol.*

She transferred Plymouth to Lady Leith's arm and grabbed her husband's hand. "Come on Tom, let a country girl teach them how things are done!"

Pennywhistle knew the first dance should be led by a royal: decorum was serious business even at a social event. But he also realized that the crowd had ingested enough alcohol that they would trade etiquette for amusement. The Congress danced, so why not practice dancing diplomacy? By putting on a diverting show, he and Sammie Jo could establish an *entente cordiale* with the crowd for the entire evening.

Pennywhistle noticed the crowd looking toward the worldly Razoumovsky for his verdict. His eyes smiled approvingly at Sammie Jo.

He followed her eagerly on the floor, put his arm round her waist, and began to lead with graceful steps.

"Pretty good for a backwoods better half, born in a log cabin," Sammie Jo whispered. "Cinderella would be jealous."

"There are princes here who would love to trade places with me."

John Danielski

"No one could ever replace you, Sugar Plum."

There was a muffled chorus of *oohs, ahhhs,* and *oh's* from the crowd; two thirds approving and a third giving the opposite verdict.

Sammie Jo's attire, as well as her previous conduct, ensured that everyone recognized the couple.

Pennywhistle and Sammie Jo danced in graceful synchronization with the music. Their movements were sensual, flowing, and easy, distinctly at variance with the practiced artifice of the Congress. Their slow swirls and ardent twirls mesmerized the crowd.

Marvelous creature! thought the Czar.

I must learn more about these Americans, thought the Emperor Francis.

I wish I were a few years younger! thought Razoumovsky.

Tonight, she truly is a princess, thought Lady Leith.

At least she dances well, thought Sagan.

Trip! thought Bagration.

Would that I could move with her grace, thought Lady Castlereagh.

I wonder if she would teach me how to dance, von Murrenberg thought wistfully.

Ingrid took a bold risk and entered the ballroom from the corridor. She knew she shouldn't, but wanted to see how her target danced. She had to admit that the American moved beautifully. Then she felt pangs of jealousy and resentment. It should have been her and Klaus on the floor, leading those of lesser rank.

Pennywhistle's eyes sparkled with a passion returned tenfold by his partner. For the duration of the dance, he forgot the desperate actions that lay only a few hours ahead. The grace of their movements became, not just a testament to skill, but a tribute to love.

The music swelled to an energetic climax and then ended with a flourish. The dancers' natural artistry had won over the audience, which narrowly restrained itself from bursting into applause.

As the orchestra prepared for a new piece, Pennywhistle spotted Metternich and Talleyrand exiting the room together. They undoubtedly wanted to speak with advisors, and it was quite possible they would seek an informal late-night meeting with Castlereagh.

The orchestra changed the pace with a stately minuet, the dance favored by courtly guests after an exquisite dinner. Minuets were slow dances that did not disturb digestion; they also allowed quiet conversation between partners. Best of all, from the point of view of many guests, the dancers change partners multiple times.

The minuet was followed by an energetic country reel. Sammie Jo relished it, as it reminded her of the dances of her youth, though the pace tonight was less frenetic than the Maryland barn dances. She put this down to the absence of bumblebee whiskey—the kind that packed a real sting.

The orchestra paused for a few minutes when the reel concluded, giving a chance for winded participants to catch their breath. The hairs on the back of Pennywhistle's neck stiffened and prickled. He had a strong feeling that they should leave *now*. But the plan was to depart at midnight, and Sammie Jo was enjoying the dancing. He decided to ignore the urging.

The next moment, a deep voice in heavily accented English caused Sammie Jo to turn around. "Might I have this next waltz, Lady Pennywhistle?" It was the Czar, dressed as a

Cossack, yet sporting reams of medals that belonged on a dress uniform. He had dispensed with a mask, probably because he did not want his handsome face obscured.

Sammie Jo looked him straight in the eye, which caught him off guard, since you were never supposed to confront a sovereign's gaze. He detected none of the deference that his presence usually provoked. Strangely, that excited him.

Sammie Jo was awed, for about half a second. She then saw him as just a richer version of the swells she had fended off back in Maryland. Alexander acted as if he were in love with his self-image and deemed his charm to be contagious, but she had seen a lot better specimens of manhood, and there was none better than her husband.

She looked Alexander up and down like he was a prize bull, giving him the kind of evaluation that men often accorded her. She saw the confusion in his face and knew she had done the right thing. "I'd be right pleased to dance this li'l old next one with you," she said with a *howdy pardner* voice that exaggerated her native drawl. "Y'all be careful not to step on my toes with those boots of yours."

"I-I promise to be careful," stammered the Czar at her breezy, insouciant response. She had not used his title.

The music swelled and Sammie Jo allowed the Czar to guide her in a box step. His lead was uncertain, his motions slow and heavy, and rhythm was not his friend. She narrowly restrained herself from assuming control and felt like a thoroughbred leading a mule. She saw a bulge in the front of his breeches and knew his mind was not on his dancing.

After several whirls, his hand glided down toward her buttocks. He squeezed them quickly and furtively. Sammie Jo's eyes blinked and squinted, becoming daggers that jabbed into Alexander's blue eyes. She bared her teeth, and her whispered words were venom spat by a cobra. "I ain't your property so get your hand off my arse. Try that stunt again and my knee will polish your family jewels so hard you'll be spitting them from your mouth."

The Czar's hand flew to his side as if retracted from a hot stove. This woman was mad! She might be a spirited bedmate, but there were many other less dangerous fish in the sea tonight. He behaved for the remainder of the dance. She would be the one that got away.

As the final note died away, Alexander bowed and spoke with face-saving gallantry. "I shall never forget this dance."

Sammie Jo noted his breech flap was now a plain rather than a peak. She curtsied. "Someday, I will tell my children about this waltz." Her ambiguous eyes and voice left it unclear whether that story would awe or amuse.

The Czar departed with unseemly haste.

Chapter 46

Pennywhistle had declined to watch his wife dance with Czar Alexander and had made his way to the west end of the ballroom to fetch himself a glass of champagne. He knew he had no cause for jealousy, but the sight irritated him, nonetheless. As he took his first sip, he noticed a quartet of women in furs entering the ballroom from the east end, walking so quickly that it was just short of running. He gathered that they, like half the attendees, had gone outside, either to get optimal seats for the midnight joust or to rehearse their parts in *le tableau vivant* that would follow, The Burning of Moscow. Other guests, who preferred pleasant frights to dancing, had migrated to a separate room to tell ghost stories.

The quartet's hurried gait triggered Pennywhistle's sense of alarm. He followed their progress as they made their way to Razoumovsky. They spoke earnestly to him, and the Count's cheerful expression changed to one of horror. The Count walked briskly over to the orchestra. He seized a pair of cymbals and clashed them together loudly, once, twice, a third time. Throughout the room, conversations paused and strolling couples came to a halt. Everyone's attention rested on Count Razoumovsky.

"Ladies and gentlemen!" he called out, "A problem has been brought to my attention. It is with regret that I announce that it is imperative for everyone's safely to evacuate the ballroom and the palace, and it will be best for all if we proceed directly out of doors. Please remain calm. However, there is a fire below, almost certainly originating in the kitchens, that may or may not be spreading. I ask you to follow my directions as my retainers lead you to the south lawn. If there is, indeed, any danger, you will be able to take to your carriages from there."

Pennywhistle's nose now informed him: there was a faint smell of burning. Looking down at a vent near his boot, he saw thin wisps of smoke emerging. Fire was indeed cause for concern. The palace was constructed of stone, but the furnishings were flammable. The count was still speaking.

Pennywhistle spotted Sammie Jo because of her height, but a sea of humanity stood between him and her.

Sammie Jo spotted her husband at the same moment and waved her arm over her head. A moment later, to his bafflement, she disappeared.

The fire had furnished Ingrid the perfect opportunity, and she had taken it. Ingrid grabbed the bird first; his claws gouged her hand, but she ignored the pain and fixed the cord holding the ransom note round its neck, then released him. He squawked angrily, then flew off.

Sammie Jo had just started to turn when Ingrid clamped the drugged cloth over her face and clasped a strong arm around her shoulders to contain her struggles. Reflexively, Sammie Jo inhaled deeply, preparing to shout or fend off an attack. Instead, she sagged into Ingrid's embrace as the drug took effect, never seeing the face of her assailant.

The Count moved through the human sea, banging his cymbals. Four trusted retainers followed him. "Stay calm, stay calm, there is time to get you all out, if you follow my directions. Let my retainers form you into lines. We will follow the protocol of rank." His calm voice and authoritative demeanor steadied the crowd, and they obeyed him.

Plymouth landed on Pennywhistle's arm in a flurry of bright wings, neck extended to present the note and the offending cord. Pennywhistle quickly untied the note and read it, his face darkening with anger. Now her strange disappearance made terrible sense. The crowd was moving towards the exits, carrying him along with it. Frantically, he tried to turn and force a way back towards where he had last seen Sammie Jo, but the tide of humanity was inexorable.

As he struggled, a tall, older man wearing the white and red uniform of an Austrian field marshal took him firmly by the arm. "Now, sir," he remonstrated in a deep voice, "nothing you left behind is worth risking your life during a fire. Come along now, and don't start a panic." Pennywhistle realized he was speaking to one of Bonaparte's most formidable antagonists, Prince Karl von Schwarzenberg. His commanding presence radiated calm. As Pennywhistle's head cleared, he realized that whoever had kidnapped Sammie Jo would already be beyond his ability to overtake. And he knew exactly where his wife would be taken, Kreigshammer Castle.

Now all that mattered was getting out and away to the river as swiftly as possible. The planned operation would go forward, only now it would be a rescue mission. The trouble was, there was a solid wall of slowly advancing royalty, high-ranking officers, and diplomats between him and the doors.

Attaché Extraordinaire

Ingrid decided to use the Count's kindness against him. She had enlisted the help of another woman by murmuring that Sammie Jo was a consumptive who had fainted, and the two women bore the woman along, moving towards Razoumovsky, now in the business of directing traffic. Ingrid repeated her story that her friend was a consumptive who would die of smoke inhalation unless she was immediately rushed from the room.

Ingrid's feigned concern and apparent devotion won over the Count: he placed the trio at the head of line one. They soon exited the room and disappeared into the large crowd milling about the grounds. The fire was visible from outside, flames shooting outward and upward from the kitchens beneath the palace. Vehicles had begun clogging the streets close to the palace, disgorging occupants who'd arrived to watch an artistic holocaust. Ingrid led the way to her husband's waiting carriage. The Good Samaritan helped bundle Sammie Jo into the back, refused Klaus' offer of a gratuity, and departed. Klaus drove the carriage away, using the alleys.

Pennywhistle was desperate. Dale on the *Queen Charlotte* would already be waiting for them. He was still nowhere near an exit, and by now, the roads leading to and from the castle would be thronged, making a quick passage to the docks impossible. Suddenly he remembered that odd moment he'd experienced earlier. It had been a premonition, he realized, help from the Other Side. If he had heeded the warning, he and Sammie Jo would be at the wharf by now. But the Other Side offered multiple opportunities for redemption; if the first was ignored, other possibilities sometimes presented themselves; one just had to pay attention. Pennywhistle exhaled, inhaled deeply, then exhaled, relaxing the tensed muscles of his neck and back, and paid attention.

Sometimes suggestions from the Other Side could seem counter-intuitive, but it was wise to trust them completely. Following a prompting, Pennywhistle moved athwart the crowd moving towards the doors, until he was behind everyone else.

He recollected that palaces were always built with hidden passages. Some of these were intended for servants, allowing them to travel from room to room without disturbing the residents as they bore away dishes and laundry, a network of corridors. But other passages were designed for discreet movements and rapid egress. He needed to find one of these. Pennywhistle's frustration caused his soul to cry out.

The response spawned goosebumps on his arms, dried his lips, and caused the hairs on the back of his neck to rise as if stimulated by a low-level current of electricity. The electricity came in pulses and waves of varied length. It had a soothing, velvety softness and represented a non-verbal communication with a presence that was wise as it was unsentimental. The presence embraced him like an old friend and his mind flooded with knowledge not his own. His vision shimmered, then sharpened to crystal clarity.

His Second Sight guided his eyes to a section of the blue alabaster column opposite him. That portion glowed with a soft light that flowed from an unearthly realm, illuminating a series of musical notes rendered as a plaster frieze. He moved close and hummed the first notes, realizing they were the start of the Razoumovsky Quartet. But he was not being directed here for musical appreciation and looked more closely at the notes; the first four had ridges on top. He instinctively pressed each note in sequence. A five by five foot panel at the base of the column retracted slowly as it swung inward, revealing a flight of stairs.

He followed the narrow passage for what seemed an eternity, finally emerging into the palace's laundry room. He quickly found a door that exited onto the South Lawn and raced toward where Gabriel was waiting with the carriage. As he ran, he decided to stop at the residence. After changing his clothes and donning a pair of steel toed boots, he would pluck up the real codebook. He was prepared to trade it for Sammie Jo, but the next owner would not enjoy it for long. He had coated the book with chemicals to make it so flammable that the smallest spark would ignite it.

Pennywhistle had no idea that he had been followed; Peter Wilson had been nearby when the fire broke out, and his instinct for safety told him to watch Pennywhistle. He'd navigated the passage a minute behind Pennywhistle. As soon as he reached fresh air, he vomited. His scalped ticket had nearly cost him his life.

Chapter 47

The smell of smoke woke Sammie Jo. Her nose was baffled; it was not the smell of hearth fire and home. It was the smell of coal fire, not wood. Wherever she was, she was moving.

She felt dizzy, and strangely weighed down. Her last memory was of a peculiar aroma, and something clapped tightly over her face. She opened her eyes slowly; her vision was as if she were viewing objects through a screen of fine gauze. A face with red hair and blue eyes gradually came into focus, reminding her of a predator contemplating prey. She instinctively made a fist to strike a blow and discovered both hands restrained by leather straps to the armrests of an exceedingly heavy chair the size of a throne. Her legs were secured as well.

"You sockdologizing old witch! Where'd you hide your broomstick and black cat? You look like the hindquarters of bad luck."

"What an ill-bred greeting," said Ingrid haughtily. "Just what I would expect from one who is merely impersonating a lady. But I anticipated an uncouth response." She produced a small pocket pistol. "We are going to talk, and this will be an inducement to civility on your part. I shall only wound you if you misbehave, but I assure you, it will be painful."

Attaché Extraordinaire

Sammie Jo noticed four distinctive claw marks on the back of Ingrid's hand. Wildly she looked around. *Plymouth!* "Where is Plymouth?" she demanded angrily.

Ingrid was baffled. What an odd question! "Across the ocean, but what—"

"Not the harbor, you biddy! My *parrot*! What in tarnation have you done with Plymouth!"

Ingrid nearly laughed aloud. This ridiculous creature was worried about a pet! In a flash, Ingrid saw an opportunity to inflict real pain on the woman she hated. It was a fitting punishment for the loss of Medusa and Klaus's rage when the falcon did not return. "That annoying bird? Dead, of course. I killed it with my own hands." She sneered down at her prisoner.

Sammy Jo fought back a sob, but tears slid down her cheeks and her eyes swam. When she cleared her throat, her voice was a tempest of rage. "You'll fry in hell for that. That bird had more humanity in his beak than you have in your whole body."

Ingrid's lips thinned in anger. Deliberately, she raised her pistol in her right hand and fired. The bullet passed inches away from Sammy Jo's shoulder. "The next one will bite your flesh." Ingrid walked to a nearby table where a powder flask, wads, and lead balls were neatly arrayed and calmly reloaded her pistol.

As Sammie Jo watched, she realized she needed cool cunning, not the fire of emotion. Ingrid was already as crazy as popcorn on a hot griddle. "All right, you win. Now, what shall we talk about?" she said, trying to sound submissive, but then she continued archly, "Fashions, food, housekeeping hints? Your career as a realtor?"

"You know perfectly well what you are here for. We each know who the other is, so let us dispense with pretense. Your husband practiced a deception upon my husband."

Sammie Jo noticed a discarded black dress, upon which lay a Hela mask. "So, you're a snake that just shed her skin, and you're itchin' to bite."

"Cease trying to provoke me. I will make matters plain. My husband and I want the real codebook. We are willing to trade you for it. By now, your husband has received a note of our demands and has twenty four hours to respond. Should we receive no response to our request for an exchange on public and neutral grounds, you will be executed. It's that simple."

"Where am I now?"

"We are on a steam launch, the *Eulenspiegel*. We shall soon dock at our destination, which is an isolated and guarded fortress, so you may forego any thoughts of escape or untoward actions. If you behave, you will not suffer. If not, the fortress has its dungeons."

Sammie Jo knew Ingrid meant Kreigshammer. Her opponent had inadvertently given her a useful piece of information. Ingrid expected a civilized response within twenty four hours and had no idea that a violent one was going to arrive far sooner. Ingrid also assumed the fortress was escape proof—evidence of arrogance and unimaginative thinking. Tom had told her the best way to conquer a conventional fortress guarded by conventional thinkers was to devise an unconventional solution. An aerial assault circumvented defenses rather than challenging them. Tom would already be on his way. He would come for her, but she needed to stall for time and figure out a way to signal him exactly where she was being held.

Attaché Extraordinaire

She had a bargaining chip of her own, because Tom believed in always having a supplementary plan if the main one miscarried. He had made her memorize the tenth table. If necessary, she could translate the letters.

For now, it made sense to give the human firetrap in front of her what she wanted.

"My husband will make the right choice, Madame von Steinwehr, so I will cooperate."

"You will address me as Countess."

"As you wish, but as far as I know you ain't one.

"Official acknowledgment is a mere formality, whereas I feel the truth of it in my blood and bones."

"I don't need to skulk behind no fancy title, and I am just fine being plain old Sammie Jo."

"Americans," Ingrid said in disgust," such impudent, boorish upstarts."

"Napoleon was an upstart, and he didn't do too bad for himself," countered Sammie Jo.

***

On the deck of the *Queen Charlotte*, Owens had been growing more and more restless. He turned to Dale. "You said Sir Thomas was famous for his punctuality. He's late."

"In my experience—"

Dale's response was interrupted by a carriage clattering madly up to the dock. The door was flung open and Pennywhistle leaped to the cobblestones, then dashed up and across the gangplank.

Dale was shocked by Pennywhistle's expression. It was as dark as the battle rig into which he had changed. He looked as though he were in a towering rage.

"Sarn't Major, assemble the men," Pennywhistle said tersely. "I have information they must hear."

"Aye, aye, sir," said Dale. His response was automatic from years of military service, but he was still trying to puzzle out the mystery of the major's emotions. Then he noticed Pennywhistle was alone. *My God, something has happened to Sammie Jo!*

"I apologize for being late, but the streets were blocked by crowds watching the fire. Our mission has now become one of rescue. The blackguards we will face tonight have taken my wife and are holding her hostage."

A murmur of anger rippled through the assembled men. It was one thing to make war on men, but it was beyond the pale to wage it on women. "We will get her back for you safe and sound, Sir Thomas, don't you worry," consoled Jones.

"Taking your wife will be the last mistake they ever make," offered Rhodes.

"Our valor shall make an ordinary fight seem like a prayer meeting! exclaimed Miller.

"Thank you all," replied Pennywhistle. "I could not ask for better men. We will follow the plan, but must exercise some extra caution to discover my wife's whereabouts."

"How will we know her?" asked Benson."

"She is tall, and dressed as an American frontierswoman for the costume ball. She will want to assist in her own rescue, so do not expect a fainting violet."

Montgomery hurried up to Pennywhistle. "Taking you wife is disgraceful. But that explains the *Eulenspiegel* being out tonight. She sped by an hour ago. My guess is your wife was aboard."

"What's the *Eulenspiegel?*" inquired Pennywhistle fiercely.

Attaché Extraordinaire

"The other steamer on the river. She usually hauls private mails. She is a lot smaller than the *Queen* but uses the same Boulton and Watt engine. I wish I could tell you we could catch her, but because of her small size, she is almost twice as fast as the *Queen,* and she has an hour lead. But the *Queen* is primed to go, boilers heated and coalers ready to shovel."

"How much speed can you get out of the *Queen*, if you push her boiler right to the edge?

"Eight knots, if I want to maintain a safety factor: nine if I do not."

"Pop her rivets if you have to."

"Consider it done, Sir Thomas. The ice chunks will make things a little dicey, so I must allow additional time for maneuvering. I can get us to our destination in ninety minutes."

"I trust that you will make every exertion, Mr. Montgomery."

A second carriage thundered to a halt next to the dock. The Earl and Lady Leith descended and hurried over the gangplank.

Lady Leith embraced Pennywhistle. "We could not find you or Sammie Jo once we got out of the palace. All we could think to do was come here."

"Von Steinwehr's taken her," said Pennywhistle gravely. "And I mean to get her back."

"We guessed something untoward had happened," rumbled the Earl.

Montgomery spoke. "Shall I hoist the gangplank now, Sir Thomas?"

"Yes."

"Wait! Not yet! I'm going with you!" The voice belonged to Gabriel, who had dismounted from the first carriage and now ran up the gangplank, a large sack slung over his shoulder. He had purposely waited until the last possible second to announce his presence.

Pennywhistle looked startled as Gabriel jerked to a breathless halt in front of him. "No, Gabriel, you are too old for this."

"I figured you'd say that, always looking out for my welfare, but my job is to take care of you and remember the things you forgot. You been thinking so hard on how to defeat people that you plum forgot about dogs. This fella that done took your wife will have mean ones, trained and hungry. Probably big Rottweilers, but I got an answer."

"God's Death! I am a perfect idiot!" He clapped his hand to his forehead. "I never considered a canine guard." Pennywhistle's nose perked up as he scented the contents of Gabriel's sack. It smelled like highly spiced steaks. "So, a sirloin solution?"

"It's an old recipe used against the dogs of slave patrols. The steaks be poisoned, but are coated with a batter that contains scents that dogs cannot resist: basil, lavender, orange, lemon, ginger, and rosemary. The strongest ingredient is female piss. Guard dogs all be male and mating is much more natural than biting people."

"Very well, you are part of the expedition. Hoist the gangplank, Montgomery. Gabriel, your operation will have to take place before the main assault." He massaged his chin, then flashed a sardonic smile. "Operation Dog Gone, it does have a ring to it!"

"What the hell?" Owens shouted. He had begun spreading out the shell of the hot air balloon. "Damn it! The balloon has a tear in it. No; it's not a tear, it's a burn. Looks like a stray fragment from the palace fire was blown onto it by the wind."

Curses rose to everyone's lips, except Lady Leith's. "Let me have a look at it," she said briskly. "The balloon is silk, is it not? I learned to sew silk as a girl." She bent down and examined the balloon shell. "I could definitely repair it, but I would need a large needle and heavy thread."

"I can help with that," said Montgomery. "We have sailcloth, needles, and thread aboard in case the engine dies, and we need to improvise a sail."

"How long would it take?" inquired Pennywhistle.

"To cut a patch to the right size and thickness, then double stitch it into place would require careful work. Maybe an hour, but there is no reason why I cannot work while the Queen is moving."

"Damn!" exclaimed Pennywhistle. "We are already far behind schedule. I don't even like to think of what Sammie Jo is going through right now."

Pennywhistle turned to Montgomery. "I will need every knot you can coax out of the *Queen*."

"Messieurs Bolton and Watt are yours to command, Sir Thomas."

"Unleash their powers, Mr. Montgomery."

Chapter 48

Ingrid had confined Sammie Jo in a large room that was in the modernized part of the castle, with grey oak paneling and two large windows, neither of which was useful for an escape, because the Danube lay five hundred feet below. The door was heavy, solid oak, barred and locked on the outside.

The room contained a bed, writing, dining, and end tables, a wash basin, a chamber pot, and plenty of linens. Servants had brought Sammie Jo a supper of soup, beef, bread, and wine, though she had little appetite. She wished she had a time piece; waiting was a tedious business, and time seemed to have slowed to a crawl. She tried to guess how long it would take Tom to arrive and hoped it would be before dawn. She had considered attempting to escape — it would have been easy for her to overpower the servant who brought supper—but much as it galled her, her best option was to wait. But perhaps she could still help Tom. The original mission had been to destroy the Clarke Letters, and finding where they were hidden had always been the weak point in the plan.

Sammie Jo wanted to be in the same room with the letters, and she needed a plausible explanation for why she would collaborate with the enemy. As an idea formed in her mind, she smiled slowly. She could play foolish, which was how Ingrid already thought of her, and desperate, willing to do anything to spare her husband from the risk of harm. But now she had a fresh problem. She needed to attract Ingrid's attention.

"Fire! Fire! Fire!" Sammie Jo pounded frantically at the door for all she was worth.

There were sounds of shouting, voices, and rapid footsteps, then the door flew open and Ingrid stood framed in the doorway. She sniffed the air and swiveled her head. There was no sign of fire, only the prisoner standing in the middle of the room. "What is the meaning of this ridiculous disturbance? I see no fire!"

"I had to get your attention some way... uh, Countess. Please listen to me. I got a proposition."

"What could you possibly have to offer?"

"Countess, I can save you and your husband a heap of time and trouble. I can translate those letters."

"That's nonsense."

"No, I can! My husband made me memorize the tenth table, in case anything ever happened to the book. That's the table you need. The knowledge," she tapped her head, "is right here."

Ingrid looked at her suspiciously.

"I can prove it. Bring me a single letter and let me translate. You watch while I do it."

"Why would you do this unless to give a false translation, to muddy the waters?"

"Because I want to get out of here without putting my husband at risk!" She made her voice sound anxious and twisted her fingers. "I figure once you have what you want, you'll let me go, and you won't have to send someone to get the book from Tom. I am the wife of a diplomat, so it would make no sense to harm me and cause a scandal."

Ingrid knitted her eyebrows in deep thought. *She probably is lying, but I have nothing to lose by testing her.*

"Very well, I will give you a chance to prove yourself, but be warned: any deception will result in you being removed to the dungeon. The rats there are most unpleasant."

Sammie Jo moaned, cringed, and made a motion. "Cross my heart and hope to die, this ain't no hornswoggle. I ain't going to play any tricks on you."

***

When the *Queen* departed Vienna, Montgomery accomplished the impossible by coaxing ten knots out of the Boulton and Watt engine for part of the journey. The *Queen's chug, chug, chug* attracted no shouts of alarm and Montgomery halted his vessel behind a headland that concealed them from any prying eyes at Kreigshammer. Lady Leith studied her repair work; the patch was strong and could withstand the air pressure.

The men held their breath as the balloon inflated, but the patch held. Pennywhistle, his four companions, and Johnny stowed their gear in the basket, then jumped in. He waved to Montgomery. "Release the tow ropes." Montgomery complied and the balloon rose slowly. It picked up speed quickly once it caught the full force of the night wind. Below them, the *Queen* shrank to the size of a postage stamp.

Pennywhistle periodically adjusted the blast valve on the burner to keep the balloon rising. When they reached what he guessed was 2,000 feet, he switched the burner off. He estimated the wind at fifteen knots, WNW, blowing them towards the castle. He unfurled his Ramsden and spotted the torches on Kreigshammer's parapets, a mile away. The moon disappeared behind clouds, making the small torches stand out.

He had reluctantly allowed Johnny to ride along. He hated putting him in danger, but the boy was the only one who had been inside the fortress. He gave the boy a short course in how to work the burner and valves. They were not difficult to understand, and Johnny was a quick study.

Sammie Jo took an hour to translate the first letter, pretending to have difficulty with the long words and Latin phrases. She was astonished and horrified by the revelations. A member of Parliament had murdered his wife, a junior member of the royal family was a pedophile, and one of George III's sons had committed sodomy. If the rest of the letters contained similar material, the letters were political volcanoes which could, indeed, bury the royal family and the current British administration. She hated giving up the information to Ingrid, but by doing so, she established her bona fides. She also realized that without the actual letters as proof, merely reporting their contents would be dismissed as vile and malicious rumors. And Tom had explained to her the severity of British law when it came to slander and libel.

Sammie Jo realized she was of two minds. On the one hand, she was trying to help Tom. But if what was in this letter was true, she wanted the truth brought to light, and wrong-doers held accountable! It was like the preacher back home all over again, privilege blocking responsibility. Her knuckles whitened as she translated.

***

Pennywhistle and the balloon floated to within half a mile from the castle. He and the four others checked their air rifles, which were suspended from slings like those employed by cavalrymen. They would be difficult to operate in flight, but the torches would at least provide aiming points. His men then strapped on their parachutes.

"Remember, the descent rate will be a thousand feet a minute, so you should land in just under two minutes. Count '1001, 1002' once you are clear, and then pull the rip cord. Keep the gun slings tight against your body until after your chute inflates."

Pennywhistle felt a moment of pure, naked fear when he looked over the side of the basket. Jumping out of a perfectly good balloon in the middle of the night ran completely counter to the survival instinct. He had done something similar once before, but that had been in broad daylight from a much lower altitude, descending upon men who were already beaten.

"Get ready. Five, four, three, two, one! Now!"

The men jumped at four-second intervals; Pennywhistle counted and jumped last. The wind cooperated, but one parachute did not. Starnes's chute failed to open, and he vanished into the night, falling to his death without a cry. The rest were luckier, and the wind bore them to the stone ramparts.

Phut Phut! The guard on the West Tower heard a sound — and died. Barton landed hard beside the corpse five seconds later.

Phut Phut! The guard on the East Tower lost the top of his head to a bullet fired from 150 feet above him.

Pennywhistle made a snap decision and altered his trajectory. With Starnes gone, there was no one to remove the guard roaming between the two towers. Pennywhistle would have to be executioner in addition to planting the anchoring pitons. The roving guard came into view, and he fired from 100 yards. His aim was true, and the guard collapsed.

Attaché Extraordinaire

Pennywhistle landed softly and rolled to disperse the impact. He dashed the hundred yards to the rear of the front parapets. He swiveled his head and checked for stray guards. Satisfied that he was alone, he pulled out the four pitons and began hammering for all his worth. The noise sounded terribly loud. Barton, Johnson, and Soames joined him, and each began hammering a piton.

Pennywhistle glanced up and saw the balloon approaching. He could see the tow ropes hanging over the side, now fully lowered. The last piton went in. He checked to make sure all four were solid as Gibraltar.

The balloon was now fifty yards away. If they failed to grab the tow lines at the right height and moment, the mass of the balloon and force of wind would rip the lines from their hands, or possibly yank them skyward, and he had planned for five men to grasp the ropes, not four.

The balloon was twenty yards out. He heard the hiss as Johnny released the air valve, and the balloon dropped lower. Pennywhistle and his men reached up and caught the ropes. They yanked down hard with all their might, then wrapped each rope around two pitons, tying the ropes off with bowline knots.

Johnny hurled a wide ratline from the basket. Pennywhistle and his men ascended it quickly. Once inside, each man took a rectangular pack of equipment and strapped it to his back. The five descended slowly, with Johnny bringing up the rear. The packs contained rope for the tow line and other accoutrements.

Now was the moment of truth. The balloon was their only means of escape if the job misfired, but it was also a huge anomaly if the moon came out from behind the clouds. Pennywhistle pulled at the bowline knots, the towlines came free, and the balloon rose and floated away into the darkness. They were committed.

A lance of pain sparked a grimace. The jump had torn something. He put a hand to his back and touched blood oozing slowly. His adrenal glands kept the pain at a distance, but that would not last. Sammie Jo had given him a laudanum ball, "just in case". He reached for it, rotated it slowly in his hand, then angrily shoved it back in his pocket.

***

"I am satisfied that your translation is correct." announced Ingrid, her voice still tinged with suspicion. Ingrid picked up the letter and the translation and departed. Sammie Jo rubbed her eyes and sighed. She could make this task last many hours, trusting her husband would arrive before her work was completed. But how could she signal her location? Could she come up with a reason to work by an opened window? But an illuminated window would not be enough; it would be one of several. Then it came to her: she had been thinking entirely along the wrong lines. She had been searching for a visual signal, but she had an audio one at her disposal: a bird call. She and Tom had used them to communicate back in Maryland. The call of a Baltimore oriole was distinctive, and if Tom heard it, he would know it could only come from one throat.

Ingrid returned and spoke with the anticipation of a dream nearly realized. "I have here one-third of the letters. If you complete the task, we move on to another set. I will stay with you while you translate, no matter how long it takes. I have no intention of letting these letters out of my sight."

I wonder where the rest of the letters are? thought Sammie Jo. She made a show of shaking her head and scrubbing her eyes, then said plaintively, "This is hard and heavy work, Countess, but I want to get it done for you as quick as ever I can. I wonder if I might open the window just a mite for some air?"

"Hmph! Anything that speeds your work along."

Chapter 49

Pennywhistle instructed his men to apply perfume from vials of his wife's that Gabriel had brought along. One drop daubed on the neck would effectively block dogs from detecting their scent. His men then assembled a six-foot-tall wooden pylon that consisted of two three-foot sections fitted together with large wood pins. They anchored the pylon to the four pitons they had pounded in earlier. A large, horizontally-rotating drum fitted with paddles was attached to the top. The men then spliced together several sections of heavy rope into one large cable, using seaman's knots, and rove the cable through two ship's blocks that would act as pulleys. The cable was looped around the drum and its ends were cast over the parapet.

Three quick mirror flashes reflecting the same number of candles blinked from the parapets of Kreigshammer. Sergeant Ames, who was hidden near the entrance to Kreigshammer Cove, saw them and relayed the message with his own signal mirror to Owens and Dale on the *Queen's* deck.

"Mr. Montgomery, move the *Queen* into the cove, but not too close," said Dale. The riverbed shoals rapidly close in and we do not want to run aground." Montgomery looked at him with a cynical expression that said, "and you think that I did not know that?"

Attaché Extraordinaire

"One of us is going to have to take an icy little swim to get the lines to the boat," said Owens to Dale. "Do you want to do it or shall I?"

"Rock, paper, and scissors?" inquired Dale.

Owens nodded. "Loser goes for a swim. On the count of three. One, two, three."

Dale guessed at Owens's response, since he was as solid as granite. Dale's flexibility triumphed as paper encased the rock.

Owens took a deep breath and dived into the icy water, which stung like a regiment of hornets. Pennywhistle's toss of the rope ends was good, so Owens's swim was a mercifully short twenty five yards. He grabbed the rope ends, quickly reversed course, and was soon hoisted aboard the *Queen Charlotte*. He handed the rope ends off to Dale, while his men threw heavy woolen blankets on him to stop his shivering. Once he warmed up, he changed into a spare uniform, which turned out to be a size too small.

A smaller version of the ship's paddle wheel, mounted atop a six-foot pylon bolted to the deck, provided power to crank the rope. Dale ran the cable ends over the paddles and tied them together, forming a continuous elliptical cable. Satisfied that the cable was taut, he pushed a button, and the paddles began to rotate, moving the improvised tram line upwards at a 45-degree angle. Dale waited a minute to make sure the movement was sure and steady, then gave the order for the men to form up; they had already blackened their faces with coal soot.

Each man was issued a magnetized iron grip with handles, which could be secured around the tram line. The grip resembled the Greek letter Omega, and once the two open ends were pressed together, the magnetic loop closed and formed a tight seal around the rope, strong enough to bear the weight of a man. Even with the handholds, the six-minute ride would be a test of endurance, since a man's arms would have to bear his entire weight. Fortunately, years of military service had given these veterans exceptionally strong limbs and hands.

"Chain One, go!" said Dale. The first man closed his grip over the cable and stepped off into the night. His three mates followed at two second intervals.

"Chain Two, Go!" The next four men clipped on and rose into the darkness. When all of the chains had departed, it became the turn of the Other Ranks.

"I wish you would stay, Robert," said Lady Leith in a pained voice. "They can do this without you."

"I have to do this," replied the Earl. "I could not live with myself if I stayed behind. You would not want to be married to a man who could not look himself in the mirror."

Lady Leith sighed in acceptance. "At least be careful! Very, very careful."

The Earl nodded, then took his place behind Owens, Dale, and Thynne. The Earl, like Gabriel, lacked the fitness of the rest of the assault force, so Dale had repurposed two parachutes into improvised slings. The older men were carried upwards.

The men on the parapet waited with boathooks, ready to pull in each incoming man and release the magnetic clamps.

The tram, while efficient, was slow. Pennywhistle checked the rear frequently, worried about stray guards and prowling dogs. He let out a huge sigh of relief when the transport process was completed.

He cut the cable and it dropped into the Danube. Three quick flashes of his hand mirror instructed Montgomery to proceed to the pickup point, a wide landing a mile below

Attaché Extraordinaire

Kreigshammer's main gate. He had warned Montgomery that his men's arrival might be hasty and uncoordinated, with a close pursuit by some very bad men.

Pennywhistle checked his watch. It was just after four am, the time of night when a man's reflexes were at their lowest ebb and his senses dullest. The men did a silent weapons check. Orders were issued via hand signals. The men had memorized the layout of the castle and the mission's timetable.

Each chain had a distinct task. Chain One was Pennywhistle's own, search and rescue. Find Sammie Jo, the letters, and destroy von Steinwehr. Chain Two was weapons, clear stairs and hallways of armed resistance. Chain Three was demolition, their target was the powder magazine. Chain Four's destination was the barracks containing most of the garrison. Chain Five's job was escape, to secure the gate and the winter conveyances in the outlying shed. Chain Six's job was to provide additional support to any team that needed it.

Pennywhistle had decided not to issue an abort order to Chain Three, no matter how well the mission went. A power-mad killer had taken his wife and had done God knows what to her. Once Sammie Jo was rescued, he would put an end to von Steinwehr, once and for all, and make sure the letters stayed buried forever.

Pennywhistle's next order provoked some grins. "Apply scent!" he whispered as he walked along the line, distributing vials of his wife's perfume. The perfume served another purpose besides befuddling the dogs' sense of smell: Sammie Jo would recognize the aroma and know help was on the way. "Praise the Lord and pass the perfume," grumbled Joel Tubbs, an evangelical preacher's son.

"It makes good scents," Johnny quipped.

"Do I pass the sniff test?" Dale asked.

Pennywhistle's eyebrows arched in amused approval.

Pennywhistle directed the chains to lie down and and do a final weapons review. Each man checked to see that his buttstock air reservoir was securely fastened, then placed a rapid reload tube in his pocket. Pennywhistle issued the next order. "Gabriel, get your show underway."

Gabriel opened his steak sack. A dog's sense of smell was ten thousand times keener than that of a man, and canines could identify a single scent as precisely as a man could identify an individual color in a painting. Gabriel began to lay out a dozen steaks in a pattern, twenty feet in front of the prone chains. Johnny scurried over to help. The wind was blowing away from them; the aroma should travel quickly. Sure enough, the final steak was barely on the ground before he heard noises that told him the lure had worked. The dogs were converging on them. A rapid clicking of claws on stones was accompanied by eager whines.

Pennywhistle's men gripped their rifles tightly but obeyed his orders not to fire. Dark shadows closed the distance.

The guard dogs reached the line of steaks. Eight Rotweilers, each weighing approximately 130 pounds, each capable of knocking a large man down and tearing out his throat, had been driven delirious by the aroma of Gabriel's concoction. Frenzied dogs whimpered, snuffled, and panted, then began devouring the meat. The men watched, air guns leveled, wondering if they would be next on the menu. Gradually, the sounds changed from chewing to choking as the poison took effect and constricted canine airways. There was no howling or barking—the poison worked quickly—but there was much thrashing in the form of convulsions. All of Pennywhistle's men loved dogs, but they shed not one tear for the fate of these beasts. The thrashing gradually grew less intense, then stopped entirely.

The moon came out from behind the clouds, revealing eight canine casualties. Both to be merciful and be sure, Pennywhistle ran the narrow blade of his colichemarde sword through each dog's head. The sword was designed for just this purpose: to dispatch a wounded animal after a hunt.

"One day I shall have to invent a faster working venom," said Gabriel, who had moved alongside. "I hate seeing animals suffer."

Johnny had pointed Pennywhistle to the north tower, where he had seen the letters. "We'll take it from here, Johnny," said Pennywhistle. "Wait here with Lord Steven, the Earl, and Gabriel until I signal the way is clear. You are part of my strategic reserve." Johnny nodded, but his face made clear he was not pleased.

The chains set off in their different directions to their appointed tasks. Pennywhistle led the men of Chain One towards the tower by way of the western parapet.

McAfee commenced spiking the six twelve-pounder guns that lined the parapet overlooking the river, hammering steel pitons into the touchholes so that no spark could ignite the main charges. The castle's cannons were reduced to the equivalent of birds with clipped wings. McAfee then headed for the rally point at the storage shed.

***

Sammie Jo's eyes felt strained, and she put down her pen. "Might I take a break, Countess? These letters are hard work."

"You may take a ten-minute respite and pour yourself a cup of tea. I am not without a heart."

I beg to differ! Thought Sammie Jo.

She poured a cup of tea and walked toward the partially opened window; the cold night air might revive her flagging energy. Suddenly her nostrils flared. Her favorite perfume! It was a signal. Tom was here!"

She looked back at the countess who was staring at the letters as if willing them to translate themselves, lost in dreams of forthcoming glory and paying Sammie Jo no mind. Sammie Jo moved close to the window. She gave the call of the oriole three times in rapid succession.

Ingrid looked up in surprise. "What was that noise you just made?"

Sammie Jo faced her captor. "It is an old Indian ritual. The Piscataways say that making the sound of an oriole brings luck to a difficult endeavor, and this here letter work sure is difficult!" She whistled again.

"How very stupid!" *And to be expected from a bumpkin who believes in aboriginal superstitions.* "There, you've had your tea. Back to work. I want to hear what this letter describes!"

***

Pennywhistle heard an oriole call and his face lit up. What on earth was Sammie Jo doing in the tower? He had been dreading the search for Sammie Jo, fearing that she would be held, not in guest quarters as a hostage but in a dungeon as a prisoner. But here was a lit room, an open window, proximity to the letters, and his wife! It came to him in a flash: Sammie Jo must have offered to translate the letters so as to put herself in the path of rescue. Resourceful woman! He felt a swell of admiration that warmed his heart and dispelled his worst fears.

Attaché Extraordinaire

***

Johnny was frustrated. Nearly everyone else had real work to do but he had been left behind. He wandered off towards the east parapet, determined to conduct a personal reconnoiter. He hoped Sir Thomas would have good luck finding the letters. But what about Lady Pennywhistle? He yearned to help rescue the lady who had convinced her husband to give him a second chance.

He rounded the corner, and then froze. Something was there. Something turned a large head. Two huge, almond shaped eyes of yellow confronted him, and the air rumbled as the creature emitted a deep growl. The castle had an additional sentinel. Even in the darkness, Johnny could see the paleness of its fur and realized it was a white tiger, a living version of the emblem on the castle's largest banner. His eyes widened and his throat went dry.

"Nice Kitty, nice kitty, it's way past your bedtime."

The tiger wasn't the least bit sleepy. This was its prime hunting time and it had scented meat in this direction, but the thirty-foot long chain that restrained it to the east parapet had thwarted its investigations. Now a meal on two legs whose hands reeked of several tantalizing scents, had presented itself. The tiger growled, clubbed Johnny with a heavy paw, and stood over him, jaws wide for a first bite.

Johnny closed his eyes and prayed. The animal's breath was fetid, and its saliva dripped onto his face. Then he heard an odd slicing sound, followed by a thud that made the stones under his back reverberate.

He tentatively opened his eyes and heaved a sigh of relief when he saw Thynne holding a bloody saber.

"Saving your life is getting to be rather a habit, isn't it" said Thynne cheerfully. "Never expected to be hunting big game.

John Danielski

This pelt would look well on my study floor. Alas, I haven't the time. I shall settle for the head as a trophy."

***

The Demolition Chain's destination was the powder magazine, contained deep in the bowels of the castle. The lower the men descended into the castle, the more rank the air became; their passage alarmed the local populations of mice, rats, and cockroaches; sending them scampering and scuttling. The chain moved slowly down the dark corridors and stairwells, until a dim light ahead signaled that they had reached their destination.

Magazine guard duty was never a favorite assignment, but it was an important responsibility. Two guards were assigned to the antechamber, and a third stood in the doorway, all three armed with swords. Since powder separates into its component ingredients over time, one of the guards' duties was to shift the barrels about on a rotation of ten barrels a night. This had to be done carefully, so it was a time-consuming task. Furthermore, each barrel weighed ninety pounds. It was a back-breaking duty.

Davies was on point; he rounded the corner of the passageway, and his air rifle whispered its distinctive *phut phut,* striking the guard in the chest. Davies expected other guards to come charging out, but there was only the one dying guard, slumped in the doorway. Griffiths strode forward and pulled the body into the corridor, and Davies advanced into the antechamber, Griffiths close behind. By the light of a lantern on a table, they saw the doorway to the magazine was slightly open. A murmur of two men's voices issued from the room, and the sound of barrels being moved. The two chain

507

men strode to the doorway, flanking the opening, air guns readied, then waited.

"We're done. Let's go." The door of the magazine swung wide and the guards exited. They never even saw their assailants in the shadows. Two air rifles discharged: two men collapsed.

Miller and his team examined the magazine and counted one hundred barrels. The sum of their explosive force could vaporize a squadron of ships-of-the line. Against the masonry of a castle, the effect would be less drastic, but it would still finish Kriegshammer as a fortress. Miller laid out multiple fuses designed for underwater demolition—gunpowder mixed with pitch and tar, which lessened the chance of sputtering out, or being extinguished by a frantically stamping foot.

The original plan had been for the fuse to be ignited and the chains to rendezvous at the departure point. That had been when the only objective had been to seize or destroy the letters. Now there was a hostage, and Miller would only light the fuse after he received a message that Lady Pennywhistle was found, or if an overwhelming enemy force attempted to retake the magazine. In that case, he would lock the outer doors with the dead guard's keys, light the fuse at the shortest distance, and go up in flames with the castle.

Barton eyed the winding length of fuse and calculated the time it would take to reach the barrels, and how far Miller would have to travel on the run to rejoin them. "Pennywhistle is cutting things pretty close," he said.

"His face is his philosophy. He likes close shaves." Griffiths remarked.

"We're done here," Miller said. "Now make for the rally point as fast as you can. Go!"

John Danielski

Reluctantly, Barton and Griffiths turned to go, unwilling to leave Miller behind. But Davies had been exploring, and his voice rang out. "Sergeant! Come have a look at this!"

Davies had found the means whereby the cannon on the tower were supplied: an artillery dumbwaiter designed to lift cannon balls and heavy barrels of powder to the main parapet. A long lead pipe ran down the length of the shaft, equipped with a mouthpiece at the end: a speaking tube. Seeing this, Miller's face broke into a manic grin.

"Never mind the stairs, lads! In you go, up to the tower and let the others know what we found. Call down word when Sir Thomas is ready. Then I'll light the fuse and I will join you above. On your way, now, and heave!"

***

Benson's Escape Chain reached the main courtyard. Three members fired single shots, eliminating the two guards pacing the fire-step above the main gate and the sentry in the guard box next to it. Two opened the main gate only wide enough for all to exit single file. The chain sprinted to the storage shed and examined the variety of conveyances. Since several men had served in Canada, they chose toboggans as the escape vehicles. They laid out eight of the front-curving wooden conveyances, each capable of carrying four people.

***

On his way to check on the progress of the translation, von Steinwehr heard noises and stopped short. He ducked into an alcove, clutching the third bundle of the Clarke Letters in his hands. He heard thuds, and then racing footsteps. Hard men in dark clothing raced past him, brandishing guns of a kind he had never seen before. He scowled as he realized that the

Attaché Extraordinaire

thuds had been caused by dead guards. Pennywhistle! How had he breeched the castle? No matter, Pennywhistle was here and must be dealt with. He raced up two flights of stairs, knocking down every torch in his path as he did so. He knew the castle and could navigate it perfectly well in the dark. He drew his pistol.

He threw open the door of the translation chamber, his expression that of the devil being told that a soul had weaseled out of his contract. "Ingrid! Ingrid!"

"Klaus! What's wrong?" gasped an astonished Ingrid.

Sammie Jo smiled.

"There are intruders in the castle. In my castle! We must get you and her," he stabbed his finger at Sammie Jo, "out of here. I shall stay behind and deal with this meddling Englishman."

"You won't have to come looking for me," A deep, challenging voice floated through the open doors; reflecting a white-hot anger mixed with Arctic reason and resolve.

Von Steinwehr blinked and started.

"Drop your pistol," barked Pennywhistle.

Von Steinwehr angrily complied.

"You deserve no mercy," snarled Pennywhistle, "but I will grant it if you surrender the letters immediately." Pennywhistle had a good idea of his opponent's response; his eyes nudged Sammie Jo's.

Her eyes flickered briefly in acknowledgement. *I'm ready to move.*

"You seem to forget, Sir Thomas, that I am not without resources." Von Steinwehr gestured at his wife, seated at the table across from Sammie Jo. Ingrid raised a pistol she had concealed in her lap and pointed it at Sammie Jo. "It seems we have a standoff. You have a choice. Your duty or your wife. The first would be foolish. Your Prince Regent is a corrupt buffoon, hardly worth the saving, whereas your wife will likely give you the heir that every man of consequence needs."

Involuntarily, Pennywhistle's left eyebrow quivered at the comment about an heir.

"Ah, I see," chortled von Steinwehr triumphantly. "One is already on the way. Now you have an additional reason to do as I say. I suspect you brought the codebook with you as a precaution; you strike me as a man who plans for contingencies."

"I try to anticipate the unexpected and unwelcome. I do love my wife dearly, and from what I have heard, your love for your wife is as deep seated."

"Ingrid is my True North," said von Steinwehr with unexpected emotion. "Why not give me the book and let me return your wife? I will grant you and your men safe passage out of the castle once the exchange is made."

"Do I have your word, as a German... gentleman of honor?" Pennywhistle nearly gagged as a sneer crept into his voice. He flexed his foot slightly, gauging the weight of the steel-toed boots he wore. He shot a glance at the wooden floor and located two large nail heads a few inches from his foot. One would do just fine.

"Since I shall shortly be a ruler again, it is important that my word be considered sacred."

Pennywhistle leaned his rifle against the wall. "I shall reach into my pocket for the codebook now. Do not interpret this as an untoward action."

Sammie Jo tensed. She knew the words were meant for her and that her husband was indeed planning an untoward action. It was therefore time to plan an untoward action of her own.

Pennywhistle drew the book from his pocket slowly, in the manner of a stage magician focusing the attention of his audience on a shiny object. Von Steinwehr's eyes narrowed and glowed with the anticipation of a dream realized. Pennywhistle half expected him to start drooling.

"Your prayers have been answered," said Pennywhistle. "God says... no!" Pennywhistle let the book fall from his hands and rasped his boot on a nail-head. The two surfaces of metal generated a formidable spark just as the chemically doctored book fell upon them.

Sammie Jo shut her eyes.

There was a bright flash as the pages ignited. Pennywhistle kicked the book into the air. It made hissing sounds as its pages turned to airborne ash.

Von Steinwehr staggered back, aghast, then reached one frantic hand towards the flaming book. Pennywhistle kicked, going for the knee, and aimed a raking strike across the eyes. Von Steinwehr was soldier enough to move, so that the blow landed on the side of his shin instead. He staggered but kept his grip on the letters.

Eyes dazzled, Ingrid fired blindly, but Sammie Jo had rolled to the side and the shot missed her.

At that moment, shots broke out and muzzle flashes blinked like fireflies in the hall. Von Steinwehr's personal guard had arrived. Von Steinwehr retreated toward the sound of their weapons and one of his men pulled him from the room.

Pennywhistle heard shouts and Welsh insults. He made for the door after von Steinwehr, but found the way blocked by guards engaged in a brisk exchange of fire with the men of the second chain.

Meanwhile, Sammie Jo had seized the letters on the table and thrust them into the flame of the lantern. 1/3 of the Clarke Letters began to go up in smoke.

Ingrid saw that things were not going well. "Go, Klaus, save yourself!" she cried. "Think of the children!"

Sammie Jo charged at Ingrid, her long arms reaching for the other woman's shoulders. The collision propelled both of them onto the end table, which collapsed. The pair rolled once, then Ingrid slammed an elbow into Sammie Jo's chin, causing her to see stars.

Ingrid jumped to her feet, grabbed an inkwell, and hurled it at Sammie Jo, who jinked left, and the object missed. Then Ingrid seized a pen knife and slashed three times at her opponent's chest. Sammie Jo retreated a step each time, gauging her enemy's stride and rhythm. When the fourth slash came, Sammie Jo sidestepped, looping and locking her own left arm under Ingrid's elbow. She grabbed Ingrid's wrist and swung her hard in a semi-circle, redirecting her momentum toward the nearest wall, adding the impetus of her own anger.

Ingrid glanced off the stone wall, dazed. The knife flew from her hand and skittered away. She snapped a back fist into Sammie Jo's temple, sending her reeling back. Ingrid lurched toward her nemesis, sheer rage keeping her on her feet. Sammie Jo dodged a punch and then thrust one of her legs behind Ingrid's as she grabbed her wrist and jerked backwards.

Ingrid hit the floor, but her scrabbling fingers found her lost knife. Grasping it, she surged to her feet. "The child in your belly will never be born!"

Attaché Extraordinaire

Sammie Jo condensed into a pure warrior. *This is mother against mother.*

The window overlooking the Danube was only a foot away, and Ingrid had her back to it. Sammie Jo folded herself into a crouch and her long right leg lashed out, directed upward. Her boot connected solidly with Ingrid's solar plexus, lifting and propelling her violently backward. Ingrid smashed through the housing of the baroque window. The hem of her dress snagged on the broken shutter, giving Ingrid just the split second for one hand to snake upwards and clutch the shattered window frame. The only things preventing a five-hundred-foot submission to the laws of gravity were the sturdiness of closely woven linen and her convulsive grip on the jagged wood that lacerated her palm.

Sammie Jo picked up the pen knife. Two pair of wolf eyes met and conveyed what was in their owners' hearts: no compromise was possible. Ingrid broke the silence. "I believe the appropriate vulgarism is 'fuck you'.

"Ya'll got that right. Fuck you, too." Sammie Jo slashed through Ingrid's dress. A bloodied hand lost its grip. The woman dropped silently into the night.

"I don't think she's headed for Valhalla," Pennywhistle said somberly.

"What about her husband?"

"He got away, damn it!"

"We must find him, Sugar Plum. He still has most of the letters."

"And we don't have time to search the whole place."

"Sir!"

Pennywhistle turned to find a perspiring Sergeant Griffiths in the doorway, who had clearly been running hard. Griffiths snapped to attention and executed a smart salute. "My mates and I were on our way out when we heard the sound of shooting. We figured we might lend a hand. I see you found Lady Pennywhistle."

"Indeed, but the letters are still at large. I take it Miller has set the charges?"

"He has, Sir Thomas. He is waiting for you to give the word to light the fuses."

"Excellent. Proceed to the assembly point after you have told Captain Thynne and the reserve to come here. We shall pursue von Steinwehr and relieve him of the letters. Your mates can lend my chain additional firepower. Rather than wait for Thynne and company, we shall mark our route. We shall daub fuse tar on the walls below the torches we pass. Give Miller the signal before you begin to follow our trail."

"Aye, aye, sir." Griffiths saluted and was gone.

Barton entered the room, carrying The *Widowmaker* and passed it to Pennywhistle. "I thought you might need your old right arm," said Pennywhistle to Sammie Jo, handing her the rifle.

"Damn right; next to you, it's my best friend," Sammie Jo said. "Now let's finish this blasted business and go home."

***

Griffiths ran for all he was worth, quickly reaching Thynne and his group and tersely relaying Pennywhistle's orders and providing directions to the room where Lady Pennywhistle had been captive. Thynne, the Earl, Gabriel, and Johnny set out.

Griffiths reached the egress of the artillery dumbwaiter and shouted down the speaking tube. "Light the fuses, Sarge! This contraption works both ways; I can operate it from above. Hop on the platform when you are done, and I will get you out."

Attaché Extraordinaire

"Got it!" hollered Miller. He quickly lit two fuses: one the primary and the second as insurance. Satisfied both were burning properly, he called up the speaking tube, "Get this thing moving!" He jumped on the platform.

Griffiths pulled on the rope that operated the dumbwaiter's pulleys and the platform began to move slowly up the shaft. When the dumbwaiter reached the surface, Griffiths clapped Miller on the shoulder and both raced off toward the rally point outside the castle.

***

Sammie Jo was domesticated. Sort of. Kind of. Mostly. But she had once warned Pennywhistle that she was so ornery that "she'd fight a rattlesnake and give him the first bite," and killing Ingrid had liberated a dark genie that set her heart racing. She strode down the corridors, following the blood trail left by von Steinwehr's guards moving in haste. Many of them had been injured in the exchange with Pennywhistle's chain. Dale barely needed to mark the walls with tarred fuses, but was doing so methodically.

Two guards appeared from a side corridor, stunned by an enraged Amazon leading a pack of renegade Prussian Artillerists. Sammie Jo fired *The Widowmaker* from the hip and kept moving. Her round took the first guard in the stomach. The second turned to flee.

"Not so fast, you bastard." She didn't have time to reload. Instead, she reversed the weapon and swung it like a club. She aimed for the back of his skull. There was a sharp crack and the man crumpled to the floor. Her blazing eyes reminded Pennywhistle that hellcats sometimes assumed human form.

***

John Danielski

Von Steinwehr had rallied. In his quarters, he gathered up the translated letters and secreted both batches upon his person. It was imperative now that he depart the castle before any more of Pennywhistle's men showed up. He felt sick about Ingrid, but she would have understood. He had to save the letters. Reichenau came before people. Part of being a ruler was a willingness to sacrifice that which you held most dear. He armed himself with a pistol and sword, then picked up his spyglass. Leaving his chambers, he made his solitary way towards the courtyard.

One of Von Steinwehr's guards had fired the alarm rockets that signaled they were under attack and had roused the sleeping garrison. Those men had hastily thrown on clothes, grabbed their equipment, and charged their muskets, but had been met by a well-staged ambush when they cascaded from the barracks into the courtyard.

Pennywhistle's men lay on their bellies and were nearly impossible to see. The large air gun magazines allowed a continuous barrage that made their opponents think they were facing twenty times their actual number. The Prussians sought to return fire but were confused by the lack of sound and muzzle flashes.

Von Steinwehr heard the sound of musket fire and approached the courtyard cautiously, concealing himself in the shadows of an archway. He gasped at the sight of his men being cut down by invisible fire. It was an eerie sight. Clearly, this exit route was untenable.

However, there was a secret door at the rear of the castle that opened onto a ski trail. He had tried the newly developing sport, liked it, and had grown proficient. He'd had no idea then that he would now be betting his life on a hobby.

Chapter 50

Sammie Jo was reloading when she felt her husband's hand on her arm. "It's time for you to go. I don't want you anywhere near when this place blows sky high. You must depart with the speed of Mercury."

"No, Tom, I ain't going. My place is at your side. I ain't affixin' to jaw about the point. And don't even think about laying me out with a punch 'for my own good' like you done back in Maryland."

He put his hands gently on her shoulders and looked deeply into her eyes. His voice flowed with a quiet strength designed to calm an emotional tempest. "This is not about you, Hawkeye, but our child. I can't be worried for his... or her safety and finish this business the right way. The best way to have my back is to leave as fast as you can. I can only draw upon your strength if you are not present."

A look of surprised understanding crossed her face and her anger evaporated. "Lordy! Lordy! You are right. I got to live for our child, not fight everybody." She threw her arms around him then pulled back and fixed his eyes with a stern look. "You damn well be careful! I ain't planning on raising this young'un by myself! This child's future is our future." She kissed him hard. "I love you!"

Pennywhistle smiled. "I got that idea! Now get moving!"

John Danielski

Dale motioned Sammie Jo to follow, and she did so without hesitation. The two joined the group running for the main gate.

The Earl was not among them. He lingered, concealing himself behind a tall stack of roofing shingles. He had his own agenda and figured if he followed Pennywhistle at a discreet distance, sooner or later, Pennywhistle would lead him to von Steinwehr.

The moon had emerged from the clouds and the snowpack amplified its effects sufficiently to give objects the illumination of early morning.

Johnny and Thynne jogged a dozen paces behind Pennywhistle, Thynne clutching the tiger's head close to his chest. Gabriel brought up the rear; his pace slowed with each footstep and his rasping breaths warned him that he was in danger of collapse. Because he had fallen behind, he saw something Thynne and Johnny had missed. He shouted a warning that was a split second too late.

A barrel-chested gamekeeper leaped from atop a wooden shed, armed with a long, serrated hunting knife. The tiger had been his pet and best friend, and the discovery of its death enraged him. He landed square on Thynne's back, knocking the wind out of him and propelling him into a stack of firewood. The tiger's head dropped to the snowy ground, white on white. The gamekeeper grabbed the glassy-eyed cavalryman with one hard hand and swung him round. His other hand raised the knife.

Johnny hesitated not a second. "Ahhhhhhhhh!" he screamed as he bent low and barreled into the gamekeeper's knees. Johnny might be a bantam, but the force of his fury was prodigious, and the gamekeeper stumbled sideways. But he righted himself quickly and his lips tightened in a snarl as he redirected his wrath at Johnny. His knife was within an inch of Johnny's chest when Gabriel grabbed his collar, jerking him backwards.

Though he was in his sixth decade, Gabriel hands were exceptionally strong. He dragged the man away from Johnny, held him outthrust at arm's length, and applied vice-like pressure to the man's windpipe. The gamekeeper flailed frantically, and one spasming leg kicked Johnny in the head. The boy dropped aside, dazed.

The gamekeeper tried to twist away three times, but each time his struggles grew less violent. He stabbed desperately behind him, slashing his opponent's forearm. The serrated blade scored deep, and blood began to flow. Even so, Gabriel continued to apply pressure. His arm muscles started twitching, then spasming. He felt a sharp pain in his chest as the iron crab extended his tentacles. His shaking hands opened and fell to his sides. "God, no!" he rasped.

The gamekeeper sucked in three deep breaths and turned to confront his attacker. He raised his knife. Gabriel fended off the strike, but he was weakening and gasping for breath.

Thynne, on the ground, shook his head and his vision cleared. Rolling onto his back, his eyes widened at the sight of Gabriel's struggle. Strength had returned to his arms, but his legs needed more time. He wrenched his Pattern '96 Light Dragoon Saber from its scabbard and slashed wildly with the energy of desperation. The curved 36-inch blade severed the gamekeeper's hamstrings. With a yell of pain, the man fell backward. The knife fell from his hand and slid across the snow to stop at Johnny's hand. Johnny grabbed it, then pounced on the gamekeeper like a terrier on a rat.

"You bastard! You bastard!" He shouted in rage and grief. Fiercely he stabbed the gamekeeper in the chest a dozen times in quick succession. Thynne's hand stopped the thirteenth stroke. "Stand down! Stand down," the cavalryman's voice held the studied authority of an officer calming a hysterical recruit. "He died seven strokes ago."

Johnny dropped the knife, but his hand would not stop shaking. Thynne helped Johnny up and both moved close to Gabriel, who had collapsed. He shuddered and wheezed as he tried to speak. Thynne applied pressure on his wound with one hand, but the blood flow continued unabated. Tears filled Johnny's eyes and Thynne's trademark nonchalance deserted him. Thynne whispered urgently to Johnny. "Get Sir Thomas here fast!" Johnny nodded and was gone like a flash.

Thynne spoke gently to Gabriel. "That was a brave deed, my friend." Thynne tore his waistcoat into strips, covered the wound, and pressed hard. The effort seemed to succeed, but only momentarily; the cut was too ragged and deep.

Gabriel managed a wan smile. "Johnny has always reminded me of my son that got sold down the river. Never found out what happened to him or his Ma. My life for his seems a fair trade. Truth is, the old ticker has been acting up the last few months and I didn't want to tell Sir Thomas until I could find my replacement."

Pennywhistle and Johnny dashed up. They fell to their knees and moved close, since Gabriel's breathing grew shallower and fainter with each passing second. His fingertips, nails, and earlobes had turned a wan grey.

"Glad you could make it for my Great Getting' Up Morning, Sir Thomas."

Pennywhistle's eyes moistened; he grimaced to dam up his tear ducts. "Oh God, I am so sorry. I should never have let you come."

Attaché Extraordinaire

"No, Sir Thomas, I came by my choice. And you gave me back what the slavers stole: my dignity. Ain't nothing more important than that. Johnny—" He coughed blood. "Johnny," he gasped, "gets my portion of the salvage money and my shares of the Black Robin." He gripped Pennywhistle's sleeve. "Make sure of that!"

Pennywhistle placed his hand gently on top of Gabriel's and murmured assent.

Johnny was sobbing. "No, no!" His head dropped onto Gabriel's chest, which shuddered unsteadily. Gabriel raised his unwounded arm and stroked Johnny's head. His touch was soothing, and Johnny felt his pain and grief subside. He hiccupped and took a deep breath, hugging the man he loved like a father.

Gabriel shivered violently, then suddenly stilled. His eyes filled with love, fixing on a distant, invisible horizon. "Do you see them, Sir Thomas? Do you see them? Praise Jesus!"

Pennywhistle saw nothing but knew a portal had opened to the next life, one intended only for Gabriel.

"My boy! And my wife!" Gabriel's eyes clouded as their light began to fade. He squeezed Pennywhistle's hand tightly and spoke in wonderment. "Hallelujah, Hallelu..." His fingers released their grip and the luminosity in his eyes flickered and vanished; Pennywhistle knew that he was now looking at an empty shell. His heart ached, but he stowed his tears and his face turned hard. "Steven, get Johnny to safety as fast as you can. I have an appointment with von Steinwehr."

"Right!" Thynne grabbed Johnny's hand and turned to go; he paused to scoop up the tiger head. The two dashed toward the main gate. Pennywhistle tore off in the opposite direction, anger over Gabriel's death quickening his pace.

John Danielski

Pennywhistle unfurled his spyglass and spotted von Steinwehr shoving off on skis. He had abandoned his men, who were losing their firefight outside of the barracks. For a man who wished to rule, he was certainly contemptuous of his subjects.

Pennywhistle had not skied since Norway, years ago, but he had been good then and he should at least be adequate now. He spied a shortcut to the exit, through a part of the castle under reconstruction. He would have to dodge scaffolds and buckets. He broke into a run.

He had just entered the canyon of scaffolds when something slammed his head with the force of Zeus swatting a fly. He flew sideways, seeing stars, and hit the ground hard, landing next to the broken pommel of his sword ,whose blade was bent. A huge hand ripped the strapped air gun from his shoulder, and with a *snap,* the gun was broken over a massive knee. Pennywhistle's vision cleared, and he confronted a face that made Beelzebub look like Adonis. The man charged like an enraged bull.

Pennywhistle rolled aside. Boris was big, but not nimble, and his momentum carried him past. Pennywhistle staggered to his feet and looked for a weapon. His colichemarde blade was fatally bent, useless. He was skilled in unarmed combat, but he felt like a pygmy confronting a colossus. The explosion clock ticked loudly in his mind, and he was far too close to the epicenter. If the explosion didn't kill him outright, falling masonry would bury him. Worst of all, von Steinwehr was getting away with the letters.

He seized a long, stout pine board. As Boris reversed course and charged again, Pennywhistle sidestepped and slammed the board into the back of his opponent's legs. Boris pivoted and glared down at him.

Attaché Extraordinaire

Pennywhistle blinked and his eyes spoke the expletive that his wife was working to suppress. The Bulgar lashed out with a punch that split the board Pennywhistle raised as a shield. Next Boris threw a vicious right hook that the Marine ducked. Pennywhistle kicked him in the knee and added a left hook and right cross to his chin. Boris smiled contemptuously. Pennywhistle slugged him in the nose, swiveling his hips for extra torque. The Bulgar shook his head and widened his smile. Was the man indestructible?

A fist crashed into Pennywhistle's head, lifting him off his feet, and he landed near a pile of bricks, barely conscious. He shook his head hard; his vision was blurry, and his head rang like a bell. One more blow like that and he would be finished. His fingers scrabbled on the hard ground and connected with a brick. He forced himself to his knees and threw it with all his might. It simply bounced off Boris's chest.

Boris laughed mightily, with the contempt of a tiger confronting a field mouse. He was enjoying his work and wanted a second or two to contemplate his achievement before finishing his prey. His hubris bought Pennywhistle the time he needed.

Pennywhistle noticed that the scaffold behind Boris was wobbly, very, very wobbly. He grasped a brick. He had had the right idea but the wrong target. He threw the brick as hard as he could then rolled fast in the opposite direction.

The brick hit a damaged joint of the scaffold. There was a dull roar and the structure collapsed. Several tons of wood, metal, and miscellaneous oddments rocketed toward the ground, and Pennywhistle's last vision of Boris was of a flailing scarecrow in an avalanche. When debris settled, there was a mound where the Bulgar had stood.

Pennywhistle breathed in and out slowly, trying to regain his energy and his senses. The pain in his back had spiked to insane levels. He desperately wanted that laudanum ball, but relief meant death; he needed his mind clear and his reflexes sharp. He checked his watch; ten minutes to go. He forced himself to his feet. He walked briskly, then as his senses righted themselves, transitioned to a trot, then broke into a run. His back was in agony.

As he raced toward the hidden door, he saw the last two chains withdrawing from the fight at the barracks.

Pennywhistle reached the hidden gate and found three sets of skis and poles attached to a long wooden rack. He selected the pair best suited to his height and weight. He attached the steel clamps of the skis to his boots and satisfied himself that the fit was sound and tight. He tried to remember everything he had been taught about skiing. The knowledge was proving elusive, but muscle memory remained.

He schussed off into the night, remembering to keep his knees bent, movements small and supple, and lean into turns. The slope was steep, and he gathered speed quickly. Air zipped through his bared teeth. The trail zigzagged, and the incessant bobbing and weaving nearly caused him to lose his balance several times. The pine forest whizzed by; he guessed he was averaging forty mph.

Schisk! Woosh! Wuff! The snow varied in depth, smoothness, and consistency.

He did not know that he had a tail. The Earl was a good skier and had decided to use Pennywhistle as his pathfinder.

Pennywhistle reveled in the sensation of speed in the cold night air. It palliated his pain far better than laudanum. Much as he loved his books, it was moments like this that he felt most alive. A dangerous mission, a formidable opponent, and a cause that was just. He could not ask for anything more, save a woman who loved him. And he certainly had that.

Swoosh, swoosh, swoosh, his skis sang a chorus with owls hooting the counterpoint.

Suddenly, the trail ended in a precipice. He was going too fast to stop, so he folded himself into a crouch and tucked his arms and poles tight to his sides. He flew off the edge, dropped ten feet, and landed with a hard thud, seconds later.

The trail continued for a hundred feet and another cliff loomed. He dropped an additional fifteen feet.

A third precipice made him feel like a jack-in-the box, but he managed to stay upright. A fallen pine caused him to jink hard to the left and he immediately ducked his head to avoid a low-hanging branch.

A buck with outsize antlers dashed across the trail. Pennywhistle swerved violently to the right. Dead ahead, he spotted an object that resembled a six-pound cannonball: a pressure-activated mine. He swerved away, but the rear edge of his right ski nicked its top. The explosion splintered his skis, but they absorbed most of the impact. His poles flew from his hands as he sped through the cold night air.

He landed with a hard plop, stars pinwheeling in front of his eyes. His vision cleared and he did a quick mental inventory of his body parts: all appeared to be intact. He unclamped the broken skis from his boots and slowly pulled himself to a sitting position, only to find himself staring down the barrel of a pistol, wielded by a large angry man.

Von Steinwehr's face was so misshapen by rage that he truly did resemble a gorgon. "You have interfered with my plans for the last time! This is something I should have done a long time ago!" He pulled the trigger, but instead of a *clack woosh bang,* there was just a loud click.

A misfire—probably wet powder, Pennywhistle realized. Von Steinwehr stared at the pistol in puzzlement. He re-cocked it and pulled the trigger again with the same result. The actions consumed only a few seconds, but it was enough time for Pennywhistle to stagger to his feet and backpedal five paces.

Von Steinwehr hurled the pistol at his head. Pennywhistle caught it in his right hand by pure luck and hurled it back. It struck his opponent on the right cheek. Von Steinwehr started and touched his bruised face. He snarled and drew a short hunting sword. He charged, the 22-inch blade aimed straight at Pennywhistle's heart.

Pennywhistle dropped to his knees since the blast had robbed him of most of his strength. The blade passed a half inch from the top of his head. Pennywhistle rolled hard to the right and grabbed the remains of his left ski. He corkscrewed to his feet and waved it in challenge.

Von Steinwehr had recovered and charged again. Pennywhistle swiveled sideways at the last second and brought the ski club down hard on his enemy's right wrist. Von Steinwehr dropped the sword, but his massive left hand fastened itself around Pennywhistle's throat.

Pennywhistle shot two quick jabs into von Steinwehr's diaphragm, followed by a knee to his groin. An ordinary man would have buckled, but von Steinwehr merely sagged. The pressure on Pennywhistle's throat slackened.

Pennywhistle's right-hand chop broke von Steinwehr's grip. He palm-heeled his opponent's nose and heard the sound of collapsing cartilage. His right hand curled into a backfist that smashed into von Steinwehr's chin.

Attaché Extraordinaire

Von Steinwehr staggered but refused to fall. Pennywhistle grabbed his throat, thrust his right leg behind, then shoved with all his might. This time, von Steinwehr went down.

Pennywhistle dove at him, but von Steinwehr rolled aside. Both men lurched to their feet. Von Steinwehr lunged at him, grabbed hard, and pulled him close and tight. Pennywhistle was strong, but the pressure of the bear hug was overwhelming and unbreakable.

Von Steinwehr poured every ounce of his rage into that bear hug as Pennywhistle's fists hammered helplessly at his opponent's sides. The Marine gasped for breath, again saw stars, and knew he was close to passing out.

BOOOOOOOOOM! A huge explosion shocked the silent snowscape. Chunks of the castle flew skyward in spectacular plumes of fire and stone that would have shamed Vesuvius. The stupendous noise reminded Pennywhistle of Trafalgar, the deafening sound of thousands of cannons fired at point-blank range.

The wooshing fragments triggered Pennywhistle's emergency reserve of energy. He stomped his right foot on von Steinwehr's left. This did not break von Steinwehr's hold, but the sudden pain caused him to incline his head backward several inches. Those few inches saved Pennywhistle's life, for a sliver of masonry struck von Steinwehr's forehead. His grip slackened and he stumbled backwards. Pennywhistle collapsed, then passed out.

When Pennywhistle regained consciousness, he saw his opponent sitting six feet away, rubbing a large, deep gash in the center of his forehead. He rocked slightly from side to side, in the manner of a bewildered child upset by his nanny's absence.

Pennywhistle slowly rose to his feet and advanced toward him cautiously.

"Do I know you, sir? I should welcome your assistance," said an oddly docile von Steinwehr.

Pennywhistle understood little German, but his opponent's tones sounded reasonable, even submissive: a lost soul seeking guidance. Pennywhistle decided to test a theory.

"We have met, sir. I am Thomas Pennywhistle."

Von Steinwehr's eyes remained glassy, and unfocused, with no hint of recognition. If this was an act, he belonged on a stage in Drury Lane.

"Do you recall your name, sir? Do you know where you are?"

"I am Klaus von Steinwehr, Landgrave of Reichenau," he said in English, "but have no idea how I came to be here, wherever here is." He rubbed his head. "I think I may have done some... some... some... bad things that may account for my present discomfiture. All I can remember is the image of a book that burned up." His normally powerful voice was that of a questing five-year-old, astonished to learn that a greater world existed beyond the nursery.

From talking to brain injured officers at Trafalgar, Pennywhistle knew that memory loss was often selective. Some could recall their names and backgrounds but nothing of the battle. Others could recall details of the battle but nothing of what had happened before it. A few were reduced to babbling children with no memories at all.

"It is all very confusing. I need to go home and put things right. I think I might have left my wife behind. So wrong."

A man with skewed morals rediscovering his conscience in the wake of an injury was the strangest of paradoxes. But would the change be permanent or would his memory return?

Attaché Extraordinaire

Pennywhistle wondered. An inspiration hit him. *"Herr Graf,* you have something on your person that I entrusted to you earlier. It is a packet of letters. If you could return them to me, I should be most grateful and shall see to it they are returned to their rightful owner."

Von Steinwehr fumbled through his pockets and located the letters. He handed them to Pennywhistle with no more concern than if he had been giving him old newspapers. Pennywhistle considered the act a crowning irony. He had accomplished his mission with a simple request. Justice had been administered by physics rather than a court of law.

Pennywhistle bowed as he accepted the letters. Von Steinwehr returned the gesture, then beamed like an adolescent rejoicing that he had made a new friend.

Pennywhistle hesitated; slaying a monster who might have no memory of his crimes felt wrong.

"I will take it from here, Tom," boomed a familiar voice that he should not have been hearing. The menace in it made plain the intention of its speaker.

The Earl stood behind him, pointing a pistol at von Steinwehr's head. "You have done your job, Tom. Now let me do mine."

"Don't do this, Robert! Let us think this out! He looks to be out of his head and may have no idea of his misdeeds. From what I have heard of your son, he would never have shot a man who belongs in an asylum. If you wish to honor his memory, holster your pistol."

"All true, Tom. If I were a better man and we were speaking in a hall of philosophy, I might heed your words." The Earl's aristocratic face suddenly assumed the countenance of an executioner. "You may forgive him for killing your brother, but he murdered my greatest joy and my brightest hope." He took a deep breath. "This is for Algernon!" He pulled the trigger and a jet of flame shot out. The shot took von Steinwehr in the temple and he dropped to the ground without any of the drama that had been a key feature of his life.

"That pays a great debt," sighed the Earl, and his face resumed its usual phlegmatic expression.

Pennywhistle shook his head sadly, regretting he had to witness a good man make a bad choice. He gripped the letters, ripped them into tiny fragments, and consigned them to the four winds.

Awareness of pain returned, and this time he placed the laudanum ball in his mouth and sucked it gratefully. He had earned it, just as he had earned a real convalescence.

Huge bolts of lightning blazed across the sky, followed by hollow booms of thunder; as if the Heavens were acknowledging a mission accomplished. Pennywhistle realized it was thundersnow, a rarity that he had heard of but never witnessed. It gave him an idea.

"I disapprove of your action, Robert, yet I understand. This must stay between us. What is done cannot be undone, but let the falling snow entomb your mistake forever."

The Earl remained unrepentant. "A monster is dead, my son is avenged, and the world is a better place. I can finally get a good night's sleep."

"Let's go home," sighed Pennywhistle. "To the women who love us, in spite of our considerable shortcomings."

"God bless them both," said the Earl.

Pennywhistle appropriated von Steinwehr's skis. He and the earl made their way carefully down the remainder of the slope, sighting the *Queen Charlotte* a little after dawn. The pair were met with tears of joy by Sammie Jo and Lady Leith,

Attaché Extraordinaire

who raced down the gang plank to shower them with kisses. Plymouth hopped from Sammie Jo's shoulder to Pennywhistle's chirping, "Good, good."

Montgomery distributed blankets and everyone except the boat's crew stretched out in search of sleep. Johnny curled up next to the Earl and Lady Leith.

As Sammie Jo drifted off in Pennywhistle's arms, she murmured, "Hell of a New Year."

Count Razoumovsky thought the same thing, as he stared at the burnt-out shell of his palace. Hunched in a ball with his arms wrapped around his knees, he rocked slowly back and forth, sobbing. "What have I done, what have I done?"

Chapter 51

The Earl Grosvenor and Lady Leith wed at nine' o clock in the morning on January 5, 1815. The ceremony was a small one held at the British Embassy. Both had been married before, in elaborate weddings, and the two septuagenarians desired to quickly solemnize their love and get on with their lives. They wanted their nuptials to be a private event with only people who mattered to them, rather than a social one that swarmed with titled people who came only to see and be seen.

Pennywhistle served as the Earl's best man while Sammie Jo acted as Lady Leith's maid of honor. Lord and Lady Castlereagh stood as witnesses. The short Anglican ceremony was performed by the Reverend Peter Parkinson, a friend of Lady Leith's: a rotund, jolly soul who never let his religious duties intrude upon his fox hunting schedule. The British veterans of the Kreigshammer assault acted as an honor guard for the Earl, though it was years since he had been a serving officer and he dressed for the ceremony in a civilian tailcoat of black with grey breeches. The NCOs all wore splendid new scarlet uniforms, paid for by Lord Castlereagh and carefully tailored by a local firm that specialized in military attire.

Attaché Extraordinaire

Lady Leith wore a conservative wedding dress of azure satin with a high neck and short train. Rather than dazzle with gemstones, she chose a discreet pearl necklace.

Sammie Jo wore a dress of yellow silk with a frilly neck and puffy sleeves. The gold necklace that circled her throat had been a gift from The Governor General of Bermuda, a reminder of her own wedding. Pennywhistle wore his Royal Marine dress uniform.

Thynne, Johnny, Dale, Deborah, Andrew Junior, and Grimsby attended. Gabriel's presence was sorely missed, but Johnny remarked that he could feel his spirit close by.

While the wedding was a simple affair, the evening reception for it was folded into something greater: a Peace Party at the Spanish Riding School celebrating the Treaty of Ghent. The event also incorporated the festivities associated with Twelfth Night, the end of the Christmas Season.

As with so many events in Vienna, the party was more than it seemed. The end of the American War had released the full range of Great Britain's military and financial resources to Castlereagh, and the party was designed to let Vienna know this in a spectacular way. That development had convinced France and Austria to sign a secret treaty of alliance with Great Britain on January 3. With Pennywhistle's help, Castlereagh had placed informers among the thousand guests, all tasked with striking up "chance" conversations with specific targets, ensuring Alexander would soon know the full implications of a treaty designed to rein in his ambitions. It was of a piece with the strange logic of the Congress, to pretend that widely known knowledge was still a secret.

Though the party was laid on hastily, it became an event not to be missed, since the invitations promised a full jousting match. Memories of the Razoumovsky Ball were still fresh among Vienna's elite, and they welcomed a chance to banish the memory of loss in a display of spectacle and chivalry.

The Razoumovsky disaster had been of collateral benefit to Pennywhistle. Because all of Vienna had mourned the loss of a famous art, book, and music collection, there was little interest in the destruction of an obscure castle on the same night. The general assumption was that a New Year's celebration at the distant castle had gotten out of hand; fireworks interacting with lightning to set off a powder magazine.

Pennywhistle had heard that the Czar had been making inquiries about von Steinwehr but they had stopped abruptly. Pennywhistle gathered that the twin storm clouds of Ghent and the triple alliance had given Alexander something else to think about.

A double line of Christmas trees welcomed guests to the main entrance of the Spanish Riding School. This was the first year that Christmas trees, "the Berlin Custom", had made an appearance in Vienna. The trees were decorated with colorful glass-blown balls and candles—a fire hazard kept in check by Mother Nature, as falling snow repeatedly snuffed out the flames that servants struggled to keep lit.

The Party opened with a boys' chorus singing English wassailing songs that were traditional on Twelfth Night. Some of the pronunciations were barely recognizable as English, but no one cared, since the boy's voices were tonal perfection. "God Rest Ye Merry Gentlemen," was particularly well done.

Four gigantic Twelfth Night cakes were cut with swords by men dressed as medieval knights, and pieces were distributed to the crowd. Prince Alfred found the bean in one piece and became king for the evening, while the Countess Zichy found the pea and became queen for the evening.

Attaché Extraordinaire

After the cake, people took their seats in the balconies surrounding the large central arena. Colorfully dressed heralds strode in and blew ear splitting trumpet blasts. Twenty four knights followed the trumpets. After making a promenade of the arena, the knights split into groups of four and gave demonstrations of knightly skills, such as spearing suspended rings, slicing hanging apples, and decapitating wax figures made to resemble Saracens.

Real jousts commenced shortly after and lasted an hour. Several participants were not just unseated but knocked unconscious. Many ladies screamed then swooned when Prince Lichtenstein was carried insensate from the arena. The festivities concluded with a short equestrian ballet, of the kind for which the Spanish Riding School was famous.

Sammie Jo and Pennywhistle skipped the show. They had started the new year with real violence and had no wish to be confronted with a mock version of it.

"Well, Sugar Plum," said Sammie Jo, "I guess this Ghent Treaty means you and I ain't official enemies no more."

"True," chuckled Pennywhistle. "But without this war, we would have never met."

"You know, Tom, I ain't seen hide nor hair of Robert and Margaret since they got into their carriage after the wedding. Lady Castlereagh asked me where they were, because she wants to organize a reception line for them."

"The Earl told me that he was tired of crowds, and Margaret agreed with him. I should imagine that their carriage is *en route* to Paris at this very moment."

"Frankly, if it weren't for your official position, I would have been happy to skip this party. Now that your job is done and von Steinwehr is out of the way, don't you think it's time to head for home?"

· "How would you feel about staying on for a while, Sammie Jo? Could you stand another few months of parties and balls? Lord Castlereagh has made it clear that he very much wants me to remain in my current post. Says I have become a trusted confidant. The future of Europe is being decided for many generations to come, and I should like to tell my child that I played a part."

"I have learned a lot about running a household in my time here and I would like to apply it to one of my own in England. But..." Sammie Jo sighed. "You wouldn't be happy knowing you'd missed history in the making, and I'd hate to have you moping around or devouring every newspaper you could lay your hands on to find out the latest goings on in Vienna. And I never did get a chance to throw my big ball. If I am here for a while longer, I will make it a sleigh ride party, the like of which this city has never seen. Besides, Dale and Deborah are staying, so she can continue covering the Congress for the London papers, so I suppose I could see my way clear to soldiering on until the curtain comes down on this particular show. That reminds me, something important I forgot to tell you. Deborah told me she wants to adopt Johnny when they return home. He and Andrew Junior have become great friends and she thinks he is an ideal candidate for a printer's apprenticeship."

"What a splendid idea!" said Pennywhistle with enthusiasm. "He is a worthy lad and deserves a real family. I will help by investing the money bequeathed him by Gabriel in government bonds. That will give him a small but reliable income for life."

Attaché Extraordinaire

"As I live and breathe!" exclaimed Sammie Jo, looking over Pennywhistle's shoulder." She smiled and boomed out, "Steven Thynne! You never said Sarah was in the city!" Lady Sarah Winters was Thynne's finance; the choice of his family, not himself. Sarah clutched Thynne's arm like a conqueror showing her conquest.

"She arrived just after the wedding, complete surprise, and well...uh..."

"We're married, Sammie Jo!" Sarah proudly held up a finger with a diamond ring. "Just an hour ago. The best hour of my life so far," she burbled.

Pennywhistle blinked in surprise and stared at Thynne, dumbfounded. The cavalryman had managed to avoid the arranged marriage for two years.

Red-faced, Thynne explained, "Well, everyone I know seems to be getting married: you, Dale, and the Earl. I did not want to be the odd man out. Rescuing Sammie Jo got me thinking that maybe a wife is a good thing to have. Sarah showing up out of the blue just after I had seen how happy the Earl and Lady Leith were... well... I figured fate was sending me a message. Reverend Parkinson was at loose ends, so I pressed him into service. Besides, eloping gets me out of being the centerpiece at the huge wedding circus my family had planned."

Sarah burst out, "I plan to tell his family that he was badly injured in the line of duty. And that I had to marry him before he died on me."

Thynne added, "And I did get a nasty scratch on the arm. You never know when gangrene could appear."

"What's that in your other hand?" Sammie Jo asked Sarah.

"Wedding present. It's a French cuirrassier's breast plate. Isn't it grand?" Sarah flourished it about.

Pennywhistle looked at Thynne in surprise.

"Owens is selling war souvenirs to the guests outside; making a fortune. Sarah just had to have this, so I obliged."

***

Twenty feet away, three of the most powerful men in Europe were talking about something very different from domestic bliss.

"Interesting that Alexander has declined to attend a celebration of peace," remarked Castlereagh.

"Just as I expected," said Metternich.

"A good thing," added Talleyrand. "He is worried."

"He certainly knows we three have been talking about an alliance and will soon realize that we have made informal ententes official," said Castlereagh, "I do not think the Czar will get much sleep tonight."

"We are taking a grave risk," replied Metternich.

"Agreed," responded Talleyrand, "but I do not want all of Europe speaking a barbaric tongue like Russian when the graceful melodies of French serve Europe's needs so much better."

Castlereagh allowed himself a rare smile. "People say the Congress dances. I believe we have called just the right tune to make Alexander dance to our step."

Attaché Extraordinaire

Epilogue

Castlereagh's gamble worked: the secret treaty saved Saxony and restrained Alexander.

The Congress was set to conclude on March 10, 1815. It had settled most of the issues confronting it with success, but nothing approaching perfection. Castlereagh was called home in February and replaced by the Duke of Wellington.

Pennywhistle had everything packed by March 7 and was ready to depart for England the next day. An unexpected reward from a grateful Prince Regent had arrived at noon: promotion to lieutenant colonel. This was the third time in his career that his deeds had allowed him to bypass an antiquated promotion system based on seniority.

He was chatting pleasantly with Sammie Jo about turning the fortress of Whistlestop into a residence when Grimsby knocked on the study door. "Come."

Grimsby entered with an agitated lieutenant that Pennywhistle recognized as an aide to Wellington. "Message for you from His Grace, Sir Thomas. Most urgent." The lieutenant handed him a sealed letter. "I am directed to convey an immediate response."

Pennywhistle broke the red wax seal and quickly unfurled the document. His face turned white.

"What is it?" asked an alarmed Sammie Jo.

"Napoleon's escaped!"

THE END

Tom Pennywhistle will return in
The Gibraltar Threshold: Pennywhistle at Waterloo.

Author's Note

The key diplomatic and social figures described in *Attaché Extraordinaire* had varied fates after Vienna.

Castlereagh's career went downhill when he returned to Britain. Much of what he had done at the Congress had been on his own hook and was opposed to the growing isolationist elements in Lord Liverpool's Administration. Many influential members of Parliament shunned long term foreign commitments. Castlereagh became increasingly isolated and anxious, believing he had secret stalkers. He slowly sank into a mental delirium and was put on a suicide watch in 1822. Despite being kept away from weapons, he managed to smuggle a pen knife into his study, with which he slit his throat at the age of 52.

Metternich was narrowly dissuaded from challenging Alexander to a duel and continued as Austria's Chief Minister for more than thirty years, becoming one of the key arbiters of the European balance of power. Henry Kissinger referred to the years following the Congress as "the Age of Metternich." Though he enjoyed many diplomatic successes, he became increasingly rigid and out of step with new realities as the years wore on. He was ousted from power in 1848, part of a wave of revolutions that swept many European nations. After spending an exile in London and Brussels, he returned to Vienna in 1851. He died there in 1859 at the age of 86.

Talleyrand held a series of largely ceremonial posts after 1815 and acted the role of elder statesman behind the scenes. He played a key role in the July Revolution of 1830 that brought Louis Philippe to the French throne. He was appointed Ambassador to Great Britain by Louis, a post he held until 1834. Though his health declined quickly after returning home, he continued to play whist from a wheelchair and took an active part in educating his illegitimate daughter, Pauline. His strategy of making France the leader of a coalition of smaller powers would be adopted by Charles de Gaulle in the 1960's. He died in 1838, at the age of 84.

Czar Alexander gradually shed his Enlightenment ideals, descending into a reactionary mysticism. He formed The Holy Alliance with several powers: dedicated to suppressing any political movements that he viewed as threats to Christian rulers ordained by God. He purged schools in Russia of foreign teachers, encouraged nativist perspectives, and put a stop to liberal reforms. The outlook of his later years has much in common with the current Russian ruler, Vladimir Putin. He died of typhus in the Crimea in 1825, at the age of 48.

The Duchess of Sagan was greatly in debt by the end of the Congress. She contacted Metternich about selling off her jewels and he happily assisted. Much is known about the romance between Sagan and Metternich because of a discovery at a Slovakian Monastery in 1949. During a renovation, a locked strongbox was found that contained all six hundred of the letters written by Metternich to the Duchess, carefully bound and perfectly preserved.

After leaving Prince Alfred, Sagan began an affair with Charles Stewart. She departed Vienna in straightened circumstances in May,1815 but returned in 1819, to marry an Austrian Major, Prince Karl Rudolph von Schulenberg. She divorced him in 1828. She served as a foster mother to several girls but was never able to reconnect with Vava, something which troubled her to the end of her life. She died alone in Vienna in 1839, aged 58. She was found at her dressing table, preparing for a ball.

Princess Bagration was almost penniless by the end of the Congress, but a Sicilian, The Duke of Serra Capriola, came to her rescue and paid her bills. She later married a rich Englishman named John Howard Caradoc and moved to Paris, where she continued to live lavishly, spend extravagantly, and conduct fashionable salons. Even in her sixties, she favored sheer, low-cut dresses. She died on a trip to Venice in 1857, at the age of 74.

Dorothée Talleyrand-Perigord, Sagan's sister, had an illegitimate daughter by Count Clam-Martinez in 1816, and in 1820, gave birth to a second, Pauline, believed to be Talleyrand's. She formally separated from her husband, Talleyrand's nephew, in 1818, but not before producing a legitimate heir, Louis Napoleon. She lived with Talleyrand until 1830 but still took lovers and acquired a reputation as a formidable seductress. She gave birth to a third girl, Julie, in 1826 and fourth, Antonina, in 1827, each the product of a different father. She was at Talleyrand's bedside when he died in 1838 and he entrusted her with the care of his papers. Upon Talleyrand's death, she became the Duchess of Talleyrand. By special order of the King of Prussia, she became the ruling Duchess of Sagan in 1845. She died in 1862, at the age of sixty-nine, after a carriage accident. Her final wishes expressed in her will, that her heart be buried in Talleyrand's grave, were not followed. She was instead buried in the same tomb as her sister, Wilhemine, and her son, Louis-Napoleon.

Prince Alfred von Weideschgratz eventually became a field marshal in the Austrian Army.

Charles Stewart inherited the title of Viscount Castlereagh after his brother's death but chose to go by another that his brother did not use: The Marquis of Londonderry.

Barbara von Krudener, better known as the Baroness de Krudener, was a Baltic mystic and Pietist Lutheran religious reformer. She was a key advisor to the Czar, but they did not actually meet until after the Congress. During the Congress, however, they carried on an extensive and detailed correspondence, on which the Czar came to rely; the Czar often said her letters made him feel that she was actually in the room with him. She convinced him that he was born with a special messianic calling; to save, not just the people of Russia but those of Europe, from various kinds of spiritual and moral rot.

Count Razoumovsky died a broken man in 1836. Despite a loan of 700,000 Florins from the Czar, he never regained his former status. He is best remembered as the man who commissioned Beethoven's Razoumovsky Quartets (Opus 59), the most ambitious and difficult string quartets written up to that time. More than anyone, he convinced Vienna that Beethoven was a genius, not just a talented musical artist for hire.

The Four Elements Ball happened substantially as described but the Razoumovsky Ball represents a composite of several balls and is designed to give an idea of the huge scale on which Viennese entertainments operated. There were not one, but two, Razoumovsky Balls; the first on December 9, 1814, and the second on December 31, 1814. Beethoven attended the first but not the second. The Palace burned during the second one, creating a spectacle that the entire city turned out to watch. The Palace was later rehabilitated and served as the Federal Geological Office of Austria until 2005.

The palaces described in the book were real. Though the Palm Palace, home to Sagan and Bagration, was demolished in 1857, the others described in the book still exist. The Palais Starhemberg that served as the British Embassy is, today, home to the Austrian Ministry of Art and Education. The Pennywhistle residence, the Palais Auersperg, is owned by a private family and is often rented out for balls, fetes, and concerts. Talleyrand's residence, the Kaunitz Palace, is now home to an educational institute.

The largest of Vienna's palaces is the Hofburg, with 2550 rooms followed by the Schönbrunn, with 1441. By comparison, Versailles has 2310 rooms, Buckingham Palace 775, and the American White House, first described as "The President's Palace," has a mere 132. The honor of grand champion in size among European palaces goes to the Palais Royal in Madrid. It has 3,418 rooms.

Jewels were an obsession with fashionable women at the Congress and drove a number into bankruptcy. The six million livre dress covered in diamonds that Princess Esterhazy wore was never forgotten. Though the city, at one point, endured a meat and wood shortage, a diamond shortage developed as well. Sagan once cannibalized Metternich's Order of the Golden Fleece to add a few more diamonds to her dress.

Countess Zichy, one of the greatest salonières, spent so much on diamonds that she had to ask Czar Alexander for a loan. He gave it, but she never repaid the debt.

Lady Castlereagh really did wear her husband's Order of the Garter as a hair ornament.

The waltz danced at the Congress was slower than the one the ones made famous by Johann Strauss.

"Pumpernickel principality," was a phrase originated by Winston Churchill to describe insignificant states.

Politically, the Congress of Vienna is often seen as a reactionary gathering, but it prevented a pan European war for 99 years. It made the balance of power a key feature in European diplomacy for the rest of the 19th century. It also formalized the diplomatic protocols still in use today, such as immunity of diplomats from criminal prosecution as well an embassy being considered the sovereign soil of the country it represents.

The Congress marked a fundamental departure from 18th century diplomacy. Treaties and agreements had usually been for the life of a particular sovereign; lapsing when that sovereign died and requiring renegotiation. After the Congress, they were made among states, and the death of a ruler would have no effect on their continuance.

The diplomatic issues discussed in the book were real and the concerns of the Great Powers unfolded substantially as I have presented them.

60% of Saxony was given to Prussia, but the state survived, and her king kept his crown. A semi-autonomous Poland was created at the edge of the Russian Empire, known as Congress Poland, but a series of revolts led to it be absorbed by Russia in the 1830's. A truly independent Poland did not reappear until 1918.

Nationalism emerged from the Congress as a powerful and enduring force. By reducing the number of German states, the Congress made possible the unification of Germany under the aegis of Prussia. A similar consolidation of political entities in the Italian Peninsula eventually led to a united Italy in the 1860's.

Prince William of Orange, son of the last Stadholder of the Dutch Republic, became King William I of the Netherlands on June 9, 1815. That Kingdom included Belgium until a rebellion in 1830 resulted in it being split off as a separate country. Dutch and Belgian troops furnished an important component of Wellington's Army at Waterloo.

The Congress produced a general denunciation of the slave trade, but its actual abolition was not accomplished until much later. Britain took the lead in ending it because she had the world's largest navy, and it was a popular cause with influential members of Parliament. The British paid prize money to crews who captured slave ships as well as head money for each African liberated.

The Spanish did ask Britain to help secure the return of the Louisiana Territory in return for supporting the abolition of slavery. The British bought them off with a payment of £400,000.

The International Rivers Committee was real. It greatly reduced tolls on European rivers but did not eliminate them. Travel by water was far faster, cheaper, and more comfortable than travel by land. The explosion of canal building in the early nineteenth century sparked a revolution in both travel and trade. The building of railways from the mid-nineteenth century on made topography irrelevant and ultimately reduced locks and toll ways to secondary status.

If the Congress had a winner, it was Britain, who emerged as the world's foremost power. Yet none of the rest of the Big Five could be considered losers, because three of them acquired substantial territories, while France remained a key diplomatic player, thanks to Talleyrand.

Reichenau never existed but was based upon the tiny state of Speyer which disappeared during the Napoleonic Wars. Its rulers made a substantial portion of their income by charging Rhine bargemen heavy tolls and were true "robber barons." A surviving micro-state continues to exist because of a sole industry. Lichtenstein, like Reichenau, is 62 square miles with 38,000 people and sustains itself by serving as a tax haven for billionaires.

Kreigshammer is fictional but was inspired by two real castles; Hohensalzburg and Hochosterwitz.

The Dolphin rescue described in the prologue is based on solid fact. Dolphins have protected swimmers from sharks and given them rides to shore. They have even been known to save drowning dogs by grasping their necks with their mouths and then depositing them on shore.

The description of Plymouth's capabilities is based on the research of Dr. Irene Pepperberg who conducted a lengthy series of tests on hundreds of parrots in a controlled, laboratory setting. One African Grey exhibited a vocabulary of over 1800 words and understood their meaning. The term "parroting," implying a mindless repetition of sounds, is a misnomer.

The Clarke scandal was real but rather than circulating the letters themselves, Mrs. Clarke published her memoirs based on them in 1809. The firestorm of controversy generated by the book resulted in the forced resignation of the Duke of York as Commander-in-Chief of the British Army. She was not prosecuted because a legal suit would have resulted in a legal discovery process that would have proven embarrassing to many influential members of Parliament. Her direct descendant, British novelist Daphne du Maurier, was sufficiently fascinated by her to create several characters based on her personality.

Both the Amusette and the Girandoni air rifle were real. Each saw limited service and never caught on because of the reasons Pennywhistle explains. A recreation of an *amusette* may be viewed at Castillo de San Marcos National Monument in St. Augustine, Florida and the Girandoni used on the Lewis and Clark Expedition is on exhibit at the Museum of American History, in Washington, D.C.

Ballooning was a popular spectator sport in the 19th century, though it was usually only the well-off who could afford to take rides. Marie Blanchard, Napoleon's favorite female aeronaut, became a national celebrity. Sadly, though vague descriptions exist of her parachutes, no specimens have survived, and I was not able to discover any drawings of them in use.

Skiing as a sport was just beginning its development, yet Danish-Norwegian troops had been conducting large scale military skiing exercises as far back as 1747.

Napoleon's escape caught the Congress by surprise, although Metternich had predicted that outcome, almost exactly a year before. No one had paid any attention to Bonaparte's grumbling that France had still not paid him any part of his two million livres annual stipend. His unofficial minder, Sir Neil Campbell, was visiting his doctor in Italy when Napoleon departed Elba on February 26. He landed in France on March 1 and entered Paris three weeks later. When the Congress got the news of his escape, most had no idea his destination was France. They expected it to be northern Italy, where they assumed he would try to raise an army before marching into France. The Congress immediately had him declared an international outlaw and pledged themselves to form a coalition to rid Europe of him once and for all.

The Congress stayed in session until June 9, 1815, nine days before Waterloo ended Napoleon's last hurrah.

Though it was said that the Congress danced rather than deliberated, few diplomatic conferences have had such a significant and lasting impact on history. If nothing else, the Congress gave a convenient separation point for the countless two semester university courses titled "Introduction to Modern European History."

Suggestions for further reading:

The Pursuit of Glory: The Five Revolutions That Made Modern Europe: 1648-1815 by T.C.W. Blanning. The best single volume explaining the world that led up to and included the Congress of Vienna. This large, well-written book covers much more than politics. The first section deals life and death and includes people, communication, trade, manufacturing, and agriculture. The second covers power and includes rulers, elites, reform, and revolution. The final section is devoted to religion and culture and includes churches, court and country, palaces and gardens, and compares the Age of Feeling to the Age of Reason. The book does a fine job of emphasizing just how uncertain and precarious life was for the ordinary people of Europe and how disruptions in the day-to-day patterns of living lead to political upheavals. As an example, the bad harvest of 1788 caused widespread hunger that played a key role in the start of the French Revolution.

The Napoleonic Wars: A Global History, by Alexander Mikeberidze. Despite its title, this book is much more about politics than war. It is a truly global history showing how the Napoleonic Wars impacted places as far afield from Europe as Iran, Arabia, and China. It also contains cutting edge research on the period that I have found nowhere else. It is a lengthy book, but you will be well rewarded for the time you expend reading it.

Vienna 1814: How the Conquerors of Napoleon made Love, War, and Peace, by David King. A pop history book that has a pleasant gossipy tone, but the research is sound. Lots of fascinating portraits of entertaining people and much good information on the social aspects of the Congress; parties, balls, dinners, sleigh rides, hunts etc. Much of the book is a tale of extravagance and excess so fantastic that no novelist could have invented it.

The Rites of Peace: The Fall of Napoleon and the Congress of Vienna, by Adam Zamoyski This book occupies the middle ground between pop and scholarly history. Focused mostly on the politics of the Congress, it also provides compelling portraits of Alexander, Metternich, Talleyrand, and Castlereagh.

1815: Regency Britain in the Year of Waterloo", by Stephen Bates. Not terribly detailed, but it will give you a good general survey of Jane Austen's England and the mindset of the Britons attending the Congress of Vienna.

Waterloo: The Campaign of 1815: From Ligny to Quatre Bras. Volume 1, by John Hussey. For only the most serious students of the period, the book contains a great deal of useful background information on the effect of the Congress's decisions in ending Napoleon's Hundred Day return to power.

The books are available on Amazon.com and all have audiobook editions.

About the Author

John Danielski worked his way through university as a living history interpreter at historic Fort Snelling, the birthplace of Minnesota. For four summers, he played a US soldier of 1827; he wore the uniform, performed the drills, demonstrated the volley fire with other interpreters, and even ate the food. A heavy blue wool tailcoat and black shako look smart and snappy, but are pure torture to wear on a boiling summer day.

He has a practical, rather than theoretical, perspective on the weapons of the time. He has fired either replicas or originals of all of the weapons mentioned in his works with live rounds, six-and twelve-pound cannon included. The effect of a 12-pound cannonball on an old Chevy four door must be seen to be believed.

He has a number of marginally useful University degrees, including a *magna cum laude* degree in history from the University of Minnesota. He is a Phi Beta Kappa and holds a black belt in Tae-Kwon-do. He has taught history at both the secondary and university levels and also worked as a newspaper editor.

BLUE WATER SCARLET TIDE

BY

JOHN DANIELSKI

It's the summer of 1814, and Captain Thomas Pennywhistle of the Royal Marines is fighting in a New World war that should never have started, a war where the old rules of engagement do not apply. Here, runaway slaves are your best source of intelligence, treachery is commonplace, and rough justice is the best one can hope to meet—or mete out. The Americans are fiercely determined to defend their new nation and the Great Experiment of the Republic; British Admiral George Cockburn is resolved to exact revenge for the burning of York, and so the war drags on. Thanks to Pennywhistle's ingenuity, observant mind, and military discipline, a British strike force penetrates the critically strategic region of the Chesapeake Bay. But this fight isn't just being waged by soldiers, and the collateral damage to innocents tears at Pennywhistle's heart.

As his past catches up with him, Pennywhistle must decide what is worth fighting for, and what is worth refusing to kill for —especially when he meets his opposite number on the wrong side of a pistol.

PENMORE PRESS
www.penmorepress.com

King's Scarlet

BY

John Danielski

Chivalry comes naturally to Royal Marine captain Thomas Pennywhistle, but in the savage Peninsular War, it's a luxury he can ill afford. Trapped behind enemy lines with vital dispatches for Lord Wellington, Pennywhistle violates orders when he saves a beautiful stranger, setting off a sequence of events that jeopardize his mission. The French launch a massive manhunt to capture him. His Spanish allies prove less than reliable. The woman he rescued has an agenda of her own that might help him along, if it doesn't get them all killed.

A time will come when, outmaneuvered, captured, and stripped of everything, he must stand alone before his enemies. But Pennywhistle is a hard man to kill and too bloody obstinate to concede defeat.

PENMORE PRESS
www.penmorepress.com

Capital's Punishment
by
John Danielski

The White House is in flames, the Capitol a gutted shell. President Madison is in hiding. Organized resistance has collapsed, and British soldiers prowl the streets of Washington.

Two islands of fortitude rise above the sea of chaos—one scarlet, one blue. Royal Marine Captain Thomas Pennywhistle has no wish to see the young American republic destroyed; he must strike a balance between his humanity and his passion for absolute victory. Captain John Tracy of the United States Marines hazards his life on the battlefield, but he must also fight a powerful conspiracy that threatens the country from within.

Pennywhistle and Tracy are forced into an uneasy alliance that will try the resolve of both. Together, they will question the depth of their loyalties as heads and hearts argue for the fate of a nation

PENMORE PRESS
www.penmorepress.com

BELLEROPHON'S CHAMPION

BY

JOHN DANIELSKI

Deep within each man, lies the secret knowledge of whether he is a stalwart or a coward. Three years an un-blooded Royal Marine, 1st Lieutenant Thomas Pennywhistle will finally "meet the lion," protecting HMS Bellerophon at the Battle of Trafalgar.

Not only will Pennywhistle be responsible for the lives of 72 marines aboard Bellerophon but their direction will fall entirely on his shoulders since his fellow Marine officers consist of a boy, a card shark, and a dying consumptive. If he has what it takes to command, it will take everything he's got.

In the course of battle, he will encounter marvels and terrors; from valiant foes to women performing miracles, from the skill of acrobats to the luck of the ship's cat, from a dead man still full of fight to a coward who has none. He and his marines will meet enemy élan will with trained volleys and disciplined bayonets. Most of all, he will meet himself; discovering just how dark his true nature really is.

Europe will be changed forever by Trafalgar, and so will Pennywhistle.

PENMORE PRESS
www.penmorepress.com